HUNT THE STARS

HUNT THE STARS

A NOVEL

JESSIE MIHALIK

HARPER Voyager
An Imprint of HarperCollinsPublishers

HUNT THE STARS. Copyright © 2022 by Jessie Mihalik. All rights reserved. Printed in the United States of America. No part of this book may be used or reproduced in any manner whatsoever without written permission except in the case of brief quotations embodied in critical articles and reviews. For information, address HarperCollins Publishers, 195 Broadway, New York, NY 10007.

HarperCollins books may be purchased for educational, business, or sales promotional use. For information, please email the Special Markets Department at SPsales@harpercollins.com.

Harper Voyager and design are trademarks of HarperCollins Publishers LLC.

FIRST EDITION

Designed by Paula Russell Szafranski
Interior art © Shutterstock.com

Library of Congress Cataloging-in-Publication Data has been applied for.

ISBN 978-0-06-305103-4

22 23 24 25 26 LSC 10 9 8 7 6 5 4 3 2 1

To my mom,
who taught me to love reading
from a very young age and took me to
the library to check out towering stacks of books.

And to Dustin,
who makes my books possible.

ACKNOWLEDGMENTS

Turning a story into a book requires an entire team of people working together, and I'd like to thank everyone who made it possible!

Thanks to Sarah E. Younger, my badass agent, who is a continual delight to work with. I'm so glad you're in my corner!

Thanks to Tessa Woodward, my outstanding editor, who always knows exactly what my manuscripts need to be the best versions of themselves. I don't know how you do it, but I'm so glad you do! And thanks to the entire team at Harper Voyager for everything you do. This book wouldn't exist without you all!

Thanks to Patrick Ferguson and Tracy Smith for reading early drafts, putting up with the inevitable "it's garbage" wailing, and generally supporting me through the ups and downs of producing a story from thin air, imagination, and stress. You all are the best!

Thanks to Bree, Donna, Ilona, and Gordon for all the help, support, cheerleading, and encouragement.

All my love and appreciation to my husband, Dustin, whose unwavering support keeps me going even when the story refuses to cooperate, and I feel like becoming a hermit in a shack in the woods. I love you!

And finally, thanks to you, readers! This book was written during the pandemic of 2020, and while it was incredibly difficult to write, it was also a much-needed escape. I hope the world is in a better place by the time you read this, but I also hope the story still serves as a pleasant escape. Happy reading!

CHAPTER ONE

I leaned against my ship's cargo ramp and watched with narrowed eyes as four soldiers in Valovian armor stalked through the landing bay. This was a human station in human space—Valoffs shouldn't be here. Yes, we were at peace—*for now*—but both sides had made it clear that they preferred it when everyone stayed in their own sectors.

The soldiers advanced from ship to ship. At each, the group leader spoke to the ship's captain for a few minutes before continuing on. They moved like Valoffs rather than like humans wearing stolen armor, so I raised my mental shields as they approached. It wasn't easy for a human to learn to shield against Valovian abilities because we had no natural defenses, but I'd learned the hard way during the war. Certain death provided excellent motivation.

The leader was male: tall and muscular, with thick black hair, dark eyes, and skin a shade or two lighter than my own golden tan. He looked vaguely familiar, but I couldn't immediately place him. He was encased in layers of synthetic black armor from neck to feet, and I knew from experience that it would deflect all but the strongest plas pistols and blades. It had exactly two weaknesses, and you had to be within reach to exploit either of them.

The group stopped several paces away, but even at this distance, their leader looked almost human. In general, Valoffs had a wider variety of hair and skin color and were a little taller than humans, with a slightly finer bone structure. However, their eyes were the biggest giveaway. Their irises were often threaded with multiple vibrant colors, and they had better-than-human night vision. They spent a lot of time in the dark—days on Valovia were only ten hours long.

There were a few other minor differences between us, but at a glance, most Valoffs could be mistaken for human easily enough. Scientists had confirmed that they *were* nearly human, a branch that had diverged several millennia ago. The constant debate was whether they'd settled Earth and created the human branch or if some long-forgotten humans had hitched a ride to Valovia.

Or maybe an unknown third party had created us both. The speculation and conspiracy theories were both varied and unending.

I felt the slightest brush of a mind against mine. It felt cold, as always, even though I didn't think it really had a temperature. When he encountered my mental shield, the leader raised an eyebrow. He was all hard angles and harsh beauty. Sharp cheekbones, strong jaw, straight nose.

And a mind that could kill with a thought.

Three soldiers in full armor—including the battle helmets that covered their faces—waited behind him. I couldn't tell if they expected trouble to find them or if they were prepared to *be* the trouble.

"Are you the captain of this ship?" the Valovian leader asked in lightly accented Common.

I straightened away from the ramp. I wasn't particularly tall, and I had to look up to meet his eyes, which added an annoyed bite to my tone. "Yes."

"I am Torran Fletcher. I want to hire you."

Now I understood why all of his previous conversations were so short. This one would be, too. "No."

"Why not?"

"I'm a bounty hunter. I hunt criminals and murderers; I don't work for them." And I *especially* didn't work for one of the top Valovian generals who'd led the war against the Federated Human Planets, commonly shortened to FHP or Fed. No wonder he'd looked familiar. He'd been one of our priority targets, but as far as we knew, he'd never been anywhere near the front lines. Disgust pulled at my lips. *Coward.*

His piercing gaze seared me. "I know you. Lieutenant Octavia Zarola, hero of Rodeni," he said with mocking reverence before his expression hardened. "*Slaughterer.* You are worth a lot in Valovian space."

Memories of blood and death and war and betrayal caused my mental shields to falter. Torran's expression went carefully blank—the look of a Valoff using their ability—and once again I felt his mind touch mine. I slammed up my shields and locked away the pain.

I hoped that whatever memories he'd glimpsed gave him the same nightmares they gave me.

My palms itched with the desire to grip a weapon. The enemy stood at my door and there wasn't a damn thing I could do about it unless I wanted to cause an interstellar incident—*which I did,* very much. But the thought of my crew stayed my hand. I couldn't go and get myself killed for a vengeance that was three years too late, not when two people still depended on me.

I returned to the conversation, pretending the lapse hadn't happened and that I hadn't imagined sinking a plas blade into his armor's weakest point. My smile was not kind. "Then it's good that we're not *in* Valovian space. And I know who you are, too, General Fletcher. You're not worth anything at all, but station security might make an exception on principle alone."

Torran tilted his head as he considered me. "I could tear through your flimsy shields in half a second. You can barely maintain them as is."

"Try me," I taunted with a careless shrug. "You will be dead before they fall. As you mentioned, I've fought your kind before." And they'd always, *always* underestimated me. It was why I was alive and they were not.

He stared for a few moments longer before apparently coming to a decision. "I will pay you two hundred thousand Federated credits to retrieve a missing item for me. Half up front, yours to keep as long as you make an honest effort, and half on successful delivery."

I blinked at the number, certain I'd misheard. Just the up-front half was ten times more than the largest bounty we'd ever landed. It would keep us in food for over a year, allow me to hire an actual mechanical engineer or two, *and* provide for the ship upgrades that Kee, my systems engineer, desperately wanted. There had to be a *huge* catch or every other captain in the landing bay would've snapped up the offer, Valoff or no.

When I didn't say anything, Torran frowned. "Did you hear me?"

"I heard you just fine. I'm waiting for the catch."

"My team and I will accompany you for the duration of the search."

Uncomfortable, but not so much that the other captains would turn down a fortune, especially if they were smart enough to limit the search to a set amount of time. There had to be something else.

"And the search will begin on Valovia."

Ah, there it was. Valovia was the heart of the Valovian Empire, and humans who ventured into Valovian space tended to disappear. That, plus the bounty on my head, meant that I wouldn't fly there even for the fortune on offer. I mentally blew a farewell kiss to the most money I'd ever almost earned. "I decline. I suggest you find a Valovian crew to help you."

"I can offer you and your crew safe passage for the duration of our contract. You will not be bothered and once the contract is complete, I will accompany you to whichever human station or planetary system you prefer."

"I would have to trust your word *and* the fact that you are even able to offer safe passage. I don't, for either. So my answer remains the same."

One of the soldiers behind Torran stepped forward, their body language furious, but Torran held up a hand and the soldier fell back. Ah, right. It was an insult to question a Valoff's honor. They were all about to be very, very insulted, then.

"A human stole a family heirloom," Torran said. "I want it back. And I want the thief caught."

Whatever had been taken must be beyond priceless if

he was willing to pay so much for its retrieval. But the thief had probably long since fenced it, meaning it could be anywhere in the universe. It was an impossible task, and one I didn't relish tackling while a Valovian general breathed down my neck.

This mission was a hard pass from me. Dead women couldn't spend credits.

Still, I couldn't stifle my curiosity. "Why not have your own people look into it?"

"We need a human crew to track a human thief." I could hear the subtle sneer beneath the words. It took all of my strength not to point out that a human had gotten the better of him and that now he was asking humans for help. The irony was not lost on me, but apparently it was on him.

"Why did they all turn you down?" I asked with a wave toward the other ships. I knew some of those captains. At least two or three were stupid enough to take this job.

"They didn't turn me down. I didn't ask them. They were clearly incompetent. You are . . . less so."

My comm implant crackled to life before I could tell him exactly where he could shove his faint praise. I held up a finger, so Torran would know that I wasn't just ignoring him, even though I'd like to. The implant piped Kee's voice directly into my inner ear. "Tavi, don't say no. We have to help. They must be desperate if they're coming to us."

It didn't surprise me that Kee was eavesdropping. She was plugged into every system on the ship and could easily hack her way into the whole station if she felt like it. Hell, she was probably linked in to my personal comm and listening through my microphone, never mind that that was supposed to be impossible.

Kee's heart was like the finest china—proudly displayed, incredibly delicate, and easily broken. She'd never met a creature she didn't want to help. I'd known her for years, and she was one of my closest friends, but I still didn't understand how the universe hadn't shattered her yet. Somehow, no matter what happened, she just kept putting herself back together and believing the best of people.

If everyone were like Kee, the universe would be a far better place. Unfortunately, it was filled with vicious bastards like me and General Fletcher.

"No," I responded subvocally.

My subvocal microphone was a tiny, flexible sensor patch stuck to my throat with clear adhesive. It was barely visible, and if anyone noticed it at all, it looked like a small, silvery tattoo.

Thinking about words was enough to move the throat muscles by minuscule amounts. Together with my comm implant, the patch picked up these subvocal movements and translated them into words using my personal voice sounds. The transmitted result was close to my speaking voice, and no one standing next to me could tell that I was communicating.

Not even a Valovian general.

Using a subvocal microphone well took quite a bit of practice and calibration. The trick was to think loudly about the words you wanted to send and very quietly about everything else, unless you wanted your whole squad to get a running monologue of your internal thoughts.

When we'd first started there had been a lot of embarrassing incidents, but now we tended to leave them on all day without issue. Subvocal comms were a crude form of synthetic telepathy, but they would never match the natural telepathy the Valoffs enjoyed.

"Come on," Kee wheedled. "We need that money, and it'll give me a chance to study Valovian tech up close. And everything I'm seeing says that Fletcher *does* have the authority to offer safe passage. He's kind of a big deal in Valovia now; a war hero turned rich noble or some shit. And his ship is broadcasting a diplomatic registration."

Kee might be all emotion and sunshine, but she knew me well enough to use more pragmatic levers to move me. She had wanted equipment upgrades for years, but I kept putting her off because I didn't have the money. We barely earned enough to keep us in food and supplies.

But if I accepted this job, I could afford the upgrades and more, even if I didn't find the stupid heirloom or the thief who'd stolen it.

I'd risked my life for far less, and if Kee's research said his offer was good, it was good. I sighed in silent defeat, and she let out a delighted whoop. "Don't get your hopes up," I warned quietly. "We'll see how negotiations go. And I'm not committing to an indefinite wild-goose chase. They get eight weeks, max."

"Give 'em hell," she agreed cheerfully. "If you can raise the price enough, I can get *two* new processing units and drag this scrap heap into the current century."

I patted my ship lovingly. *Starlight's Shadow* wasn't the newest or fastest or prettiest, but she got the job done—kind of like me.

Torran stood silently waiting for my answer with the kind of coiled strength that could flash into deadly action at a moment's notice. His gaze never wavered from me. Behind him, his soldiers kept careful, discreet watch on everything in the landing bay. They moved like a team who had been together for a long time. If Torran wasn't a general anymore, who were *they*?

Had he, like me, tried to keep his squad together after the war? I laughed under my breath. Of course not. He'd been a general. He didn't have a squad—he had underlings.

I centered myself and *focused*. The three soldiers behind Torran were not suppressing their power and their auras sparkled and danced around them in beautiful jewel tones: ruby, sapphire, and topaz. Torran was another matter entirely. His aura limned him in brilliant platinum that sparkled with hints of color, like light hitting a prism.

I'd never seen an aura like it. Of course, humans weren't supposed to be able to see auras at all, but in the last, desperate years of war, the FHP had come up with an experimental augmentation, and I'd volunteered in a reckless attempt to save my squad.

Most of the test subjects had lost their minds from the strain. I had not, but it had been touch and go. Chunks of my memory were still hazy.

Ultimately, it didn't matter. Aura colors didn't seem to be directly related to power levels or abilities, at least not in any way we'd been able to determine with our admittedly limited study. Maybe the FHP knew more now, but I'd cut ties and ensured they stayed cut by making myself scarce. I'd served my time. I wasn't giving them any more to be a test subject.

I stopped focusing and my head throbbed. It'd been a while since I'd used that particular ability and my body wasn't used to the strain anymore. Or maybe time had softened my memory of the constant pain of war.

The soldier with the ruby aura turned their head toward me but didn't attempt to enter my mind. Had they felt me looking at their auras?

I mentally shook off the past and met Torran's dark eyes. I wasn't close enough to see all of the colors, but a clearly visible line of silver traced a vibrant lightning bolt pattern across both of his irises. I forced myself not to look away. "What was stolen?"

"A family heirloom. I will explain further once we've reached an agreement."

His tone said he wouldn't elaborate, but I pressed anyway. "It's hard for me to agree when I don't know what I'm hunting. If the thief stole a unique, easily identifiable piece of art then finding it is far easier than if they stole a generic piece of jewelry."

Torran said nothing. His team's subtle movements highlighted his incredible stillness. He could've been carved from stone. And, indeed, I'd met rocks that were more forthcoming.

I tried again. "How long ago was your mystery item stolen?"

"Approximately eight standard days." The tiniest curl of his lip told me exactly what he thought of referring to human time units as the standard.

I wrinkled my nose, both at him and at eight days. More than a week was a long time for a trail to go cold. We'd gotten lucky picking up older bounties in the past because of Kee's ability to find information, but that might not help us on Valovia. "Kee, you finding anything?" I asked under my breath.

"I'm looking, but I'm not seeing anything. Either they haven't reported it, or the Valovian police force is better at keeping secrets than the FHP. And based on what I've seen before, they're not."

"Did you get the authorities involved?" I asked Torran.

There was the tiniest crack in his calm facade, and his glare became even fiercer. "No. This is a family matter."

"Who assessed the crime scene?" I asked, my limited patience running dangerously thin.

"I did," he replied.

"And? Did you find any leads?"

"Yes."

When he didn't say anything else, my patience snapped. "So you expect me to agree to help you find an unknown item stolen by an unknown thief over a week ago with nothing more than your word that this isn't just an elaborate plot to lure me and my crew to our deaths in Valovian space?"

He stiffened and his glare turned icy. "I already offered you safe passage and agreed to explain after the contract is signed."

"So you said." I blew out a frustrated breath. I didn't like going into a contract blind, but with half of the money up front, I would make a tidy profit even if the task was as impossible as I feared.

I knew what I had to do, but I still didn't like it. Working with the enemy felt like betrayal, and bitterness filled me. I tried to think of it as relieving a Valovian general of as much of his money as possible.

It didn't help.

Before I could change my mind, I spoke. "Double the price and deliver a signed guarantee of safe passage, and I'll give you four standard weeks of my crew's best effort.

If we haven't recovered the item or the thief by then, I keep the first half of the payment and we go our separate ways—after you've escorted us to safe territory. You and your team will be allowed on my ship, but you must respect my crew and follow my orders. Rifle through anyone's head without permission and I'll dump you into space. Do we have a deal?"

Torran's expression remained frustratingly blank. I would have better luck reading a painting. My patience was shot, but I had stubbornness in spades. I stared him down.

Finally, after an age, he said, "Give me twelve weeks and I'll give you two-fifty."

I laughed in his face. A Valovian squad on my ship for three months? No thanks. "Eight weeks, three hundred thousand credits. That's my final offer. Take it or leave it."

When he didn't respond, relief chased disappointment. Kee *still* wouldn't be getting her upgrades, but at least I wouldn't have to deal with Torran and his squad for two months. I tossed him a mocking farewell salute and turned to my ship. I'd been waiting for Eli, my first officer, to return from a supply run, but I could just as easily wait inside.

I was halfway up the ramp when Torran stirred. "Wait."

The extra height from the ramp meant he had to look up at me. It was petty, but I enjoyed it anyway. "Yes?"

Torran raised his chin. "I accept."

Fucking hell.

CHAPTER TWO

Eli showed up while Torran and I were in the middle of heated contract negotiations. Torran had refused my standard bounty hunting boilerplate and now he was trying to give me an aneurysm from sheer rage and frustration.

My first officer parked his levcart at the bottom of *Starlight*'s ramp and circled around toward me, his face set in granite lines. He was tall and heavily muscled, with deep brown skin and warm brown eyes. He wore the dark pants and black shirt that had become his working uniform. When he wasn't scowling, Eli was incredibly handsome, so much so that Kee and I gave him shit for it. People took one look at his face and underestimated him, even with his build.

"Problem?" he asked quietly.

Eli, Kee, and I had served together during the war, and while I didn't *need* the support, having him at my side loosened some of the tension I'd been carrying. Eli and Kee were the siblings I'd never had, and the bonds we'd forged in blood and death were diamond hard.

If I needed help burying a body, Eli would silently grab a shovel and start digging while Kee erased all evidence of the crime.

I would do the same for them.

"This is General Torran Fletcher," I said with a wave at the Valoff in question. "He's trying to hire us, but my standard contract isn't good enough for him, so we're negotiating. Rather, he's dictating, and I'm ignoring him."

At the name, Eli's eyes darted to Torran. I knew that look, so I tensed to intercept an attack, but Eli merely growled something nasty under his breath. He looked at me, and his voice came through my comm, picked up by his subvocal mike. "I hope you know what you're doing."

"Blame Kee."

Eli shot me an exasperated look and heaved a long-suffering sigh.

"Yes, blame me for forcing Tavi to accept more money for eight weeks of work than we'd normally make in two years," Kee said over the comm, her voice tart. "Woe is us."

I covered my laugh with a cough. Torran had to know we were communicating with each other, even if he couldn't hear us, but his expression remained unreadable. "General Fletcher, meet my first officer, Elias Bruck. When I'm not around, you'll follow his commands while aboard *Starlight's Shadow*."

A curt nod was Torran's only response.

"You may want to move this somewhere more private," Eli said. "You're starting to draw interest."

I'd noticed the increasing frequency of people walking by, but for all of our furious disagreement, Torran and I had kept our voices down.

"They're not setting a single foot on my ship without an ironclad contract," I growled with an impatient wave toward the Valoffs. "It's not my fault the general refused a perfectly good one."

"My ship is—" Torran started, only to stop when I made a disbelieving noise. I *certainly* wasn't setting foot on a Valovian ship, contract or no.

For the first time, frustration showed in Torran's expression. Welcome to the party.

Without warning, one of the Valovian soldiers broke from the group and headed toward the landing bay's exit into the station. Eli stepped protectively closer to me. We were both a little jumpy with so many enemies nearby.

"Chira is going to secure us a neutral location," Torran explained.

This was a Fed station, so as long as we remained in the station itself, it was unlikely to be a trap. And if it *was* a trap, well, then more fun for me.

"Message *Starlight* when you have the location. My team and I will meet you. And I suggest you think about accepting my boilerplate, or at least compromising on some of your ridiculous requirements, or this discussion will go nowhere, and you'll just waste our time."

Torran's mouth tightened, but he inclined his head a fraction of a centimeter. Without another word he and his remaining team turned as one and headed for the door.

Well, that wasn't creepy as all hell or anything.

Eli waited until they had cleared the airlock into the

station before he spoke. "Do you really think this is a good idea?"

"No. But Kee's right—it's more money than we'll make in two years and that's if we fail to retrieve the item. If we get lucky and find it, we'll be set for a while."

"Damn straight," Kee chimed in over the comm.

"Or we could all die," Eli said drily.

Kee huffed out a breath but held her tongue. She and Eli were the opposite sides of the same coin. Kee was optimistic and idealistic while Eli was more pessimistic and pragmatic. They balanced each other, and they'd learned long ago that neither would change the other's mind.

"Kee, keep digging for info while General Fletcher finds us a meeting room," I said. "Eli, grab the levcart and I'll help you unload the supplies. I want us to be ready to fly as soon as the meeting is over, whether or not we get the job."

THE SUPPLIES DID NOT TAKE LONG TO PUT AWAY. THE LEV-cart had been less than half full and most of it had been food, cheap staples that went a long way for not a lot of money. This month was especially lean. If we didn't nab a bounty in the next few weeks, I wouldn't even be able to buy us rice and generic protein next month.

I docked the levcart in its place in the cargo bay and then entered the main part of the ship. As soon as I cleared the hatch, I was attacked by a leaping ball of white fur. I caught Luna before her claws could find purchase in my tender flesh. She chittered at me as longing and a vague picture of a small rabbit-looking creature—Luna's idea of food—flooded my mind.

Luna was a burbu, a mildly telepathic animal native to

the Valovian sector. She communicated with simple emotions and images. The combo she was giving me right now meant she was hungry. When I didn't move toward the galley, she sent me another image, this time of her empty food bowl. That one was relatively new, proving that she could learn and adapt her images.

"I'm going, I'm going," I grumbled. Nearly a quarter of our food budget went to an animal that weighed less than five kilograms. "I just fed you this morning. Where do you put it all?"

Luna whined at me and rested her head against my chest. I snuggled her closer and buried my nose in her fur. She looked like a cross between an arctic fox, a small house cat, and a ferret, with a long slender body, a pointed snout, four slim legs, and a fluffy tail. Her fur was dense, soft, and as white as freshly driven snow.

Big violet eyes and adorable rounded ears that swiveled made her look harmless, but she had sharp, retractable claws and even sharper teeth. We'd all been gently nipped when we'd displeased our imperious mascot—usually by not feeding her fast enough.

I'd found her injured and alone while we were on a mission deep in enemy territory. I would have left her behind because I'd been having enough trouble keeping my squad safe, but then her pitiful plea had breached my mental barriers and it was all over. I'd had our medic patch her up, and I'd carried her kilometers in my pack, sure that she was going to die before we were safe.

She hadn't.

She had also resisted all of my efforts to release her back into the wild once she was healthy. And she'd taken an instant dislike to being left behind, which meant many of our missions were accompanied by a white shadow. My commanding officer had looked the other way only because Luna turned out to be an excellent tracker and early warning system.

Kee popped her head out of the large utility closet she'd converted into her personal engineering control room and systems hub. Her pale skin and rainbow-colored hair glowed in the overhead lights. "Don't believe her. I just fed her thirty minutes ago."

I pulled back and looked in Luna's eyes. "You sneaky little devil. No more food for you until dinner."

Luna chirruped at me, a lilting trill that sounded like no animal I'd ever heard, and sent me another wave of longing. I shook my head at her. "Not going to work. Dinner."

Luna squirmed in my arms and I put her down. She sent me a baleful look and leapt two and a half meters straight up to the narrow walkway I'd installed along the top edge of the hallways for her. She liked to be tucked up against the ceiling—the better to ambush her prey.

After Luna stalked out of sight with a final twitch of her tail, I turned to Kee. "Find anything interesting?"

She grimaced. "Not much. Whatever is going on, Torran's people are keeping it close."

Eli came in behind me. "Or nothing is going on and it's an elaborate trap."

I held up a hand before they could devolve into arguing again. "Assuming it's not a trap, who do we need to hunt a thief?"

"Lexi," they both said at once.

"I agree. Kee, track her down, see if she's available, what her current rate is, and where she is."

"You know she'd do it for free, if only to see the look on

the Valoffs' faces when a human does what they couldn't," Eli said.

Lexi had been in our squad during the war, and she had no love lost for Valoffs. When it became clear that bounty hunting wasn't going to make us rich, she'd struck out on her own with my blessing. We still helped each other out occasionally, but Lexi was doing far better than we were. If many of her jobs were questionably legal, we all pretended not to notice.

"I'm on it," Kee said. "You want me to go to the meeting with you or stay here and keep an eye on things?"

An extra gun would be handy if things went sideways, but Kee was even more powerful when she was plugged into her systems. "Stay here. If things go wrong, be ready to launch in a hurry."

She nodded and disappeared back into her room.

"How long do you think we have until they secure a location?" Eli asked.

"Not long. My guess would be in the next fifteen to twenty minutes."

"I'll get ready."

I did the same. I always wore a few weapons when we were on-station, but a few more wouldn't hurt, especially with our counterparts in full Valovian armor. I secured a plas blade to my right leg. The twenty-five-centimeter energy blade wouldn't activate unless I held the grip and pressed the switch, which meant it didn't need a sheath.

The energy blade defaulted to a lethal cutting edge, but it could also be set to deliver a nonlethal stun. I could draw it and switch modes in a heartbeat, a move drilled into us by countless military instructors because the line between life and death could flip in a fraction of a second.

A plas pistol went on my other hip. I wasn't as strong shooting with my left hand, but my left-handed knife skills were shit, so this was my strongest configuration for close fighting. I peeled off my short-sleeved shirt and strapped on a lightweight, flexible armored vest. It wouldn't stop much, but it was the most inconspicuous armor I owned. When I put my shirt back on, it was difficult to tell that I was protected.

I pulled my long hair up into a tight bun. The dark, curly strands fought containment, but I ruthlessly pinned them in place. Long hair was a liability in a close fight, but I refused to cut it off—my hair was easily my best feature. It set off my golden tan skin and pale blue eyes and gave me a hint of softness that my face lacked.

As the last pin slid into place, a soft *ping* rang through my cabin. The ship had received a new message. A glance revealed it was from Torran and that he'd secured a private room at a nearby restaurant.

I hit the ship's intercom. "Kee, the meeting details are in the ship's log. Eli, be ready in two."

They both confirmed and I released the intercom. Time to see if this was a trap or a legitimate offer.

THE RESTAURANT TORRAN HAD CHOSEN WAS ONE OF THE nicest in the area. It was the kind of place two CEOs would meet to discuss mergers and acquisitions. The few patrons I saw from the entrance were well-heeled and well-dressed.

The maître d' flicked a glance from my head to my feet— including my visible weapons—and then did the same to Eli, who sported even more weapons. Her gaze stopped on his face, and she just stared for a second before she remembered to smooth her expression. "May I help you?"

I suppressed my smile, well aware of how Eli affected some people. "I'm meeting someone in the private dining room."

"Your name?"

"Tavi Zarola."

She made a subtle gesture and a young man in a black-and-white uniform appeared beside her. "Please follow him."

I inclined my head in thanks. Eli and I followed the server deeper into the restaurant. We skirted the main dining room, which was broken into small, intimate spaces with nooks and alcoves, the best of which had a view of the floor-to-ceiling window.

Distant stars sparkled against the velvety darkness of space, and a faint nebula smudged color across the wide expanse. I knew the window was at least as strong as the metal and composite of the rest of the station, but it looked delicate and fragile. And standing next to it, staring out into the black, one was reminded just how precarious our place in space truly was.

The server led us down a short, secluded hallway. He swung open a wood-paneled door and gestured us inside. Torran sat on the far side of a long table. Behind him, the floor-to-ceiling window offered the same breathtaking view as in the main dining room.

An advanced antireflective coating meant I could still see outside even though the room was far brighter than the view beyond the window. It also meant that I couldn't use the window as a mirror to see anyone who snuck up behind me. If I sat across from Torran, my back would be to the door.

A glance around the room revealed that Torran's group

had lost a member. The two remaining Valoffs stood behind Torran and remained hidden beneath their armored helmets, so I didn't know if these were the same two who had accompanied him in the landing bay. I could check their auras, but it wasn't worth the headache.

Torran took in my weapons with a sweep of his gaze. His expression shifted, but before I could identify the emotion driving the change, he smoothed it away. "Thank you for joining me, Lieutenant Zarola," he said stiffly. "Please have a seat." He gestured at the chair in front of me, the one directly across from him.

"It's Captain Zarola now," I corrected. "I'm no longer part of the FHP military." And instead of sitting in the indicated chair, I moved left and sat at the head of the table with a wall at my back. Eli stood a step behind me on my right. We both had an unobstructed view of the door and the rest of the room.

"I've got eyes on you," Kee said through our group comm. "I'll let you know if any surprises show up."

The server who had led us to the room hovered by the door and Torran begrudgingly turned to me. "Would you care for something to eat or drink?"

The air I was breathing was the only thing I could afford in this restaurant, and that was only because they hadn't figured out how to charge for it yet. "No, thank you."

Torran waved the young man away, and the server bowed and withdrew. He closed the door behind him, leaving me trapped in a room full of enemies, so I decided to go on the offensive. "Have you reconsidered your objections to my standard boilerplate?"

Torran ignored me. "I brought a contract for you to review." He slid a slate across the table. Made of Valovian tech, it was a wafer-thin flexible display about the size of my two hands held side by side. I heard Kee's soft exclamation over the comm and bitterness twisted through me—not at her, but at myself. Despite my best efforts, I couldn't afford to get her the tech she wanted and needed.

But if I took this job, that would change.

With that in mind, I focused on the slate. It displayed a long wall of text, written in legalese. I read the contract twice, then slid the slate back to Torran. I clenched my fists, fury burning away the bitterness. "I will not sign that."

Torran's expression didn't change. "Why not?"

I had many problems with the contract, but I listed the worst first. "It gives you the right to take over my ship and my crew in the event of an emergency—an event you can define however you like. So if I refuse to do something I think is stupid or dangerous, you can declare that to be an emergency and take over. If I continue to refuse, you can lock me—*and my crew*—up. Any captain who signs that contract is not qualified to be called captain. If that is what you expect, then we're done here. Find someone else."

Torran stared at me for a long moment, but I didn't feel the telltale brush of his mind against mine. We were closer than we'd been earlier, and I could see hints of copper and teal in addition to the silver in his irises. If he thought he could cow me into agreeing by staring at me, he was about to be disappointed.

"I don't appreciate being jerked around," I said when he continued to hold his silence. "This does not bode well for our future working relationship, and I have serious doubts about our ability to work together. So here is my offer: we start with my boilerplate. I will give you an hour of my time to modify it until it is satisfactory to both of us. If we can't reach agreement in an hour, we'll go our separate ways."

Torran pulled the slate closer and tapped on the surface. The text changed and he slid it back to me. "These are the modifications I require."

My clenched fists tightened. *We desperately need this money.* I had to keep reminding myself or I'd tell him exactly where he could shove his modifications.

I pulled the slate toward me and started reading. It was my standard contract, modified in a few places with some of the changes we'd discussed in the landing bay. The modifications were not unreasonable. I glanced at Torran, who sat staring at a second slate.

Without his eyes on me, he was handsome, in a harsh sort of way. His features benefited from the fine bone structure common to Valoffs, which kept his face on the attractive side of brutal. He looked like someone who could take a fist to the face without breaking stride.

Right now, I would very much like for someone to test that hypothesis.

I returned to the slate, modifying Torran's changes until I was happy with the resulting contract. Before I slid it back to him, I had to ask, "Why did you start with the other contract if you already had this one ready?"

His gaze met mine and I fought the urge to look away. "If you had signed the first contract, you would've proven that you were the wrong person for the job."

I scoffed. "No one would sign that contract."

Torran's mouth thinned. "You'd be surprised."

It took us another thirty minutes to nail down the minutiae. But at the end, I had a signed contract, a promise of initial payment later today, and a start date of tomorrow morning. Torran had pushed for starting today, but I still had a few things to finish up before we left.

Tomorrow, we would head directly for Valovia with a single stop to pick up Lexi, if she could join us, which meant I had less than twenty-four hours to resign myself to the fact that I'd be hauling around a squad of Valoffs for the next two months.

Lucky me.

CHAPTER THREE

We returned to the ship and Kee met us in the cargo bay, her eyes bright. "Lexi is in. She has to finish up a job and will meet us at the Bastion station."

"Good." Bastion was the last human system before Valovian space. We'd have to travel through it anyway, so it was a good place to meet. But I wondered why Lexi was so close to the border.

Kee clasped her hands in front of her and sent me a pleading look. "Now that we're getting paid, can I order a new processing unit?"

"How much?" I asked.

"Forty thousand."

I couldn't quite suppress my wince. That would be almost a third of our initial payment, and I still had to pay Lexi and hire a mechanical engineer or two, at least temporarily. If we were heading into Valovian space, then I wanted to ensure that we would make it back out again, no matter what happened.

"It's top-of-the-line," Kee wheedled. "It usually goes for over twice that, but someone special ordered it and then ghosted, so my contact is willing to cut me a deal. It would be a *huge* upgrade for every system on the ship—including nav and defense."

I moved the numbers around on my mental spreadsheet. I could make it work. It meant we wouldn't have as much cushion as I would like, but we'd make do. We always did.

"Can you get it up and running by the time we pick up Lexi?" I asked.

Kee bounced on her toes, hope shining on her face. "Yes!"

"Then order it—*after* General Fletcher's payment goes through." Kee nodded and turned for the main part of the ship. I called after her, "And find me some mechanics who'd like a temporary job and can serve as muscle in a pinch!"

She gave me a thumbs-up over her shoulder as she disappeared through the hatch.

"You're a softie," Eli accused with a grin.

I laughed. "You try saying no to that face. I've been putting it off for years, and this is probably the only time we'll have the spare capital. I hope you weren't planning to retire soon."

"Early retirement isn't in my plans. You want me to help you screen the mechanics?"

"Would you rather do that or go back and get more supplies? We're going to need more food. We'll do a final stock up in Bastion, but we'll need supplies to get there."

Eli's nose wrinkled as he thought. "Supplies," he said at last. "Should I get anything special or just our usual?"

Valoffs could eat human food as easily as humans. It might not be their first choice taste-wise, but if they wanted something special, they'd have to provide it themselves. "The usual. And restock the medbay. Double up on bandages, medicine, and trauma kits. Wait for the payment to go through."

Eli left to check the medbay's current stock of supplies, leaving me alone in the cargo bay. I sucked in a deep breath and slowly let it out. I felt like I was getting ready to go to war.

And perhaps I was.

I SPENT ALL AFTERNOON INTERVIEWING MECHANICAL ENGIneers. A couple of them had been very promising, but they'd balked when I told them our destination. I rubbed my tired eyes. Taking a crew of four into enemy territory wasn't my first choice.

"You Captain Zarola?" an unfamiliar voice asked.

I'd turned the cargo bay into my impromptu office. A woman stood at the base of the cargo ramp. She was tall and muscular, with light brown skin and curly black hair, cut short. She wore a green tank top, long black pants, and thick boots.

At my nod, she said, "I heard you're looking for a MechE."

"I am. It's a temporary position and we're heading into Valovian space. I'm looking for someone who can also fight if circumstances call for it." Three interviews ago I'd decided to lead with the information most likely to terminate the interview. And all three candidates had thanked me and moved on.

The woman didn't run. "Permission to come aboard."

I waved her in and watched her climb the ramp. She moved like a soldier, efficient and light on her feet. She looked around with a scowl. "If you have a MechE now, they're shit," she said without prompting.

"Thanks," I responded drily. "And you are?"

"Anja Harbon. I spent six years as an FHP grunt and survived. That was followed by four years as a mechanical engineering specialist. I was booted out after I punched my commanding officer."

"Did they deserve it?"

Her smile was fierce. "Yes."

That smile told me that she'd happily punch them again. "Are you going to have a problem following my orders?"

Her eyebrows rose. "Are you going to give me stupid orders?"

"Quite possibly. We're going to Valovia with a squad of Valoffs. Most would argue that was stupid at the outset."

"I looked you up," she said quietly. "You're the reason my company made it out of Rodeni."

I shook my head. "It wasn't just me."

Shadows darkened her face. "No, but you're the one who volunteered to risk everything, and your entire squad went with you. You won't have to worry about me following your orders."

Memories crept around my mental block. I'd volunteered because it was that or die. It didn't make me noble—it made me reckless. I'd snatched victory from the jaws of defeat, but only at a terrible cost. General Fletcher wasn't the only one who thought I was a monster.

"Show me the rest of the ship. Hopefully it's in better shape than this," Anja said with a wave around the cargo bay.

I laughed, shaking off the memories. "Don't get your hopes up."

ANJA MUTTERED THE ENTIRE TIME I SHOWED HER AROUND the maintenance level of the ship. In the engine room, she patted an open maintenance hatch and murmured, "Poor baby. I'll fix you up in no time."

After the tour, we returned to the cargo bay to discuss details. When she quoted me an extremely low salary requirement, I raised my eyebrows and waited.

She broke eye contact. "I need to leave this station," she said. "I'm not in legal trouble, and it won't affect my performance, but by taking me along, you'd be doing me a favor."

"Am I going to have a crime syndicate on my ass?"

She shook her head. "Nothing so dire. Just a messy breakup. This station is only so big, and I don't have the funds to leave right now."

"Will trouble follow you?"

"No." A wealth of bitterness infused that statement, and I got the feeling that the breakup wasn't Anja's idea.

"If you were going to fight a Valoff in armor, where would you attack?"

Her eyes narrowed. "At a distance or up close?"

"Both."

"At a distance, the armor is nigh impenetrable. A high-powered plas pistol or rifle can occasionally punch through, if you get lucky. Up close, a plas blade will penetrate under the jaw or up through the groin joint, but it's hard to get it right."

Either her story about being in the military was true, or she had done her research about Valovian armor. Either way, it was enough to give her a trial—and to help her get off this station.

"We leave in the morning, and we're heading to Bastion. Prove yourself on the way and I'll hire you for the full job. Fuck up, and I'll leave you at the station with a week's pay and a ticket to wherever you'd like to go."

She smiled faintly. "Sounds like you're incentivizing me to fail."

"Maybe," I agreed, "but I don't want anyone on my ship under duress—it only leads to more problems later, so I'd rather find out early. My systems engineer will be digging into your history tonight, so if you have anything you'd like to add, now would be the time, because she *will* find it."

Anja looked down and away, avoiding my gaze. Ah, so there was something else. I waited for her to gather her thoughts.

"It was the station master's wife," she blurted. She looked up, distress clear. "I didn't know who she was, or even that she was married. We dated for months. I thought . . ." She trailed off, swallowed, and shook her head. "It doesn't matter. The station master found out and shadow banned me from every available job, ship, and resource. If I stay here, I'm as good as dead."

And if I gave her a lift, the station master would likely ban me, too.

The commanders who oversaw the space stations scattered throughout the galaxy had an enormous amount of power over the people under their care. The best treated it as the responsibility it was and ensured everyone prospered. The worst let the power go to their heads and declared themselves supreme ruler, helping a select few who then maintained the status quo while everyone else suffered. Clearly this station's commander fell into the second category.

I sighed. Getting shadow banned sucked, especially at a station like this that was the only thing around. But there was nothing for it. I couldn't leave her behind.

"I'll work for free," Anja offered gruffly. She was fighting hard not to show just how desperate she was. "I can fix everything on your ship by the time we arrive at Bastion. You won't owe me anything other than transport."

"We leave in the morning. The terms remain the same: a week's pay if you want off at Bastion or if you fail. Otherwise, we're headed to Valovia, so bring your weapons and gear." I paused in thought. "In fact, bring everything you have." I waved an arm around the mostly empty cargo bay. "We have room for it. If you decide to stay on, we'll figure out what to do with it."

She nodded once, sharply, and turned to leave. She paused at the top of the ramp. "Thank you," she murmured without turning around. She didn't wait for me to respond before she continued on her way.

I activated my subvocal mike. "Kee—"

"I'm on it," she confirmed. "So far, her story checks out. I'll let you know if anything comes up."

"Thank you."

The initial payment had landed while I was in the middle of interviews. I still couldn't quite believe it, but I'd authorized Eli and Kee to buy what they needed. Eli was still out getting supplies, so I headed into the main part of the ship to take stock of my own equipment. I wouldn't mind another weapon or two before we hit Valovian space.

A few meters into the ship, Luna leapt at me from her walkway along the top of the wall. Used to her antics, I snagged her out of the air, and she grumpily chirruped at me. When we were in space, I wore a padded shoulder guard that she could jump onto without ruining my clothes or skin. And she was smart enough to know not to jump on me without it, but we'd been on this station for a few days, and she was getting bored.

"I know, darling," I said soothingly, "I'm ready to leave, too. But soon you'll have more people to attack, and I'll totally let you sink your claws into the Valoffs as often as you like." I snuggled her close and scratched behind her ears.

Luna tilted her head, closed her eyes, and sent me a wave of affection. I returned the sentiment a thousand times. I didn't know if her telepathy worked both ways, but I hoped she knew how much I adored her.

I gave her one last scratch. "How about I get my shoulder guard and then we go check the crew quarters?" I asked her. Despite her intelligence, Luna couldn't answer, not really, but I'd gotten used to talking to her—we all had. I often overheard Kee working on a problem aloud while Luna chirped back at her.

I turned down the hallway toward my quarters and Luna stayed happily snuggled in my arms. That was answer enough.

Starlight's Shadow was a moderately small ship, with room for twenty regular crew and overflow bunks for another dozen. The crew quarters lined both sides of a long corridor. At the far end, set apart from the rest of the quarters, four rooms served as the captain's and officers' quarters with single bunks and en suite bathrooms.

At this end, eight double bunks shared two large,

communal bathrooms. The double bunks were divided into two sets of four, with the bathrooms between them.

I would put Anja and Lexi in the rooms at this end of the corridor—the farthest away from mine. I would usually put Lexi next to me, in the officers' quarters, but I needed to put Torran there. I didn't want to, but there was some truth to that old saying about keeping one's enemies close.

The rest of the Valoffs would share the middle set of rooms. That way I would have friendly eyes on both exit points, just in case they decided to try something.

I stopped outside my door. Eli, as my first officer, had the cabin directly across the hall from me, and Kee's quarters were beside his. They could both help keep an eye on this end of the corridor. The door next to mine seemed too close for comfort, but I would just have to deal. Separating Torran from his squad was also a good idea.

Luna chirruped and butted me with her head. I stroked a hand through her soft fur. "I know. I don't have to like it; I just have to do it."

The door slid open at my touch, and I wrinkled my nose in frustration. When the Valoffs arrived, I would have to start locking it again, which meant I'd have to find another way for Luna to enter and exit.

My quarters were larger than the others, with a bedroom and bathroom tucked away in separate rooms behind a small office. The additional space meant I could talk to people in private without having to invite them directly into my bedroom.

But every square meter on a ship was precious, and even though I had a bit more space than everyone else, my office was cramped. I'd managed to fit in a tiny desk and chair, a comfy guest chair, and a small bookcase. Heavy paper books were a luxury that I could ill afford, but I couldn't bear to part with them, either.

The office was painted a bright, sky blue that always made me smile. I moved through to my bedroom, which had deeper blue ombré walls, the color of the sky brightening just before dawn.

Luna jumped to the bed and curled into a circle, her fluffy tail over her nose. She watched me with one curious eye. When I pulled out my shoulder guard, her head popped up and she chirped at me.

I stripped off my shirt and armored vest, then replaced the shirt and strapped on the shoulder guard. As soon as it was in place, Luna launched off the bed. I smiled and braced as she landed perfectly on the guard. Her claws dug into the soft top without being able to pierce the flexible armor underneath.

"Ready?"

She chittered at me, so I set off. First, I checked the cabin next to mine. The bedroom was painted bright green, a leftover from Lexi, but all of the other personal adornments had been removed. A double bed dominated the space, with a small chair and side table tucked in the corner.

All of the crew cabins were included in the routine cleaning of the ship, so the room was clean, if bare. I pulled linens from the wardrobe and stacked them on the bed. Torran could put on his own sheets.

The double bunk rooms had a single bed built into the wall on each side, with a curtain that could be pulled to divide the space in half. The beds themselves also had blackout curtains so one person getting up wouldn't wake the other. Each side had a small, built-in wardrobe and a pull-out chair. These rooms were cramped, which made the other common spaces on the ship more important.

Torran was bringing three people with him, but the agreement we'd signed allowed him to bring up to five. I prepared three rooms. There was no reason to double up until it was necessary. It would be far easier to keep the peace if everyone had a private place to retreat to when needed.

I also prepared rooms for Lexi and Anja. I was hoping to hire another mechanical engineer on Bastion, so I made up a third room next to theirs. The bathrooms would be the demarcation between Valoffs and humans.

Luna had stayed with me, exploring the rooms that she didn't often see. I clicked my tongue and she leapt up to her perch on my shoulder. I stroked her head. "I suppose it's time to figure out what we're having for dinner."

She perked up at the magic word. It had not taken her long to learn all of the food-related words.

"Come on, you little glutton. Let's get you fed, then I'll see what I can do for the rest of the crew."

I often took cooking duty because I enjoyed it. Eli and Kee took turns at cleanup. I wasn't sure if the Valoffs had ever washed a dish, but they were about to learn. Everyone on *Starlight's Shadow* did their share—unwelcome guests included.

I stopped by the hydroponic garden on my way to the galley. The garden was mostly self-contained, but I enjoyed spending time in the greenery. One of the first things I'd done after I bought the ship was install a little table and a few comfy chairs in the back corner. I'd planted honeysuckle and trained it to climb a lightweight arbor over the space. The vines draped over the entrance, creating a little oasis of green.

Luna headed straight for her perch in the arbor. I decided I could spare five minutes for mental health, so I followed her and sank into a low chair with thick padding. The blossom-heavy vines waved gently in the room's ventilation and blocked some of the bright overhead grow lights.

The distant rumble of the fan merged with Luna's low purr of contentment. I closed my eyes and let the soothing sound and the sweet smell of honeysuckle flowers melt away my stress.

After a few minutes, I reluctantly climbed to my feet. If I stayed any longer, I would fall asleep. I checked on the plants. Vegetables and herbs in various stages of development grew on shallow, multilevel racks filled with circulating, nutrient-dense water. The lights automatically simulated a day-night cycle.

A hydroponic garden was expensive, in terms of both weight and space, but it also helped both the air and water scrubbers. And sometimes eating fresh vegetables in deep space made all the difference—along with sitting in the bright sun lights and admiring the greenery.

Thanks to Eli's supply run, we had a lot of fresh vegetables already, so I harvested only some herbs. Tonight I would make a veggie paella, which would provide us with plenty of leftovers for lunch.

Kee was vegetarian, so most of our meals were made with synthetic, plant-based protein. Eli and I rarely bothered with meat now, even when we had the money to afford it. It'd taken a bit for me to dial in my recipes—I'd turned out some truly abhorrent meals in the early days—but now

I was as comfortable cooking vegetarian as I had been cooking with meat.

I called Luna and she reluctantly emerged. She loved this room. After I'd made sure she wouldn't mess with the plants, I'd put a sensor on the door so that it would open for her from either side. When she disappeared from the rest of the ship, the odds were good that I would find her asleep on her perch in the vines.

The galley was empty when I arrived. It was a large space, with seating for twenty around two big tables and a food prep area tucked away in the back. If the ship was running with a full crew, at least two full-time chefs would be aboard to cook for multiple shifts. With just the three of us, I usually cooked dinner, and everyone fended for themselves for breakfast and lunch. We ate a lot of leftovers and meal replacement bars.

I should probably hire a chef now that our numbers were going to more than double, but a mechanic was the more pressing need. If Torran and company didn't like my food, they could cook for themselves. Or they could starve. Either way was fine with me. I ignored the twinge of sympathy I felt at the thought of someone suffering.

My heart was a damn nuisance.

CHAPTER FOUR

Both Kee and Eli showed up just as I was putting the large skillet of paella on the table. I laughed at their impeccable timing. Sometimes I thought they were part bloodhound.

"Oooh, smells good," Kee said. "New recipe?"

"Veggie paella, but I tried some new spices this time. It was good when I tasted it, but you'll have to let me know if I overseasoned it."

She waved a hand at me. "I'm sure it'll be delicious."

Eli went to get plates and silverware while Kee filled glasses with water. We usually ate family style and the simple domesticity filled me with peace. Even Luna was curled into a content ball on her high platform, watching us with sleepy violet eyes.

But tomorrow, everything would change.

I slid into my usual seat and Kee and Eli sat across from me. Kee closed her eyes after the first bite and declared, "Divine!"

"Thank you. Did you get the new processing unit?"

She nodded. "And I persuaded the seller to throw in a few extras, since I was doing them a favor."

"Weren't you already getting a huge discount?" Eli asked between bites.

Kee smiled. "I'm an excellent negotiator."

Eli huffed out a laugh and nudged her with his elbow. "Did you blackmail them?"

"Not everyone has to be blackmailed into being nice, you know."

"That's not a no," I said.

Kee pointed her fork at me. "Quiet, you."

Eli and I nodded at each other. "She totally blackmailed them," we agreed.

Kee sniffed. "I merely pointed out that I was a good customer and that I hadn't asked any inconvenient questions. A little kindness goes a long way."

She managed to keep a straight face until Eli burst into gales of laughter. Then she smiled, winked at us, and kept eating.

EARLY THE NEXT MORNING, ANJA WAITED JUST OUTSIDE THE range of the ship's proximity warning. She stood next to a levcart piled with boxes. I wouldn't have known she was there, except I did a visual sweep of our surroundings as part of my morning routine.

I remotely lowered the cargo ramp and spoke to her over the intercom. "Park your stuff in the cargo bay. I'll meet you in five."

I finished getting ready and then went to meet her. She

stood at stiff attention next to the levcart. She didn't look like she'd gotten much sleep.

"How long were you waiting?"

She glanced away. "Not long." When I raised my eyebrows and waited, she conceded, "A while. I didn't want you to leave without me."

"I promised you a job. I wouldn't leave you behind," I said as gently as I could, then I clapped my hands and changed the subject. "Let me show you to your quarters and then you can decide what you want to keep with you and what you want to store here. Is the levcart a loaner?"

She nodded, and I waved for her to follow me into the ship. Once inside, I kept a sharp eye out for Luna. I'd left her sleeping on my bed, but there was no telling where she was now. I didn't want Anja's first meeting to involve claws.

I slid open the door to the cabin I'd mentally assigned to Anja and led her inside. "It's not much, but you won't have to share."

She looked around, her face expressionless. Her voice, when it came, was very quiet. "It's more than I was expecting."

"Don't worry, you'll earn it. You saw the state of the ship. We haven't had a mechanic in over a year. I'm pretty sure we're running on hope and composite tape at this point."

Finally, she laughed. "I've seen worse. Not *much* worse, mind, but some. Don't worry. It's nothing I can't handle." She looked around again. "Do you care if I stack a few things on the other bed?"

"Nope. It's your space. You'll have a woman across the hall once we arrive at Bastion, but the cabin next to yours is empty. The Valoffs will be on the other side of the bathrooms. No one should have to double up unless we have to take on rescues."

She nodded. The one law that both the Valovian Empire and the FHP had easily agreed on was the obligation to pick up passengers from ships in distress. With the vast distances in space, no one could afford to ignore a distress call, no matter how far out of the way it was. Ships were required to carry extra rations for just such an emergency.

"I think everything will fit in here," Anja said. "That way I won't take up cargo room."

I shrugged. "It's up to you. We have plenty of cargo space. I'll help you carry."

Her eyes flew to mine, to see if I was serious. "You don't have to—"

I waved her off. "I know. But it'll go faster. First, I want to introduce you to Luna, our resident troublemaker. She's a burbu." I saw a flicker of recognition at the name and continued, "She likes to hang out on the walkways near the ceiling. She knows she's not supposed to jump on people unless they're wearing a shoulder guard," I said, pointing at mine, "but sometimes she forgets."

"Will she attack?"

"In play," I said firmly. "If you're quick, you can grab her out of the air before she lands on you. She doesn't mean to hurt you, but she will claw you while she's finding purchase. Catching her stops that."

"She won't bite?"

My smile had a wry edge. "Not usually. And never hard enough to draw blood."

"Your reassurance needs work," Anja said drily.

"She should calm down once she gets to know you,

but sometimes new crew members get extra attention for a while."

I led Anja to my quarters. In the office, I saw Luna just before she jumped, but she was aiming for me, not Anja, so I let her land on my shoulder guard, used to absorbing her momentum.

Anja gasped, but didn't move.

I turned, so Luna was closer to the MechE. I reached up and scratched the burbu under the chin. She purred in greeting. "This is Luna. She's spoiled rotten, as you can see."

Luna watched Anja with quiet patience. Anja reached out a tentative hand. "May I?"

"Of course. She loves to be petted. Behind her ears or under her chin are her favorites. Don't pet her tail or belly unless she's in your lap and very calm."

Anja petted her for a few seconds, then froze and looked at me with wide eyes. "Did she just—?"

Luna butted her hand and Anja absently started petting her again.

"She mildly telepathic, if that's what you mean. She can project emotions and simple pictures at you. Was it a picture of food? She hasn't had breakfast yet and food is her favorite."

"It kind of looked like a bunny."

I chuckled. "Yeah, that means food. You'll get used to it because you'll see it a lot."

"I saw a few burbus during the war, but I never got close. I had no idea."

"I think they are protected in the Valovian Empire. The FHP had a shit fit when I told them I was keeping her, but after I showed them how I'd tried to return her to her natural habitat, multiple times, without success, they relented. Still, I would appreciate it if you didn't advertise her presence."

Anja nodded. "Of course."

I led Anja back out into the hallway and Luna came along for the ride. "Might as well do a quick tour while we're here. I'll stop by the galley to feed this little mischief-maker, then we'll carry boxes. Sound good?"

When Anja agreed, I pointed at the two doors across the hall from mine. "Kee and Eli. They're both enjoying their last day of sleeping in, so I'll introduce you later. Kee is my systems engineer and Eli is my first officer. If you need anything while on board, either of them can help you."

This end of the hallway led to the bridge, so I started there and worked my way through the ship. We stopped in the galley to feed Luna. We left her with her food and continued with the tour. The ship had three levels, with the main level at the top.

The main level contained the crew quarters, bridge, galley, and garden. The middle level housed the medbay, gym, and rec room. The bottom level was the maintenance level with all of the mechanical systems that kept us alive and flying.

The gym took up around 40 percent of the middle level. Strength and flexibility made bounty hunting easier and burning off excess energy was good for mental health out in deep space. I had installed multiple cardio and resistance stations, and there was a large open space with a padded floor that we used for stretching and hands-on combat training.

The rec room was as large as the gym, but the room was divided into smaller spaces with lightweight, movable half walls. Comfortable furniture in various groupings gave everyone a place to relax and unwind, either alone or together. We spent a lot of time here, watching vids, reading, and just quietly hanging out together.

The last stop on the middle level was the medbay. It was relatively small, with four beds and an autostabilization unit. We didn't have a dedicated doctor, but Eli, Kee, and I had all had extensive first aid and trauma training.

"Is that a third-gen autostab?" Anja asked, using the shortened name we'd all picked up in the service. When I confirmed, she whistled under her breath. "No wonder the rest of your ship is in need of repair, all of your money is in here."

She wasn't wrong. The tech was incredibly expensive. But when medical help was sometimes days or weeks away, an autostab could be the difference between life and death. It was worth it not to watch another friend die.

"Have you had to use it?"

I nodded. "Once." Kee had caught a stray plas pulse during what should've been an easy pickup. I shoved down the memories of blood and fear. The autostab had saved her life, even if the slow journey back to civilization had taken a decade off mine. I swallowed and continued, "It paid for itself."

Anja's expression turned grim and her mouth tightened in sympathy. She, too, knew about loss.

I mentally shook myself. "Let's skip the bottom level, since you already saw it yesterday. Any questions before we start carrying boxes?"

"What's the ship schedule?"

"We usually run on a standard day cycle with everyone on a single daytime shift unless we're in dangerous territory.

You will be expected to help with general cleaning in addition to your mechanical duties, but everyone gets plenty of downtime. We'll add you to the dinner cleanup schedule, which is shared by everyone who doesn't cook. If you enjoy cooking, let me know, and I'll swap days with you."

Anja laughed. "You don't want me in the kitchen."

"Fair enough," I agreed with a smile. "Dinner is communal, and while eating together is not required, it's encouraged."

"Will the Valoffs eat with us?"

I grimaced before reluctantly nodding. "I'd rather keep an eye on them, so yes. Is that going to be a problem?"

"No. I can be civil, but I doubt we're going to end up best buds."

"Civil is all I ask."

BY THE TIME WE'D MOVED ANJA'S STUFF INTO HER QUARTERS and returned the levcart, both Kee and Eli were awake. I found them in the galley. Kee sat at the bar while Eli worked the stove. Luna was nowhere to be found. She liked to nap after meals, so she'd likely be in the garden.

Eli turned to slide eggs out of a pan and onto two plates. "You want some?" he asked when he caught sight of us.

"No, thanks." I'd grab something later when I got hungry. "Anja?"

Her stomach growled, but still she hesitated.

"If you don't like eggs, you're welcome to have something else," I said. "There's plenty of leftovers in the fridge, or we have meal bars."

"Don't listen to our fearless captain. I make a mean scrambled egg—far better than some tasteless meal bar."

Eli's smile was warm and welcoming, and it took me a second to remember the effect he had on others.

Anja blinked and rallied enough to say, "Eggs would be great, thank you. I can clean up."

"I've already volunteered," Kee said with a bright smile. She handed one of the plates to Anja and kept the second one as Eli returned to cooking. "But I wouldn't mind if you wanted to keep me company. I'm Kee, systems engineer. And that ugly brute is Elias, first officer, but we all call him Eli. Welcome aboard!"

"I'm Anja, mechanical engineer. Nice to meet you."

"Have you ever replaced a processing unit?" Kee asked. "I could use a hand, and these two are terrible at delicate, fiddly work."

"Don't fall for her rainbow hair and sunny smile," Eli advised over his shoulder. "She is completely ruthless when it comes to her systems. Once, I made a tiny little mistake and she refused to talk to me for a week. *A week!* That's like three lifetimes in Kee time."

Eli's mistake had taken out the navigation system. He hadn't meant to, of course, but Kee had been furious—and worried. Without nav, our chance of finding our way out of deep space was basically nil. It had been a long week.

Kee sniffed. "That's how long it took me to fix your mess. You deserved longer, but I couldn't stand your sad eyes. And you made me apology cookies. You know I can't resist cookies."

"I've never replaced a processing unit, but I'm good with fiddly tasks because my job involves a lot of them." Anja paused and looked back and forth between them. "But what kind of cookies? Just in case."

"Snickerdoodle is my favorite, but I've never met a

cookie I didn't love. Eli made me chocolate chip, with the chocolate bar he'd been hoarding for two months. That's when I knew he was really sorry."

Eli plated the last of the eggs and joined them at the bar. "I *was* sorry. I told you that about a million times."

Kee's smile was gentle. "I know. But actions speak louder than words, and I was mad at you."

The proximity chime cut off whatever Eli was going to say. "Show me," I said, moving to the nearest screen.

Torran Fletcher had arrived without so much as a message of warning. As I watched, he climbed the cargo ramp, three Valoffs in full armor behind him, each of them pushing a levcart piled with supplies.

I growled under my breath.

"Problem?" Eli asked, his earlier playful mood wiped away, leaving the hard-faced soldier.

"Our guests have decided to arrive early and make themselves at home." I waved him off when he would've left his breakfast. "I will go say hello. You stay here. If they murder me, avenge my death."

"Not funny," he said with a scowl.

"I'm kidding." *Mostly.* I looked at Anja. "You okay here?"

When she nodded, I took my leave and used the short walk from the galley to the cargo bay to compose myself. I needed to be calm and cold and professional, even if Torran's audacity made me furious. And I needed to practice my mental shielding.

By the time I made it through the hatch into the cargo bay, the Valoffs had the levcarts mostly unloaded. Torran carried boxes beside his soldiers, which surprised me. I expected him to stand and point. They had neatly stacked their supplies out of the way against the starboard wall. I considered making them move everything just for the hell of it, but such pettiness was beneath me.

Torran turned at my approach and inclined his head. "Captain."

"General. Your comm must have failed to deliver the message that you planned to arrive early and board my ship without permission."

His eyes narrowed. "We had an agreement."

"The agreement doesn't override common curtesy. Would you board a Valovian ship without informing the captain?"

"I apologize," he said stiffly. "I should have warned you that I would arrive early to give my crew time to make another trip back to our ship. I was going to wait outside with the cargo, but with the ramp down, I thought you expected me." He looked like the words tasted foul, but I didn't detect any deceit.

The three soldiers with him finished unloading the levcarts and waited, unmoving. It was creepy as fuck because I couldn't see their faces. I made an instant decision. "Ship dress code is civilian clothes. If your soldiers don't have any, have them pick some up."

Torran straightened, trying to use his height to intimidate me. "They are comfortable in armor."

The top of my head might have come up only to his nose, but I was hard to intimidate. "Good for them. They'll also be comfortable in civilian clothes. My ship, my rules."

His mouth firmed into a flat line. When I didn't budge, he nodded once, sharply. The three soldiers behind him moved at the same time, pushing the carts out of the cargo bay and down the ramp without a word.

"They will return with the rest of the gear and appropriate clothing. It will take them approximately thirty minutes."

I desperately wanted to leave him standing in the cargo bay for the next half an hour, but he had agreed on the armor. I could also be civil. "Would you like to see your quarters while you wait?"

He stared at me for long enough that I thought he wasn't going to respond, but finally he inclined his head in agreement. I waved for him to follow. It made me itch to have him at my back, but it was better to find out now if he was going to gut me where I stood.

We were nearly to our destination when I caught a flash of white out of the corner of my eye. I'd been keeping watch for Luna, but I hadn't been careful enough.

"Luna, no!" Before I could turn and grab her, she froze, held in the air by an invisible force.

CHAPTER FIVE

Telekinetic. I assessed the threat with new eyes. Fighting a telekinetic Valoff one-on-one was a good way to die. I clutched the grip of the plas blade on my hip but didn't draw it. "Let her go," I demanded.

Luna, for her part, did not seem to mind the midair hover. She was a little above shoulder height, held by nothing but air and Torran's power. She blinked sleepily at me and started to purr. It was all I could do not to snatch her out of the air, but I didn't know exactly how his ability worked and I didn't want to hurt her.

"How *dare* you," Torran seethed. His eyes blazed with fury, and as I watched, the silver and teal expanded, bleeding through the darkness of his irises. I could *feel* the power roiling off him.

My nightmares had come to life in the hallway of my ship.

I drew my blade but didn't activate it. I would fight for

Luna, even if I was hopelessly outmatched. I poured energy into my mental shields. I would have one shot and if he sensed it, I was done.

Luna chirruped at him and cocked her head, her ears swiveling between the two of us. He met her eyes, and I got the distinct impression that they were communicating far better than I'd ever communicated with her.

Jealousy reared its ugly head. What if she liked him more because he could understand her? Hurt punched me in the stomach, but I kept my weapon hand steady.

"Are you okay?" Kee asked quietly, her voice coming through my comm implant.

"I don't know," I responded subvocally. "He's telekinetic. Stay back for now. Relay the message."

"Eli is around the corner behind you. He has a plas rifle. If shit goes down, duck to your right."

I wouldn't, not if it left Luna in the line of fire. But Kee knew that, as did Eli. They would compensate.

Slowly, the brilliant color drained from Torran's eyes until his calm mask was back in place. Luna was gently lowered to the ground, then released. She looked between us, then leapt for my shoulder. Her familiar weight was almost enough to send me to my knees in gratitude.

She chose *me*.

But even that relief couldn't temper the fury still coursing through my veins. I glared at Torran and did not put away my plas blade. "What. The. Fuck." I took a breath to prevent the rest of the rage from spilling out. "Explain, now."

"Burbus," he said, his accent lilting over the word, "are highly protected, as I'm sure you know. They are not pets for offworlders. The punishment for stealing one is death, and all Valoffs are authorized to carry out the sentence."

"So you're executioners without the need for judge or jury. Sounds about right."

"You're still alive," he pointed out quietly. "Luna, as you call her, has chosen you as her family. That takes something extraordinary and cannot be coerced."

"I found her nearly dead, thanks to your soldiers. After she healed, she wouldn't return to the wild. I tried." I didn't owe him anything, but I felt compelled to explain myself.

Torran nodded, his earlier anger either forgotten or carefully hidden. I had a feeling it was the latter. "She would mourn your death and separation is not an option. You are responsible for her now."

I snorted. "I've *been* responsible for her for years. We were fine long before you arrived."

Luna curled her tail around my neck and rubbed her head against mine. She was trying to soothe me. I reached up and scratched behind her ears while I tried to get my anger under control. We'd found out early on that she could sense emotions better than we could.

"If I'd tried to grab her out of the air, what would have happened?"

"I would have killed you," Torran said without inflection.

I huffed out an unamused breath. "I am not so easy to kill. Would I have been able to move her?"

He pointed at the ground. "I could kill everyone on this ship without moving from this spot," he said flatly. It wasn't a boast so much as a statement of fact.

Cold chills broke out along my spine, raising the hair

on my arms. All Valoffs seemed to have some telepathic ability, which was dangerous enough. Telekinetics were less common, and strong telekinetics were rare, thankfully, because just one could turn the tide of battle.

A strong Valovian telepath could take out a squad of humans without mental shields. A strong telekinetic could take out *a battalion,* and the shielding didn't matter. If they couldn't pierce your mind, they could crush your body.

Luna shifted restlessly and chirruped at Torran. He tilted his head and listened. After a moment, he continued the conversation as if he hadn't just threatened to kill everyone on the ship. "You would not have been able to move her unless I had let her go. You could have hurt her. And you can tell your man behind the corner that he is no longer needed."

I was happy for Eli to remain exactly where he was, so I responded to the first part of Torran's sentence. "*You* could've hurt her."

"She was in no danger from me."

The sentence was perfectly neutral, but I heard everything he'd left unsaid. Inviting him onto my ship had been a colossal fucking mistake, and one I couldn't fix without bankrupting us.

"You wear the shoulder guard for her?" Torran asked, changing the subject.

"Yes." The word was clipped and cold, but civility was beyond me right now. I started down the hallway toward his quarters, then stopped and spun back to him. Luna purred louder, but I was beyond soothing. "Threaten my crew again and I will invoke the hostile client clause on the spot. Are we clear?"

Torran's eyes narrowed. When I didn't back down, he inclined his head in agreement.

The clause was a standard part of my contract, but one I'd expanded just for this job. It gave me permission to confine them to quarters until a suitable station could be reached, and it broke the contract in such a way that I kept the initial payment.

If the Valoffs objected, a neutral arbitrator would be hired at the destination station to determine if the clause had been invoked with cause. Threatening to kill my crew once might be allowed to slide, but repeated threats were certainly cause, and Torran knew it. If the arbitrator ruled against me, then I'd be forced to pay back the initial payment and make an additional hardship payment, so invoking the clause wasn't something I would do lightly, but I *would* keep my crew safe.

Torran's eyes moved over my shoulder, and I turned to find Eli leaning against the wall, with a plas rifle held loosely in his arms. His lips were pressed into a flat line and his eyes were clear and cold. It was his killing look, and I hated that Torran had put it on his face.

"We're fine," I said, my voice calm and soothing. "Go help Kee with her project."

"Who do you think sent me here?" he asked softly, his gaze still locked on Torran.

"I have the situation in hand," I said, sinking command into the words.

Luna hopped down from my shoulder and went to sit in front of Eli. When he ignored her, she chirruped at him. He glanced down and sighed, his mask breaking. He patted his T-shirt-covered shoulder. "Come on, you little menace, let's go see what Kee is doing." Despite his wording, his voice was soft with affection.

Luna leapt up with a happy chirp and Eli didn't flinch,

though I knew just how sharp her claws were. Eli nodded to me, gave Torran a flat look, the threat clear, and then turned and disappeared around the corner.

"Kee," I said, subvocally.

"I'm on it. I'll put him to work. And I've got eyes and ears on you."

I led Torran to the room next to mine. Yesterday, I'd thought myself so clever, keeping my enemies close, but now I wished that I'd put him somewhere much, *much* farther away. Like a black hole at the edge of known space.

That *might* be far enough.

I opened the door. "Here's your cabin. Your crew will be in the nearest rooms," I said with a wave back the way we'd come.

I stepped inside and Torran followed. He took in the bright green walls without comment. The door slid closed behind him. The room felt claustrophobically small in a way it never had before, and my head throbbed.

After a second, I dropped my extra mental shields. I needed the practice, but giving myself a migraine on the first day wasn't beneficial. And I had the sinking feeling that no amount of shielding would protect me from Torran if he ever truly wanted to do me harm.

I shoved the thought aside and focused on the here and now. "You have private facilities, so you won't have to use the crew head. Extra linens are in the wardrobe. If you need anything else, ask me or Eli." I glanced at the stack of linens on the bed and eyed him dubiously. "You *do* know how to make a bed, right?"

One corner of his mouth tipped up. The tiny grin transformed his face, softening the harsh lines of his features.

He went from a beautiful, coldly distant statue to a warm, handsome man made of flesh and blood.

The change sent a jolt through my system. I ignored it.

"I can make a bed," he confirmed. "This, at least, is not so different."

I gave Torran the same spiel I'd given Anja. To my surprise, he didn't balk at the assumption that his people would join in shared crew duties such as cleaning, but his eyes narrowed at the communal dinner. "Is that a problem?" I asked.

"You cook for everyone?"

"We occasionally trade off, but yes, I usually cook dinner."

"You would cook for us, too?" he asked, something odd in his tone. His expression had turned flat again, so it was no help.

"Yes," I said slowly, "assuming you can eat what we eat. It's easier to prepare one big meal than a bunch of small ones. But if you would rather cook for yourselves, you can, though I would still prefer if you ate dinner at the same time as the rest of the crew. It helps build camaraderie. If you need your own food, you should ask your people to pick it up while they are out."

"We brought food with our supplies. Most of it is human fare we picked up along the way, which you are welcome to use. If my crew gets restless and homesick, I will cook for them from the supplies we brought from Valovia."

"You cook?" I asked in surprise.

He stiffened in offense, and his tone was biting when he said, "Leaders provide for those under their care."

Not often enough. I kept the words locked behind my

teeth. "I'm sorry. I didn't intend the question as an insult. I figured you had people who cooked for you."

He didn't look any less insulted. "It is my honor to feed my crew. Are you not the same?"

"Me, personally, or humanity in general?" I asked, then waved and continued without waiting for a response. "I enjoy feeding my crew, but in general, humans have a more ambivalent attitude toward cooking. Some enjoy it, some loathe it. Is it going to cause some sort of interstellar incident if I cook for your people?"

He considered me for a long moment. "No."

Well, that wasn't exactly reassuring.

He turned his head toward the cargo bay, and his eyes went distant. "My crew has returned."

A second later, the proximity warning alerted me to their presence. I wondered if they had contacted him, or if he was mentally keeping track of everyone in the area. Could he even do that? There was so much we didn't know about Valovian abilities.

I hoped that lack of knowledge wasn't something I would come to regret.

CHAPTER SIX

In the cargo bay, the Valoffs were busy emptying the lev-carts of boxes, crates, and trunks. A few large soft-sided duffels were in a pile off to the side. Without a word, Torran started carrying supplies. I sighed and did the same.

The nearest Valoff jerked in surprise when I picked up a box, but I ignored them. I'd never been one to stand around and watch while work needed to be done, and I wasn't going to start now. As much as I might regret the decision, the Valoffs were still my clients for the next eight weeks.

A minute later, Eli joined us, scowl firmly in place. He growled out a barely civil greeting and picked up a crate, muscles flexing. One of the Valoffs in armor stared for a second before turning their attention back to their own crate.

With all of us working, the carts were quickly unloaded. I swiped an arm across my forehead, wiping away the light sheen of sweat. The landing bay was warm to-day, but I didn't close the cargo ramp. We'd be shut in soon enough. Might as well enjoy the fresh air while we could. Well, fresh-*ish*. The recycled air carried the bitter tang of mechanical grease and hot metal.

Torran's crew left to return the levcarts. While waiting for them, I caught sight of a tall woman in a station security uniform heading straight for *Starlight*. She was flanked by a half dozen guards.

"Any idea what that's about?" Eli asked quietly from my right.

I rubbed the side of my face. "Unfortunately."

Torran stepped up on my left. "Is there a problem?"

"Most likely." There wasn't time to say more.

The security liaison and her entourage stopped at the bottom of the cargo ramp. She was a bit younger than me, perhaps in her late twenties. Her brown hair was pulled back into a severe bun. Her eyes flickered over Torran and Eli before landing on me. "Octavia Zarola?"

"Yes?"

"Security footage from this morning revealed that you are harboring a dangerous fugitive. Turn over Anja Harbon immediately or face sanctions."

I sighed in frustration. The universe owed me a good turn, but today wasn't my day. "What is she accused of?"

The woman blinked. "It is none of your concern."

"I disagree. Anja is my mechanical engineer. As her captain, I have the right to demand details as well as proof of a crime."

That earned me a sneer. "She is a traitor. If you refuse to hand her over, you will share her fate."

"Why don't you tell the truth: she's being shadow

banned because the station master's wife failed to mention that she was married, and the station master is pissed and trying to save face by punishing someone who doesn't have the political power to protect herself."

The security liaison went livid. Bright red color bloomed in her pale cheeks and her hands fisted. Behind her, the guards shifted restlessly.

Next to me, Torran stood statue-still, but I could feel the power swirling around him. I couldn't explain how exactly, but it felt angry, much like it had earlier when he'd found out about Luna. Hopefully that anger was directed at the security liaison or the station master, because if not, we were going to have a real problem.

Eli shot me an exasperated look before turning a blinding smile on the security liaison. "I'm sure this is all just a little misunderstanding," he coaxed, smile still firmly in place. "Why don't we discuss it in private?"

She blinked and swayed slightly before steeling her spine. "There is nothing to discuss. Turn over the fugitive immediately."

Captains had a lot of autonomy on their own ships, even when those ships were parked in a station's landing bay. She couldn't force me to turn over Anja because the station didn't have any proof of a real crime. But she *could* force me to leave and Torran's crew wasn't back yet. "I've yet to see any evidence against her. Come back when you have some and we'll talk."

"If you refuse to cooperate, then your docking authorization is revoked, as is all future station access. Leave immediately. If you delay or return, you will be arrested."

"While I would be very happy to leave your station behind, I am waiting on additional crew."

Her eyes lit and her lips twisted into a cruel imitation of a smile. Crew away from the ship didn't have the same protection as crew on board. "How unfortunate," she murmured. "I'm sure they can catch up with you at the next station."

"You would interfere with a Valovian diplomatic mission?" Torran asked, his voice cool.

"*Starlight's Shadow* does not hold a diplomatic registration," the woman sneered.

"Perhaps not. But *I* do, and I am a paying client of Captain Zarola."

"And you are?"

"Torran Fletcher, diplomatic envoy of Empress Nepru."

That would've been good to know. As an envoy, he had far more power than as a simple general, no matter how high-ranking. "Kee," I growled quietly.

"I told you his ship had a diplomatic registration," she said over the comm, "but my initial search didn't turn up his status. They must be keeping it quiet. I'll find out why."

At the bottom of the cargo ramp, the security liaison flinched and paled. I guess I wasn't the only one who'd heard of General Fletcher. After a second, she gave Torran a short bow. "Envoy Fletcher, I humbly apologize for the inconvenience, but I must insist on retrieving the traitor."

"No." He stared down at her. "Return to your superiors before I report this diplomatic breach to Her Imperial Majesty." When the liaison didn't move, Torran barked, "Now."

The liaison jumped. She took one look at Torran's expression and bowed again. Her eyes cut to me, filled with impotent rage. The meaning was clear. I was *super* banned, and if I set foot off of my ship before we left, she would happily lock me up and lose the key.

She turned and marched across the landing bay, the soldiers following her. Once she was far enough away, Torran's people slid around the side of *Starlight* and slipped into the cargo bay like silent shadows.

I turned to Torran, who watched the retreating liaison with a frown. "Thank you," I murmured.

His frown deepened. "She will still ban you from the station."

My laugh was bitter. "Oh, I know. I knew that before I hired Anja. I'll report them to the FHP for abuse of power, but it likely won't matter."

"We should get out of here," Eli suggested.

"Tell Kee to get ready for launch and to corral Luna. We don't need another incident before I can explain. I'll lock things down here and then show our guests to their quarters. I'll meet you on the bridge."

Eli paused, clearly uneasy leaving me in the company of four Valoffs. I gave him a minuscule nod and tilted my head toward the hatch. After another searching glance, he tossed me a lazy salute and left.

"Do you have everything you need?" I asked Torran. When he nodded, I closed the cargo ramp. I eyed the pile of cargo on the starboard side of the bay, then pulled out straps and netting. "Any cargo that is remaining here needs to be secured. If you are planning to take things to your quarters, put them off to the side."

The Valoffs moved the duffel bags farther away from the rest of the pile. Together we lashed the cargo to the various tie-offs scattered around the bay. It wasn't strictly necessary because we should have life support, including gravity, for the duration of the trip, but cutting corners on safety was a good way to invite bad luck aboard.

Once the cargo was secured, the Valoffs silently picked up their duffels. The sooner they were out of their armor, the better. Seeing myself reflected in their helmets brought back too many memories I'd rather forget.

I led the way to the crew quarters and pointed to the three rooms I'd set aside for them. "Here are your cabins. You can decide who stays where. The shared bathroom is there." I pointed at the door back the way we'd come. "Change into civilian clothes and then come to the bridge for crew introductions. I'm going to get us launched."

The soldiers said nothing, but they each turned for a separate door. *Not human.* I suppressed the shiver.

Torran followed me farther down the hall until we came to his door. "*Lotkez,* my ship, will be shadowing us to Valovia."

I stopped abruptly and turned to him. "What?"

"My ship will—"

"I got that part. Why?" Not only would I have a Valovian general breathing down my neck, but I'd also have his warship on my ass. Fantastic.

"Time is of the essence. Your ship has approval to enter Valovian space, but *Lotkez* will escort you directly to Valovia so that you don't have to wait through the checkpoints. It will also ensure safe passage."

"So why aren't *you* on your ship?"

He gave me an unreadable look. "Would you have followed me into enemy space without me aboard?"

I grimaced. No, no I wouldn't. Not even for the fortune on offer. I had to remember that General Fletcher was a brilliant tactician. He might choose to lead from the safety of the back, but at least he'd always sent his troops into battle with a solid plan. I needed to be careful or I would be outmaneuvered *again*.

"Very well, I will keep an eye out for your ship. Anything else?"

He shook his head.

"Make sure your crew knows about Luna. I don't want another *misunderstanding*."

I left him standing in the hallway and made my way to the bridge. The large space had half a dozen terminals for the various crew I didn't have. At the front, a wide screen showed a divided view of the outside cameras. The safety perimeter was already raised around our ship, warning of an imminent launch.

Kee, Eli, and Anja were all in place. Anja looked at home at the engineering terminal. Eli was in his usual spot at the tactical terminal, but his station had become more of a catch-all for everything that we didn't have crew for. Kee glanced up from the nav terminal, where she also handled the ship's systems. "I have a route to the wormhole," she said. "We've got clearance to launch. They told us not to return."

Anja winced.

"Yeah, I figured as much," I said as I settled into the captain's terminal. I smiled at Anja. "No worries. We'll just stock up before we head through this part of space again. I wouldn't want to give them my money anyway." I turned to Kee. "How long to Bastion?"

Kee sent the route to my terminal. "Five days if we don't have to wait too long for wormhole access."

Starlight's Shadow was not the fastest ship in the galaxy—it wasn't even close. Torran had probably made the trip in less than half the time if *Lotkez* was a newer Valovian ship, but he would have to settle for a slow return trip. No matter how essential speed was to the investigation, *Starlight* could only go so fast.

Our route crisscrossed through space, taking us through three wormholes. Getting from point A to point B was never straightforward—not if you wanted to arrive in less than a millennium. Earth still hadn't received any radio transmissions from the Valovian Empire that hadn't been relayed through the wormholes by ships, drones, and satellites, and the Valoffs' territory also resided within the Milky Way.

Space was unimaginably vast. Without the wormholes, humans wouldn't have been able to venture much beyond our small solar system. It was pure luck—*bad* luck, some would say—that we'd run into the Valoffs more than a century after humanity's first successful wormhole round trip. Up until that point, humans had thought that we were alone in the universe. Or at least in our galaxy.

The initial meeting had not gone well. Subsequent meetings were not any better.

And, as far as we could tell, Valoffs also relied on the wormholes for space travel. They jealously guarded the ones in their territory. If they'd developed standalone faster-than-light technology, they hadn't used it during the war.

They had their own type of anchors that stabilized their wormholes, but their overall level of technology was eerily similar to our own, which only fed the conspiracy theories. I found it hard to believe that the Valoffs had somehow spied on us from thousands of light-years away, yet had achieved spaceflight only because of technology stolen from humanity, but logic wasn't necessary for conspiracy theorists.

I accepted Kee's proposed route and went through the prelaunch checklist. While the various system checks ran, I went through my final mental checklist. We had plenty of food and supplies, but if something went wrong, we'd pass fairly close to two more stations before we reached Bastion.

All of the prelaunch checks came back green. *Starlight's Shadow* was ready to fly, and I was antsy to leave this station behind. "Ready?" I asked.

Kee, Eli, and Anja murmured their assent.

I eased the ship off the deck and out of the landing bay. As we passed through the atmo barrier and entered open space, my muscles unclenched. I loved being in the black. Some people found space travel claustrophobic and anxiety-inducing—and it certainly could be—but I loved the endless possibilities.

The farther we got from the station, the more I relaxed.

When the traffic around us dwindled to almost none, I turned on the autopilot. Technically it could've guided us from launch, but I liked to have manual control around stations. Call me paranoid and old-fashioned, but I wanted my ship to be in *my* control when we were navigating around a bunch of obstacles that could kill us.

"We've got company," Eli announced a few minutes later. "A Valovian ship is shadowing us."

"Is it *Lotkez*?" At his nod, I continued, "That's General Fletcher's ship. According to him, they plan to escort us all the way to Valovia."

"Well, that's not concerning at all," he muttered.

"See if you can find out anything about their capabilities, but be subtle about it. I don't want them to know we're prying."

Kee's eyes lit and she turned to her screen with determination. Eli said, "It doesn't appear to be a warship, at least not on the surface. It's a little bigger than *Starlight*, and it's broadcasting a diplomatic registration."

He sent a series of images and a 3D model to my terminal. *Starlight* might not look like much, but she had excellent sensors. The other ship was nothing but a black shadow on the visual cameras, but the sensors had captured it in detail. I rotated the 3D model. *Lotkez* had the sweeping curves typical of Valovian design. I might not care for them, but they made beautiful ships.

If *Lotkez* was armed, and I assumed it was, then the weapons were carefully hidden.

There were two approaches to safety in space: a plethora of visible weapons or none at all. The first option was the one most captains used. I didn't know if the Valoffs had to deal with pirates or not, but human pirates were less likely to try to take a ship with better weapons.

The second option required a lot of mettle because pirates *would* try to take it on the off chance that it was actually unarmed. If a captain wanted to hunt pirates, they would hide their weapons. And while a diplomatic registration might smooth the way on stations and at checkpoints, it just made a ship a more interesting target in the black.

Fighting pirates was a risk that took time and paid nothing, so *Starlight* fairly bristled with visible weapons. Our current route was reasonably safe, so combined with our weaponry, I hoped it would be enough to keep us off the menu until we reached Bastion. If it wasn't, then I hoped *Lotkez* knew how to fight because I would absolutely leave them behind to fend for themselves.

Unless Torran wanted to pay me an additional fee to protect them.

I laughed to myself. Maybe pirates wouldn't be so bad after all.

The door to the bridge slid open, and knowing who it had to be, guilt wormed its way through my system. Wishing ill on someone just so I could make a profit wasn't the kind of person I wanted to be, no matter who the targets were. We were no longer at war with the Valovian Empire. I needed to remember that.

I stood and met Torran's gaze. He had changed out of his armor. A quick glance showed that civilian clothes suited him. He wore black pants, a dark gray shirt, and heavy boots. Muscles that had been obscured by the armor were now apparent.

And he had a lot of them.

He wasn't bulky like Eli, but he had defined arms, a sculpted chest, and a flat belly. He had far more muscles than any general should, considering his job was to sit behind a desk and order people to die.

Two men and a woman waited behind him, and while they weren't quite standing at attention, the military bearing was obvious. They all wore the same style clothes as Torran, with color being the only variation. Their expressions were carefully blank, but none of them looked particularly happy to be on my bridge.

I addressed the group. "Thank you for coming. I'm Octavia Zarola, the captain of *Starlight's Shadow*. I answer to Octavia, Tavi, or Captain Zarola. This is my crew." I pointed at each person as I introduced them. "Elias Bruck, first officer."

Eli held up a hand in greeting, but his expression remained cool.

"Next is Kee Ildez, systems engineer and navigator."

Kee waved and gave them a bright smile. "Welcome aboard."

"And finally, Anja Harbon, mechanical engineer." I didn't mention that she might leave in Bastion. She was here now, and that was all that mattered.

Anja inclined her head. "Nice to meet you."

"If you need anything, come to me or Eli. Kee and Anja are going to be busy until we get to Valovia."

I'd expected that to generate curiosity, but I'd been wrong. Their faces remained expressionless. I blew out a slow breath. It was going to be a long damn eight weeks.

"I am Torran Fletcher and this is my team." He stepped aside and pointed to the woman. "Chira Pelek, first officer."

Chira stepped forward and bowed. She had on a deep garnet shirt. She was as tall as the men beside her and sleekly muscled. Her skin was so pale that it appeared to have a faintly blue undertone. Her straight, shoulder-length hair was silvery white, which looked like its natural color. Her eyes were pale, maybe blue or gray, with dark streaks.

Chira stepped back and Torran continued, "Varro Runkow, weapons specialist."

Varro stepped forward. His shirt was black, leaving him in unrelenting black from neck to toe. He was more muscled than Torran, with tan skin, curly dark blond hair, and eyes that were a medium shade, maybe hazel or brown, with darker streaks. He inclined his head in silent greeting and then stepped back.

Torran pointed to the final man. "Havil Wutra, medic."

Havil wore a dark blue shirt. He stepped forward and

bowed. He was leaner than Varro, which the armor had concealed. In armor, the three of them had looked nearly identical. Havil had deep brown skin, straight black hair, and dark eyes, likely brown or black, with lighter streaks.

I wondered if Havil's medical training would be applicable to human physiology, because if so, it would be nice to have a trained medic on board.

I took a moment and focused on the group. The headache was immediate and intense, but their auras wavered into view. Chira's aura was sapphire, Varro's was topaz, and Havil's was ruby. Torran's aura remained an unusual platinum with hints of other colors.

I let the focus go and clenched my hands against the urge to rub my temples. I needed to start practicing again. I'd gotten lax because we'd stopped dealing with Valoffs after the war.

Havil frowned. "Are you okay?" he asked, his voice a smooth tenor.

I narrowed my eyes at him. What had he sensed? I waved off his concern. "I'm fine." I needed to be more careful in the future. I hadn't felt the brush of his mind, but that didn't necessarily mean anything.

I addressed the group. "Welcome aboard. Did General Fletcher tell you about Luna?"

Their expressions shifted but not enough for me to catch what emotion drove the change. All three nodded.

"Good. If you do anything to hurt or frighten her, I will put you in a spacesuit and send you for a walk outside. If you're lucky, *Lotkez* will pick you up. If not, not my problem. We clear?"

"We would never harm a burbu," Chira murmured, outrage clear despite her soft tone. "We understand."

"Good. Same thing goes if you start poking around in our heads without permission." I paused, thinking about Havil's question. "I know some of you may be empathic and can't help picking up stray emotions, but if you actively try to read us, you will break the contract, and I will happily keep your money as I sail off without you."

"I have briefed them on the contract requirements," Torran said. "They will abide by the terms."

"If nothing slows us down, it's five days to Bastion. I'll work up the duty roster tonight, but for now, you can settle in and familiarize yourselves with the ship. Kee will show you around."

Kee hopped up from her station and beamed at the group of unsmiling Valoffs. Kee looked delicate and harmless, and she was, unless you threatened her or hers. People always underestimated her, but she was perfectly capable of defending herself long enough to call for help, even outnumbered.

I hated sending her out as bait, but if we were going to be double-crossed, it was better to know now.

"Come on, I'll give you a tour and show you the best places to hang out." She headed for the door, talking as she went. "And we'll let Luna out of the galley on our way by so you can meet her before she ambushes you."

I tensed at the mention of Luna. The Valoffs already knew about her, so it wouldn't be a surprise, but Torran's volcanic reaction was still fresh in my mind.

Kee continued talking as she led Chira, Varro, and Havil from the bridge. "Luna likes to jump on people, but her claws are really sharp, so we made these little shoulder guards for her to use as landing pads. You should get Tavi to show you how to make one, too."

The door slid closed, cutting off Kee's bright voice and leaving me with the intense urge to follow her. Instead, I got to deal with Torran, who'd remained behind. I painted on a pleasant expression and reminded myself that he was a paying client.

I could be civil for two months. But it was going to be a challenge.

CHAPTER SEVEN

Torran remained by the door while his sharp gaze cataloged the bridge a section at a time. *Starlight* wouldn't give up her secrets so easily, but it was better to distract him before he started digging deeper.

"Not interested in a tour?" I asked him.

His eyes cut to me and my skin prickled at the reminder of how they had looked when he was angry. "I've reviewed the ship's map."

I rubbed a tired hand over my face. It was barely lunchtime of the first day and I was already ready for a break. Only fifty-five and a half days to go. "Do you have any questions?"

"No."

I held on to my remaining patience with both hands while Eli and Anja pretended to be busy at their terminals. I knew they were pretending because *Starlight* was flying under autopilot and didn't need their input.

Summoning every shred of civility I had left, I asked, "Did you need something else?"

Torran tilted his head a fraction of a degree. It wasn't enough to notice normally, but when he focused on something, he stood so still that every movement was magnified. "No."

Civility snapped. "Then why are you still on my bridge?"

He frowned and glanced around as if he were looking for something, and suddenly I understood. He was used to being in control, and a captain's default position was on the bridge.

I'd spent hours and hours staring out at the black for no reason other than I liked sitting at my terminal. With a tap, I could verify that everything was working as expected. I knew that the ship would alert me at the first sign of trouble, no matter where I was on board, but it wasn't the same.

And I also got antsy when I was on someone else's ship.

I took pity on him. "Come on, I'll show you where we store food in the galley and then you can help me with dinner prep. Usually I don't start this early, but I'm making lasagna tonight and it takes a while to assemble and cook."

"Please tell me you're going to make enough for leftovers," Eli pleaded, proving that he'd been paying more attention to the conversation than he'd let on.

I grinned at him. Lasagna was one of his favorites and we hadn't had it in a long time because some of the ingredients were expensive and highly perishable. "I'm making two giant pans. There should be plenty for leftovers." It would take me a while to dial in the required amount of food for the additional people on the ship. Until I had it right, I would err on the side of too much.

Eli looked between Torran and me. "You need any help?"

His meaning was clear, but we'd all have to get used to being alone with the Valoffs. "No, thanks. I'm going to put General Fletcher to work. We have a few hours until the first wormhole traversal. Stick to your usual duties until I update the roster. And keep an eye on the ship while I'm busy."

Eli dipped his head in understanding. He knew I really meant for him to keep an eye on Kee until she was done with the tour.

That sorted, I turned to Anja. "You're welcome to take the day to familiarize yourself with the ship. If Kee doesn't need you, then I'd appreciate an inventory of what you think needs fixing and a priority for each task."

She nodded. "I've already started a mental list, but I'll head down to maintenance and make you a formal list."

"The initial list doesn't need to be exhaustive. You won't have time for a full accounting before Kee needs your help. Focus on the highest priority issues and note any tasks that you could use help with. I'll work it into the roster."

"Will do."

I took one last look at my terminal, then waved for Torran to follow me out of the bridge. He did so with an unreadable expression. I couldn't tell if he was angry or bored or happy, but I doubted it was that last one.

I turned left and headed for the garden. I needed some fresh basil. Torran followed me, a nearly silent shadow. He moved quietly, even in boots. My body was apparently fresh out of adrenaline because having him at my back barely gave me a twitch.

The door to the garden slid open, and Torran made a

soft sound of surprise. "This is the garden," I said. "Keep an eye out for Luna. She likes to hang out in the corner." I waved to the back corner with the little green arbor.

When Torran didn't say anything, I turned around. His face was alight with something like longing before he caught me looking and wiped the expression away. "This reminds me of home," he said simply.

I wavered, torn, then my damn traitorous heart made the decision for me. I knew longing. "Come on, it gets better."

I led him to the arbor and gently swept aside the hanging vines. Luna was on her perch, curled into a ball with her nose tucked under her tail. Apparently she thought a nap in the greenery was better than a tour with Kee. The burbu opened one sleepy eye and chirped at me. "Go back to sleep," I said softly. "We're just going to be here for a minute."

Torran stood frozen behind me, so I pointed at one of the chairs. "Sit there and relax while I gather some herbs. It helps."

He folded his long frame into the low chair and for the first time, I saw some of the tension drain out of him. He tipped his head back and closed his eyes. When he wasn't busy glaring at everything, he really was beautifully built. I let the vine curtain fall closed before my wayward thoughts got me in trouble.

Normally, gathering basil was super quick, but I puttered around the garden for ten minutes before harvesting what I needed. I returned to the arbor and peeked inside. Torran had slouched down in the chair and Luna was curled up on his chest, purring, while he gently stroked her with one hand.

A riot of emotions clamored through my system.

Sprawled in the chair like an indolent king with his distinctive Valovian eyes closed, he looked like a heartbreakingly handsome man who had been conjured from the ether specifically for me. And the illusion didn't shatter as much as I thought it would when he cracked one eye, his expression as open as I'd ever seen it. "Finished?"

I cleared my throat, trying to find my voice. "Yes. But if you want to stay here, you can. I can manage dinner on my own."

That brought back the emotionless mask, and I mourned the loss for a moment before I remembered why that was a cosmically stupid idea. I could appreciate that he was handsome—I had eyes, after all—but I had to avoid letting my heart get involved. He was responsible for the deaths of thousands of humans in a senseless war that the Valoffs had started. I couldn't forget that.

He sat up straight, holding an arm under Luna so she wouldn't tumble off his chest. "I will assist you," he said coolly. He looked down at the burbu cradled in his arms and she cocked her head at him, looking for all the world like she was listening.

It was incredibly adorable.

I hardened my heart against all the soft emotions that tried to rise. *No.* He'd threatened me earlier. He was not adorable; he was a stone-cold killer wrapped in a pretty package.

Luna stood on his arm and shook herself. She looked at me, judged the distance, and launched herself at my shoulder. After she landed, she sent me a mental picture of her empty bowl and a wave of longing.

I laughed and scratched her under the chin. "I already

fed you breakfast, you little glutton, and I *know* Eli gave you a treat when he put you in the galley. You're just going to have to wait until dinner like the rest of us."

Torran stood, bringing him far too close. Startled, I looked up at him. His irises were deep gray, nearly black, with a vibrant slash of silver running through them. Smaller streaks of copper and teal branched in interesting patterns across the dark background. The colors seemed to move and change, growing and lessening in intensity. Was that even possible?

I shivered and let my gaze drift over the rest of his face. His dark brows slashed across his forehead. A long, straight nose led to firm lips. His cheekbones were high and sharp, a Valovian trademark, but a strong square jaw balanced them out.

I shook myself out of my frozen perusal with a blink. Torran's fathomless gaze swept over my face, his expression closed. I wondered what he thought of *my* eyes. They were pale blue, with a darker ring around the outside. By human standards, they were pretty. By Valovian, they were completely uninteresting.

Exactly how I liked it, I reminded myself firmly.

I stepped back and let the vines fall closed between us. The strange spell broke and I wondered if he had been messing with my mind, but I dismissed the thought almost immediately. I hadn't felt the telltale brush of his mind against mine.

No, I feared the truth was far worse: he hadn't done anything at all.

That was all me.

CHAPTER EIGHT

Despite my firm insistence that I wasn't going to feed her, when Luna rode all the way back to the galley on my shoulder then jumped down next to her bowl and stared up at me with huge violet eyes, I caved.

"Fine, fine," I said, "you can have *one* more treat, but that's it." I pointed a finger at her. "If you eat all of our food before we reach Bastion, we'll have to eat *you*." It was an entirely empty threat, and she knew it.

"In Valovan, *burbu* is the word for 'hunger,'" Torran said. "Modern standard Valovan is based on an older dialect. Different regions have different names for burbus, but many of them revolve around their appetite."

"Doesn't surprise me. When I got out of the service, I took her to three vets to ensure I was feeding her enough because it seemed like she was always hungry. But when we left extra food out, she didn't eat it. I worried that something was wrong, but they all said she was healthy." I rummaged around in the dry goods cabinet and pulled out a piece of jerky.

Luna sat by her bowl, her round ears pricked toward me. "This is it until dinner," I said sternly. "No more begging."

She tensed, ready. I waited a beat, then tossed the jerky high. Luna leapt and snagged it out of the air. She twisted around to land on her feet, then leapt again to the rail along the top of the wall. She disappeared out of the room, prize clamped between her sharp teeth.

I turned to Torran. "Do you or your team have any dietary restrictions I need to know about? Kee doesn't eat meat, so most of our meals are vegetarian. Is that going to be a problem?"

He shook his head. "That is fine. We do not have any restrictions."

"If you give me a list of your team's favorite meals, I'll put them in the rotation if we have the ingredients."

Torran gave me an unreadable look, but he inclined his head with something like grudging respect. "I will get it to you tonight."

"Are you okay with chopping vegetables?" When he nodded, I grabbed the small wire basket near the walk-in cooler door and gestured for him to follow me. I pulled the door open and cold air slapped me in the face. Goose bumps rose on my arms. The cooler was sized for a full ship and even with the extra food we'd bought, the shelves were more than half empty.

"Most of our vegetables are stored in here," I said, "along with other perishables. Frozen food is through that door," I said with a wave at the door on the back wall of the cooler. "You are welcome to eat anything we have in here, but if you finish something, add it to the list on the wall outside."

I worked quickly, gathering the vegetables we'd need for lasagna while explaining what each one was to Torran, just in case they were unfamiliar. This recipe was vegetable heavy. Doubling it made it even heavier, and the basket's handle dug into my palm. When I went to switch hands, Torran reached out and effortlessly plucked the basket from me.

"Allow me," he said, oddly formal.

I glanced at him, but his face was set in its usual mask. "Thank you." I made a mental note to do some research on Valovian food customs because something weird was going on, and he wasn't being very forthcoming.

If Torran felt the strain of holding the heavy basket, he didn't show it. I swiftly grabbed the last of the ingredients, then stared at the basket, trying to remember anything I'd forgotten. When nothing jumped out at me, I led Torran out of the walk-in.

"Put the basket there," I said, pointing at the counter. I pulled out a cutting board and a chef's knife, then placed them beside the basket. I also grabbed a big bowl.

Torran silently watched me, and his gaze missed nothing. I had no doubt that if I asked him to grab a knife, he'd know exactly which drawer to use.

"This should be enough to get you started. You're welcome to look in any cabinet here, so if you need anything else, just dig around until you find it." I made two stacks of vegetables. "Small cubes for the first stack and medium-thick slices for the second stack. They can all go in the same bowl."

We worked in surprisingly comfortable silence—after I got over the fact that Torran was standing behind me armed with a knife. The rhythmic sound of the knife on the cutting board was the only thing that let me know he was there.

I made the sauces and started precooking the veggies he had already chopped. Each cube and slice was militarily precise. Once everything was ready, we layered the ingredients into two pans. I did the first while Torran copied me on the second. With his help, it'd taken less time than I'd expected, so I covered both pans and put them in the cooler. I set a reminder for an hour out.

"Thank you for your help," I said, and I meant it.

"You are welcome." He looked like he wanted to say something else, but his head jerked to the side as if he'd heard a distant sound, and he frowned.

"We've got a problem," Kee said over the comm at the same time.

Dread tightened my stomach. "What kind of problem?" I asked subvocally.

"Eli's going to flatten Varro if you don't get down here. We're in the gym."

"He'd better fucking not," I growled, sprinting for the door. I tried to raise Eli's comm, but he'd disabled connections. I was vaguely aware of Torran on my heels. Rather than taking the stairs, I slid down the access ladder, landing hard on the deck below. My bad knee twinged, but I ignored it.

I slammed into the gym and took in the scene in a single glance. Chira and Havil stood off to one side. Chira was scowling but not intervening. Havil winced with every blow. Kee stood on the other side, biting her lip. In the middle of the room, Eli and Varro circled each other on the sparring mats.

They were equally tall and muscular. The fight might

have started as sparring, but now they looked like they were trying to beat the shit out of each other. Both had split lips and Eli's eye was already swelling. Varro's jaw was red, and he favored his right side.

I considered letting the stupid idiots fight it out, but I needed to get this situation under control immediately or the Valoffs would never respect my command. Without a word, I drew my plas blade, flicked the setting to nonlethal, and activated the energy blade. It came out blue, confirming its nonlethal status.

I waded into the fray and walloped Eli with the blade. He went down with a surprised shout. It might be nonlethal, but it still hurt like being struck by lightning. Varro rounded on me and threw a punch. I shifted to take it on my shoulder, but it never landed. Varro stood frozen, his eyes wide.

I turned to Torran. "Let him go," I bit out.

Torran narrowed his eyes at me, expression tight. "No."

All of the tentative camaraderie I'd felt for the last couple of hours evaporated. "My ship, my rules, General Fletcher. Let him go, or I'm going to shock him where he stands."

Varro shifted back, holding up his hands. "I didn't—"

I hit him with the blade, and he joined Eli on the mat with a pained groan.

Eli chuckled through split lips.

My rage turned incandescent and I pointed the blade at him. "Do you think this is funny, Bruck? Do you think I *wanted* to come down here and put you in time-out because you couldn't act like a damned adult for two seconds?"

Eli froze and his eyes flashed to mine. Whatever he saw in my face caused him to wince, but I was too mad to care. "No, Captain."

"I might've expected this from them, but I expected better from you. What happened? Why aren't you on the bridge?"

"He insulted Kee."

Ah, that made more sense. Eli would let insults run off him like rain, but he'd go to war for those he cared about. I deactivated the plas blade and clipped it back into place against my leg.

"I meant no insult," Varro rasped with a cough.

Kee's expression was bright with worry and her gaze kept flickering between the two men on the ground. "What did he say?" I asked her.

Her eyes slid away from mine. "Nothing important."

Whatever it was had hurt her. No wonder Eli had lost his head. I sighed and pressed my fingers to the spot between my eyebrows. My head hurt, my knee hurt, and my rage had burned out, leaving weariness behind.

"A week's extra cleaning for everyone involved, including the spectators. This ship will damn well sparkle by the time you're done. Kee, take Eli to the medbay and patch him up. Havil, take Varro. After that, all of you are confined to quarters until dinner. If I see you out of your room, you'd better be on your way to the head."

I looked at each of them. "I will not tolerate insults and fighting on my ship. If you have an issue, come to me. If you want to spar, that's fine, but you will take appropriate precautions to prevent injuries. You *won't* duke it out like meatheads in a bar fight. Next time, I won't be so lenient. Am I clear?"

One by one, they nodded. The Valoffs had the slightly distant look they got when they were communicating. Their expressions remained impossible to read, but I didn't see any open mutiny. Kee and Eli both looked abashed, but they didn't argue about the punishment. They were my family, but they knew that a captain had to run the ship, and they'd fucked up.

"Clear out. I'll send an alert when dinner is ready. I don't want to see any of you again until then." I glanced at Kee and Havil. "Let me know if these two are more hurt than they let on."

They nodded, and the room slowly cleared. The plas blade packed a punch, and both Eli and Varro moved with careful deliberation. They nodded warily at each other on their way out the door. They weren't bosom buddies by any stretch, but their shared pain bonded them in that strange way common to soldiers. I set a reminder to check on them both in thirty minutes. I didn't want them in pain just because they were too proud to ask for help.

I closed my eyes and heaved a sigh. This was going to be a very long trip.

"You were reckless. You could've been hurt," Torran said from directly behind me.

I nearly jumped out of my skin. I thought he'd left with the others, and I hadn't heard him move at all. I spun and my already tender right knee send a bolt of pain lancing through my leg. I gritted my teeth against the urge to curse. And the urge to tell him exactly where he could shove his commentary.

Torran took one look at my face and his brows drew together. "You *are* hurt."

"Just an old injury acting up from when I landed wrong. Did you need something, General? Perhaps you'd like to undermine my authority again?"

Torran's eyes went distant then cleared. "Havil will

look at it once he's done with the other two. And I did no such thing."

I waved off the offer. "There's nothing to look at. And you did."

"Havil will look at it," he repeated, voice firm.

I rolled my eyes, but I didn't have the energy to fight him about it. He was a client. If he wanted his medic to look me over, then I could spare the five minutes it would take for Havil to find nothing wrong that ice and time wouldn't fix.

"Would you have preferred for me to let Varro hit you?" Torran asked, genuine curiosity in his eyes.

"No," I said honestly. "I appreciate that I won't have a bruised shoulder. But then I gave you an order and you argued with me. If you don't respect me, your team won't either."

Torran's mouth flattened. He looked like he would like to argue again, but finally he dipped his chin in acknowledgment. "You are right. I apologize. I will ensure that my team understands that my failure should not be emulated."

Torran spoke flawless Common, but sometimes his phrasing was oddly formal. Still, I got the gist. "Thank you."

I walked in a slow circle. My knee throbbed with each step, but the pain didn't get any worse. I could walk without a limp if I focused, but it wasn't super fun. Getting old sucked sometimes. At thirty-four I wasn't exactly ancient, but after more than a decade of war, I *felt* old. Minor injuries that wouldn't have phased me at twenty now took me days to recover from.

Torran watched me with his arms folded across his chest. On my second lap, he said, "I did not expect you to include your crew in the punishment."

I talked while continuing to walk. "It takes two people to fight, and one of them was mine. Kee could've stopped Eli, if she'd been thinking straight. Your team could've stopped Varro. No one did, so they will all share the punishment. If nothing else, it'll give them something to complain about together."

"Varro didn't know he was attacking you."

I glanced back at Torran and found him scowling, whether at me or Varro, I didn't know. "I gathered that," I said. "If he'd knowingly thrown a punch at me, his punishment would've been far worse."

"He could've hurt you."

I chuckled drily. "This wasn't my first fight, either as participant or referee. I know how to take a punch. Of course, I'm not as young as I once was. Or as stupid, I hope. There was a time when I would've waded in with bare fists. Now I let technology shoulder some of the burden."

"You stunned him even though I had him contained."

I shrugged. "He deserved it, especially after throwing a blind punch. As you said, he could've hurt someone. And the shock was the extra punishment he and Eli got for being the ones stupid enough to start throwing punches. Maybe next time they'll think first."

A grin tipped up the corner of Torran's mouth. "Maybe."

The grin transformed his face, and I ordered my wayward pulse back to its normal rhythm.

A whisper of sound from the door announced Havil's arrival. Kee popped her head in behind him. "Eli is fine. We're headed up to our quarters. Anja is down in maintenance if you need something. I sent her an update." She looked meaningfully between me and the two Valoffs in the room.

"Thank you. I will see you at dinner."

Kee gave me a solemn nod and disappeared.

Havil stopped next to Torran. "Where are you hurt?"

"Right knee. It's an old injury that I aggravated. I just need rest and ice."

"I would like to examine it, if that's okay with you," he said quietly. "I may be able to help."

I sighed. I just wanted to go to the bridge, put my leg up, and stop moving, but I said, "Let's go to the medbay. I'll have to take my boots and pants off."

The two Valoffs froze.

"Is that going to be a problem? If so, I'm happy to just head upstairs. I would prefer it, actually." I started edging around them, intending to do exactly that.

"No, it's not a problem," Havil quickly assured me. "But you shouldn't walk on the leg until I get a chance to look at it. There's no reason to injure yourself further."

"I've been walking on it for five years. I'm fine. As I already told General Fletcher."

"*Udwist,*" Torran muttered under his breath. Before I could ask what it meant—because it didn't sound like an endearment—he bent and swept me up in his arms.

Now it was my turn to freeze. My breath caught in my throat at his easy strength. My left side was pressed against the hard wall of his chest. And by the time I remembered I shouldn't let him haul me around like a sack of potatoes, we were already in the hallway.

Torran's long stride ate up the short distance to the medbay—which he found without direction. I guess he really had studied the ship's map.

He gently placed me on the examination table and stepped back.

"Thank you," I murmured. "But next time, a little warning first, please."

One eyebrow rose. "Would you have agreed had I warned you?"

He had me there. Rather than answering, I hopped off the table—landing on my left leg—and bent to unlace my boots. I stood and toed them off with a wince. Torran remained rooted in place.

I started undoing my belt. "Are you going to stand there and watch?"

He straightened and focused on me. I had the feeling that I'd pulled him from his thoughts and he hadn't been looking at me at all. I squashed the mild sense of disappointment before it could grow into something unhelpful. Torran turned and left the room. The door slid closed behind him, leaving me with Havil.

I dropped my pants and climbed back onto the table. Nudity didn't bother me, and my underwear covered everything anyway. The area around my right knee was a constellation of faded white scars against skin that remained light golden tan even in the black of space. The scars were a vivid reminder that I was lucky to have kept the leg.

Havil examined me with the cool, impersonal touch of a medical professional. This close, I could see his eyes. They were deep brown with wide tawny streaks. He had kind eyes, I decided, even if they were distinctly Valovian.

When he was done with the exam, he met my gaze. "What do you know of Valovian abilities?"

I wasn't sure why he was asking, so I went with the most basic answer. "Most of you are telepathic."

His eyes crinkled at the corners, but he didn't press me for a more thorough answer. "That is true. In the same vein, some of us can heal. I can't do anything about the scars, because they are already healed, but I can help with the internal injury, with your permission."

"It's as old as the scars," I said, stalling. I'd never heard of a healing ability, not one that had been proven. There were rumors that the Valoffs had far more abilities than we knew about, but most people dismissed them as just that: rumors.

"It didn't heal properly, and you've irritated it enough that I might be able to help with more than the minor swelling. It still won't be fully healed, but it should be an improvement."

"Why would you help me?" I asked, deeply suspicious. He had not only casually confirmed an ability that the FHP would kill to have, but he was also willing to use it on me.

Havil's expression was gentle. "I'm a healer and you are in pain," he said simply. He hesitated for a moment before continuing. "I can *feel* your pain, and it would take more energy to shield against it than it would to heal you. I healed Eli and Varro earlier. You can check with Eli if you have concerns."

I filed away the information that he was empathic and then did exactly as he'd suggested. Over the comm, Eli confirmed that he felt great and that the whole thing had "tingled" but otherwise wasn't invasive.

I let Eli go and reinforced my mental shields. I nodded at Havil. "If you are willing to try, then I would appreciate your help."

He put his hands on the sides of my knee. "You might feel some prickles, but it shouldn't be unbearable. If it is, let me know and I will adjust."

Warmth turned into a mild burn, complete with the

tingles Eli had mentioned. They intensified to stinging pain, and I sucked in a breath. My shields remained untouched.

"Sorry," Havil murmured. "Just a little more, if you can bear it."

"Do it," I gritted out. I gave him a strangled laugh. "At least it's better than the field surgery."

Time stretched. Eventually the burning pain receded back to a mild warmth, and some indefinite interval later, Havil removed his hands. Sweat had broken out along his forehead and his deep brown skin had taken on an unhealthy pallor.

I reached out to steady him when he wavered on his feet. Despite my help, he started to list. I slid off the table and wrapped his arm over my shoulder. I clutched my other arm around his waist as he continued to slide downward. He looked lean, but he was surprisingly heavy. I needed to get him on the table, but I wasn't strong enough to do it alone. "Torran!" I yelled.

"I'm okay," Havil whispered. "Just overdid it. Give me a minute."

The door opened and Torran took in the scene with a glance. Havil's weight disappeared from my shoulders. "Move back," he said. "I have him."

It felt wrong to let go of someone who could barely stand, but I carefully slid out from under Havil's arm. I held out my hands, ready to catch him if he toppled, but he didn't fall.

"I'm fine," Havil insisted again. "Let me go."

"I don't think that's such a great idea, doc," I said. "Why don't you sit on the table for a bit until you recover."

I didn't know how much Torran was assisting, but

Havil slowly climbed onto the edge of the exam table. I handed him an electrolyte drink from the tiny cold storage unit built into the wall. I wasn't sure the drink would help, but based on the sweat, it wouldn't hurt.

With Havil stabilized, Torran's gaze flickered over me before snagging on my legs. My *bare* legs. Or maybe it was my scars that interested him. My knee was the worst, but other scars marred my skin, mapping the horrors of war across the canvas of my body.

I might not mind nudity, but I felt strangely vulnerable with my scars on display under the bright lights of the medbay. I pulled on my pants with shaky hands.

I met Torran's inscrutable gaze, relieved that I saw neither triumph nor pity in his eyes. "If you will look after him," I said with a head tilt at Havil, "I will go check on the others."

He nodded, so I pulled on my boots, lacing them only enough to allow me to escape without them falling off my feet. I just needed a minute to collect myself, to once again lock away thoughts of war and death.

It was only after I'd left the medbay that I realized that my knee didn't hurt at all, not even a tiny twinge. And my head felt better, too.

I was completely pain free for the first time in five years.

CHAPTER NINE

I checked on the crew confined to quarters, let Anja know that it was safe to come up from mechanical if she wanted to, and put the lasagna in to cook. By the time I made it back to the bridge, we were nearly to the first wormhole.

The massive circular anchor enclosed a piece of space that didn't match the surroundings. It bulged out, darker than the space outside the anchor's circumference. The anchor's green glow visually assured me that we were on the correct approach. Wormholes appeared spherical, but going through one at the wrong angle wouldn't do anything at all.

The anchors stabilized the wormholes and made microadjustments to ensure ships would be put on the correct course to traverse the path to the other side. They also controlled traffic flow. No one knew what would happen if two ships collided in a wormhole's interior—or if it was even possible—but ships *had* collided at the entry and exit points, with devastating results.

I confirmed our course and the anchor put us in the holding pattern. Only two ships were ahead of us. A few minutes later, *Lotkez* entered the pattern directly behind *Starlight*. Torran's ship wasn't going to let us get too far out of sight, which I supposed was for the best if they were our ticket to Valovia.

Luna stalked into the room, her tail bristling. I'd left the door open for her. I didn't know *how* she knew we were close to a wormhole, but she always did—and she didn't like it. She jumped into my lap and burrowed against my stomach.

I ran a soothing hand down her back and whispered nonsense to her. Truth be told, I appreciated her company. Usually Eli and Kee would be on the bridge with me when we traversed a wormhole. It wasn't dangerous, per se, but it carried more risk than open space.

The first ship ahead of us had just disappeared from *Starlight*'s sensors when I heard the intentional scuff of a boot on the deck. I turned to find Torran standing in the doorway. His face was set in harsh lines of tension.

I frowned at him. "What's wrong?"

He didn't answer. Instead, he asked, "May I enter?"

I waved him in and pointed at the empty comm terminal. "You are welcome to use that station for the duration of our contract. The terminal is set to read-only and access is logged."

Torran nodded and settled into the chair. He glanced at the screen, but he didn't relax.

"How is Havil?" The medic hadn't been back in his room when I'd checked on the rest of the crew.

"He's recovered. He has returned to his bunk until dinner." His tone did not invite further conversation.

Luna raised her head and chirruped at him. When he didn't respond, she stood and stretched. She sent me a lingering wave of affection, then left my lap—unheard of, this close to a wormhole—and jumped onto the comm terminal.

When Torran tried to gently move her out of the way so he could use the terminal screen, she nipped his fingers with a low hiss. He glared at her and she glared right back, then she flopped over so even more of her body covered the screen.

That drew a rusty chuckle from him. *"Acha torva,"* he murmured. He sat back in his chair and she crawled into his lap.

I stealthily pulled up a Valovan dictionary and guessed at the spelling. *You win.* I smiled. Luna often won, even when you didn't know you were in a battle. Earlier he'd called me *udwist.* The spelling was trickier, but he'd either called me *stubborn* or *wizard.* I kind of hoped it was the latter, but I figured it was the former.

If he was going to keep speaking Valovan, then I needed to look into a real-time translation module for my comm implant. It wouldn't be a bad idea before we landed on Valovia anyway. I added it to my list of supplies to acquire on Bastion.

The second ship in front of us in the pattern disappeared into the wormhole. Three minutes later, the anchor gave *Starlight* the all-clear to approach. I double-checked the course settings and then locked in my approval. The autopilot would take us through. A traversal technically *could* be manually piloted, but this was one case where the autopilot was an improvement. A tiny misalignment could be the difference between success and failure.

The ship automatically sounded the wormhole warning. Usually traversals were relatively smooth, but occasionally they got rocky. In case the Valoffs didn't understand the alarm, I hit the intercom. "Two minutes to wormhole traversal. Secure yourselves."

Over our group comm, Kee, Anja, and Eli let me know that they were secure. Kee also assured me that she was keeping an eye on everything from her quarters.

I let out a deep breath. They might not be *here* with me, but they were still with me. I took my own advice and shrugged into the harness attached to my chair. The odds of needing it were incredibly small, but it didn't hurt anything. Torran did the same, then he placed a protective hand on Luna, cradling her close.

I absolutely refused to find it endearing.

The wormhole loomed large on the main screen. The closer we got, the more distorted the view, as if space was compressed in concentric rings, tighter and tighter. I focused on the terminal in front of me. All systems were running well within spec.

Starlight's engines ramped to full, and a minute later, we pierced the plane of the anchor.

The ship picked up a vibration that had nothing to do with the engines, and time seemed to stretch thin and compress at the same time. The light from the stars spun out into strands that danced around the ship. It was beautiful and nauseating.

Torran clutched Luna closer.

The ship juddered one last time and then we were through. A new set of stars greeted our exit from the wormhole. *Starlight* remained at full power as we moved out of the danger zone. Ships *usually* came out at the same point every time, but sometimes one went astray, and I didn't relish a literal run-in with *Lotkez*.

I took slow steady breaths and let my heart rate settle. One down, two to go. Then we'd be on Bastion, and I'd get to see Lexi for the first time in nearly a year.

We were well out of the danger zone when *Lotkez* appeared on the sensors behind us. "Your ship made it through," I told Torran.

He rolled his shoulders and some of the tension drained out of him. "Thank you."

Luna jumped to the ground and gave me a plaintive look. I knew that look, even if she wasn't sending me pictures of empty food bowls. I pointed at her. "No more food until dinner. We agreed, remember?"

She told me exactly what she thought of our agreement with a flick of her tail as she stalked from the room.

I laughed and sent her a wave of affection.

Torran shifted in his seat but showed no signs of leaving the bridge. That was fine, I needed to work on the duty roster, and I could do that as easily here as in my office.

And if my gaze drifted Torran's way more often than it should, no one would blame me for keeping my enemy in sight.

Right?

I FED LUNA, THEN PULLED THE LASAGNA FROM THE OVEN and let it rest while I fixed a big salad to go with it. Greens grew quickly and could be stacked fairly close together on vertical shelves, so we often had salad with our meals.

Anja and Torran sat at the bar in cool silence. Anja had finally emerged from the bowels of the ship with a frighteningly long list of necessary repairs. Luckily, most of it was either low priority or easy, but there were a few things that needed to be addressed as soon as possible.

And none of them was cheap.

At this rate, I was going to have to actually catch the thief for Torran in order to come out ahead, which meant I needed to talk to him about the details. My mental to-do list just kept getting longer and longer.

"Would one of you mind setting the table? Silverware is in the drawer. Plates and glasses are in the cabinet," I said with a wave in the correct direction, "and the extra faucet by the sink dispenses chilled water. I'm going to cut the lasagna and call the others to dinner."

Anja and Torran silently worked together, opening cabinets and drawers until they found what they needed. By the time I was done slicing the two pans of lasagna, the table was set. I put the salad in the center of the table and a pan of lasagna on either side of it.

I hit the ship-wide intercom. "Dinner is ready. You're all released from your quarters. Come and get it before it gets cold."

"Where should we sit?" Anja asked.

I studied the table. If Kee, Eli, and I sat in our usual spots, we would have humans clustered at one end and Valoffs at the other, which might be comfortable, but it would do nothing to build camaraderie.

"We'll interlace everyone. You sit at the end of this side. Varro will sit next to you, then me, then Chira. The other side will be Havil across from you, then Kee, General Fletcher, and Eli." Adding Lexi would break the pattern a little, but I'd worry about that when it happened.

Seating Varro across from Kee was a gamble. If he really hadn't meant to insult her, then he'd have a chance to apologize and make it up to her. But if he couldn't keep his insults to himself, then he'd be eating in his quarters, right after I buried a sharp elbow in his ribs.

The others began trickling in and I directed them to their seats. Eli grumbled under his breath, but since I couldn't hear *exactly* what he was saying, I let it go.

Torran approached me as the last of his people settled into place. He handed me what appeared to be a large bottle of wine, but the bottle itself was far more ornate than the bottles I usually bought. "To celebrate our contract," he said.

I frowned at the bottle. I didn't remember having it in our small collection. We usually drank beer or cider if we were going to drink. "Where did you find this?"

"I brought it with us. Chira retrieved it for me."

I turned it over and noticed the label written in Valovan. I couldn't read the language, but I could recognize the characters and some common words. I looked at him with wide eyes. "It's Valovian wine?"

He inclined his head.

Valovian wine was renowned across the galaxy. It was also hideously expensive. Bootleggers had made a killing during the war, and now semilegitimate distributors were doing the same. But perhaps it wasn't so costly for a high-ranking general who made his home on Valovia.

"Thank you," I said. "Would you mind opening it while I get out the glasses? Do you need a corkscrew?"

Torran shook his head. "Our bottles don't use cork."

Neither did ours these days, but we still used a corkscrew to open them. I let it go.

He pulled the thick, waxy covering from the top of the

bottle and then removed a delicate composite stopper. The stopper had a built-in grip and what looked like a one-way valve. It was as pretty as the rest of the bottle.

Torran poured the wine into glasses and I distributed them to the table. He handed me the next-to-last glass and then picked up the final one for himself. We returned to the table, and he raised his drink. "To success."

We all raised our glasses and then drank. The first sip slid down my throat like liquid velvet—smooth and rich. It was like no wine I'd had before and probably never would again. It was too rich for my meager bank account, but now I understood why people paid ridiculous amounts of money for it.

Kee made a delighted sound. "Keep bringing wine and you can stay as long as you like."

"Considering how much this wine sells for, I would agree to that deal," I replied with a grin. "But that means you can't drink it all."

She clutched her glass close with a dramatic flourish and laughter rippled around the table.

We passed the food and everyone served themselves. The Valoffs were more hesitant, but Kee and Eli dug in with gusto and I did the same. I hummed in delight. It was a good batch, and it'd been a long time since we'd had lasagna.

It reminded me of home.

I hadn't seen my parents in over a year, but we kept in touch with asynchronous video or text messages, depending on how deep in the galaxy I was. And I carried fond memories of their tiny, warm kitchen and my mom's loving smile with me wherever I went.

Chira, who sat on my right, made a faintly surprised sound after trying a bite of the lasagna. "This is good."

"Tavi's lasagna is the best," Eli confirmed. His first serving was nearly gone, and he was already eyeing his second. Luckily for him, we hadn't put much of a dent in the two big pans, so there was plenty left.

"Thank you. I'm glad you like it. I've never cooked for Valoffs before, so you'll have to let me know if things are too spicy or too bland or otherwise don't agree with you. You won't offend me. I'll be far more upset if you're hungry and miserable in silence."

I tried not to notice that while Torran had eaten his salad, he hadn't touched the lasagna on his plate.

On my other side, Varro ate in silence. Across the table from him, Kee chatted with Havil and Anja, and even occasionally drew Torran into the conversation. The only person she pointedly excluded was the silent Valoff next to me.

So he hadn't apologized.

Poor bastard.

Kee shined brightest of all of us, and her attention was like basking in sunlight. Take that attention away, and the world turned a little darker and colder. It was as if the sun decided to shine on everyone but you. Eli and I both had been on the receiving end before, but we had been smart enough to apologize, promptly and profusely.

We'd see how long it took Varro to learn the same lesson.

WE ALL HAD A SECOND GLASS OF WINE, AND THE DELICIOUS alcohol was just strong enough to lower guards and smooth some of the group's hard edges without tipping anyone over into belligerent drunkenness.

And so we survived our first dinner without resorting to threats, violence, or insults.

Torran eventually ate his lasagna without a single word or expression to indicate what he thought about it. Not that I was watching him *that* closely, but all of the other Valoffs had expressed their appreciation for the meal. I reminded myself that it didn't matter what he thought, as long as he ate.

The newly minted duty roster put Eli and Chira on clean-up duty. It was partially as punishment for the fight earlier, because as first officers, they should've known better. It would also show the Valovian crew that they weren't doing anything that the first officers hadn't already done.

As people started to stand from the table, Kee bounced to her feet. "I got the new episodes of *Crash Crush* while we were on-station." She turned to Eli and me. "Rec room in thirty?"

We both nodded. The romantic drama was Kee's latest obsession. We'd watched the first episode two weeks ago because Kee had randomly grabbed it with her last media download. Then we'd had to wait until we were closer to a distribution server to pick up the newer episodes. Kee was *dying* to know what happened to the female lead who'd accidentally wandered into enemy territory—and straight into the male lead's arms.

"I love that show," Anja said. "What episode are you on?"

"The first one," Kee wailed. "I've been waiting *forever* to see what happens." She waved a finger at Anja. "Don't spoiler me."

Anja mimed locking her lips.

"Would you mind if I joined you?" Havil asked tentatively.

Kee beamed at him. "Of course not! Are you a fan of the show?"

Havil shook his head with a rueful smile. "I've never seen it, but I have enjoyed other human productions. Maybe you could recap the first episode for me before you start the second?"

She grabbed his hand with an excited little hop. He stilled, but she didn't let it deter her. "Even better, we'll watch it while the others clean up." She looked around, skipping straight past Varro. "Anyone else want to join?"

I caught Chira's brief longing glance before she dropped her eyes to the dishes in her hands and remained silent. Varro's mouth was set into a firm line as he looked anywhere except at Kee.

I sighed quietly. I swear, sometimes my job was half therapist, half mediator, and half de facto ship parent, with a few other halves left over for captaining, negotiating, and bounty hunting.

"Why don't we all start over with the first episode in thirty minutes?" I suggested. "I could use the refresher, and Eli and Chira can get caught up, too, if they want to join."

When Chira's surprised look bloomed into a smile, I knew I'd made the right call. "Thank you," she said. "I would like that."

I drained the last drops of the delicious wine from my glass. "Until then, I'll be on the bridge if anyone needs me." I gave Eli and Varro a warning glance. "Stay out of trouble."

Eli tossed me a jaunty salute. "Aye aye, Captain." He was not deterred in the slightest when I glared at him.

Varro settled for a stiff nod.

I left them to it. I couldn't constantly watch them, so they were going to have to figure out how to tolerate each other.

The bridge was dim and silent. Stars dotted the display

as *Starlight's Shadow* slid through the emptiness of space. After three years, the background hum of the engines was easy to ignore, a heartbeat that was noticeable only when something was wrong.

I dropped into my seat with a deep sigh. It had been a long time since the ship had carried more than Eli, Kee, and me, and the thought was bittersweet. I'd never expected to haul our former enemies around the universe.

Life was funny sometimes.

After checking that everything was truly okay with the ship, I leaned back and put my feet up on my terminal. It wasn't the most dignified way to sit, but it was comfortable.

While there was always some traffic on wormhole routes, this wasn't a highly popular—or profitable—one. There were no habitable planets and only a handful of remote mining stations in this sector. The ships in front of us at the wormhole had taken other routes, so the only other ship in sensor range was *Lotkez,* and they weren't likely to hail me. I could sit however I liked.

The next wormhole traversal wasn't until the day after tomorrow, in the early hours after midnight. Then, two days after that, we'd traverse the final wormhole before Bastion and arrive at the station in the early hours of the fifth day.

After we restocked and picked up Lexi, we'd pass through the heavily guarded wormhole that divided human space and Valovian space. Then we'd travel for a day before the final traversal spit us out close to Valovia itself. If everything went according to schedule, we should be on-planet by the eighth day. As far as space travel went, it was almost speedy.

Now if only we could catch the thief as quickly.

Why would a human go all the way to Valovia to steal something from Torran? It didn't make sense. There were plenty of less risky targets in the human sectors.

The door to the bridge slid open while I was pondering possibilities. A glance over my shoulder revealed the Valoff in question. Torran nodded in greeting and then slipped into the comm terminal. He did a cursory check of the ship's systems and then settled back in his chair.

"Why didn't you hire a bounty hunter at Bastion?" I asked. Not only would it have saved him several days of travel, but it also would've offered a much better selection.

Torran glanced at me before returning his attention to the comm terminal. "There are too many ears on Bastion," he said at last. "I did not stop."

So he really was trying to keep the theft quiet. "What was stolen?"

His gaze cut to mine, and I saw calculation in his eyes before he masked his expression. "A family heirloom."

"If you want my help—and you appear to, with the amount you're paying me—you're going to have to give me more than that. Or we can agree it's an impossible task, and I can keep the initial payment and let you off on Bastion."

Torran sighed, and for the first time, he looked worn and worried. "I want your help," he murmured. "The thieves stole a very old, very important ring. It's engraved with my family's insignia, and possessing it gives the holder the right to access the family's accounts and properties."

"Shit," I breathed as the full implication hit me. "Can you invalidate the transactions because the ring was stolen?"

One shoulder lifted. "Perhaps, but it will not be easily done."

"Have they already accessed your accounts?"

He paused, clearly debating whether or not to tell me the truth. "They tried. I moved the vast majority of our assets into protected accounts as soon as I learned of the theft."

"How many assets are still at risk?"

Torran stared at the stars on-screen for a long moment. "Enough."

"If the ring is so important, why wasn't it secured?"

"It was."

I snorted. "Then your security sucks." I talked through the heist. "So a team of—do you know how many thieves were involved?"

"At least four."

"So a team of four breaks into your . . . house?" At his nod, I continued, "Breaks into your house, defeats whatever security you had protecting the ring, and makes off with it. You lock your accounts, and they try to access them. Presumably they know that not everything is locked down and are systematically trying to find something to steal. Which means they have to be close enough to access it."

I looked at him in dawning comprehension. "You think they're still in Valovian space, possibly on Valovia itself." I followed that train of thought. "And you can't involve the Valovian authorities because you are trying to keep it quiet. Why?"

Torran's jaw hardened. "I can't tell you."

"Why not?"

"I am bound by an oath."

"Of course. That would make this entirely too easy," I growled. "Instead, let's let the humans go on a wild-goose chase without enough information to find anything. That's *way* better."

My sarcasm was not lost on him. He glared at me. "It was not my decision."

Now *that* was interesting. As far as I knew, there were not too many people on Valovia who could override General Torran Fletcher. "Are you the head of your household?"

Torran's eyes gleamed and he inclined his head.

"So it wasn't someone in your family. The government?"

He said nothing.

"Kee will find out, oath or no," I warned him.

"I hope so," he whispered so quietly that I wondered if I'd imagined it.

CHAPTER TEN

By the time I made it down to the rec room, Kee had Havil and Eli rearranging the furniture. The number of seats in front of the vid screen had doubled, and the individual seats we usually used had been replaced by couches and loveseats from the other parts of the room.

When I quirked an eyebrow at her, Kee gave me an innocent smile. I didn't believe it for a second.

I felt Torran arrive, his presence heavy at my back. He hadn't mentioned joining us when I'd left him on the bridge—after I'd quietly ensured all of the terminals were sufficiently locked down. I shifted out of the doorway and he stepped up beside me.

He watched Kee directing the others for a moment before softly asking, "Does she always get her way?"

I chuckled. "Pretty much." Kee drew people like bees to honey, and Eli and I were not immune. It wasn't just her cheerful optimism and delicate build—it ran deeper, some indefinable quirk that was all her. If Kee ever put her mind to it, she could manipulate nearly anyone, but the thought never occurred to her. And 99.8 percent of the time, she was incredibly easy to get along with.

Varro continued to find himself in the uncomfortable .2 percent.

When everything was arranged to her satisfaction, Kee flopped into the middle seat of a couch. She patted the seat to her right and Havil joined her. Eli moved to take the seat on her left but before he could get there, Varro slid into it.

When Kee side-eyed him, he gave her a challenging look. She retaliated with a smile full of teeth, then turned her back on him to talk to Havil. Varro's jaw clenched.

I almost contacted Kee over the comm to tell her to stop antagonizing him, but I stopped myself at the last minute. She had the right to be upset. If he still hadn't apologized in a few days, I would have to intervene for everyone's sake, but for now, I'd let her handle it.

I claimed a spot on the loveseat in the back so I could keep an eye on everyone. It should not have surprised me when Torran sat down on my right—it was the best tactical position, after all—but it did.

Something in my expression must've given me away, because he quietly asked, "Would you prefer for me to sit elsewhere?"

I shook my head. The loveseat was small, but a half dozen centimeters still separated us. I needed to take my own advice and act like a damned adult. He didn't need to find another seat just because I was inconveniently attracted to him.

Eli, Chira, and Anja took the last sofa and once everyone was in place, Kee turned on the screen and dimmed the lights. I slouched down in my seat then sat up with a dissatisfied noise. I needed a place to put my feet. My normal chair reclined with a built-in footrest.

A footstool was just out of reach on my left. I stretched for it without getting up, and I nearly had it when it suddenly slid back a few centimeters. It surprised me enough that I almost fell onto the floor, but a hand on my right arm steadied me.

A glance back revealed Torran wore a solemn expression of concern, but his eyes were full of laughter.

I sat back with a huff. "You move it, then," I whispered. I lifted my legs and waited. And waited. *And waited.* I was just about to give up and get the damn thing myself when it silently slipped under my legs. I lowered them gingerly, aware he could move it away as easily as he'd moved it into place.

The footstool stayed put, and I slouched back down into my preferred viewing position. I was hyperaware of Torran for a few minutes until *Crash Crush* sucked me in. I already knew what happened in the first episode, but I still sighed in satisfaction when the male lead rescued the female lead from discovery with a smooth move that resulted in them pressed up against a wall together.

Kee cheered, but Varro scoffed. "No Valoff would react that way."

The two sides in the show were based on some ancient human war, not the Valovian war—that conflict was still far too raw. There were starting to be more human-Valoff couples, including a handful of minor celebrities, but it wasn't yet common, especially in the sectors farther away from Bastion and Valovia.

Kee rounded on Varro, her eyes flashing. "What is your *problem?*"

"I don't have a problem."

She huffed. "The stick up your ass suggests otherwise."

Apparently that insult translated well enough because Varro's eyes narrowed.

Before he could say anything, Kee returned her attention to the vid screen. "You're not worth the time," she said dismissively. "If you don't like the show, you're welcome to leave."

Varro opened his mouth, then clicked it shut. His shoulders were a taut line. I glanced at Torran, to see what he thought of the exchange, but his gaze was focused on Varro and his expression was distant.

Maybe I wouldn't have to intervene after all.

The second episode was just as good, and before we knew it, Kee had us watching a third. Even Varro's tense posture relaxed as the show drew him in. It was sweet and funny and romantic, and the actors were excellent. This was one of Kee's better picks.

I climbed to my feet before she could start a fourth episode. "It's late, and I happen to know you all have an early morning of cleaning scheduled tomorrow." I checked the time and corrected myself. "Today."

Eli opened a group comm with Kee and me. "Are we going to take watch shifts?"

"No. I'll have *Starlight* monitor for movement and alert me if anyone leaves the crew wing. Get some sleep while you can because I think we're going to be spending some time on Valovia and we'll need to be more careful then."

They nodded and dropped the comm.

I pulled Havil aside as the room started to clear. "Are you okay?"

He inclined his head. "I am fully recovered."

"I'm glad to hear it." I swallowed and met his eyes. "Thank you for healing me. If there's anything I can do to repay you, let me know."

His smile was as kind as his eyes. "You are welcome. I am glad I was able to help. There is no debt between us."

"You healed a pain I've been living with for five years. There is *definitely* a debt between us."

He shook his head. "I was given my gift to help others, not to accumulate favors."

"How did you endure the war?" I murmured to myself, but Havil caught the words and his expression darkened.

"I was lucky to be assigned to Torran."

Which meant he hadn't been near the front lines, so he would've avoided the worst of the suffering. But if healing and empathy were Valovian abilities, then others hadn't been so lucky. I'd had enough trouble living with my own feelings during the hardest years. If I'd also had to live with the constant pain of those around me . . . . I let the thought go with a shudder. I wasn't that strong.

"I'm sorry. I didn't mean to pry. If you need anything while you are here, let me know." I waved when he would've protested again. "Not as a debt, but as gratitude."

He smiled. "Very well. I will let you know, if *you* promise to let me know when your knee starts bothering you again."

I could tell from his expression that no amount of arguing would change his mind, so I inclined my head. "Deal. Sleep well."

"You, too." He bowed slightly and turned for the door.

The room had emptied except for Torran, who leaned

against the wall next to the door. Havil exited with a nod, leaving Torran and me alone in the room.

Torran's attention focused on me and a shiver danced over my skin.

"Did you need something, General?" I asked as I approached. "Or were you just staying to ensure I didn't eat your medic for dessert?"

A brief smile touched his mouth. "I don't think he would be very delicious."

It was a clever dodge of the question that surprised a laugh out of me. "True enough."

Torran's expression warmed briefly before settling back into polite detachment. "I've instructed Varro to stay away from Kee."

My eyebrows rose. "All he needs to do is apologize— and mean it—and she'll forgive him. But if he can't do that, then I suppose distance is the next best option. I was planning to intervene if they hadn't worked it out in a few days. Do you know what he said to her?"

Torran shifted. "I believe he may have inadvertently implied that she was unintelligent."

"How do you accidentally call someone stupid?" I demanded, outraged all over again on Kee's behalf. No wonder Eli went ballistic.

"I don't know. He wouldn't say."

I blew out a breath. "Is he usually this much of an asshole?"

"No," Torran said slowly. "He is occasionally curt but never cruel."

"He apologizes, sincerely, before we get to Bastion or he's off my ship. You can find someone else to replace him."

Torran stared at me for a long moment before bowing his head. "Agreed."

THE NEXT MORNING CAME TOO EARLY. THE SHIP HAD ALERTED me three times during the short night. The first was right after Torran and I had returned upstairs to the crew quarters. The Valovian general had left his room and walked a lap of the ship. He did not try to enter the bridge.

Later, Chira had gotten up in the middle of the night to visit the garden. I'd fallen back asleep waiting for her to leave, and the ship hadn't alerted me again, so I assumed she was still asleep in the arbor.

And a few minutes ago, Varro had headed for the galley.

I started my day early, but not this damn early. However, now I was awake, and my alarm was set to go off in forty-five minutes anyway. I dragged myself out of bed.

Luna made a disgruntled noise and curled more firmly into the covers, tucking her nose under her tail.

I chuckled at her and then dressed in workout clothes. I pulled my hair up into a long ponytail. I might as well get some exercise in while the gym was empty.

On my way downstairs, I stopped by the galley. Varro sat at the table, staring into the distance. When he heard me, his head jerked up.

"Good morning," I said, fighting to keep my voice neutral.

"Good morning. Did I wake you?"

I shook my head. "I'm on my way to the gym. Just stopped by for water."

We had a shared stash of reusable water bottles, so I

pulled one from the cabinet and filled it from the chilled water faucet. Behind me, Varro remained silent.

I capped the bottle and moved to leave the room. I was steps from the door when his voice brought me to a halt. "Captain Zarola, may I ask you a question?"

I turned back to him. "Yes."

He swallowed. "How do humans apologize for words that hurt?"

"Telling the person you are sorry is a good first step. Take responsibility for your actions, and promise to work on doing better."

"What if that doesn't work?"

I settled into the chair across from him. "Are you talking about Kee?"

He nodded.

"Did you say, 'I am sorry,' or did you try to weasel out of it?"

"I told her that I didn't mean any insult." He ran a frustrated hand through his hair, tousling his curls. They softened the hard lines of his face. "She is still angry."

I sighed. "You might not have *meant* to insult her, but you still did. You hurt her feelings. You have to own that. How would you apologize to another Valoff?"

"I would say *lota chil vetli* and if the insult was grave, I would bring them *vosdodite,* an apology gift."

"Are you sorry that you hurt Kee's feelings, or are you just trying to apologize because General Fletcher ordered you to?"

Varro looked away. "I did not mean to hurt her," he said stiffly. "I was not ordered to apologize." He paused. "I'm supposed to stay away from her."

He was uncomfortable, but he seemed sincere. "Very

well, here's what you're going to do. First, you're going to tell her that you're sorry, and you're not going to weasel out of it. Tell her in Valovan if you have to, she'll figure it out. Next, you're going to give her an apology gift just like you would for another Valoff. Cookies are her favorite. Come on, I'll show you the recipe. You're lucky that we just restocked."

I pulled up the snickerdoodle recipe on the galley terminal. "Do you know how to bake?"

Varro nodded, then added, "Are you sure food is an appropriate apology?"

"Do you have a better suggestion?"

"On Valovia, we usually either give something the recipient desires greatly or something valuable and difficult to part with."

"Trust me, Kee loves cookies." I pointed at the screen. "Bake the cookies, give them to her, sincerely apologize for hurting her, promise to do better, and then walk away. She may not forgive you immediately, and that's her choice. Do *not* say something stupid like 'I'm sorry you were insulted.' Got it?"

He nodded again, looking a little mystified. Hopefully he'd figure it out as he went. And as long as he didn't royally fuck it up, Kee would forgive him just for making the effort.

I left him to it and took the stairs down to the middle floor. The gym was blissfully empty, so I cranked up a playlist with a heavy beat and got to work. I'd designed my workout to go easy on my knees, with low impact cardio and a full body resistance routine. Even so, I usually felt at least some pain or tension.

Today, I had none.

I was on my last few reps on the rowing machine when

Eli strolled in, looking bright and fresh in his loose shorts and tight tank. I could feel the sweat dripping down my face, and my shirt was plastered to my back. At least he would be just as grimy once his workout got started.

He turned down the music and said, "You're up early."

I grimaced. "Unfortunately." I finished the set and paused to catch my breath.

"Want to train?" Eli asked with a head tilt toward the sparring mats.

"You just want an excuse to beat me up because I ruined your fun yesterday," I said without heat.

Eli's grin was sharp and quick. "Varro is fast as fuck," he confided. "It was a good match." The grin wiped away. "Too bad it was necessary." Eli looked at me. "Did you know he's making apology cookies?"

I rolled my eyes. "Where do you think he got the idea? He seems sincerely sorry. If he's not, Kee will eat him alive. Either way, she gets cookies."

Eli offered me a hand up, then easily pulled me to my feet. "You're too soft. Let's toughen you up."

"I will enjoy making you eat those words, Bruck, even if I have already done an entire workout while you got your beauty sleep."

He grinned and tossed me a pair of hand wraps. I snagged them out of the air and wrapped both hands with the ease of practice. I jabbed at an imaginary foe, testing my muscles. I'd gone hard this morning, and I could feel the fatigue. Eli would eat my lunch if I let him get close.

I removed my shoes and socks and stepped onto the mat. Eli was nearly twenty centimeters taller than me, with a much greater reach. He was stronger, and for all of his muscled bulk, he was fast, too.

In other words, he was the worst type of opponent, which made him the best for training.

I tapped my wrapped knuckles to his and then danced out of reach. I had to keep moving. Once he got me on the ground, this would be over embarrassingly fast.

He feinted at me, but I dodged the real blow and retaliated with a quick jab to his flank on my way by. "Getting slow in your old age," I taunted.

"If I'm old, then you're ancient," he said.

I laughed. He was only two months younger than me.

"Make sure you tell everyone that an old crone beat you up," I said, darting under his guard to land a light blow on his abs. We weren't trying to hurt each other, so the strikes were just hard enough to let the other person know that they'd been hit.

He clipped my shoulder when I wasn't quite fast enough on the escape, and he grinned at me. "Now who's the slow one?"

We kept circling, trading taunts and blows in equal measure. I was decent at hand-to-hand combat, but in a real fight, Eli would mop the floor with me. But because we trained together, I knew how to take on a much better opponent, which had saved my skin more than a few times.

After fifteen minutes, I flopped down on the floor and tapped out. My muscles had picked up a fine tremble and I sucked in great gulps of air. "You win this round, Bruck. Don't let it go to your head."

He grinned down at me, barely winded. "I win every round."

I tried to sweep his legs out from under him, but he jumped back with a laugh. "Enjoy your nap. Some of us are here to work out."

"At least help me up, you monster," I growled at his retreating back. "Respect your elders!"

"You got yourself down there, you can get yourself up."

I stared at the ceiling and tried to get my breathing under control. I really was going to be moving like a little old lady once the muscle soreness set in, but at least my thoughts had settled.

We were going to Valovia and it seemed like we might be there for a while. Allies would be few and far between. I needed to ensure that Torran and his crew saw us as indispensable before we landed. And I needed to strengthen the ties between our crews.

So all I had to do was personally overcome more than a decade of war and distrust, and then persuade two teams of people to do the same. In the next week.

I blew out a heavy breath. Sure, no problem.

CHAPTER ELEVEN

By the time I'd stretched and then dragged myself to my feet, the gym had gotten busier. Chira was running on a treadmill in shorts and a tank. Her pale skin practically glowed in the overhead lights, and she'd pulled her silvery hair up into a short ponytail. She moved at a steady clip, her breathing deep and even.

Eli was working his upper body on the resistance press, and he had finally started sweating. A glance at the resistance setting showed that it was because he was pressing far more than my body weight.

My gaze snagged on Torran, who was rowing. His resistance setting was also incredibly high, but that's not what had grabbed my attention.

It was the flex of the muscles in his back and shoulders during every pull.

Which I could clearly see because his sleeveless shirt clung like a second skin.

I took a moment to appreciate the sheer beauty of all those muscles working in unison. Rowing was a full body workout, and it took practice to make it look so easy. But his smooth rhythm never faltered, not even when I looked up and realized he was watching me in the mirror.

I didn't know how long I'd been caught staring because his expression was inscrutable, but I could feel the blood rushing to my cheeks. His eyes flickered over me and I hoped I didn't look as bedraggled as I felt.

Of course, the mirror killed those hopes. I was flushed and sweaty and the curls in my ponytail had frizzed so much that it looked like Luna's fluffy tail. On her it was adorable . . . on me, not so much.

I needed a shower and breakfast, maybe not in that order.

When I started unwrapping my hands, Torran stopped rowing and approached. The view from the front was just as fine, with his chest and abs lovingly defined under his shirt. He nodded at my wraps. "Do you need an opponent?"

A shiver raced over my skin at the thought of sparring with Torran, but I shook my head. "No. Eli already kicked my ass this morning. I was just gathering enough energy to take these off and head upstairs."

Torran frowned. "Are you injured?"

"Nope, just tired." I slowly unwound the wraps and realized just how true that was. I'd been slacking off on my workouts and it was showing. "If *you* need an opponent, Eli would probably enjoy sparring with you. He's a good partner as long as you don't go around insulting the people he cares about."

I hung the hand wraps from a clip on the wall. They weren't quite dirty enough to wash yet, but I didn't want to put them back in the clean basket. I would use them again tomorrow. I needed to get back into my normal routine.

"I am finished," Torran said. "I will accompany you upstairs."

I eyed him. "Are you really done or are you just worried that I'll fall on my face? Because I don't need a babysitter."

"I am not babysitting; I am protecting my investment. If you become incapacitated, your crew will not go to Valovia without you, and I do not have time to hire another crew."

I wasn't sure that was better, actually, but it didn't matter. I was his ticket to reclaiming a family heirloom, and he was my payday. We had agreed to a simple business transaction. I needed to keep that perspective.

And if he already saw me as an investment, then my plan to ensure my team and I were considered indispensable before we arrived on Valovia was already well underway.

There was no reason at all to be disappointed.

THE NEXT FEW DAYS PASSED PEACEFULLY AS BOTH CREWS settled into *Starlight*'s routine. There were no more fights, and three days after he'd insulted her, Kee forgave Varro. She didn't hold grudges, so she treated him like everyone else, joking with him like nothing had happened. If he remained extra reserved around her, she pretended not to notice.

Kee and Anja had gotten the new processing unit installed, and as expected, it was a huge improvement over the old one. When I'd marveled at the improved nav plotting times, Kee had just smiled smugly and given me her best I-told-you-so look.

Overall, the trip was going very smoothly, which made me a little wary. I'd expected more issues. I felt like I was sitting atop a bulging volcano, just waiting for the eruption, so it was a relief to make it through the last wormhole before Bastion without any trouble. *Lotkez* followed a few minutes later, and some of the tension unknotted. Maybe I was worried for nothing.

I looked around the crowded bridge. Even though it was after midnight, both crews had stayed up for the traversal. I could see the same relief I felt reflected on more than one face. Wormholes didn't bother me too much, but the Valoffs seemed much less comfortable around them.

"Everyone should get some sleep," I said. "It'll take a couple of hours to arrive, maybe more if their docking department is backed up again. Then we'll do a quick restock, pick up Lexi, and hopefully leave by tonight."

"Have you heard from her?" Eli asked.

"Not yet, but the last comm broadcast was yesterday morning. We should be getting a refresh from the station momentarily."

Long-distance communication was slow at best. Comm drones traversed the wormholes to broadcast messages and news to the next set of drones and ships. In highly trafficked areas, the drones might cross the wormholes six or eight times a day. Out here, it was closer to once a day unless you were sending military or government messages. Stations also kept a two-month queue of received messages, since ships were often out of range.

Urgent messages could be sent via special delivery on high-priority drones, but it got very expensive, very quickly.

"Lexi should've arrived late yesterday," Kee said.

"If I don't hear from her in the next refresh, I'll send

her a message in the morning. No reason to wake her up now."

Kee yawned and stretched. "Sounds good. You going to fly us in?"

"Yes, then I'm going to try to sleep until a reasonable hour."

People slowly trickled from the bridge, leaving Anja and Torran. Anja stopped by my terminal. "Should I pack my things?" she asked quietly.

"Do you want to?"

"No."

I smiled at her. "I hoped you'd say that. Kee already threatened to mutiny if I let you leave on Bastion and she has to go back to working with Eli."

Anja looked down. "I barely did anything. And I didn't get as much done in mechanical as I'd hoped."

"You did plenty." And she had. She'd worked her ass off this week. It wasn't her fault that there were so many issues that needed fixing. My expression sobered. "We are heading to Valovia, likely for weeks. Be very sure that is something you want to do." I held up a hand to stop her when she would've interrupted. "I'm not trying to dissuade you. I want you to be sure, so take tonight to think about it."

She murmured her agreement and left the bridge, leaving me alone with Torran. Luna had left riding on the improvised shoulder guard Chira had fashioned for her. The burbu seemed to be picking a new Valoff for every traversal, and Chira was tonight's winner. She had snuggled Luna close as we crossed through the wormhole.

But no matter where Luna spent her day, or with whom, I always found her curled up on my bed every evening, waiting for me. Tonight, she would have a long wait.

Torran also seemed to be settling in for a long wait. He'd made himself at home at the comm terminal over the last few days.

"You don't have to stay up," I said.

He glanced at me. "Neither do you."

I tipped my head at him, conceding the point.

The autopilot would take us most of the way, so I checked the settings, then settled back and put my feet up. I stared at the main screen and let my mind wander. I was mentally working through my third set of backup plans for what I would do if things went bad on Valovia when Torran stirred.

"I figured you would try to stay on Bastion longer."

"You are paying for my time, and the sooner we get to Valovia, the sooner we can start hunting," I said. It also meant that we could *leave* Valovia sooner—and hopefully richer.

Torran hummed in agreement.

"Plus, Bastion is expensive. They have a corner on the market and they know it." I stared at the web of stars on-screen. "Will I be able to buy supplies in Valovian space?"

"Yes, but only if I barter for you." At my skeptical look, he elaborated, "You're human, and worse, you're infamous. Merchants will not sell to you. They might sell to one of your crew, but it would still be expensive."

I made a note to stock up with three months of emergency staples. We might not *enjoy* eating rice and generic protein for that long, but it would keep us alive if we had to leave Valovia in a hurry and needed to take a roundabout route home.

I turned my head sideways on the headrest so I could

see him. "Why are *you* willing to work with me?" I asked, my curiosity getting the better of me.

"You're well known in other circles, too. The people who have worked with you say you're honorable and stick to your agreements. And that you are good at finding lost things."

Unfortunately, that fame hadn't been enough to keep us in credits. I was picky about the jobs I took, and the ones that paid the most were often the shadiest.

Case in point: we were heading to a place where people wanted me dead.

"Were you looking for me specifically?"

His lips compressed into a flat line. "You were the first marginally qualified crew I found. I didn't have time to search further."

I snorted. "You can be kind of an asshole sometimes— you know that, right?"

He leveled an unreadable glance at me. "You would not be the first to call me that."

"I'm sure I won't be the last, either," I muttered under my breath.

EARLY THE NEXT MORNING, I DRAGGED MYSELF TO THE GALley for a much-needed hit of caffeine. Our arrival at Bastion had been delayed by over an hour, so I'd had a very short night, and my head ached with the lack of sleep.

I scowled at my coffee cup and silently urged the stimulant to work faster. When Kee bounced into the room, bright and energetic, I transferred my scowl to her.

She winced in sympathy. "Short night?"

"Three hours. And Bastion is charging us a fortune to dock. The sooner we can leave, the better."

"I saw Lexi messaged. Have you contacted her to let her know we're here?"

I nodded. "I sent her a message a few minutes ago with our location, so she should turn up later. I also need to go round up some more supplies because General Fletcher says we might not be able to buy anything in Valovian space."

Kee frowned. "He's not going to feed us once we hit dirt?"

"I don't know, but I'll feel better if we're prepared for the worst."

Kee glanced toward the door, then leaned in and whispered, "Speaking of, now that we're closer to the border, I checked on your Valovian bounty. It's been temporarily suspended with no listed end date."

That wasn't as good as a total cancellation, but it was better than nothing. I would still have to be careful once we crossed into Valovian space because some less than reputable hunters would pick me up anyway, if they got the chance, just in case the bounty returned to active.

"Thanks for the update. Let me know if anything changes as we get closer. I've authorized Anja to buy a few things she needs for the repairs, so I'd appreciate it if you could also help her find the best deal and get her set up to draw on our funds—with a reasonable limit. And tell Eli to keep an eye on *Starlight* while I'm gone."

"You should take Eli with you," Kee said. "The station isn't dangerous, exactly, but it's rougher than it was the last time we were here."

"Send him with Anja. The parts are more important. You stay and look after the ship, and I'll look after myself."

Torran entered the galley wearing his synthetic black armor, minus the helmet. "I will accompany you," he said.

"Not wearing that, you won't," I said, waving at his armor. Bastion still carried scars from the war. Lucrative trade deals with the Valoffs had bought a measure of tolerance, but most of the people on the station were still understandably wary and suspicious.

Torran looked down at himself. "What's wrong with this?"

"Everything. If you wear that, everything I buy will cost three times as much, and it's already overpriced to begin with."

His eyes narrowed. "I will pay the difference."

"Or you can just remain here in comfort and no one will have to pay extra. I will return in an hour or two."

Torran glared at me. "I will accompany you. If you can't afford to purchase supplies because of my presence, then I'll pay for them in their entirety."

I bristled at the implication that I couldn't take care of my people. In my peripheral vision, Kee shook her head. "Oof. Wrong move, buddy," she muttered.

"I can buy my own supplies," I bit out. "I neither require nor desire your assistance, General Fletcher. Stay here, stay out of trouble, and stay out of my way."

I turned to storm away, but Torran stepped into my path. His eyes glinted in the light and his expression told me that he wasn't going to back down. "I am merely protecting my investment, Captain," he reminded me softly. "I *will* accompany you, one way or another. You should take the deal I've offered."

The threat was clear, and my already simmering temper flared into an inferno.

Kee grabbed my arm and hauled me across the room before I could act on the riot of emotion. "He's a client, Tavi," she whispered urgently. "Venting your anger might feel good right now, but you'll regret it later."

"I definitely won't," I promised.

"Let him accompany you." When I scowled at her, she held up a hand. "Hear me out," she wheedled. "Get the food you wanted *and* the parts for the ship. *All of them.*"

It took a second for her words to sink past the fury. When they did, I turned to her with wide eyes. She gave me an impish grin. "You would've thought of it, too," she said, "once you calmed down. I'm just speeding up the process."

She was right. If I hadn't lost my temper, I *would've* thought of it. Everything on the repair list would cost a fortune—even before the additional markup because he was a Valoff. But Torran had offered me the deal, and I was going to use his honor against him.

Eventually he would learn to stop threatening me or he would go bankrupt, and either way, I won.

"Keep an eye on the ship," I told Kee. "And let me know when Lexi arrives. Make sure she knows I've put her in the room across from Anja. I'll be a couple of hours, at least, so feed Luna when she wanders in. Any requests?"

"Chocolate," Kee said at once. "Something good."

I nodded and pivoted back to face Torran. "Very well, I accept. You may accompany me as long as you pay for the supplies. Are you ready to go?"

When he inclined his head, I dropped my coffee cup in the sanitizer, then led him to the cargo bay. Despite the early hour, I'd dressed to go out, so I was wearing flexible armor under my shirt, and I was carrying both a plas blade and pistol. I hoped neither would be necessary.

Torran did not appear to be carrying any weapons. Though when your mind was a weapon, everything else was a little superfluous.

I downloaded Anja's list of parts to my personal comm. The screen was cracked, and the back was held together with composite tape, but it got the job done. Maybe if we found Torran's missing ring, I would allow myself to upgrade to a model made sometime in the last decade.

Or maybe I'd keep using this one until it completely failed. We weren't short on areas that needed an infusion of credits.

If Torran noticed the state of my comm, he wisely kept his mouth shut.

I pulled the levcart from its dock and opened the cargo bay door. None of Torran's team had joined us. "Your people aren't accompanying you?" I asked.

He shook his head. "They will remain with the ship."

"I'm surprised they're letting you out on your own. I figured they were your security team."

A brief smile touched Torran's mouth. "If anything, I'm *their* security team." As if to prove his point, the levcart rose over my head, did a barrel roll, and then settled back to its normal hover height so gently and precisely that it didn't even need to make an adjustment.

My eyes widened and I fought the urge to freeze in place. In a hostile situation, the levcart could instantly become projectile, shield, or battering ram. Telekinetics were battlefield specters for a reason.

Still, I couldn't quite help my curiosity. I'd never met a telekinetic before—which was one of the reasons I'd survived the war. "How long could you hold the levcart in the air?"

Torran's gaze flickered over my face. "It depends on the circumstances," he said slowly. "But in the easiest case, I could hold it long enough that sleep would become the bigger concern. I have to be awake to maintain the hold."

Goose bumps rose on my arms as a shiver worked its way down my spine. Not only was he a telekinetic, he was a *powerful* telekinetic. If he ever turned on me, I would have a split second to act, then I would be dead.

Torran watched me, expression unreadable. "Would you prefer it if I didn't use my ability while aboard *Starlight*?"

"No. I would prefer it if you didn't *attack* while you're on board, of course, but otherwise you're free to do as you like." My eyes narrowed. After the footstool prank, I'd barely seen him use his ability. As powerful as he was, using it would be a habit—one he must be fighting. "You've already been limiting yourself."

He nodded once. "It tends to make humans uncomfortable."

He wasn't wrong. Still, my sense of fairness made me offer, "Maybe don't fling around a tornado of knives or something equally terrifying, but you don't have to hobble yourself. We'll get used to it."

The corner of his mouth tipped up. "'A tornado of knives'?"

"You could, right?" When he shrugged noncommittally, I continued, "Once Kee gets used to you, she'll have you juggling full glasses of water while she tosses random things at you, just to see if you can catch them."

The grin bloomed, softening the harsh planes of his face. "She would've liked my childhood tutor."

It was hard to imagine Torran as a child. I wondered if

he'd always been so quiet and serious or if something had happened to spark the transformation. I bit down on the questions I wanted to ask. Torran was a payday and nothing else. Anything more was far too dangerous.

I pushed the levcart out of the ship and down the ramp without another word.

CHAPTER TWELVE

During the war, Bastion had been the Fed's main operating base. It was two wormhole traversals from Valovia itself, but only one from the edge of inhabited Valovian space. Late in the war, FHP troops had eked out a forward operating base on the other side of the first wormhole, but Bastion had remained the stronghold.

Today, the forward base was gone while Bastion continued to grow. It was now one of the largest stations in human space, with the civilian population nearly matching the number of full-time military personnel. The nearest habitable planet—one of the reasons FHP forces had fought so hard for this sector—was over a day away.

The landing bay was full to nearly overcrowded. Ships were squeezed together with the bare minimum safety clearances, leading to tight, winding walkways. We joined the steady stream of people heading into the station.

Torran's armor got us more than a few dirty looks. By

the time we made it to the main airlock into the station, a two-meter gap of clear space separated us from the rest of the crowd. If Torran noticed—and how could he *not*—I couldn't tell from his expression, which remained cool and distant.

We had docked in an older part of the station that had been repurposed for civilian use after the war. It was smaller and grimier than the newer sections, but it also offered better prices. Here, the original military design was evident: everything was arranged for maximum efficiency and minimal aesthetics—functional but ugly.

"Turn right," Kee said over the comm. "I figured you'd want the ship parts first. The best prices I found are two levels down, but you can skip the first elevator. I'm sending the info to your comm."

"Thank you," I said subvocally.

"I'm looking at food prices next. I'll let you know what I find. Yell if you need anything else."

"Will do."

I turned right and bypassed the line for the first elevator. The crowd thinned as we moved away from the landing bay door. By the time we made it to the second elevator, the line was only a few people deep. I pulled out my comm and checked Kee's directions while we waited.

I was used to monitoring my surroundings no matter what I was doing, so I saw the moment the man in front of us decided to become a problem. His leer at me turned into a scowl as he caught sight of Torran.

He stared at me. "Dirty Valoff fucker," he muttered, loud enough that he wanted to be heard.

He had dark hair and naturally pale skin made even paler by years in the black. He was thickly muscled, likely either a soldier or mercenary. When he caught me looking, his lip curled up.

I deliberately looked back down at my comm, dismissing him completely.

"Didn't you hear me, Valoff fucker?" he persisted.

The few people around us edged back. I sighed and put my comm away. This was another reason I hadn't wanted Torran to accompany me. His presence created as many problems as it solved.

"If you're trying to insult me, you're going to have to do better than that. It's good you have all those muscles, because clearly no one is hiring you for your brainpower."

The man's mouth opened, then clicked shut. I could see the mouse wheel of his mind slowly turning, then his cheeks flushed red with outrage. Bullies didn't like it when the tables were turned and insults started flying back toward them.

"You stupid little c—"

The man's mouth clicked shut again, but by the way his eyes widened, he wasn't the one responsible. When the elevator opened, he slid two meters to the left, terror plain on his face. With his removal, space opened for me to push the levcart into the lift.

Torran's expression never changed.

One brave lady who had been in front of us ducked into the elevator, but everyone else suddenly decided they didn't need to change levels after all.

After the doors swished closed, the lady warily eyed Torran. "Thank you," she murmured. "I know you didn't do it for me, but that creep was harassing me before you showed up." She gave him a shy grin. "It was nice to see someone shut him up."

Torran inclined his head. "You're welcome."

We exited the elevator without causing any more potential interstellar incidents. As soon as we were alone, I turned to Torran. "If he reports you, then we're going to have bigger problems than an asshole who likes to run his mouth."

"There is nothing to report."

"You used your ability on a human who wasn't a threat. That breaks at least a half dozen laws."

"He *was* a threat, I did not injure him, and I have diplomatic immunity." Torran's narrowed eyes and icy tone told me that he would do the exact same thing again, given the opportunity.

I rolled my eyes. "You insisted on coming with me because you didn't have time to waste if something happened. Even with diplomatic immunity, it'll take time for the station authorities to let you go if you cause trouble."

"If there are repercussions, I will deal with them," Torran said, "but I will not let someone hurl insults at you when I can prevent it." He slanted a questioning glance at me. "This is why you did not want me to accompany you."

I sighed. "I didn't know that this would happen, but it doesn't surprise me. Bastion was heavily involved in the war and memories are long. I didn't want trouble."

When Torran didn't respond, I relented a little and grinned. "But did you see that asshole's expression when he realized he couldn't talk? *Priceless.* So thank you for that."

Torran searched my face for a moment, then he smiled. My breath caught. He was always objectively handsome, but he was gorgeous when he smiled. "You are welcome," he said softly.

I dipped my head and focused on the levcart. "Let's get what we need and get off this station," I murmured.

NOW THAT MY ANGER HAD WORN OFF, MY CONSCIENCE wouldn't allow me to take *complete* advantage of Torran's generosity, no matter what I'd said earlier. I picked the high-priority parts that Anja needed, but I left the rest for another day—one when I'd be paying my own bill.

Still, the total was high enough that I winced in sympathy for his bank account.

He paid without a whisper of complaint.

Before we left, I checked on the price of a translation module for my comm and grimaced. This close to Valovian space, they were in high demand, and I couldn't justify the massive expense. Kee and Lexi spoke the language well enough to get us through. For anything else, I'd have to keep looking up Valovan phrases the old-fashioned way.

With a sigh, I led Torran out of the shop. Kee directed us up one level to the nearest reasonably priced grocer. She also let me know that Lexi had arrived safely.

I blew out a relieved breath. Lexi could take care of herself, but I still worried about her. If Kee or Eli ever struck out on their own, I'd worry for them just the same. The four of us had forged unbreakable bonds in the midst of war and death, and I felt responsible for all of them, no matter where their lives took them.

This job might be terrible and impossible, but I was glad for the excuse to hang out with Lexi for a few weeks.

At the grocer, I stocked up on enough shelf-stable supplies to last us for three months, then began picking out perishable and frozen food for the next few weeks. "Do you have any requests?" I asked Torran.

"I've enjoyed all the meals you've prepared."

I waved a hand. "I'm not fishing for compliments. It's okay to have a preference. Do you want me to make something again? Do you have a recipe you'd like for me to try? Do you want supplies to cook something for yourself? Now is the time to speak up."

He tilted his head, thinking. "I enjoyed the lasagna."

Warmth blossomed. I might not have been fishing for compliments, but I appreciated it when someone liked my food. I added the lasagna ingredients to the growing mountain of food.

I added a few chocolate bars and other treats that I thought both crews would enjoy, then I pulled out my comm to quietly prepay. As expected, the total was far higher than it should've been.

Prices were listed on the shelves, but that was merely a suggestion, and the owner had the option to adjust them on the fly—which they had, dramatically. If I thought I could get a better deal somewhere else, I'd unload everything and leave.

But there were no better deals to be found, not with Torran shadowing my steps.

The total bill wasn't much compared to the parts for the ship, but it didn't feel right to make him pay for this, too. Except that when I tried to pay, it wouldn't let me because Torran had *already* paid.

When my eyes flew to his, he met my gaze, unflinching. "I promised to pay," he said quietly.

I shook my head. "I wasn't going to hold you to it. The parts were already too much."

His spine stiffened and his expression closed. "You told Kee you'd get everything on the list, but you didn't," he said, his tone cool. "Why not?"

He'd heard our not-so-quiet conversation. I shifted uncomfortably. "I was only going to buy a few things before you waltzed in and started issuing orders," I said. "Denting your bank account sounded good when I was angry, but then I calmed down, and you took care of that asshole, and . . ." I trailed off and shrugged. "Buying more just because you were paying didn't seem right."

He stared at me for a long moment, then his eyes went distant. My mental shields were not at their strongest, so I braced for the feel of his mind touching mine, but it never came.

His expression cleared. "Do you need anything else?"

I considered the food stacked on the levcart. If we had to stay on Valovia for the full eight weeks, we would be okay even if no one sold us supplies. We would be out of fresh food, but between the garden, the pantry staples, and the frozen food, we wouldn't starve.

"I have everything I need," I said. "If you're done, let's head back to the ship so I can put all this stuff away before it melts."

He inclined his head in agreement, and we made our way back to *Starlight's Shadow*. This time, the trip went smoothly, and Torran's presence deterred anyone from getting too curious about what was under the levcart's cover. An armored Valoff wasn't a foe to take lightly, despite what the jerk earlier had thought.

Starlight's cargo bay was empty when we arrived. The levcart was too wide to fit through the hatch into the main part of the ship, so I parked it as close as possible. I would have to carry the food to the galley.

The hatch opened, and Kee bounced out with her customary bright smile. Lexi followed at a more sedate pace, but her smile was just as bright.

"It's good to see you, Lex," I said as I pulled her into a hug.

"You, too," she said.

I squeezed her tight, then stepped back to look her over. She was a half dozen centimeters taller than me and nearly a dozen taller than Kee, with the kind of sleek, flexible strength that people often underestimated.

This week, her chin-length, curly hair was a pure, gleaming blond, several shades lighter than her natural strawberry blond. Her pale skin had taken on a faint golden glow from time in the sun—she'd recently spent a significant amount of time on-planet.

Depending on her agenda, Lexi could go from pretty-but-forgettable to absolutely stunning in fifteen minutes flat. Today, her makeup played up her hazel eyes and minimized the rest of her features, and she wore a pair of slim charcoal slacks with a sapphire blouse.

I raised my eyebrows. "Did you come straight from a job?"

"Just wrapped it up," she confirmed.

"Do I want to know?"

She shook her head with a grin, then her gaze darted over my shoulder and her expression smoothed into professional politeness. "Is this the client?"

Lexi tailored her persona to her clients—or her marks. She switched between charming, smart, vapid, and cunning—and everything in between—as easily as others changed outfits. Until she found which worked best, she usually stuck with professional reserve.

I was interested to see what she would pick for Torran.

I turned so I could wave a hand at Torran. "Lexi Bowen, meet Torran Fletcher." I gestured back at Lexi. "General Fletcher, Ms. Bowen."

They nodded coolly at each other. Lexi's gaze traveled from Torran's head to his toes. She sent me an inquiring glance. "You let him go out on the station dressed like that?"

I huffed out a laugh. As if I had the ability to *let* Torran do anything. "I advised him to change or remain behind. He declined."

Lexi's eyes narrowed. "Did you run into trouble?"

I hesitated, which did me in as surely as admitting it. At the pause, Kee's head snapped up. She had been examining the chocolate I'd bought, but now her stare locked on me. "What happened?"

"Just some asshole, being an asshole. It was dealt with, no one was hurt, and station security *probably* won't want to talk to us, but maybe we should get an early start, just in case. Is everyone on board?"

Kee looked like she wanted to press more, but I silently shook my head and she subsided. "No," she said. "Anja, Chira, and Eli left to get some additional parts."

"For the ship?" When Kee nodded, I asked, "Did Anja forget to put something on the list?"

"She didn't say. I didn't have time to set up her credit account, so Eli went with her, and Chira decided to tag along, too—thankfully *not* in her armor. Between the three of them, they'll surely be able to manage."

I murmured my agreement. Eli wouldn't buy something

outrageous without consulting me first. I hoped that Anja hadn't found more issues, but she must've if she needed more parts. I sighed and rubbed the spot between my eyes. I'd put off maintenance for too long, and now that decision was costing me.

The main hatch opened, and Varro stepped out into the cargo bay. His eyes landed on Kee first before flitting over the rest of us. Without a word, he moved to the levcart, hoisted two heavy bags of rice onto his shoulder, and then vanished back through the hatch.

"How did he even—" Lexi started, then paused and glanced at Torran. Her mouth compressed into an unamused line.

"Let's get the rest of this stuff put away," I said before she could comment further. "Leave the parts for now and focus on the food."

By the time all the food was put away and the parts had been hauled down to maintenance, Eli, Anja, and Chira had returned, pushing a borrowed levcart piled high with additional items.

I met them in the cargo bay and pulled Eli aside. "How much did this cost?" I quietly demanded.

As soon as he looked at me sideways, I knew I wasn't going to like the answer. "Nothing," he said slowly. "Chira paid for everything out of Torran's account."

I closed my eyes and strove for patience. "Whose idea was it to get more parts?"

Eli frowned slowly. "Yours?" It came out as a question. When I sighed, he continued, "Chira said that you and Torran weren't able to get everything, and that we should get the rest."

I didn't say anything, and Eli cursed. "You didn't know."

"I didn't know," I confirmed. "This was all Torran's doing."

"Why?"

"It's a long story." And the truth was, I wasn't entirely sure *why* Torran had decided to buy the rest of the parts. The weight of this new obligation pressed on my temples, aggravating the headache I'd been fighting all day.

Eli met my eyes. "Do you want me to take everything back?"

The petty, stubborn part of me absolutely *did* want him to return everything, but I bit down on the response. Even if he returned it, the shopkeeper wouldn't refund all the money, so I'd still be in debt and have nothing to show for it. I silently shook my head.

"Go have something to eat while we unload this stuff," Eli suggested gently. "You look like you're about to fall over."

My stomach growled at the mention of food. It was nearly lunchtime and I'd been running on caffeine alone for far too long. "Once you're done unloading the parts, make sure everyone has everything they need, then get us ready to fly. The sooner we leave, the better."

"You don't want to hire another engineer?"

I sighed. I'd spent last night going over our finances while waiting for docking permission. Things weren't as bleak as they had been last week, but we were also spending money far faster. It made me nervous.

"Ideally we'd have another engineer, but we're already burning through the budget. Anja confirmed she wants to stay on, so we'll be okay until this job is done. If we find the heirloom and get the second payment, I'll reevaluate."

Eli nodded and went back to carrying parts, but not

before giving me a pointed look and tilting his head toward the galley.

"I'm going, I'm going," I grumbled.

I moved into the ship, keeping an eye out for Luna, but she didn't launch herself at me. She was probably napping in the garden. Maybe I'd join her after I grabbed a meal bar.

The air in the galley smelled delicious, rich with butter and spices, and my stomach growled. Torran stood at the stove with his back to me. Luna clung to the guard on his shoulder, watching him cook. She turned and chirruped at me in greeting.

Torran glanced at me. "Are you hungry?" The question was casual, but his body language was not. He'd changed out of his armor, so I could see the tense line of his shoulders.

A thousand questions and accusations flickered through my mind, but I was too tired to fight right now, so I gave him the simplest answer. "I'm starving."

"May I cook for you?" The question was oddly formal, and I still hadn't looked up Valovian food customs. But I'd been cooking for him for nearly a week without incident, so the opposite probably wouldn't cause any new problems—I hoped.

"Sure," I agreed, "if you don't mind. But if it's too much work, I can grab a meal bar."

He pointed at the bar. "Sit. I'm nearly finished."

I frowned. "I don't want to eat your lunch," I protested. I edged toward the pantry. "A meal bar is fine."

A barstool slid back by itself. "Sit," he said again. "There is more than enough food to share."

I gingerly perched on the seat and propped my elbows on the bar. Torran moved around the space with an easy familiarity. I tended to eat lunch at odd hours, grabbing left-overs or a bar whenever hunger finally pulled me from my task list, so I hadn't noticed that he'd been cooking.

And he appeared to be good at it.

He slid the pan's contents onto two plates, and then put a little bit on a small saucer and blew on it. Once it was cool, he set it on the floor and Luna jumped down with a little chirp. She butted her head against his leg, then turned to the food.

My heart threatened to melt, but I very firmly reminded it that Torran was the enemy.

Wasn't he?

The more time I spent around him and his crew, the less sure I became. It was hard to think of the people you shared meals with as the enemy—that was the whole point of the shared meals—but for me, it had worked a little *too* well.

Eli was right, my heart was too soft. I was beginning to think of the Valoffs as allies, maybe even friends. And that was potentially a very dangerous mistake to make.

Before I could figure out how to fix it, Torran set a plate in front of me, then handed me a glass of water to go with it. He joined me at the bar with his own plate and drink.

"Thank you," I murmured. The dish appeared to be noodles and veggies in a dark sauce. I took a bite and flavor exploded on my tongue—sweet and spicy, with just a hint of sourness to balance it out. He'd combined familiar spices in a way that I never had, but the combination worked in-credibly well.

I glanced at Torran in surprise, only to find his eyes already on me. "This is delicious. Will you share the recipe for the sauce?"

He inclined his head.

We ate in silence. Luna finished her snack and leapt up to her perch to watch us, just in case we planned to give her more. Unfortunately for her, I was too hungry, and the food was too good. There were no leftovers.

I felt better after eating. I cleaned up while I organized my thoughts into reasonable arguments instead of irrational shouting. Still, Torran beat me to it.

"You are upset about the parts," he said quietly from his seat.

I turned and met his eyes. "You knew I was going to be upset, or you wouldn't have gone behind my back."

His expression didn't even flicker. "The parts were the payment I promised for allowing me to accompany you. You might not expect me to keep my word, but I will keep it nonetheless."

I blew out a slow breath. "You had *already* bought parts. Your promise was fulfilled."

Torran shook his head. "I heard your conversation with Kee. You agreed only because she persuaded you to get everything you needed at my expense. My promise was not fulfilled."

"That doesn't explain why you went behind my back."

One of his eyebrows rose a millimeter, but he remained silent. His look spoke volumes, though.

I huffed out an unamused laugh. "If you had explained that it was a matter of honor, I would have agreed to let you buy the rest. Unlike Valoffs, I can't read your mind. You have to communicate using words. If you fail to communicate, then you can't be surprised when I get upset."

He stared at me for a long moment before his chin dipped in agreement.

I tried to shake off the uneasiness I felt about the additional parts. Torran didn't view it as an obligation that I would be forced to repay. In his mind, he had fulfilled *his* obligation by purchasing them. But knowing didn't always translate into feeling.

"Do you need anything else before we depart?" I asked.

"No, I am ready to leave when you are. If we are departing soon, I will let *Lotkez* know."

I'd almost forgotten the Valovian ship that had tailed us from the previous station. "Do you want to go see your crew before we return to open space?"

Torran shook his head. "I spoke to the officers earlier. They do not require my presence."

I needed that reminder that the people he'd brought with him were his underlings, not his friends. "Let them know. I'm going to get us ready to fly."

CHAPTER THIRTEEN

Lexi found me on the bridge while I was running our pre-launch checks. She slid into the operations terminal like she'd never left.

"So, Torran Fletcher," she said at last. "I never thought I'd see the day when you voluntarily worked for a Valovian general."

I glanced over my shoulder. The door to the bridge was closed, so our conversation would be private enough. "I never thought so, either, but his money spends as well as anyone else's. And he's offering a lot of it."

Lexi laughed. "Kee already confessed that she talked you into it."

"She did," I agreed, "but it was the right call. And now we get to spend a few weeks with you. How have you been, Lex, truly?"

Her smile turned brittle around the edges. "This last

job was a lot. The client was a real piece of work, but, as you said, the credits spend the same."

"Some money is not worth making," I said gently. "If you ever need us, we'll always be there for you. And you can join us whenever you need to escape. You know that, right?"

Her expression warmed into fond affection. "I know," she said quietly. "And I love you for it." She waved a hand. "Overall, business is good, and I'm happy. This last job just got to me. But now I get to hang out with you and Eli and Kee for a few weeks while milking a Valovian general out of some of his ill-gotten gains. Has he given you any details?"

"Yes. Over a week ago, a group of four or more humans stole an heirloom ring from his house on Valovia." A thought occurred and I looked her over. "You wouldn't know anything about that, would you?"

She laughed lightly. "I'm reckless, but not *that* reckless. I haven't been to Valovia in six months." Her amusement died. "And I wouldn't be going back if it wasn't a personal favor for you."

"Is there something I need to know?"

"No. I met someone interesting, but he stole my job and left me sitting alone in a hotel bar like a dumbass." Her mouth twisted into a bitter line. "Lesson learned."

My eyebrows rose. "Someone got the better of you?"

"There's a reason I was in the bar," she said with a self-deprecating grimace.

"I'm sorry."

She waved off my concern. "Has Kee found anything?"

"No. She's hoping for better results when we get to Valovia. General Fletcher is keeping it quiet, so there's not too much information to be found yet."

"I'll poke around and see if I can uncover any details on

the heist crew," Lexi said as she stood. "I'm not as good as Kee, but maybe I'll spot something that she overlooked. I'll at least see if the rumor mill has anything."

"Thank you."

Lexi left with a wave, and I returned my attention to my terminal. The prelaunch checks came back green. I hit the ship's intercom. "Launch in five. Eli and General Fletcher, confirm readiness."

A minute later, both Eli and Torran confirmed that their teams were ready for launch. I went through my mental checklist one last time, but I couldn't think of anything else I needed from the station. At the five-minute mark, I lifted away from the deck and eased *Starlight* out into space.

It took nearly forty-five minutes before traffic thinned enough that I felt comfortable turning on the autopilot. There were two wormhole traversals during this section of the trip, and the first wasn't until early tomorrow morning.

In three days, we'd be on Valovia.

I had not ventured into Valovian space since the war, and I'd never been through the wormhole that led to Valovia itself. Now I had less than twenty-four hours to resign myself to the fact that I was leading my crew back into enemy territory. The thought sent nervous prickles down my spine.

I'd already added Lexi to the duty roster, so I decided to see if I could give Anja a hand with the maintenance. With all of the extra parts, she'd need all the help she could get.

And I needed the distraction.

BY DINNERTIME, I WAS TIRED, SWEATY, AND FILTHY, BUT ANJA and I had made significant progress on the most important fix, which involved replacing worn parts in the heating and cooling systems. I hadn't let any of the ship's routine maintenance get *dangerously* behind, but I hadn't exactly been swapping out parts early, either.

If nothing else, this job would give *Starlight's Shadow* a much-needed round of upkeep.

When it became clear that the fix was going to take longer than expected, I'd asked Eli to cook dinner.

In my bedroom, I stripped off my clothes and put them directly into the refresher. I set the cleaning cycle to run, then quickly showered and changed into clean clothes. I felt better after the shower, but my body was a collection of aches.

My arms trembled from holding parts in place for hours, and I'd put too much stress on my bad knee while trying to contort myself into the tiny maintenance crawlspaces with Anja. My knee had been so much better that I'd forgotten that Havil hadn't been able to completely heal it. I hoped I hadn't undone any of his work.

I limped my way to the galley, stomach rumbling. I arrived just as Eli finished cooking. Havil glanced my way, his brow furrowed. Shit, I'd forgotten that he was empathic.

I wasn't entirely sure how to shield pain, but I strengthened my mental shields, and he went back to helping Eli without saying anything.

At least without saying anything out loud.

Torran turned and frowned at me. His gaze flickered over me, presumably looking for the injury. When I raised an eyebrow at the frank assessment, he met my eyes, expression unreadable.

"Are you hurt?" he mouthed.

I shook my head.

His frown returned, but he dipped his chin and returned to his conversation with Kee.

Lexi and Varro were working together to set the table. Lexi had changed into stretchy dark pants and a light blue shirt, but her expression did not match her relaxed wardrobe. Her smile was too bright, too sharp.

I pulled her aside after she'd laid out the plates she held. "What's wrong?"

"It's just strange to see *Starlight* full of Valoffs," she said, her eyes troubled. "And Kee chats with them like they've been friends forever. It's like she's completely forgotten that they tried to kill us for years—and damn near succeeded. I know she could make friends with a rock, but cozying up to the enemy is too much, even for her."

"Give Kee some credit," I admonished lightly. "She is aware of who they are. The first day, General Fletcher threatened to kill everyone on the ship, and I had to break up a fistfight between Eli and Varro. Since then, we've had nearly a week to get used to it. Take the time and space you need. I was planning to seat you between Eli and Fletcher," I said, pointing at chairs, "but I can put you on the other side of Eli instead, if you would prefer."

She considered it, then shook her head. "Your original plan is fine. I'll adapt."

"Let me know if you change your mind. Have you been introduced to everyone?"

"Thank you. And yeah, Kee introduced me to the rest of Torran's crew. Quite the interesting collection of people, isn't it?" She didn't wait for a response, but at least her smile was a little more genuine when she went back to helping Varro.

I leaned against the wall and watched the two teams interact. Lexi was right—both teams were becoming more comfortable with each other. Chira and Havil helped Eli plate the food while Kee kept up a constant stream of conversation with anyone who came into her orbit.

Anja entered the room, freshly showered. She headed my way with a grimace. "I think we may have overdone it," she said. "I don't know about you, but I feel like I've gone a dozen rounds with a boxing bot."

"At least I'm not the only one," I said with a laugh. "Good work today, but go easier tomorrow. You don't have to fix everything all at once. If you've been working this hard the whole time, I'm surprised you didn't escape on Bastion."

She ducked her head. "I like your ship," she said quietly. "I wanted to ensure you would keep me on."

"Consider yourself kept. Now promise me that you won't push yourself quite so hard."

"I'll try to ease up a little. Thanks for your help today."

"You're welcome. Now that the processing unit upgrade is done, ship maintenance is the highest priority. In a couple of days, once the rest of the crew gets done with their extra cleaning, I'll adjust the roster so you have more help every day. Until then, I'll help when I can."

She waved me off. "You don't have to do that."

"I know. But I have a bit of time, and it needs to get done—without you doing it all yourself."

Eli called us all to the table, but I stared at Anja until she gave me a reluctant nod. "I won't do everything myself. But," she said, drawing out the word, "I can knock out a lot of the smaller tasks while you're busy with other things. I won't overdo it."

That was likely all of the concession I would get, so I smiled and let her go.

Torran's eyes tracked me across the room. I was positive my limp did not go unnoticed, but he didn't say anything when I sank into my seat.

Eli had made a potato and veggie dish with a cream sauce that was simple and delicious. He didn't cook much, but when he did, he proved that he knew his way around the kitchen.

The lack of sleep followed by the afternoon's work had left me exhausted. I let the conversation flow around me, soothed by the sound of my crew enjoying a meal together. I'd missed Lexi's snort-laugh when Kee said something especially ridiculous, and the way Eli gently teased both Lexi and Kee until their smiles were wide and genuine.

All of the surviving members of my squad were safely back in my care, and while I knew it wouldn't last, I would enjoy it while I could.

AFTER DINNER, THE CREW HEADED DOWN TO THE REC ROOM to get ready for the next episode of *Crash Crush* while I stayed behind to clean up. Both Eli and Lexi had offered to help, but I waved them off.

Torran was harder to dissuade—mostly because he didn't offer, he just started helping.

He cleaned the counters and stove while I loaded dishes into the sanitizer. I set the machine to run and then stretched my arms overhead, trying to work out the tightness in my back.

"You should let Havil look at you," Torran said, his voice quiet.

"I'm fine, I just did too much this afternoon, and I don't bounce back as easily as I once did. There's nothing he can do about that." I paused and dropped my arms. "Is it possible for me to shield pain so he can't sense it?"

Torran stared at me for long enough that I figured he wasn't going to answer. I mentally shrugged. It was worth a shot.

"It's possible," he said at last.

I leaned against the counter and waited, but he didn't elaborate. "Will you tell me how to do it? I don't want Havil to have to suffer just because I've overdone it."

"Havil's job is to monitor the team, but if he needs to, he can shield far more easily than you."

"When he was working on my knee, he told me it would take more energy to shield from the pain than it would to fix it."

Torran smiled faintly. "I believe he may have stretched the truth in order to secure your cooperation. Empaths have some of the strongest and most complex shields I've ever seen. They have to or they don't survive long."

"But if his job is to monitor the team—which is a subject we will definitely be returning to—then he's not going to shield, so I should still learn how."

Torran stepped closer and his gaze swept across my face. My stomach clenched with a combination of desire and wariness, but he merely said, "You want me to make you a more dangerous enemy."

"I want you to make me a more dangerous *ally*," I corrected. "We're only a few hours away from Valovian space. On the off chance that your offer is real and not just a thin ruse to lure me and my team to our untimely ends, it would be better if every Valoff we meet can't read my thoughts and tell when I'm hurt. You said my shields are shit. Help me make them better. Or at least let Havil do it."

I'd already approached the other Valoffs over the past few days, but they'd all gently demurred when I'd tried to broach the subject with them. Torran was my last chance. I probably should've started with him, but I hated showing him my soft underbelly.

Still, it would be far better to learn what I could before we landed.

Torran continued to stare at me for a long moment, then he dipped his chin. "Very well. But I will have to touch your mind to help you. Will you allow it?"

I couldn't help the grimace that wrinkled my nose. Admitting my shields were shit was far different from having him poke at them—and my thoughts. "Can't you just explain what I need to do?"

"Could you explain how to fly *Starlight* to a civilian who had never seen a ship before?"

I tilted my head and considered it. "Well, maybe with autopilot and a wide-open space. But I understand what you're saying, even if I don't like it. Will you give me your word that you'll stay out of my thoughts?"

"I will likely hear your surface thoughts while I'm examining your shield, but I won't try to delve deeper than that, and I will give you warning before I begin. When I do, start mentally naming everything you can see in the room. The more specific, the better."

"Is that effective?"

"Effective enough."

I filed that away for future reference. I wasn't sure how

thrilled the others would be to have a Valovian general poking around in their heads, so I would have to teach them what I learned.

Torran gestured at the table. "Shall we sit?"

My stomach tied itself in knots. This had seemed like a much better idea a few seconds ago when it was just theoretical. Maybe Torran's plan all along had been to get me to lower my guard so he could pry into my thoughts.

Bitter fear coated the back of my tongue.

"We don't have to do this today," Torran said, his tone surprisingly gentle.

"I'm okay," I lied. I moved to my normal seat at the table before I could talk myself out of it. This was likely the only time in my life that a Valoff would help me learn how to defend against other Valoffs, and my team counted on me to keep them safe. I couldn't chicken out.

Torran sat across from me, his expression serious. The colorful streaks in his dark eyes glinted in the overhead lights. The silver had expanded when he'd threatened me because of Luna. Would the colors shift when he used his ability this time or was it driven by emotion?

"Are you ready?" he asked. When I nodded, he continued, "Build your shield as you usually do."

"Done."

"Start naming things. If you want me to stop, just say so."

I pressed my fingers against the table and started mentally naming things. Table. Table with a scratched black composite top. Chair— The cool brush of Torran's mind distracted me, and I faltered. *Torran.* A dozen thoughts flashed through my head.

I curled my fingers into a fist until my knuckles turned white. Pale hands on a composite table. Lightweight composite chair. Walk-in cooler with a silver door.

"I am finished," Torran said a few seconds later.

I'd been so busy ignoring him that I'd forgotten to check his eyes. A peek revealed that they looked normal now.

"Your shield is decent for a human," he said. "I caught only a few thoughts. But it won't stand up to someone determined."

I tried not to worry about what thoughts he might have glimpsed. "How do I make it stronger?"

"Valovian children learn to shield instinctively. Your shield reminds me of a child's. Did someone teach you or did you learn on your own?"

I'd learned during the war because it was that or die. Without shields, a mediocre telepath could make you see things that weren't there. A strong telepath could make you turn your weapon on yourself or your allies, all while thinking your behavior was completely normal.

I'd watched more than one soldier fall to friendly fire while the shooter smiled.

I focused on the pressure of my fist against the table so the memories would stay dormant. Command had produced dozens of training videos, but none of them had worked as well as brutal experience.

"I learned on my own," I said, my tone flat and distant.

Torran nodded, as if he'd expected that answer. "How do you construct your shield?"

Heat bloomed in my cheeks. I had no idea how Valoffs protected their minds, but I doubted it would be as silly as how I did it. I swallowed my pride and said, "I imagine donning an armored helmet." I'd tried imagining many things—walls, bubbles, shiny shields, mountains—and the helmet was the only thing that reliably worked for me.

Torran's mouth quirked, but he was smart enough not to laugh.

"What do you do?" I asked. If I was going to open myself up to ridicule, it was only fair that he did the same.

"It's different for me, because my brain works differently. But at a simple level, I build overlapping nets, with each layer allowing certain things through and blocking specific threats."

"So you can communicate telepathically without others being able to read your thoughts?"

A faint smile curved his lips. "Exactly."

With the comm implants, humans had gained a fraction of that ability, but the implants still relied on technology to work. Innate biological skills would always have an advantage.

"Could you communicate telepathically with me, even through my shield?"

"Yes. And if we were close enough and I focused, I could hear your replies, too."

Curiosity had always been a weakness of mine. Before I could think better of it, I asked, "Will you show me? Not the hearing the replies part, but what telepathic communication sounds like."

Torran frowned. "Are you sure?"

I nodded, even though I really wasn't.

Torran took me at my word. I felt the slightest brush of coolness, then his voice whispered across my mind. "Octavia."

I froze in terrified wonder. It was completely different

from communicating via comm implant. I somehow knew that the thought came from Torran, but like our subvocal comms, it didn't exactly sound like his speaking voice. Unlike our comms, it was closer, more intimate, like a caress. I shivered and forced myself to start naming things in the room lest he catch the direction my thoughts had taken.

"Are you okay?" he asked.

"Yes. Thank you for demonstrating. I thought it would be like our comm implants, but it's not, exactly." I had a million questions, but I brought my focus back to the reason I'd asked for help in the first place. "If I can't build nets like you do, then what *can* I do?"

Torran took the change of subject in stride. "Can you tell when I touch your mind?" When I nodded, he continued, "I can build a shield for you, but I don't know if you'll be able to feel it well enough to figure out how to duplicate it. If that doesn't work, I can try piercing your existing shields to see if you can fix the holes that way."

I swallowed. Neither choice sounded super fun. "Are there any other options? How would you explain it to a child?" While it grated to be treated like a child, I'd take it if it kept Torran out of my head.

"In public, parents shield for young children until they learn to shield themselves. Children instinctively learn from that example."

Well, that was exactly zero help. "I don't suppose you've taught other humans how to shield?"

A flicker of emotion crossed Torran's face, too fast to identify. "You will be the first."

"Fine. Show me how you'd build a shield for me. Let's see if I can learn anything from it."

"Are you ready?"

No, no I was not, but I agreed anyway.

I stared at the scratches in the tabletop as Torran's mind brushed mine. I focused hard on my mental shield and what was presumably Torran's additional shield, but all I felt was the same coolness that I normally felt, just to a much larger degree. His telepathic voice remained silent.

I glanced up. Torran's eyes blazed with power, the silver, copper, and teal nearly obliterating the deep gray. Fierce Valovian eyes in cool, dispassionate faces haunted my nightmares, and paired with the cold feel of his power, I recoiled violently. I was on my feet and reaching for a weapon before I realized I'd moved.

Luckily, I didn't have any weapons on me, and that likely saved Torran's life—and mine.

Torran flinched as if struck, and I could no longer feel his power. He blinked and his eyes reverted to their normal state, then narrowed dangerously. "How did you do that?" he demanded.

I slowly picked up the chair I'd knocked over and wrestled the memories back into the mental box where I kept them. My hands trembled and I felt sick to my stomach. "Do what?"

"You barred me from your mind. It should not be possible."

He didn't say "for a human," but I heard it nonetheless. I slid back into the chair and tried to hide the fact that my legs had barely supported me. My pulse pounded in my temples. "I didn't do anything."

"Just before you kicked me out, you were scared, terrified. Why?"

"Do you really need to ask?" The question came out far more bitterly than I'd intended, so I took a deep breath and searched for calm. I didn't find it, but I faked it as best I could. "I fought Valoffs for a decade. During the war, shining eyes and cold power meant death, and some instincts are harder to overcome than others."

Torran's expression morphed into searing anger and bitter grief, and it didn't take a mind reader to know that he was thinking about Rodeni. It was the most infamous battle in a war full of famous battles. I'd lost half of my squad and most of my soul on that cursed planet. Others had lost so much more.

After the battle, I'd gone straight to Command still wearing my bloody uniform and turned in my discharge request, effective immediately. Lexi, Kee, and Eli had all done the same.

None of us had escaped unscathed.

"Why did you do it?" Torran asked. His voice was so quiet and pained that the words could've come straight from my own conscience.

I clenched my hands together. I knew exactly what he meant. That day in Rodeni was seared into my memory forever. "I was told the Valovian civilians had evacuated and that the military had taken over the building as a command center. We were being overrun. An attack on Valovian Command was the only way to buy our forces enough time to fall back. I volunteered to go. My squad followed me."

His gaze sharpened, pinning me in place.

The memories rose, haunting me with my failures. My stomach churned as adrenaline surged through my system, but I swallowed down the acidic taste of bile. "By the time I figured out that the building still held civilians, the charges were planted. I called off the attack and got overruled."

I didn't tell him—*couldn't* tell him—that three of my

squad had died while frantically trying to deactivate the explosives. I'd already said too much. FHP Command had lied to me, killed my people, and then left us behind to die. When we'd survived against all odds, they had used expedited discharge approvals to buy our silence and compliance while they'd paraded me around as a hero.

I would never forgive them.

I stood on shaky legs, drowning in bloody memories, and barely keeping my stomach contents where they belonged. "I'm sorry," I said through the lump in my throat. "Thank you for your help with my shields."

I fled without waiting for a response.

CHAPTER FOURTEEN

I sent my team a message telling them to watch *Crash Crush* without me and retired to my room. Luna wasn't inside and I desperately missed her. My thoughts refused to calm, so I changed into my workout clothes and headed for the gym.

I cranked the music and settled onto the rowing machine. I pushed my tired body hard, burying memories under layers of exhaustion and pain. Sweat soaked through my clothes and I kept rowing, until the stroke cadence was the only thought left.

By the time I was done, I felt wrung out, both emotionally and physically. My bad knee burned with every movement. Maybe I would just sleep on the sparring mats and save myself the trouble of trying to climb the stairs.

The music lowered, and Eli appeared at my elbow, offering me a hand up. He pulled me to my feet and steadied me when I almost wobbled over.

"You want to talk about it?" he asked quietly.

I sighed. Eli was my first officer. He deserved to know. "I asked Torran to help me with my mental shields. He didn't do anything wrong, but I reacted poorly, and that led to a brief discussion of Rodeni." Bitterly, I continued, "All of that, and I didn't learn anything new about shielding. I don't know how we'll protect ourselves on Valovia."

Eli went still. "Did he hurt you?"

My mouth twisted. "No, I managed that all on my own."

"Did you tell him anything you shouldn't have?" Eli asked, his voice quiet. There was no judgment in his gaze, but Eli always planned for the worst-case contingencies.

"Nothing that he can use against us. And if he tries, I'll deny it loudly and publicly, like the good little FHP pawn that I am. You know I won't risk you and Kee and Lexi."

"It's not us I'm worried about," Eli said softly.

I squeezed his arm. "Despite the current evidence to the contrary," I said with a wave at my sweaty clothes and aching knee, "I know how to take care of myself, too."

His skeptical gaze spoke far louder than any words.

AN EARLY MORNING WORMHOLE TRAVERSAL MEANT AN-other short night. I hadn't slept well and the dark circles under my eyes were beginning to look permanent. Pretty soon I'd be mistaken for a raccoon.

The bridge was full when I arrived. Lexi and Kee chatted quietly with Chira, Havil, and Varro. Mostly Kee chatted and the others nodded as appropriate. Eli, Torran, and Anja were all busy studying their terminals—or at least pretending to.

From my shoulder, Luna chirruped in greeting, then leapt to Havil's shoulder. All of the Valoffs had started wearing shoulder guards for her. And while Valovian expressions were often hard to read, Havil's face softened when Luna chose him.

It hadn't escaped my notice that all of the Valoffs had been slipping her extra treats. By the time this job was done, Luna would be three times her weight and spoiled rotten.

I'd worked on my mental shield in the hours while sleep had eluded me. From the way Havil frowned at me, I didn't think it was working. My whole body felt bruised. Heading into enemy territory at anything less than 100 percent wasn't smart, but I hadn't been thinking clearly.

Torran glanced up from his place at the communications terminal. He nodded at me, his expression perfectly flat. I'd made a mistake in asking for his help, but I didn't regret the decision. I would do whatever I could to keep my crew safe.

I dipped my head at him. I could pretend that everything was fine as well as anyone else.

"*Lotkez* will go through the wormhole first," Torran said. "They are already in the pattern and will ensure you won't be stopped on the other side."

It was the whole reason his ship had trailed us rather than returning at the faster speed they were capable of, but it still set my teeth on edge. I didn't know *what* awaited us on the other side of the wormhole, but another Valovian ship probably wouldn't make much difference.

I nodded my acknowledgment as I settled into the captain's terminal and checked on *Starlight*'s system. I confirmed the course and the wormhole anchor added us to the holding pattern. There were a dozen ships in front of us, including *Lotkez*.

One by one they disappeared, and the tension in the room ramped up.

Luna had abandoned Havil's shoulder for his arms, and he buried a hand in her soft fur, stroking her gently.

"What's going on?" Lexi asked, glancing around. She looked at me. "Are we about to fly into a trap?" While Lexi could be as subtle as a sylph when she needed to—and could lie better than anyone I'd ever met—her default state was one of pure blunt intensity. And so far, she hadn't adopted a persona for the Valoffs. Either she didn't have a solid read on them or her last job had been even worse than she'd said. My money was on the latter.

I lifted one shoulder in answer to her question. I didn't know why the Valoffs hated the wormholes, and I wasn't confident that we *weren't* flying into a trap. Truly, I was a stellar captain.

"You can't feel it?" Chira asked, her voice pitched low.

"Feel what?" Lexi asked.

That surprised a laugh out of Chira. "The wormhole. The field it emits. It's like a shiver down your spine, except one you can't block or ignore. The longer we stay close, the worse it gets. Traversal is worse still."

Lexi frowned and glanced at Kee. "Do you feel anything?"

Kee shook her head. "Nothing like that, but I can kind of tell when we're approaching a wormhole. Like static in the air or something."

Lexi tilted her head in thought. "I suppose that's true. Even in the belly of a battleship, I always knew when we were close."

I hadn't really thought about it, but they were right. It didn't bother me, not in the same way it seemed to bother the Valoffs, but even in my quarters earlier, I'd known we were getting closer.

Lexi slanted a look at Chira. "That still doesn't answer if we're flying into a trap."

Chira stiffened and her expression shuttered. "General Fletcher has promised safe passage into and out of Valovian space. If there is any trap, it will not be our doing."

Lexi's smile was as wide as it was fake. "Good to know."

Chira's phrasing struck me. Did she think that someone else would set a trap for us? Honestly, I wouldn't put it past the FHP, but no FHP forces were allowed on the Valovian side of the wormhole. Did she know something about the people who'd stolen from Torran?

Before I could figure out if the wording had been intentional, we got the all-clear from the anchor and *Starlight* chimed the wormhole warning.

"Everyone strap in. We're next." I took my own advice and shrugged into my harness. *Lotkez* had already disappeared through the anchor, and Torran had sent word of our arrival to the Valovian forces guarding the other side, so hopefully there wouldn't be any misunderstandings when we arrived.

But just in case, I brought *Starlight*'s active defense capabilities online. From his terminal, Eli saw the change and raised an eyebrow at me. "Expecting trouble?" he asked subvocally over the comm.

"Just being cautious," I replied.

I hoped it wouldn't be needed but being prepared never hurt. I also brought up our weapons systems. I didn't fully activate them, because there was no reason to give the Valoffs an excuse to attack, but I could bring the ship into full battle readiness with a single command.

It might buy us enough time to get back to Fed space, assuming our access wasn't blocked.

The distorted space of the wormhole filled the screen as the autopilot brought us closer and closer. The engines ramped up and then we pierced the anchor's plane. The ship picked up a steady vibration. I dropped my gaze to my terminal, but out of my peripheral vision, I could see the starlight dancing on the main display.

Time stretched thin, then the wormhole spat us out the other side.

More than one sigh of relief filled the air as I scanned *Starlight*'s sensor data. *Lotkez* was just ahead of us, outside the danger zone, and there were a handful of ships within sensor range, but only one registered as military.

Of course, it was a huge, heavily armed battleship, so one was plenty.

No one hailed us as we moved out of the danger zone. The battleship didn't target us, or even subject us to a sensor sweep. We headed deeper into Valovian space unchallenged.

The knot in my stomach unclenched.

We weren't in the clear, exactly, because there could still be a trap waiting for us on Valovia, but we'd overcome the first challenge. At least tomorrow's final traversal was at a more reasonable midmorning hour. Maybe I could get enough sleep for once.

The bridge began to empty now that the wormhole was behind us. The Valoffs appeared more relaxed. Being back in friendly territory was probably a relief for them, but I wouldn't completely relax until we'd safely returned to FHP-controlled space. I might not love the Feds—*huge, huge understatement*—but I'd still take human space over Valovian.

"You want me to stay?" Eli asked over the comm.

I'd been so lost in thought that I hadn't realized everyone except Eli and Torran had left the bridge. Even Luna had wandered off, likely in search of a sucker she could con into feeding her a second breakfast.

"No, go on. I will be okay. I'm planning to monitor for a bit, just to ensure we're in the clear, then I'm going to help Anja with maintenance."

"Shout if you need anything," he said as he stood. Then he left the bridge, leaving me alone with Torran.

I'd known that avoiding Torran on a ship of *Starlight*'s size would be impossible, but I'd hoped to be a *little* more successful than this. I could order him to leave, but that would reveal far more than ignoring him.

If only he weren't so difficult to ignore.

My eyes kept sliding his way, so it was only a matter of time before he caught me looking. He held my stare for a moment before rising and approaching. He placed a small, rectangular black box on the corner of my terminal, then stepped back.

"I am sorry about yesterday," he said quietly. "You asked for my help, and I failed." His mouth flattened. "Then I let emotion override courtesy and caused you greater pain. Please forgive me."

Of all the things I'd expected, an apology wasn't even on the list. I blinked at him for a second before glancing at the box. "What is this?"

"It is *vosdodite,* an apology gift."

"You don't need to do that," I said, gently pushing the box back toward him. "I accept your apology."

Torran stiffened and his expression shuttered.

"Let me guess," I said drily, "if I don't accept the gift, it's some sort of grave Valovian insult?"

Torran unbent enough for one corner of his mouth to tip up. "Essentially, yes. A rejected gift can mean many things. The most common is a rejection of the apology. Or it could mean that you feel insulted by the quality of the gift in relation to the offense, and that I should try again with something more dear."

"What if it just means that I accept your apology, and you really don't have to get me anything because I'm human, and we don't expect apology gifts?"

"You can accept my apology by accepting the gift."

I pressed my lips together. I was potentially about to make another mistake, but I'd thought about this last night after my talk with Eli. I hadn't *really* said enough to get us in trouble with the Feds, but they could make our lives miserable without technically violating our contract.

I met Torran's eyes. "If you want to give me an apology gift, then I will accept your promise that you will forget everything I told you last night, and that you won't repeat it. If you do, or if you try to use it against me and mine, I will vigorously deny it."

Torran frowned, a question in his eyes. Understanding dawned, and his eyes narrowed. "The FHP is hid—"

"General Fletcher, your promise, please," I said, interrupting him before he could complete the thought.

I could see the struggle in his face. The muscle along his jaw flexed as he tried to find a way around it.

I prodded at his honor. "Unless, of course, you are not truly sorry," I said with a carefully careless shrug.

"One question first," he demanded. When I warily nodded, he asked, "Did you really call off the attack once you knew there were civilians inside?"

Now it was my turn to struggle. That question would

lead to a dozen more, each of them digging deeper into an event that needed to remain buried. My squad's freedom rested on my ability to sell the lie that was the Fed's account of the battle on Rodeni. If there was even a *hint* that I planned to reveal the truth, they would lock us up and lose the key.

Already, my silence had betrayed me. I had to do damage control.

I dropped my eyes to my terminal so I wouldn't have to see Torran's face when I lied to him. "I must've misspoken," I said. The words tasted of bitterness and frustration, but I forced them out. "I was overwrought and not speaking clearly. Of course the FHP had no knowledge of civilian inhabitants before the attack. It was an unfortunate tragedy." That last part, at least, was true.

I could *feel* his gaze boring into me, but Torran didn't say anything for an endless moment. When I risked a peek at him, he frowned at me. "I don't think you misspoke at all."

I met his eyes and lied to his face. "I absolutely did. If you are finished with your apology, then I need to get back to work." I pushed the box to the edge of the terminal. "Take that with you."

"I will not use what you told me against you," Torran promised quietly. "And I will forget the conversation. But if you ever want to talk, I will listen. If you and your crew want to work on your mental shields, my people and I will help. I apologize again for the harm I caused. Please keep the gift." He bowed his head, then left before I could protest.

The bridge door hissed closed behind him.

I stared at the box he'd left behind. It was wrapped in

matte black paper embossed with a subtle, swirling design. Curiosity tempted me to open it, even though I should return it to him unopened, insult or no. I was human. I didn't have to conform to Valovian standards.

But part of me was dying to see what was inside, to see what Torran thought was an appropriate gift.

I picked it up. The box was heavy for its size and it didn't rattle when I gently shook it. The wrapping paper was folded into straight, precise lines, and I wondered if he'd wrapped it himself. Surely not. Right?

I ran my fingers over the swirling pattern, fighting the desire to open it.

After a few seconds, curiosity won.

I slid a fingernail under the paper's longest seam and popped open the adhesive. The wrapping opened in a complex origami shape that was as beautiful as the paper itself.

Nestled inside, still encased in its anti-tamper packaging, was a brand-new, high-end comm. I didn't know how much this exact model cost because I hadn't looked at prices in a while, but I knew that it had to be more than a thousand credits.

No matter how much I wanted to keep it, it was too much.

I'd been happy with Torran's promise to forget last night's conversation. I didn't need an expensive gift on top of that. I would have to find a way to give it back to him without insulting him.

And figure out why he'd had a new comm in the first place.

CHAPTER FIFTEEN

I stayed on the bridge until we were well away from the wormhole and the traffic around us had dwindled to nearly nothing. As promised, *Lotkez*'s presence smoothed the way, allowing us to bypass all of the checkpoints. No one challenged us as we headed deeper into Valovian space.

I dropped the comm in my quarters, where it would stay until I could figure out how to return it, then spent the rest of the morning helping Anja in maintenance. My body felt better with the additional movement, but my knee still ached with every twist. I'd overdone it last night, but the little sleep I'd managed had been nightmare-free, so I'd gladly take the pain in trade.

When I finally stopped for lunch, I found Luna waiting for me in the galley. She chirruped when I appeared and glanced longingly at her food bowl—her food bowl that still had food in it.

I shook a finger at her. "I'm not giving you anything

else. You still have food, probably because you conned multiple people into feeding you. If you eat all the food I bought for you before we return to Fed space, you'll be stuck with rice like the rest of us."

I grabbed a meal bar and patted my shoulder guard. "I'm going to the garden if you think you can leave your food bowl for that long."

She perked up. *Garden* was one of the words she knew. When it became clear that I wasn't going to give her any treats, she leapt up to my shoulder.

I took us on a longer path to the garden and used the time to inspect the other parts of the level. Tomorrow was the last day of extra cleaning duty and everything looked good. I didn't know if Torran had ordered the Valoffs to comply or if they'd done it on their own, but they had worked as hard as my own crew, and no one had complained.

Starlight's Shadow had needed the deep clean and the extra work had kept everyone out of trouble, so it was a win-win.

The garden door slid open, revealing the green oasis inside. I headed for the arbor. I needed ten minutes of peace while I ate my meal bar.

Unfortunately, the universe wasn't on my side because when I pushed back the vines, I found Havil waiting for me. Maybe he'd just been enjoying some peace of his own, but he must've felt me approaching. His eyes found mine with unerring accuracy. Luna chirped at him in greeting, then jumped up to her perch in the corner.

"You are in pain," he said quietly.

"Tweaked my knee yesterday," I confirmed, because I'd promised him that I would tell him if it bothered me. I had planned to stretch the bounds of that promise as far as possible, but I wouldn't lie to him. "Then I made it worse last night in the gym."

He nodded as if that was the answer he'd expected. He didn't scold me or tell me that I should've taken it easier. His expression remained open and calm. "May I look at it?"

"You don't need to," I said. "You shouldn't have to exert yourself because I was stupid. But I would appreciate a lesson in how to shield pain, if you have time."

One side of his mouth quirked up and the corners of his eyes crinkled. "My job is ninety percent exerting myself because someone was stupid," he said, not unkindly. "And I will help you learn to shield, if you let me heal your knee first."

I tilted my head and considered the request. "Should we ask one of the others to join us? Last time you overdid it. I don't want you to get hurt on my account, and I can't catch you if you're holding my knee."

Havil waved me off. "Last time I healed three people in a row, and it had been a while since I'd used so much energy in such a short time. Healing just your knee won't be a problem." When I continued to look at him skeptically, he held up his hands with a small smile. "Promise."

I sank into one of the low chairs and pulled the material of my pants up over my right knee. The joint was swollen and I winced. "Is this good enough or do I need to take the pants off completely?"

"This is fine," Havil said. "Let me know if it's too much, but it shouldn't be as bad as before."

When I nodded, he shifted so he could place his hands on my knee. I didn't think I'd ever get used to the warm, prickly feel of his power. He must've sensed my unease because he glanced up at me. The tawny streaks in his deep brown eyes had expanded, but even glowing with power, his eyes remained kind. With the chair at my back, I had nowhere to go, but my instinctive panic remained manageable. *Barely.*

He searched my face for a moment before returning his concentration to my knee. The prickles turned into fiery needles, and I held my breath.

"Just a bit more," he said.

As promised, a few moments later, a final round of prickles swept through me from head to toe, then Havil sat back. I kept a close eye on him, but he didn't look like he was going to faint away, so perhaps he had just done too much last time.

My knee already felt better, which would never cease to amaze me. "Thank you."

"You're welcome. If you hurt yourself again, come to see me. I don't mind. Healing is why I'm here."

That triggered a memory, and my eyes narrowed. "General Fletcher said you're here to monitor the team. What does that mean?"

Havil smiled. "It's not as bad as whatever you're thinking. As a field medic, I am part of a squad of soldiers who have been trained to push past pain and get the job done."

He gave me a pointed look, which I blithely ignored.

He continued, "It's my job to know when they are silently hurting, either because they're too proud to admit it or because they feel like it's too minor to bother with."

"And you report what you feel to the general? What about personal privacy?"

"My squad knows about my job, and they accept my position in the team. I would not report specifics about you unless you gave me permission, or we were in an immediate, urgent situation where the information would fundamentally change the strategy. As an empath, privacy is very important to me."

I relaxed slightly. For whatever reason, I trusted him to keep his word. It wasn't anything I could put my finger on, but I often went with my gut and my gut said he was trustworthy.

"Speaking of privacy," I said, "can you help me with my shields? General Fletcher seemed to think that empaths were excellent at shielding."

Havil's eyes darkened, but he nodded. "We have to be," he agreed quietly. "Let's see what we can do."

WE SPENT TWENTY MINUTES TRYING TO IMPROVE MY MENTAL shields with only marginal success. At least I was getting used to the touch of a mind against mine, for better or worse.

Havil stood to leave, and I stopped him with one final question. "Can I ask you about *vosdodite*?"

He nodded. "What would you like to know?"

"Hypothetically speaking, what would you do if you wanted to accept the apology but felt like the gift wasn't necessary? How would you return it without causing offense?"

Havil started shaking his head before I was done asking the question. "The acceptance of *vosdodite* is the acceptance of the apology. The person giving the gift chooses it specifically for the recipient. To return the gift is to decline the apology."

"What if the recipient is human?"

"It doesn't matter. If you give the gift back, a Valoff will assume that you don't accept the apology."

"Did Torran tell you to say that?"

Havil's face softened into a gentle smile. "No, but I've worked with him for a long time. If he gave you *vosdodite,* he wants you to have it, even if you think it's unnecessary. Don't insult him by returning it."

I huffed out a frustrated breath. "My feelings don't matter?"

"Of course they do. Proper *vosdodite* should make you feel better, not worse. If you absolutely cannot accept the gift, then I suggest you talk to him about it. But you will be hard pressed to convince him that you truly accept the apology while simultaneously rejecting the gift. If he thought *vosdodite* was necessary, then he will likely try to give you something else."

Well, damn. That did not sound promising. "Thank you."

Havil nodded and left.

I slumped back in my chair and stared at the green foliage. I would have to approach this problem very carefully or I'd make the situation worse. But Havil had given me a sliver of hope. All I had to do was convince Torran that I'd feel better without the gift—a job that would be much easier if he hadn't already seen the state of my current comm.

EARLY THE NEXT MORNING, I MADE MY WAY DOWN TO THE gym. I'd finally gotten a decent night's sleep thanks to Havil's healing and a reasonable bedtime, so I felt like a new person. I planned to knock out some exercise, then get ready for the last wormhole traversal before Valovia.

Despite the hour, the gym wasn't empty. Eli was on the resistance press, Chira was rowing, and Torran was running on a treadmill. Based on the sweat plastering Torran's shirt to his chest, he'd been at it longer than the other two. I took a moment to appreciate the sheer beauty of his lean, muscular form in motion. He made running look effortless.

He glanced up and caught me staring. He paused his workout. "Do you need a sparring partner?"

I bit off the instinctive denial and considered the offer. I'd fought Valoffs during the war, but I'd never sparred with one. Perhaps I could learn something new.

"Sure, if you don't mind," I said. "And as long as you're not expecting me to be as good as Eli. Give me a few minutes to warm up."

Surprise crossed Torran's face before he nodded. I was getting better at reading the subtle changes in his expression.

I hopped on an elliptical and eased my way up to a brisk jog. I let the movement drown out my concerns. Much like with shielding, this could go incredibly wrong, but I wouldn't know if I didn't try. And if it went *too* sideways, Eli would bail me out.

Once my muscles were warm and pliable, I left the elliptical and moved to the sparring mats, where Torran waited. I wrapped my hands and reminded myself that this was just for fun. I knew my own strengths. Torran was going to kick my ass.

Eli and Chira had given up any pretense of working out and watched us with curious eyes. Based on Eli's smirk, I expected Kee and Lexi to *just happen* to wander in at any moment.

"Have you sparred with Eli?" I asked. When Torran nodded, I continued, "I'm not as tall or as fast as he is, so please keep that in mind. Pull your punches and don't aim for the face or groin. Any questions?"

Torran touched his wrapped knuckles to mine. "Should I avoid using my ability?"

I lifted my hands in a defensive position and slid back far enough to give me space to move. "I don't particularly want to be a telelocked punching bag because I'm already at a disadvantage. That said, if you will teach me how to break telekinetic holds, then I accept."

"Breaking holds isn't easy," Torran said as he circled closer. He moved with a lazy grace that did nothing to disguise the predatory look in his eyes.

I darted in and jabbed at his flank. The hit connected, but I got a tap on my shoulder for my trouble. He was even faster than Eli. I adjusted my strategy.

"But breaking holds is *possible*?" I asked once I was at a safe distance.

"It's possible for Valoffs. I don't know about humans." He frowned at me. "I don't want to distress you."

I closed the distance between us until I was barely outside his reach. Despite the obvious opening, he didn't take it. "Is it dangerous?" I asked.

He shook his head and slid away from the blow I aimed at his abs, then retaliated with a light jab toward my left side. Rather than retreating, I deflected the hit with my forearm and tapped his ribs. His answering smile was quick and fierce.

It was all the warning I got.

He went on the offensive, and he was fast as hell. It was all I could do to block and dodge. He backed me to the edge of the mat. With nowhere left to go, I decided to fight dirty.

I feinted at him so he would put his weight on one leg,

then grabbed his arm and shoulder. I stepped into him and swept his foot out from under him while twisting him off balance with my grip. The whole move took less than a second and he landed flat on his back on the mat.

Distantly, I heard Eli whoop. His lessons were paying off.

I let go of the arm I still controlled and danced out of reach. I wouldn't win a grappling contest, so I gave Torran time to get up. And gave myself a second to forget the warm, firm feel of his skin.

Torran stayed down.

"General Fletcher?" When he didn't respond, I eased closer. "Are you okay? Did I hurt you?" The floor was padded, so he couldn't be that hurt, right? It wasn't like Valoffs had glass spines. I glanced at the group of spectators. Eli and Chira had been joined by the rest of the crew, and everyone had given up the pretense of working out. None of the Valoffs looked concerned.

Torran still didn't move.

I crept closer with a concerned frown. "Torran?"

I caught the flash of his eyes and the curve of a satisfied smile before his hand clamped around my ankle. He yanked, but I transferred my weight to my other leg and hopped closer. It was ridiculous because I couldn't *do* anything, but I was still standing. I counted that as a victory.

Torran's smile grew, then an invisible force swept my other leg out from under me. I hit the mat on my back with a surprised grunt. By the time I caught my breath, Torran had pinned me under his body, his face perilously close to mine.

The hold was solid, and I could feel him, lean and firm, against me. I was effectively trapped, but rather than fear, desire simmered through my blood.

I glanced up at him and my breath caught. He was handsome at a distance, but up close, he was *devastating*. The colors in his dark eyes seemed to shift with the light. My gaze fell to his lips. Firm, smooth. I could almost feel them against mine.

It took a supreme effort of will to drag my mind away from his mouth, but I managed it. "I would call using your ability cheating, but since I started it, I'm willing to call it a draw—if you help me up."

A grin hovered around his lips. "Perhaps I am comfortable here," he said softly.

I arched, just a bit, testing his hold. I could barely move, but his expression shuttered, and he lifted himself off me. Once he was standing, I lifted an arm and he hauled me to my feet with easy strength. He didn't step back, so we ended up nearly chest to chest. I tipped my head back to find him staring down at me, something dangerously like heat in his eyes.

"You call me by my given name only when you're worried," he murmured, his voice pitched low. "Why is that?"

The question brought me back to myself, and right now I very much needed the reminder of why I maintained distance between us. I stepped back and smiled at him, though judging by his frown, it wasn't too convincing. "We are business partners. Using your title is polite."

He made a noncommittal sound, but his searing gaze remained riveted on my face. I feared he saw far too much, so to distract him, I asked, "Will you show me how to break telelocks now?"

Both Eli and Lexi started to protest, but I silenced them with a look.

Torran frowned, but he nodded reluctantly. "Valoffs

can break a lock if they are more powerful or more determined, but like shielding, it's instinctive. You won't be able to do it the same way, so rather than focusing on my power, focus on moving your body. It's harder to hold someone who is resisting."

When I didn't say anything, he asked, "Have you been locked before?"

I grimaced. "I'm alive, so no."

Something dark and harsh flittered across his face before he smoothed his expression back into careful blankness. "Take a deep breath and nod when you are ready. I will lock you in place for five seconds so you know what to expect. Then we will focus on just your arm for practice."

"If he doesn't let you go, I'll kill him," Eli said subvocally over the comm. I appreciated the thought, but unless he had a plas rifle hidden under his workout clothes, he would have a hard time of it.

I shook out my arms and bounced in place. This was such a bad idea. Still, I sucked in a deep breath, then nodded. I felt the cold brush of Torran's power and every cell froze. I couldn't move, couldn't breathe, couldn't blink. How much power did he have, that he could lock me so precisely?

My heart beat twice as fast, as if it alone could make up the difference. I wondered if he could stop that, too, if he tried.

Panic pulsed through my system, but I locked it down. I tensed every muscle, straining to move. Nothing happened.

Five seconds had never felt longer.

Torran released the hold. I sucked in a deep breath and waved off Lexi, who'd lunged for me. When I could speak, I pinned Torran with a hard look. "How did a group of humans steal from you when you could've locked them in place with a thought?"

I'd already discussed what I knew about the theft with my team, but we needed more details if we were ever going to be successful. Now was as good a time as any to press Torran for more information.

But, unsurprisingly, he handled the change of topic without a flicker of surprise. "I was away from home."

"You didn't take the ring with you? Wouldn't it be safest on your person?" I glanced at his hands. He didn't wear any visible jewelry. None of the Valoffs did. But neither did my team. Kee wore a necklace constantly, but it was always hidden under her clothes. Eli chose tattoos over jewels, and Lexi wore jewelry only when she was going for a particular look.

"It should've been safe at my house."

"How many people knew you wouldn't be home?"

Torran laughed without humor. "Many. I spoke at a public event. My attendance had been advertised for weeks."

I sighed. Nothing about this job was easy.

"How was the ring secured?" I asked.

He glanced away, clearly uneasy. "It was locked in my office. I have security personnel as well as an electronic system."

I raised an eyebrow at Lexi. She was the best thief I knew. "Could you do it?"

She shrugged. "Maybe. Depends on the system and the guards. For a human building, yes, with enough info and prep. But when the guards can sense you without seeing you? Much harder."

"Dig into the guards," I told Kee over the comm. She was likely already working on it, but an internal traitor was my best guess at this point.

Kee dipped her head in acknowledgment.

I turned back to Torran. "Is there anything else I should know before we get to Valovia?"

Torran stared at me for a long moment then slowly shook his head. I'd never had a more recalcitrant client.

I held out my arm. "Then let's see if I can break a telekinetic hold."

Lexi edged closer, stepping onto the mat. "Can I practice, too?"

"Me, too!" Kee called. She looked a little green around the edges at the thought, but she firmed her shoulders and soldiered on.

In the end, everyone on my crew tried breaking locks, with help from all of the Valoffs. None of us was successful individually, but I finally broke the lock when Kee and Eli managed to distract Torran for a fraction of a second.

Of course, a heartbeat later, he just locked me again.

My strategy for fighting a telekinetic Valoff remained the same: avoid at all costs. If that failed, then option two was run the fuck away, as fast as possible.

There was no option three.

CHAPTER SIXTEEN

I tapped my fingers on my terminal as Valovia grew ever larger on the bridge's main screen. Yesterday's final wormhole traversal had gone as smoothly as the rest of the trip, and the lack of problems made me nervous.

It made it seem like Valovia was a little *too* welcoming.

We were mere hours away from landing, and so far, not a single ship had challenged us, but my anxiety kept creeping higher, especially as the sensors picked up more and more military ships.

Starlight had an excellent navigation system, but huge swaths of Valovian space were uncharted, at least by humans. If we had to run, we had very few escape options, and now that we were close to the planet, *Lotkez* had broken away from our flight path, so we didn't have an escort, either.

Not that I would trust Valoffs to help us while we were on the run, but I'd gotten used to seeing Torran's ship trailing us on my sensors, and the lack felt wrong. My worry rose another notch.

Luna shifted in my lap, nudging me until I resumed petting her. She seemed to sense my anxiety. Or she sensed we were close to a planet. Either way, she had been especially clingy this afternoon, and I appreciated the comfort.

I wasn't sure what I'd do with her when we landed. Torran didn't have a private landing pad capable of holding *Starlight,* so I would have to land in a public spaceport. I hated leaving Luna alone all day, but I wasn't sure taking her with us was a good idea, not with the way Torran had reacted.

Most spaceports allowed crew to sleep on the ship for as long as it was berthed, so at least we wouldn't have to pay for a hotel.

And I still hadn't decided how to return the gifted comm. I needed to talk to Torran, but after our telelock practice yesterday, he'd been surprisingly scarce. He wasn't avoiding me, exactly, but he seemed to be making an effort to be where I was not.

So maybe he *was* avoiding me.

Even now, with Valovia glowing green, brown, and white on-screen, he wasn't in his usual spot at the comm terminal. Instead, Chira had taken his place. The pale Valoff had assured me that Torran was fine when I'd asked.

Eli and Anja were at their terminals, but Kee had holed up in her control room with Lexi, searching for info on the heist, the guards, and anything else she could find. Now that we were close to Valovia, Kee had real-time access to the Valovian networks and the knowledge needed to use them, so she was taking full advantage.

The minutes crept by. *Starlight* reported our destination

to ground control and got nearly instantaneous approval to land. My anxiety crawled higher. In space we'd be hard pressed to escape, but once we were on the ground it became infinitely harder, and Valovia seemed awfully eager to accept us.

Torran finally entered the bridge when we were just five minutes from atmospheric entry. He met my stare with a level gaze, his expression smoothed into flat nothingness.

"Remember that you promised us safe passage on your honor," I said. My voice came out steady despite the nerves squeezing my chest.

I caught a tiny flicker, as if he wanted to break my gaze but overcame the urge. "I remember."

Personal honor was a cornerstone of Valovian society. Would Torran destroy his to capture a human crew? I wanted to believe the answer was no, but I wasn't exactly impartial. I *liked* Torran and his crew. Over the past week, I'd stopped seeing them as enemies.

But I also needed to be careful. I had no doubt that we would receive a very cold reception on Valovia, even if we weren't immediately murdered or imprisoned. We needed to do the job we were hired for, get paid, and then beat a hasty retreat back into safer space.

The one-minute warning sounded and everyone strapped in. Sixty seconds later, *Starlight's Shadow* sank into the Valovian atmosphere with a judder. The ship definitely was not at its best in atmosphere. It lumbered like a beast too heavy for flight.

I made some minor adjustments to the autopilot but mostly let the ship take us in. Below, the view turned green. Torran lived in Zenzi, the capital city, nestled within the planet's temperate equatorial girdle.

As we drew closer, a sprawling city came into view. The orange sun was either rising or setting, causing the taller buildings to glow on one side and cast deep shadows on the other. A check of the local time confirmed that it was early morning.

Getting used to a solar day that was ten hours long was going to be a struggle. It was only in the last hundred years or so that Valoffs had combined two solar days into one longer unit, *buratbos,* a shortening of "two sun day."

Before the widespread adoption of artificial lighting, Valoffs worked and slept in short bursts with the natural daylight. With the adoption of the longer twenty-hour *buratbos,* they worked through a day, a night, and most of another day before sleeping through the second night. It roughly translated to fourteen or fifteen awake hours and five to six sleeping hours.

I wasn't sure I would adjust, even if we were here for the full length of the contract. At least my quarters didn't have any outside windows, so I could sleep without the sun shining in my eyes.

The spaceport was at the edge of the city, a huge flat area dotted with other ships. Ground control guided us in, and *Starlight* settled on the landing pad with a final jolt.

Someone let out a quiet sigh, but otherwise, the bridge remained eerily quiet. Eli and Anja studied their screens. The Valoffs stayed in their seats. I checked the outside cameras. A few people were visible at distant ships, but no one was waiting to snatch us up.

Yet.

I shut down the engines and prepared to put the ship in standby. We were on Valovia. It still didn't feel real, despite the images streaming in from the outside cameras.

Luna stood and stretched. She sent me a wave of long-ing with a mental picture of her empty food bowl. It wasn't dinnertime yet, but we'd skipped lunch, so she was hungry.

I scooped her up and rose. The rest of the shutdown checklist could wait a few minutes. And if anyone was wait-ing for us outside, maybe they would get impatient and tip their hand.

Eli glanced up. "Going to feed the little beastie?" Fond affection took the sting out of the words.

"Yes. She missed lunch and she wants me to know about it. I'll finish the checklist when I get back. Keep an eye on things."

He nodded and went back to his screen.

I carried Luna to the galley, where she promptly sent me another wave of longing. I set her next to her bowl and scratched behind her ears. "I'm working on it, Little Miss Impatient. Give me more than a nanosecond, yeah?"

Patience had never been Luna's strong suit. She twined around my legs and nipped at me when I didn't move fast enough for her. I held the food out of reach with a stern look until she settled, then I put it in her bowl. She sent me a wave of affection before she started eating.

My heart swelled with return affection. I loved the fluffy little menace, impatience and all.

Torran entered the galley on silent feet. When he saw he had my attention, he asked, "Will you be ready to depart once she is finished eating?"

"I'll be ready once I put *Starlight* in standby."

Torran's gaze flashed to my face. "You aren't bringing her with you?"

"She'll be safer here. And she can look after herself un-til we get back later."

Torran frowned. "You're planning to return to the ship tonight?"

"Yes. There's no reason to pay for a hotel when we have perfectly good rooms here."

"I've already taken care of accommodations, and shuttling back and forth is a waste of time. Bring Luna. I've dismissed most of my staff and alerted the rest. She will be safe."

I took a deep breath and searched for calm. "Don't you think you should've let me know about the accommodations before now? If you had, I would've packed."

He looked genuinely confused for a moment before he inclined his head. "My apologies. I thought it was understood that I would provide rooms while you were on Valovia. Guests are always provided for."

"But we're not guests, we're contractors."

Torran shook his head. "It doesn't matter. My team is staying with me, so you'll have to share the guest wing with them, but you already know them. I do not have any other guests at this time."

Guest *wing*? Kee had told me that he was rich, and he was paying us a veritable fortune to find a ring for him, but I was still envisioning a house, not some monstrosity that was large enough for a guest wing.

He continued, "It will also be safer if you aren't shuttling back and forth every day."

"Are we in danger?"

"Your bounty has been suspended, but that doesn't guarantee safety. I can protect you when you're with me, but my reach extends only so far."

"I'm not exactly planning to run around announcing my presence."

A brief smile touched Torran's mouth. "I appreciate that, and I've done what I can to obscure the fact that you're here, but it will eventually get out, especially once you start investigating. Staying close will ensure your safety."

Was he really concerned about my safety or did he want to keep me away from an easy escape route? I rolled my shoulders, trying to unknot some of the tension. I couldn't constantly second-guess all of his motives or I'd be an inferno of anxiety. I needed to be cautious and prepared without tipping over into paranoia.

"I'll tell my team to pack for a week," I said. "Will we have access to a kitchen? We have some food that's going to spoil if we don't eat it."

Torran's expression shifted as some of his tension also drained away. "You are welcome to use the main kitchen."

I dipped my head in thanks and went to tell the team about the change in plans.

MY TEAM PACKED WITH QUICK EFFICIENCY. WE WERE USED TO traveling light. Most of our weapons, gear, and tech supplies were already packed in the cargo bay, so we just had to load them into the shuttle that would take us to Torran's house.

I left my bag with Eli, then went through the walk-in cooler and packed all of the food that would spoil in the next week. I'd have to make another trip later if we were going to remain on-planet longer than that.

Luna finished her lunch, then jumped up onto my shoulder guard when I patted it. "We're going on an adventure," I told her. "Don't run off and give me a heart attack, okay?"

She shifted and peered down into the box of food I picked up. When I didn't offer her any, she chirruped at me.

"You have a one-track mind, friend. No more food until we arrive." I'd very carefully hidden her favorite treats in the bottom of the box. We'd never had trouble with her stealing food, but I didn't want to tempt her, either.

By the time Luna and I arrived, everyone had gathered in the cargo bay. The ramp was lowered and the Valoffs had already transferred most of the supplies they'd brought. They all were wearing their armor. As usual, Torran neglected to wear a helmet.

I tried not to take the armor as a bad sign, but based on Lexi's scowl, she didn't share my optimism.

I pulled Kee aside. "Is the ship locked down?"

She nodded. "As tight as I can make it. And I left a few surprises for anyone who tries to access it, either physically or electronically."

"You'll know if they try?"

She didn't quite roll her eyes, but I could tell the restraint cost her. "Yes."

"Thank you."

That earned me a bright smile. "Of course. Lexi and I found a few leads, too. We'll chat later."

From the side, the waiting shuttle looked like a sleek black rounded rectangle that was designed to hover rather than fly. It had an unfamiliar looping sapphire insignia on the side. Large cargo doors on either end had folded up, allowing the Valoffs to load their supplies.

With a nod, my team started loading our gear. Luna jumped down and inspected the new transport. I didn't really worry about her running off because she'd stuck by my side through a literal war, but I kept an eye on her nonetheless. I was more worried about a Valoff spotting her and freaking out.

Once everything was loaded, Kee and I did the final lockdown on *Starlight*. The ship would keep the essential systems running while in standby, but it would take twenty minutes—ten if we rushed—to be ready to fly again.

The cargo door closed with a final *thunk* as the locks slid home.

Time to see what Valovia was all about.

This was the first time I'd set foot on a Valovian planet during peacetime. Bitter memories tried to swamp me, but I locked them down and focused on the present.

Gravity on Valovia was a little less than Earth standard, so moving was just a bit easier. It wasn't enough to affect my balance, but it would take me a few days to readjust to *Starlight*'s gravity once we returned to the ship.

The air was crisp and dry, and the pale blue sky looked washed out against the large orange sun that rose higher every minute. I found it hard to believe that it would set in less than five hours.

I returned my attention to the ground and boarded the shuttle. Luna sat on the tallest stack of crates, observing her surroundings with a keen eye. A dozen seats hung from the ceiling in connected pairs. Each pair was anchored at a single point that looked like it would pivot.

Lexi had already claimed a seat and secured herself, but Havil and Chira were demonstrating the safety restraints to Eli and Anja. Kee poked the nearest pair of seats and they swung slightly.

She caught my glance and grinned at me. "Well, that's fun."

Varro drew closer, looking like someone trying to approach a wild animal without scaring it off. "Do you need help?"

If I was generous, I would say that he had asked both of us, but he kept sneaking sidelong glances at Kee while trying to pretend indifference. Kee, who was far from oblivious, beamed at him. "Please. I don't want to end up on the ceiling."

I waited until my team was secure before looking for a seat of my own. While I'd waited, Torran had closed the shuttle's doors. Now he waved me to the last empty pair of seats, located in the back—he'd remembered my preference for being able to keep an eye on everyone.

He pointed at the shoulder harness. "Would you like me to show you how the clasps work?"

I had a pretty good idea, because we'd recovered Valovian vehicles during the war, but I nodded and let him demonstrate the buckle that slotted together at an angle and then snapped flat. The design worked well as a safety restraint because the clasp wouldn't come apart as long as there was tension on it.

I gingerly climbed into the seat and strapped in. The chair swayed as Torran settled next to me. The slim armrest between us did nothing to prevent me from feeling the heat of his body all the way from my shoulder to my knee.

"Ready?" he asked.

I twisted to glance back at Luna, who still sat on the pile of cargo like a tiny, fluffy queen. "Should I hold Luna or will she be able to ride where she is?" The little burbu had excellent balance, but if we needed shoulder harnesses, then she might need more support.

"She'll be fine there. She can dig her claws into the cargo if she needs to."

"Then I'm ready."

Torran said something in Valovan and the shuttle lifted

off its parking pads. The sides of the vehicle were lined with tinted windows, and I didn't even bother to pretend that I wasn't fascinated by the view outside.

We accelerated smoothly away from *Starlight's Shadow*. Our seats did not swing as much as I'd expected, and I wondered if the pivot was actually connected to an electronic control that activated when the transport was in motion.

Torran must've already set the destination because once we left the spaceport, the shuttle seamlessly joined the stream of ground traffic. I didn't see any transports in the sky.

I turned to Torran. "Are flying transports banned because of the Imperial Palace?"

"There are flights within the city, but they are limited to public transport and imperial business," he said. "There are also both local and high-speed underground lev lines."

If I were a thief, which option would I choose? I would probably split the team, making it harder to track everyone. I wondered if Kee could still pull surveillance video from two weeks ago.

We left the neighborhood streets and entered an elevated expressway. The shuttle accelerated rapidly. On the first corner the seats started to make sense. They swung just enough that I felt pressed into the seat bottom rather than the armrest.

In the distance, tall, glass-encased buildings stretched into the pale sky. The taller buildings lost a lot of the ornate, organic architecture of their shorter counterparts, so at this distance, Zenzi looked like any large city on a human-populated planet.

Ten minutes later, we exited the expressway and entered a residential neighborhood. At least, I assumed it was residential. The streets were wide and lined with greenery. Tall, spiky hedges and elaborate gates blocked the view, but a few roofs were just visible. Traffic was light and all of the shuttles we passed were shiny and well maintained.

As we delved deeper into the neighborhood, the gates got farther and farther apart. We finally turned onto a block with a single gate on it. It bore the same sapphire insignia as on the side of the shuttle, and it slid open as we approached.

My comm couldn't communicate with Valovian networks or positioning satellites, so I couldn't pull up a real-time map. Just before we'd left, Kee had sent us all offline maps of Torran's house and the directions to return to *Starlight*. I hadn't realized just how big his property was from the satellite imagery. We were close to the Imperial Palace and all of the estates on the surrounding blocks were reserved for high-level diplomats and advisors.

The shuttle slipped through the gate into a deep green paradise. Vibrant flowers nestled in lush foliage, and trees with long, draping branches hid the view of the house. I caught sight of the edge of a gravel path and I wanted to explore where it led.

The house, when we finally arrived, wasn't what I'd expected from something with a guest wing. On Earth, it would've been tall and stone and square. Here, it looked like it had sprung up from the greenery surrounding it. A sweeping green roof was held up with thin curved supports.

The front of the house followed the arc of the circle driveway, like two arms open for an embrace. The main entrance was clad in sapphire glass around two enormous wooden doors inlaid with the same looping insignia that was on the shuttle and the gate. The rest of the facade was a pale, translucent material that obscured the view inside.

The shuttle came to a stop directly in front of the entrance. Torran shrugged out of his harness and stood. "Welcome to my home. My staff will move your supplies while I show you to your rooms."

I stood and grabbed my personal bag, then patted my shoulder for Luna. She joined me with a questioning chirp.

Our gear crates were locked with the strongest locks Kee and Lexi could find. If Torran's people could get through them in the few minutes the transfer would take, then they deserved to poke around in our stuff. Anything we didn't want searched was already in our personal bags.

"We'll carry our bags, but I would appreciate it if your people would move the crates. The groceries need to go in a cooler. I can move them if you prefer."

Torran shook his head. "There's no need. Do you want everything chilled?"

I nodded. Luna's snacks didn't need to be refrigerated, but the cold wouldn't hurt them, and it was easier to start with everything rather than explaining what to leave out.

My team grabbed their personal bags. Eli, Kee, Lexi, and I had all worked together long enough that we knew the drill. I took point, then Kee and Lexi were lookouts in the middle. Eli brought up the rear, and he waved Anja over beside him. Once he figured out her strengths, he would assign her a more permanent position.

We all had our comms on and set to a group channel. We had to stay within a kilometer of each other for devices to stay connected using their local mesh networking. Farther than that and we'd need to be able to tap into the Valovian communication networks.

I didn't really expect an attack, but there was no harm in a little caution in enemy territory. Torran glanced at us.

It had to be obvious what we were doing, but he did not comment.

As we approached the massive front door, it swung open on silent hinges. A Valoff wearing civilian clothes stepped out with a charming smile. He was handsome, with tan skin and straight black hair that was long enough to fall over his forehead. He moved like a soldier or fighter, lithe and light on his feet.

Behind me, Lexi sucked in a sharp breath.

Unaware of Lexi's reaction, Torran introduced the newcomer. "Captain Zarola, this is Nilo Shoren, my second officer. He's been continuing the investigation while I was away."

"I'll bet he was," Lexi muttered just loud enough for the comm to pick up.

I caught the exact moment that Nilo saw Lexi. His smile died for a fraction of a second before coming back even brighter than before. The pieces connected. Twenty credits said this was the mystery man from the hotel that Lexi had told me about.

Clearly the universe still loved to vex me.

I introduced Eli, Kee, and Anja before turning to Lexi. "And this is Lexi Bowen, recovery specialist."

I had to give it to Nilo: now that the shock had worn off and his mask was affixed, it didn't budge. "It's a pleasure," he said with a charming grin.

Lexi gave him her emptiest smile. "Same, I'm sure," she murmured. She looked perfectly relaxed, but I heard the murder in her saccharine tone. Nilo Shoren had better sleep with one eye open.

"No stabbing," I warned her over the comm.

"No promises," she replied just as quietly.

CHAPTER SEVENTEEN

We made it to our rooms without anyone getting murdered. Torran's house was as beautiful on the inside as on the outside, full of curving lines and warm, cozy spaces. The front door opened into a huge kitchen, dining, and living area, showcasing the importance of hospitality in Valovian culture.

The guest wing was tucked away off the back left of the house, separated from the main building by a long, glass-enclosed hallway that offered a delightful view of the careful landscaping. And *wing* hadn't been an overstatement. There were at least a dozen small but exquisite bedroom suites lining two separate corridors, as well as a pair of doors leading outside, so guests didn't need to walk through the main house to enjoy a bit of nature.

Torran's team had taken rooms in the first hallway, so we chose rooms in the second. It gave us all the illusion of privacy, though I had no doubt that we were under surveillance.

Torran left us to unpack after our trunks of supplies were delivered. We dropped our bags in our chosen rooms and then shuffled the trunks around. Eli and I split the general supplies while Kee got her trunk full of tech goodies.

By unspoken agreement, once everything was put away, we all converged on Lexi's room. She just rolled her eyes and waved us in.

"Spill," Kee demanded.

Lexi sighed. "I met Nilo six months ago. Of course, that wasn't the name he used, and I didn't know that he worked for Fletcher. I was supposed to do a lucrative little job for a Valovian businesswoman, but Nilo stole it out from under me. Don't let the charming facade fool you. He's smart, cunning, and ruthless."

She didn't mention the hotel bar, so I didn't bring it up, but I did ask, "Is it going to be a problem?"

"For him, maybe," she said with a sharp grin. When I just stared at her, she relented. "I will be on my best behavior. It will not affect the job."

"Do you want me to try to keep you two separated?"

She shook her head. "I'm the best suited to keep an eye on him because I know his tricks."

Lexi's expression remained a little too sharp and dangerous, but I let it go. She could look after herself, and I trusted her to let me know if there was a problem. "Tell me what you and Kee found earlier."

She switched topics without missing a beat. "I scoured my usual haunts but there wasn't a peep about a job on Valovia. So we're either tracking an independent team or someone who knows how to clean up their tracks—either way, they're professionals. This isn't a rookie job." She waved at Kee. "I'll let you tell them what you found."

Kee grinned. "Because we're so close to the palace, there are more cameras on the streets here than elsewhere in the city. I did a little poking and found some surveillance footage that might be our thieves. It's hard to tell because they hit in the dark and the angle isn't the best, but it's a start."

"How many?"

"Four or five. Maybe more if they split the team. The camera I found is on the corner of the block. I'm still tracking down alternate angles."

"Excellent work. Now that we're here, I'm hoping that General Fletcher will be more forthcoming with details. His system should've caught something, too."

"I hope so," Kee said. Then she switched to sign language, her hands flashing through the words. "I am going to set up my system and breach his security. Until then, be careful because we are likely being monitored, including our comms."

Eli, Lexi, and I nodded our understanding. Kee had learned sign language during childhood because her father was deaf, and she'd taught the rest of us during the war, when totally silent, untraceable communication had been even more useful than the subvocal comms.

Anja frowned at us but didn't say anything. If she decided to stay on, we would have to teach her, too.

"I'm going to walk the perimeter while the sun is up," I said. "I know our body clocks think it's afternoon and the sun is going to set in a few hours, but try to stay up because we're in the first half of the double day. The faster we adjust to local time, the easier it will be. If you're hungry, Torran said we're allowed to use the main kitchen."

"Two sunsets in a single day will be interesting," Eli said.

"Could be worse," Lexi said. "The last planet I was on had an impossibly long day. Do you know how hard it is to sneak around when it looks like high noon outside *all the time*?"

Eli grinned. "I'm sure you made it work."

Lexi's mouth curved into a small, satisfied smile. "Damn straight I did."

I DUG A MEAL BAR OUT OF MY PACK AND SPLIT IT WITH LUNA before I ventured outside. I took the little burbu with me. We could both use the fresh air and exercise. Eli tried to join me, but I sent him off with Lexi and Anja to check the property in the other direction.

Kee had decided to remain holed up in her room with her electronics.

I understood the desire to hide away. I loved my team like family, but I needed five minutes of solitude to settle my nerves.

Torran's property was beautiful. It was carefully land-scaped but retained a wild kind of beauty with a profusion of native plants, none of which I recognized. I'd studied the offline map Kee had sent to my comm. The property had to be nearly a hectare, but it was hard to judge the size from the ground because the winding paths were obscured from each other.

I had just begun to relax for the first time since Valovia had shown up on *Starlight*'s display when Torran *just happened* to appear on the random path I'd chosen. He'd changed back into civilian clothes, though the dark slacks and thigh-length, long-sleeved tunic were far nicer than the casual clothes he'd worn on *Starlight*.

I raised an eyebrow at him. "Did you sprint down the other path so it would look like you ran into me by chance?"

He shook his head, amusement in his eyes. "Believe it or not, I was merely enjoying a walk. I've been away for a long time and while *Starlight*'s garden was nice, it's not the same." He frowned at me and looked around. "Are you alone?"

Warning tingles licked up my spine. If they felt more like anticipation than concern, I ignored it.

"Luna is around here somewhere," I hedged. "Why? Is your property unsafe? If so, you should've told me. My people are out, too, and I need to warn them."

He shook his head. "The property is safe enough. I did not think your first officer would let you explore on your own in unknown territory. He seems . . . protective."

"Eli does have an overprotective tendency," I agreed easily. "He's currently using it on Lexi and Anja." I cocked my head and thought about the snatches of conversation I'd caught over the comm. "And Havil, I believe."

Torran's eyes went distant, then he dipped his head in agreement. "And Chira."

I chuckled. "It's a party over there, wherever they are."

"Do you wish to join them? I can . . ."

I waved him off before he completed the offer. "I sent them off together on purpose so I could enjoy a quiet walk with Luna."

Torran hesitated, then asked, "May I join you?"

"If you'd like, but I'm planning to walk the whole

property, so you don't have to stick around once you've gotten enough fresh air. Do you know where the thieves gained entry?"

Torran's mouth compressed, but he nodded. "Shall I show you?"

"Just point it out when we get there."

He silently fell in beside me, letting me set the pace. We ambled along while Luna frolicked through the greenery. For all of my relaxed pace, I kept a sharp eye on our surroundings.

Torran was surprisingly good company, and the silence between us was far more comfortable than I'd expected. I let the sun and crisp air unknot some of my tension before I turned my mind back to the matter at hand.

Unfortunately, I was here to do a job. I mentally sighed and bid my relaxing walk farewell. As long as Torran was here, I might as well get some answers.

I glanced at my silent companion. "Did Nilo find anything new while you were away?"

"Nothing useful."

Which was not the same as nothing. I didn't know what it was going to take for Torran to trust me, but at this rate I needed to stop mentally spending that second payment because we wouldn't find the ring in eight *months,* never mind eight *weeks.*

I stopped and turned to him. "Why did you really bring me and my team all the way to Valovia?"

He froze and met my eyes. "What do you mean?"

"I thought you were reticent about the details because we were still in human space, and you didn't want the information leaked. But we're standing on your planet, *on your property,* deep in Valovian space, and you still aren't giving me enough information to actually do the job you hired me for. So what is your objective?"

Torran ran a hand down his face, and it was such a familiar, weary expression that my heart cracked open a little more. Whatever else was going on, he truly was worried.

"I am bound by a web of oaths," he finally said. "Navigating them is . . . difficult."

"Someone doesn't want you talking about the theft even now?" He didn't deny it, and he'd already said he was the head of his household. Who else would want to silence him? I took a stab in the dark. "Is it the empress?"

The merest flicker of his expression was all the answer I got, but it was enough. "Kee, I need you to look into General Fletcher's connection to Empress Nepru," I said subvocally over the comm. "I think she's preventing him from telling us about the theft."

"On it," Kee confirmed.

"Why would the empress care about a family ring?" Eli asked.

"Losing it makes one of her top generals look weak," Lexi said. "If she's facing opposition, this could be fuel for the rebels."

"Maybe they're having an affair and something else that would incriminate her was stolen at the same time," Anja said. Her voice was bitter.

My heart jolted a little at the thought. The empress was undeniably beautiful, but she was married and nearly old enough to be Torran's mother. As much as I hated the thought, it was possible.

I tuned out my squad as their theories became increasingly improbable. But an affair—that would explain quite of lot of things. And there was one way to find out.

I carefully studied Torran's expression. "Are you having an affair with the empress?"

His eyes widened in shock and the colors shifted as the teal and silver streaks spread. But his voice, when it came, was quiet and firm. "No."

I believed him. "Is someone in your house?"

He shook his head.

"But the empress is involved somehow."

Torran said nothing.

I growled and jabbed a finger at him. "This is the most annoying game ever, you know that, right?"

He stepped closer, until my finger was pressed into the soft fabric of his tunic—fabric that covered firm muscles. My brain short-circuited, and I almost didn't catch his words.

"I apologize," he said. "I am trying." He dipped his head, until his mouth was near my ear. "And I am not having an affair with anyone." He slid back and slanted a heated glance at me. "At the moment."

I KEPT SNEAKING SIDELONG GLANCES AT TORRAN, TRYING TO figure out if he meant that last statement the way I'd heard it, but he was acting like he hadn't said anything shocking at all.

My pulse jumped every time I remembered the heated look in his eyes. He *had* to have been flirting . . . right? Doubt and certainty warred with each other.

Luna continued to enjoy her time in the sun. She never

got so far away that I couldn't spot at least a bit of her white fur, and I wondered if she could feel my turmoil. I knew that she would be happier on a planet with plenty of room to roam, but if she decided to stay behind this time, it would break my heart.

We came upon a relatively clear piece of the outer wall, and I stopped. I couldn't see the house behind us, but it wasn't far away. Multiple feet had trampled the plants leading from the path to the wall. "Is this where the thieves got in?"

Torran's eyes glinted as he nodded.

A tall row of densely packed shrubs with sharp, spiky leaves surrounded the property, and if that wasn't enough of a deterrent, the stone wall itself was three meters tall. So how did the thieves get over it?

I mentally apologized to the gardeners as I stepped on the edges of a few plants in order to get a closer look. The wall was too tall for me to pull myself up, so I waved Torran over. "Give me a boost. I want to see the top."

"There isn't anything to see."

"Doesn't matter. If you won't do it, I'll ask Eli. He shouldn't be too far away."

Torran's jaw clenched, then he jumped, caught the top of the wall, and pulled himself up with ease. If he expected me to do the same, then he was in for a major disappointment.

"Take a deep breath," he said.

As soon as I did, his power clamped around me. My feet left the ground and he lifted me up next to him. He braced his hands on either side of me, then released the telekinetic hold. I clutched his arm as I found my balance on the narrow wall.

"That wasn't exactly what I meant," I said breathlessly, "but I'll take it. Thank you."

The wall was only twenty-five centimeters wide, but the top was flat, so moving around wasn't difficult. Next to me, the shrubs surrounding the property were hip-high but carefully trimmed back, leaving a small gap between them and the wall. Someone crawling along the top of the wall would have plenty of cover to move without being seen from the street.

The street itself was narrower than the one that ran past the main gate. I didn't see anything that looked like streetlights, so perhaps it was completely dark once the sun set. That would certainly be convenient for someone trying to sneak in.

I reached out to touch the point of one of the shrub's glossy, deep green leaves. They looked like they would tear up anyone who tried to climb through them.

Torran's warm fingers closed around mine before I made contact. "Don't. *Vomosulabr* are very sharp and the points are coated in an irritant. If it pierces your skin, it won't kill you, but it will make you wish you had not touched it."

"Do not touch the spiky shrub," I relayed to my team. "Not deadly, but unpleasant."

"I don't usually go around touching alien plants," Lexi said drily.

Well, that made one of us, apparently.

Torran still held my hand, his grip gentle and warm. I peeked up at him and found his eyes on my face. "Thank you for the warning," I said. "I passed it along to my team."

"You are welcome," he said. We were close enough that

I could see the colorful streaks in his dark eyes. The silver, teal, and copper seemed to shift in intensity, growing brighter before fading.

I stared, mesmerized.

His incredible eyes dropped to my mouth and the heat in his gaze rekindled. I might have doubted that he was flirting earlier, but this look was impossible to misinterpret—Torran wanted me. My breath quickened and I licked my lips. I wanted him, too, no matter how foolish that made me.

Torran groaned low in his chest, and his head dipped toward mine.

I lifted my face. My eyes were nearly closed when I caught a flash of movement in my peripheral vision. I instinctively spun to look and nearly fell off the wall.

Torran steadied me while heat climbed my cheeks. The transport continued down the street, unaware that it had nearly caused me to break my neck. But it was a good reminder that we were highly exposed here, standing on top of the wall.

My pulse pounded in my ears, from both the adrenaline and the desire. I reluctantly drew away from Torran and he let me go. I focused on the shrubs and tried to get my thoughts in order.

But they were still very focused on the almost kiss.

My lips tingled. I peeked at Torran's face, but his expression had returned to its unreadable natural state. This time, though, there was no doubt: I *hadn't* imagined the desire in his gaze. If not for the untimely transport, I would know how his lips felt against mine.

Damned transport.

I cleared my throat and prayed my face wasn't as red as it felt. The moment was lost, so I returned to the problem of the theft. "So how did the thieves get over the plants without getting stabbed?"

"They wore armor." Torran's voice was steady and didn't reveal any of his thoughts.

But the statement did reveal something else. My gaze shot back to his face, embarrassment forgotten. "You have video. Or witnesses."

I waved the implicit question away before he could deflect again. "Never mind, we'll discuss that once we're back on the ground." I worked through the theft in my head. I could see the side of the house from here. So climb over the wall, infiltrate the house, grab the ring . . . then what? "Did they leave this way, too?"

"No, they left via the front gate."

My eyebrows rose. "That's a bold choice. Were they injured?"

"No."

I blew out a frustrated breath. Getting answers from Torran was like pulling teeth from a tiger. It shouldn't bother me, but I actually *wanted* to find his ridiculous ring for him, and he was making it very difficult.

The line of shrubbery was unbroken in either direction, and despite standing on my tiptoes, I couldn't see the ground outside the wall. I settled back onto my heels before I fell into the shrubs and tested Havil's healing skills—again.

I'd seen enough. I still wanted to see the rest of the property in case we needed a quick exit, but now I had a mental map of how the thieves had gained entry. Hopefully I could pair it with Kee's surveillance video to start putting together the night's timeline.

And then we could figure out what Torran was really hiding.

CHAPTER EIGHTEEN

After I shimmied off the wall, thankfully without injuring my knee, Torran and I walked the rest of the property. By unspoken agreement we avoided the others, though I'm sure Havil and Chira knew when we passed them.

By the time we made it back to the side of the house facing where the thieves had entered, the sun had crossed the zenith and was quickly sinking toward the horizon.

My body clock thought it was late afternoon. Staying up through five hours of darkness was going to be a challenge. At least if I made it most of the way, I could just sleep for an extra few hours and wake up tomorrow local time.

The short solar days were going to break my brain. Nothing to do but keep busy.

I called Luna to my shoulder and turned to Torran. "How do we get to your office from here? Specifically, how did the thieves get to your office?" I gestured him ahead of me. "Show me."

Torran's eyes narrowed at the command, but he turned back down the path and ducked behind a tall, leafy plant. I followed him, unsure what to expect. The small, covered entrance was completely hidden from the trail. I heard a click, then Torran pulled the door open.

"Is this door kept locked?"

"Yes."

I rolled my eyes and prayed for patience. Loquacious he was not.

I entered the house and found myself in a pale cream hallway that I hadn't seen on our way to the guest wing. "Where are we?"

"This is the family wing. My bedroom and private office are here, as well as spare rooms for family guests."

"Do you have any family guests staying with you currently?"

He flinched, very slightly, then shook his head.

From the way his expression hardened, I wouldn't get any more information out of him about family guests, so I moved on. "Was the ring in your private office?"

"Yes."

"Show me."

Torran inclined his head in agreement, but before we made it to his office, whichever door it was, Nilo appeared at the end of the hall. He hurried our way, a wide, apologetic smile on his face.

Before he could say anything, Luna chirruped at him. His face softened into genuine warmth, and he reached out a hand. "May I?"

I nodded. "This is Luna."

Nilo closed the distance between us and reached up to scratch Luna behind her ears. She stretched forward, purring deep in her chest. Nilo's eyes cut to mine, his expression open. "She adores you," he murmured.

I smiled. "I love the little fuzzball, too." Nilo and I stood intimately close with just a handful of centimeters between us. I glanced up at him. He was incredibly handsome, with his fine bone structure and gold-streaked green eyes, but I didn't feel any of the tight anticipation that I felt around Torran.

Before I could dwell on what that meant, Torran cleared his throat.

Mischief danced in Nilo's eyes as he leaned closer to me, and I suddenly understood exactly why Lexi had waited for him in a hotel bar. His gaze invited play, and it would've been an irresistible temptation for my favorite thief.

I tipped my face up to his, interested to see exactly what he had planned. I didn't get the chance to find out, though, because in the next breath, Nilo slid back a meter and a half.

As soon as Torran's power let him go, Nilo winked at me. Torran growled something that I didn't catch, but it didn't seem to dampen Nilo's spirits.

"Did you need something?" Torran demanded. "Or did you just come to bother my guests?"

At the reminder, Nilo's apologetic mask reappeared as if the last few minutes had never happened. "I'm so sorry to interrupt," he said to me, "but I'm afraid I must speak to Torran alone."

"Is it about the theft? If so, then I would like to be up-dated as well."

"I'm afraid I can't say," Nilo said, the picture of polite contrition.

Torran's eyes went distant as he and Nilo silently com-municated. Torran frowned, then his gaze cut to me. "I'm sorry, but I must deal with this. I will show you the office later. Until then, please feel free to explore the public part of the house."

Translation: leave the family hallway so I can have a secret meeting with the person who stabbed Lexi in the back. Message received, loud and clear.

I pasted on my fakest, sharpest smile. "Find me when you're done. I still have questions about the theft—the one you hired me to solve and then refused to talk about."

Torran's expression didn't change, but Nilo watched us with sharp eyes. Torran bowed slightly and gestured toward the end of the hall. "This will take you back to the main part of the house. The guest wing will be to your right. I will message you when I'm free."

"You'll have to come find me because my comm doesn't work here."

Torran frowned at me. "Of course it does. It's dual-tech."

It took me a second to realize that he meant the comm he'd given me, the one I hadn't figured out how to return yet. Feeling vindictive after being summarily dismissed, I pulled out my original comm, battered and held together with composite tape. "It doesn't and it's not."

Torran's expression blanked into careful nothingness, and guilt slithered through my system. Spitefulness was uncalled for, no matter how frustrated I was. "I'm sorry," I said. "I will find you later to discuss the theft."

I turned to leave, but Torran caught my wrist, his grip gentle. Nilo disappeared into one of the rooms lining the hallway—presumably Torran's office—and the door closed behind him.

"Is there something wrong with the comm I gave you?" Torran asked, his gaze intense.

My eyes slid away from his. "No, not as far as I know."

His fingers flexed around my wrist. "Then why aren't you using it?"

Luna must've felt my anxiety because she purred and butted her head against mine. I appreciated the comfort she offered, even if I didn't deserve it. "I was going to give the comm back," I said. "I just hadn't figured out how."

Thunderclouds gathered on Torran's brow, so I rushed to add, "Not because I don't accept your apology, but because a gift is not necessary. My current comm is fine. I am happy that you apologized, and your promise was *already* your gift. I don't need a comm in addition."

"I told you to keep it. And I've seen your current comm. It is not fine." His eyes narrowed. "How are we supposed to coordinate if you can't receive messages?"

"Kee is working on it."

Torran's thumb stroked across my inner wrist for the third time, and I suppressed a shiver. I didn't think he even realized he was doing it, but electric tingles danced up my arm with every pass.

"Keep the comm. Use it." I opened my mouth to protest, and he silenced me with a look. "If you must, return it when the job is finished."

I pressed my lips together in thought. Borrowing a comm for the duration of my time on Valovia was far more palatable than accepting an expensive gift. I dipped my head in reluctant agreement.

"Good. Now I must speak with Nilo. Enjoy the rest of your day."

I raised an eyebrow and looked down at the wrist Torran still held. Out of the corner of my eye, I saw his mouth quirk, then he very deliberately stroked his thumb across my wrist a fourth time before letting me go.

My eyes flashed to his face, but his expression was unreadable. His eyes, however, pulsed with color.

He wasn't as unaffected as he seemed. And he'd *absolutely* known what he was doing.

This time, the shiver was impossible to suppress.

SINCE TORRAN HAD PRETTY MUCH GIVEN ME PERMISSION TO snoop in the rest of his house, I planned to do exactly that, but first, I stopped in the kitchen, which was both beautiful and unfamiliar, and poked around until I found the refrigerator and the box I'd brought from *Starlight*.

I pulled out Luna's food and water bowls and set them in an out-of-the-way corner. Luna hopped down to check them out, then sent me a wave of longing when she found her food bowl empty.

I dug around in the box until I found the container of jerky. I'd barely touched it when Luna's eyes locked on me. I swear she could hear the rustle of treats from two sectors away. I pulled out a piece and Luna tensed.

"Don't tell anyone I'm spoiling you."

She cocked her head, but her eyes didn't leave the jerky in my hand. I made her wait for a beat before tossing it high. She leapt to catch it, then disappeared out of the room with her prize. If we planned to stay here for more than a week, I would have to build her some sort of climbing tower or she'd resort to perching on whatever she could find, likely with disastrous results.

With Luna taken care of, I delved deeper into the unfamiliar part of the house. I let Kee know where I was going, just on the off chance that one of Torran's staff decided to jump out of a room and murder me. I didn't think the odds of that were very high, but if it happened, I wanted my crew to know who to avoid.

The house was far larger than it appeared from the front. The sloping roof and curving lines hid exactly how expansive it was. The guest and family wings were at the back of the building with another hallway between them that I hadn't explored yet.

The final hallway branched off from the front of the house, following the curve of the front wall. I explored it first, since it was closest to the kitchen. I expected it to be the public rooms, and the first door I opened proved me correct.

The office was pristine, with a beautiful, sculpted desk and plush chairs. Floor-to-ceiling windows offered a view of the gorgeous landscaping. The colorful, understated art on the wall reflected the colors of the flowers outside.

The room was lovely but completely lacking in personality. I doubted that I'd find a single useful piece of information, but I rifled through everything anyway. The desk didn't have any drawers, hidden or otherwise.

A long cabinet against the wall turned out to be a bar cabinet. I poked around inside but it didn't reveal any secrets except that Torran kept a lot of liquor on hand for his guests.

The rest of the wing was much the same—beautiful and cold. A sitting room, bathroom, lounge, and game room were all exquisitely decorated, spotlessly clean, and completely impersonal.

By the time I was finished with the wing, the sun had sunk below the horizon. It was only late morning local time, but my body clock thought the darkness meant that it was time for sleep. The house lights tried to compensate, blazing bright, but my body knew the sun was gone and was having none of it.

My stomach rumbled, reminding me that I'd split my lunch bar with Luna. I'd forgotten to ask Torran about the meal schedule, but I would explore the other wing, then start on dinner. My team would be ready to eat, even if it was earlier than local dinnertime.

Figuring out the kitchen on my own would be a challenge—one I'd deal with when I came to it.

I moved through the house to the final wing. When I approached, I heard Eli's voice, taunting someone. It didn't sound serious, but I sped up just in case. The last thing I needed was another fight.

Several familiar voices drifted from the first room on the left. The door stood open, so I slipped inside and found myself in a large, well-equipped gym. Eli was giving Anja pointers—some helpful, most *not*—as she and Chira circled each other on the padded sparring floor. Anja taunted Eli as often as she taunted Chira.

Both Anja and Chira had donned lightweight protective gloves and didn't appear to be trying to kill each other, so I didn't intervene. Chira had a few centimeters of height on Anja, but Anja had several kilos of additional muscle, so they were evenly matched.

Havil stood next to Eli, but his eyes spent more time on my first officer than on the two sparring women. Of course, most people's eyes were drawn to Eli. The man really was too damn handsome for his own good.

The rest of the room was empty. I figured Kee was still hiding with her tech, but both Lexi and Varro were missing, too.

"Care to go a round, Tavi?" Eli asked, without taking his eyes from Anja and Chira.

"I heard the terrible advice you gave Anja. I'm pretty sure that she'll happily kick your ass for me."

"Sure thing, Captain," Anja agreed with a grin. She dodged a quick jab from Chira and retaliated with a flurry of light blows.

"Just keep it friendly so I don't have to come back and crack skulls," I warned.

They all murmured their agreement, so I left them to it and retreated to the hallway with a wave.

Across the hall, the door slid open to reveal a tropical oasis. Plants crowded the edges of the room, and the air was warm and humid. What looked like a natural hot spring had been widened into a pool big enough for a dozen people. Heat rose from the surface of the water.

I skirted around the heated pool and found another pool hidden beyond the foliage, this one large enough for swimming. I debated it for a second and then decided Torran wouldn't have a toxic pool in his house.

Probably.

I crouched down and dipped my fingers in the water. It was pleasantly cool. I didn't have time to swim—or a swimsuit—but I really wished I did. It had been nearly a year since I'd seen this much water in one place.

I reluctantly stood and examined the rest of the room. A sauna and a luxurious locker room rounded out the amenities. I stole another glance at the pool. Maybe if I came super early, no one would notice if I swam in my underthings.

I left my new favorite room and explored the rest of the hallway. This was obviously a shared wing where both family and guests could relax and socialize. There was a game room, a lounge with comfortable furniture, and a screening room with a huge display on the wall.

The next door I opened revealed a spacious library. Lexi was leaning against the far wall, a book in hand and an innocent expression on her face. When she saw that it was just me, she snapped the book closed and went back to searching through the shelf next to her.

I caught her eye and signed, "Find anything useful?"

She shook her head.

I kept signing. "Where have you looked?"

She gestured at a good 80 percent of the room. I laughed, then switched to speaking. "I figured you'd be in the gym showing Eli how it's done."

She shrugged. "The four of them seemed to be doing fine on their own, so I decided to poke around and see if I could find a book to read."

Which meant that she had likely snooped through the rest of the hallway, same as me. "Let me know if you find anything interesting," I said. "I'm going to look around some more, then start on dinner."

At the mention of food, Lexi's stomach growled. Her smile turned wry. "Food would be good."

"Has anyone checked on Kee lately?" I asked before I left.

"I'm fine," Kee said over the comm. "Varro brought me some food earlier, so I'm not starving. I'm working on the thing we talked about. It's a little more difficult than I expected, but I'm nearly there."

"Let me know if you need anything," I said.

Kee agreed and went back to her virtual breaking and entering.

Lexi's hands flashed. "Her and Varro?"

I lifted my hands and shrugged. I didn't know.

Lexi frowned at me. She was only a year older than Kee, but she'd always treated the younger woman like a little sister—we all had. Kee was the youngest and the brightest of us all, and we were incredibly protective of her.

I had no doubt that by dinner, Lexi would know everything available about Varro Runkow.

I waved farewell and left the library. The rest of the hallway didn't have any more secrets to reveal, so I decided to try my luck in the kitchen. I'd brought a lot of perishables and no pantry items, so dinner might be a little interesting.

Assuming I figured out how to use the stove.

If there *was* a stove.

Torran had said he'd dismissed most of his staff, and other than the people who had delivered the supply crates to our rooms earlier, I hadn't seen a single person during my snooping. But if nothing else worked, I'd yell until someone came to see what the commotion was about.

I entered the kitchen and went straight to the butler's pantry around the corner, where I'd found the refrigerator. I pulled out my box of groceries and looked through it. A veggie soup would be nice with the crispness in the air. And it would keep, so people could eat whenever they got hungry.

Hopefully Torran had some sort of veggie stock and lentils or beans or potatoes—even rice or pasta would work. I just needed something filling.

Opening the nearby cabinets yielded a big pot, so I was on my way. Across from the fridge, an unmarked door opened to a giant walk-in pantry. The shelves were filled with cans and boxes with Valovan labels, as well as bins of flours, grains, and other produce. I could guess what some of them might be, but most were unfamiliar. And while I doubted Torran had poison in his pantry, making an incorrect guess could make dinner inedible.

I was about to give up and ask for help when a box with a Common label caught my eye. A multitude of items crowded the narrow shelf, most of them the same brands I'd bought on Bastion. The bins underneath were carefully labeled in Common as well, with everything I needed to cook my usual meals.

Either Torran kept highly expensive imported food around on a regular basis—and he just happened to eat vegetarian and preferred the same brands that I did—or he'd ordered extra food especially for us to use while we were here.

The fastest way to earn my trust was to take care of my people, and by providing food, Torran had done exactly that. He might be a master strategist, but this didn't feel calculated. It felt personal.

It felt *kind*.

And strategy or kindness, it was working. As much as I tried to shore up my defenses against him, he kept knocking them down.

I grabbed all of the ingredients I needed and made my way into the kitchen proper. I poked around until I turned up a cutting board and knife, then got busy with prep. Chopping had a soothing kind of rhythm to it, and I let my mind drift.

Luna, who always had a nose for dinner, even in its early stages, came and sat next to her empty food bowl. When that didn't get the result she wanted, she chirruped at me and sent me a picture of said empty bowl, just in case I didn't realize it was empty.

I made her wait while I finished chopping carrots, then I got out her food and filled her bowl. I didn't usually give her so much at once, but we were in a strange place with a different schedule. Until we all got used to it, I would err on the side of too much.

Luna dove into her dinner with her usual gusto. I watched her for a second before going back to my prep work.

Once everything was in the pot, I began looking for the stove. I wasn't completely ignorant of Valovian technology, but I'd never seen a kitchen this nice. Usually the stove was visible, just like in a typical human kitchen.

I found a trio of seams in the counter under what looked like it could be a vent hood. I waved my hands around, trying to trigger it to open, but nothing happened. I hoped whoever was in charge of surveillance was having a good laugh at my expense because this had to be hilarious to watch.

A flat control pad on the wall lit up when I reached for it. The labels were in Valovan, but it also included handy little pictograms. I pressed one and crossed my fingers.

The seamed section of counter sank down and split apart, with each piece sliding sideways out of view. The stove underneath rose until it was flush with the rest of the counter. It was pristine and I made a note to take more care than usual not to get soup everywhere.

I had just figured out how to get the burner on when my comm implant crackled to life.

"Tavi," Kee said, her voice flat, "I got into the security system. You need to see this." That tone was never a good sign from my normally bubbly systems engineer.

I turned off the stove and covered the pot. Dinner would have to wait. "Are we in danger?"

A long pause sent adrenaline flooding into my system, but eventually Kee said, "No, I don't think so. I've already alerted the others. They're on their way."

"I'll be right there."

I debated taking Luna, but if we weren't in danger, then she would be okay here. And taking her away from food was a good way to get nipped. "Stay out of trouble," I told her as I left.

The short walk to the guest wing felt like forever. By the time I let myself into Kee's room, I'd come up with a hundred worst-case scenarios.

Anja, Lexi, and Eli were already crowded into the room. From their expressions, they were also planning for disaster. Anja and Eli had changed out of their gym clothes at some point. I wondered if they'd joined Lexi in doing some snooping of their own.

Without a word, Kee turned her slate around to face us and started the video. It took me a second to recognize the hallway Torran and I had entered earlier. Four soldiers in blacked-out armor came into view from the left. With helmets, body armor, and cloth covering every inch of skin, there were no distinguishing features visible at all, but they moved like humans.

Military-trained humans.

They swept down the hall and stopped at the second door on the left. Without a word, the first soldier held up a small square device to the lock. The door slid open and all of the soldiers disappeared inside.

Kee held up her finger, silently telling us to wait.

Less than thirty seconds later, the soldiers reappeared, but one of them was carrying something. As one, we all leaned forward, trying to see what it was.

The soldier shifted and the bundle in their arms resolved itself into an unconscious, dark-haired Valovian child, no more than seven or eight. The soldiers took the child and disappeared off the left side of the screen, presumably back out the same door they'd entered.

"Oh, fuck," Eli breathed.

"That," Kee said, her voice hard and angry, "was Cien Nepru, the empress's grandson—and Torran's nephew."

CHAPTER NINETEEN

Fury turned my vision red as I stalked out of the guest wing. "Torran!" I shouted at the top of my lungs. When no one responded, I turned and started for the family wing, shouting as I went. I would shout this building down if I had to.

I was nearly to the room on the video when I heard multiple sets of footsteps behind me. I spun to find Torran sweat-slicked and shirtless. The rest of his team arrived on his heels. It looked like they'd come from the gym.

Torran scanned the area for threats before his gaze settled back on me, confusion clear.

"You," I growled, closing the distance between us with furious intent. "You lying, deceitful son of a bitch."

Torran waved, and his team silently melted away, but not before casting sidelong glances my way. Once they were gone, Torran's eyes narrowed.

"No," I said, jabbing a finger at him. "You don't get to be

insulted. You *lied* to me. We're not looking for some stupid ring, are we?" I didn't give him time to answer. "No, we're not. We're looking for a fucking child and you didn't think this information was important enough to share."

Torran's entire posture changed, transforming from confused to deadly in the blink of an eye. "What do you mean?"

I ignored the implicit threat and pointed a furious finger at the closed door. "You know exactly what I mean. You hired us to do a job. Did you think we were so incompetent that we wouldn't find out? If so, why hire us at all?"

"Who have you told?" Torran asked, a dangerous edge in his tone.

I threw my hands up. "I haven't told anyone, you asshole! We're working for *you*. We're trying to help *you*. The only one here who isn't helping *is you*." I jabbed my finger at him again, too angry to remain still. "Don't you care about your nephew?"

Torran loomed over me. "Listen to me and listen well. If this information gets out, your lives are forfeit. The empress is looking for a target, and I won't be able to protect you. So you had better make sure your team understands exactly what is at stake should they open their mouths."

Kee was monitoring this conversation, so she would relay the information to the others, not that we made a habit of blabbing about our jobs anyway.

"I don't care about the fucking empress; I care about the kid." I sighed as the anger drained away, leaving me feeling fragile and tired. "Why didn't you just tell me? A kidnapping is completely different than a theft. We would've made a different plan and worked faster. That poor kid has been held for over two weeks. He must be terrified."

Torran ran a hand down his face. "I told you what I could," he said quietly. "I hoped that it would be enough."

"Have the kidnappers been in contact? Have they demanded a ransom?"

Torran gestured and the nearby door slid open, revealing his office. At least he hadn't been lying about that part. "Go have a seat. I'll get dressed and join you."

At the reminder, my eyes drifted over Torran's exposed chest. No wonder he'd been able to pull himself up onto the perimeter wall earlier—he had plenty of muscles for it. A low-slung pair of loose pants hung from his hips. I was still furious at him for keeping his nephew a secret, but I could admire and fume at the same time. I was good at multitasking.

I spun without a word and entered his office.

"So . . . are we staying?" Kee asked over the comm.

"Yes. It's not the kid's fault. We need to work fast and bring him home safely. Keep digging. Find everything you can, including why Torran picked us out of all the available bounty hunters. Something is off."

"I'm on it. I'll also keep an ear on you. Shout if you need help."

I nodded, though she couldn't see me. Or maybe she could. I wouldn't bet against Kee now that she'd breached the security system.

Torran's office was far more cluttered than I would've expected from the simple elegance of the rest of the house. A massive, built-in bookcase lined the left wall, and the lower shelves were filled with colorful children's books in both Valovan and Common. Narrow windows along the top of the wall showed a glimpse of stars sparkling in the inky sky.

I rubbed my eyes. Today had been eternal and it wasn't over yet.

I circled the large, heavy desk and settled into Torran's chair. A pair of books, a fancy Valovian slate, a framed drawing of two people done by a child, and a handful of sparkly rocks rested on the smooth wooden surface. An elegant digital display cycled through a short series of photos, all of Torran and his nephew. I picked it up for a closer look.

In the most recent photo, Cien looked about the same age he was when he'd been snatched from this very room. My anger returned.

"What are you doing?" Torran asked from the doorway. He'd pulled on a short-sleeved shirt, but he'd kept the same loose pants.

"Snooping," I said without a hint of remorse. "It seems to be the only way to get information around here." I pinned him with a hard look. "Why didn't you tell me that you're related to the empress?"

None of Kee's original information had turned up the link. If it had, I wouldn't have taken the job, even for the fortune on offer. I did not want to be entangled with the imperial family, but it was too late now.

"I'm not." Torran stepped into the office and the door slid closed behind him. The room suddenly felt a lot smaller, but I remained sitting in his chair as he stalked toward me.

"Don't give me that shit. Cien is your nephew and her grandson."

"My sister married the empress's son, but our relationship is not common knowledge. How did you make the connection?" Torran stopped next to me and raised an eyebrow.

I smiled at him and pointed to the guest chairs on the

other side of the desk, then returned to the conversation with a shrug. "Making connections is our job."

People dismissed Kee because of her colorful hair and relentless optimism, but she was one of the smartest people I'd ever met. She could take the thinnest of threads and pull until she'd unraveled an entire tapestry.

Or an entire imperial family, hidden branches and all.

Rather than moving around the desk, Torran settled on the near edge, close enough that his legs brushed the arm of my chair, but I refused to budge.

I raised my chin and met his eyes. "So was all of that information about the ring just bullshit?"

"No. Cien *does* wear a family ring that grants him access to my accounts. Until I have my own children, he's my heir."

"Why was he alone while you were gone?"

"He wasn't alone," Torran said, then corrected himself. "He wasn't *supposed* to be alone. He had a bodyguard, and the house staff was here, too."

My interest sharpened. "Where is the bodyguard now?"

"Missing."

Of course they were. "Did the bodyguard help the kidnappers?"

"Cien's bodyguard slipped out before the kidnappers showed up," Torran said. "But it's a good bet that he helped them before disappearing, because they knew exactly where to find my nephew."

"The other staff?"

"Investigated, extensively, and they appear to be uninvolved."

My eyes narrowed. "Why are you being so helpful all of a sudden?"

"I was unable to discuss the kidnapping with anyone who didn't know about it." He sighed. "And I am still bound by additional oaths, but I will share what I can."

"Why was Cien here?"

"His parents are on a diplomatic trip. He often stays with me when they are traveling, under the pretense of learning military strategy."

"His parents *are* on? They haven't returned?"

Torran's expression darkened. "No. The empress is keeping Cien's disappearance quiet. If his parents returned early, that would cause suspicion."

I silently shook my head. It's good that I wasn't an empress's daughter-in-law, because if my kid went missing, I'd wade through hell to get them back, and fuck everyone else.

I tried to let it go. I wasn't successful, but I switched topics anyway. "I'm assuming your team has been hunting the whole time you were gone? What have they found? I want all of the information you've collected so far. In a kidnapping, time is of the essence."

A muscle in Torran's jaw flexed. "I've already told Nilo to prepare a brief for your team."

Speaking of . . . "You didn't tell me if the kidnappers have been in contact."

Torran said nothing, and I blew out a frustrated breath. "Let me guess: you can't tell me."

His chin dipped a bare millimeter.

I leaned back and propped my feet on his desk. He looked at them pointedly but didn't ask me to move, so I stayed where I was. With him looming over me, it was easier to watch his face when I was tilted back.

"I'm guessing they don't want money because you would've given it to them." I waved at the drawing and the shiny rocks. "You love your nephew, that much is clear. So they want something you're not prepared to give." I thought about it. "Or they want something the empress isn't willing to give."

Torran's expression remained flat, but the tiniest of flickers proved that I was on the right track. What could kidnappers want that a *literal empress* would refuse to provide in return for her grandson? Empress Nepru had the collective might of the Valovian Empire at her fingertips. She was smart and resourceful. The FHP delegates had underestimated her and paid a steep price.

So the kidnappers had asked for something extraordinary. And whatever it was, Torran wasn't allowed to say.

I rubbed my face. "Investigating would be so much easier if you could talk to me. Why would you agree to promises that make finding your nephew harder?" My eyes narrowed in anger. "Does someone *not* want him found?"

Torran stared at me for long enough that I thought he wouldn't answer. "Finding Cien is our main priority," he said at last. "But the situation is delicate and my options are limited. I had hoped to return to better news." His hands clenched on the edge of the desk, frustration etched into the tense lines of his body.

"What *can* you tell me?"

"Cien has been gone for too long. I need you to find him. *Soon.* I know you took this job only for the money, so I will double your completion bonus if you find him in the next ten days."

For now, I ignored the question of how he knew about my financial situation and focused on the important part of his statement. "What happens on day eleven?"

Torran's expression turned bleak, but he didn't answer.

I sighed and stood. "I'm going to finish cooking dinner because my team needs to eat. After that, I expect a comprehensive brief of everything you've learned so far. We'll get everyone together to go over the data, because maybe talking through it will reveal something new."

Torran's lips pressed into a grim line, but he nodded. On impulse, I reached out and touched his arm. "We'll find your nephew," I said as gently as I could. "My team is good at finding lost things."

His eyes were as desolate as I'd ever seen them. "I hope so," he murmured.

DINNER WAS A DECIDEDLY SUBDUED AFFAIR. THE VALOFFS didn't eat with us, despite the fact that it was dinnertime in standard time and midday local time. We'd gotten used to eating with Torran's team, and we all felt their absence.

Outside, the sky was dark. I would never get used to a "noon" that was in the middle of the night. I couldn't decide if the two-day cycle was better or worse than a single short day, but my body was certainly on team "sleep when it was dark," even though it wasn't that late in standard time.

The war had never reached Valovia, so we'd never had to acclimate to the two-day schedule. And I'd never been on any planet that had such a short solar day. It was going to completely wreck my body clock.

I glanced around the table. Everyone was concentrating on their meal, but Kee was eating with the sort of focused intensity she usually reserved for solving difficult puzzles. She was beating herself up for not finding the information on the kidnapping sooner, as if that would even have been possible with Torran refusing to help.

After dinner, we headed for Torran's private office. He intercepted us in the hallway and directed us to another room in the family wing. It looked like it had originally been a bedroom, but all of the furniture had been replaced. Now half a dozen desks with large workstation displays crowded together on one side of the room and a collection of chairs took up the other half in front of a huge wall display.

Kee sucked in a breath and looked around with wide eyes. Torran had better lock the door when we were done or Kee would spend all of her time in here.

"Please have a seat," Torran said, indicating the chairs. Nilo stood at the front of the room, next to the display, but the rest of the Valovian team was already seated. Eli plopped down between Havil and Chira while Kee bounced over to sit next to Varro. Lexi sat in the back, as far from Nilo as she could get without leaving the room. Anja looked torn, but she sat next to Chira with a smile when the other woman waved her over.

I leaned against the back wall, too wound to sit. Torran joined me. "How was your dinner?" he asked.

"Peachy," I muttered. In truth, dinner hadn't done much to blunt my annoyance at him for keeping his nephew a secret, and I was in a fighting mood, so my best bet was avoidance.

Unfortunately, Torran hadn't gotten the memo.

He frowned at me. "Is something wrong?"

"It's been a long day," I said with a sigh. "Let's hear what you've found so far."

Torran stared at me for a moment longer before turning his attention to Nilo. The other Valoff stepped forward and the screen behind him turned on. Nilo had lost some of his easygoing charm. His face was set in lines of grim determination.

"Approximately seventeen standard days ago, an unknown team broke in, tranquilized Cien, and escaped with him. We tracked them to the edge of the city, where they abandoned their transport. Flight data does not show any ships leaving the area, so we believe they took a smaller craft that remained hidden in the trees."

"We saw a team of four on the video," I said. "Were there more?"

Nilo nodded. "Four infiltrated the house with four more in lookout positions and one securing the transport."

That was an interesting split, but if they knew that Cien was alone and unprotected, it made sense to send a smaller team into the house. If four trained adults couldn't subdue a child, then more wouldn't necessarily help.

"How long was it before Cien's disappearance was noticed?"

"Three hours," Torran said, bitterness in his tone. "I found him missing upon my return."

My heart winced in sympathy. A missing child was every caregiver's nightmare. I touched Torran's arm in comfort and he nodded, once, sharply, but didn't say anything else.

When I didn't ask another question, Nilo resumed his brief. "The kidnappers have been in contact twice. Both messages originated on Valovia but from different cities each time, and each message was one-time use, with no reply address supplied."

"They don't want to negotiate," Kee murmured.

Nilo nodded. "I am not at liberty to discuss the content of the messages, but you are correct."

"What's their motivation?" Lexi asked. She sounded cool and professional, her mask firmly in place.

"I'm not at li—" Nilo began.

Lexi waved a hand. "I'm not asking you to detail exactly what they asked for. But, in general, what do they want? Money? Power? A trade?"

Nilo looked at Torran. After a few seconds of silent communication, Nilo said, "Power."

"Are they zealots or mercenaries?" Lexi asked.

A small, pleased smile curved Nilo's mouth. "Good question. We believe they are zealots."

I blew out a breath. Zealots couldn't be reasoned with. Mercenaries could be bought off with enough money, of which Torran seemingly had plenty. But zealots would fight to the end for their beliefs and money wouldn't sway them.

"So where are they now?" Eli asked. "Or if you don't know that, where are they *not*?"

"We believe they are still on Valovia, but likely not in any of the major cities. Cien is a strong telepath. Unless they are keeping him drugged constantly, he would be able to reach out to any nearby Valoffs for help."

"Is there a way to block telepathic abilities without drugs?" I asked.

Nilo's expression gave nothing away. I rolled my eyes. "You ruled out cities, but you could be making that decision on bad assumptions. Could a stronger Valoff prevent Cien from communicating telepathically?"

A disgruntled murmur rose from the Valoffs in the room, but surprisingly, it was Havil who spoke up. "It's possible," the soft-spoken medic said slowly. "But it would require at least a team of two to ensure coverage because it's not possible to block while asleep."

I nodded my thanks, then said, "I know you want to paint humans as the villains here, and I don't disagree that anyone who kidnaps a child is the worst kind of scum, but the kidnappers *already* had help from Cien's guard. It's not a huge stretch to imagine they found a few more Valoffs willing to help them out."

"So you think they're in the city?" Torran asked, his body tense. If I said the wrong thing, I had no doubt that he'd start tearing the city apart looking for his nephew.

"Not necessarily," I said. "There are a lot of witnesses in the city, so it's not ideal for a team that needs to stay hidden. But all of our base assumptions need to be examined before we rule anything out."

"How would you kidnap a Valovian child?" Nilo asked, genuine curiosity on his face.

I wrinkled my nose in thought. "I wouldn't. Putting aside the whole moral issue, there are too many variables to control. Children are already unpredictable, but add in unknown mental abilities and you have a recipe for disaster."

"If the team had help from Cien's guard," Lexi said, "then some of the risk is reduced. Presumably they knew about Cien's abilities and how to counter them." She shrugged. "With enough prep, we could do it. Kee and I could get us in, and Eli and Tavi could grab the kid. Easy."

"Lexi!" Kee growled, her tone quelling. Next to her, Varro sat still and quiet, observing the room with a sharp eye.

"Am I wrong?" Lexi asked with a raised eyebrow.

Kee silently shook her head, then turned back to Nilo. "Did you trace the transport?"

Nilo nodded. "Stolen."

Kee perked up. "Did you find video from where it was taken?"

"We don't know when, exactly, it was stolen. The owner rarely uses it and didn't even know it was missing until we showed up."

Kee was undeterred. "Surely you have the vehicle logs. Did you put a data analysis team on it?"

"The logs were wiped," Nilo said.

"I want to look at it. You didn't give it back, did you?"

Nilo's eyes narrowed, and he looked at Kee with new appreciation. "We still have it. I'll take you over there after the meeting."

"I will take her," Varro said. "You stay here and answer questions."

Nilo looked like he might argue, but Kee turned to Varro with a smile. "Thank you."

"What about Cien's guard?" I asked. "He couldn't have vanished into thin air. Where is he?"

"He left before the kidnappers showed up," Torran said. "We tracked him into the city before the trail went cold. His accounts have been flagged, as has his identity. He hasn't touched any of them."

"They gave him a new identity and a trip off-planet," I said.

Torran dipped his head in agreement.

I looked around the room. "What happens in eleven days?"

As one, the Valoffs froze and then pretended that they hadn't. "What do you mean?" Chira asked, false cheer in her voice.

"You all aren't as smooth as you think you are," Lexi murmured.

When no one volunteered any more information, I said, "We'll assume that we must find Cien in the next ten days. I want everyone to split into groups with each group containing at least one member from my team and one from Torran's. Torran's people will go over the information they've collected so far. My people will ask questions and look at the assumptions. Let's work together to see if we can find something that was overlooked."

When no one moved, I clapped my hands. "Now, people."

Varro stood and offered Kee help up. "I'll take you to the transport."

She beamed at him. "Thank you. I need to stop by my room to grab a few things," she said, then she turned to Anja. "Would you mind helping me? I'm probably going to have to take the transport apart to get to the data store. I could use another set of hands."

Anja rose with a smile. "Of course."

As the three of them left, Varro murmured something I didn't catch.

Eli, Havil, and Chira moved to one of the desks and began discussing the timeline from the night of the kidnapping. That left Lexi, Nilo, Torran, and myself. "You want me to deal with Nilo?" I asked Lexi subvocally over the comm.

She silently shook her head. "I'll deal with him," she replied. "You try to pry more information out of their fearless leader."

I laughed to myself. I'd have better luck prying information out of a locked safe deep in the heart of the Imperial Palace.

CHAPTER TWENTY

Torran and I spent the next four hours huddled together in front of our desk's workstation display. The rest of our people did the same, with the exception of Kee and Varro, who'd remained with the stolen transport after Anja had returned.

At one point, Luna wandered in, found all of us far too boring for her, and wandered back out again.

I had to give the Valoffs credit—they'd done a thorough and meticulous investigation. The timeline for the kidnapping was broken down into detailed, minute-by-minute increments.

But the kidnappers had been thorough, too, and they'd left very few leads.

There was nothing obvious that Torran's team had overlooked, and helpless frustration sharpened my temper. I hadn't felt this antsy when I'd thought we were hunting a ring, but a ring wasn't a child. Cien had already been gone for two and a half weeks, poor kid.

I stood and stretched the knots out of my back, then checked on the others. "Find anything?"

Eli shook his head. "Nothing yet. Their work is solid."

I'd hoped that my team had found something I'd missed, but Eli was right—the investigation was solid, but there just weren't enough leads. "Has anyone heard from Kee?"

"She was fine when I left a few hours ago," Anja said. "We found the data store, so she's probably still looking at it."

"If she's found something interesting, Varro will have to pull her out kicking and screaming," Lexi said. She and Nilo were at separate desks, but they appeared to be working together without stabbing each other.

"Varro says they're still in the workshop," Torran confirmed. "Kee's been staring at her slate and grumbling ever since she and Anja connected to the data."

"Kee, have you found anything?" I asked over the comm.

I got a long sigh in return. "Maybe," she said. "The vehicle logs were wiped but not completely. Recovery is slow and finicky, but I think I'll be able to piece together the data once I'm done."

"Are you at a place where you can stop for the night?" I cut off her grumbled protests. "It's after midnight standard and I need you sharp. Downtime will do you good."

"It's still light outside!"

I turned to the window. So it was. The long shadows meant the sun was low in the sky, but it was definitely still light. My body clock didn't care and demanded sleep. I'd been up for too long.

"Fine, you have until sunset," I agreed, "then I'm letting Varro drag you out."

I could *hear* her smirk. "That's not the threat you think it is."

I let my own smile seep into my tone. "If it gets you out of the workshop, I'll call it a win. One hour, Kee. I mean it."

"Aye aye, Captain." The sarcasm was heavy, but then she added, "Thanks for looking out for me."

"Always," I promised.

I turned back to the rest of my team. "I'm going to work for another hour to ensure Kee doesn't stay up all night, but the rest of you are free to bow out whenever. We'll start again in the morning."

They all turned back to their workstations. I plopped down next to Torran. "Let's go over it again."

We did, but the facts didn't change. In the first video snippet, the kidnappers emerged from an underground garage in the middle of the night. No one had been able to trace their whereabouts before that, or how they'd accessed the garage. Pieced together traffic footage showed that the transport came straight to Torran's property, dropped off a team of eight, and then took a wide, circular route that brought it back just in time for the pickup.

Then they went straight to the edge of town and disappeared into the trees.

That was it. They'd as good as vanished with the empress's grandson, snatched from a house a stone's throw from the Imperial Palace.

How?

How had they pulled it off without so much as a single hitch? The question followed me to bed and kept me awake far longer than it should've.

THE SOUND OF A DOOR OPENING IN MY DREAM. WHERE A door shouldn't have been, pulled me from a deep sleep. My eyes felt welded shut with exhaustion, but I cracked them open just enough to see. The room was pitch-black and quiet. I was almost ready to brush it off as nothing when I heard the slightest scuff of a boot against the floor.

Someone was in my room.

I thrust my hand under my pillow and grabbed the plas pistol I'd stashed there. I rolled out of bed and landed in a crouch. "Lights!"

The room turned blindingly bright, revealing Torran in the middle of the room with his hands up. He was wearing his armor. "Don't shoot," he whispered.

"What the fuck, Torran?" I demanded in a harsh whisper. "What are you doing and why are we whispering?"

"I was trying to figure out how to wake you without getting shot." He raised an eyebrow at the pistol still locked on his body.

I dropped the pistol's muzzle toward the ground and growled, "Knocking is designed to solve exactly this problem." I scowled at him. "You overrode the lock on my door."

"Get dressed and come with me. I will explain, I promise, but we don't have much time."

I glanced down at myself. I had on a tank top, panties, and nothing else. No wonder his eyes kept trying to drift down. "What am I dressing for?"

"Wear a thin base layer with warmer clothes on top."

I quickly pulled on a pair of leggings, then added my standard work wear of sturdy pants, a comfy T-shirt, and supple boots. I also grabbed a coat. I strapped on my plas blade and tucked the pistol into its holster. Finally, I picked up my comm and called Kee.

"What are you doing?" Torran demanded.

"I'm leaving with you in the middle of the night with

no explanation. I'll do it because I trust you at least that far, but I'm letting my team know that I'm going."

His mouth compressed, but he didn't argue.

Kee was not amused with the early call *or* my plan to leave with Torran to parts unknown. I told her to go back to sleep and then hung up on her. Once she calmed down, she'd find a way to track my comm and keep an eye on me. Kee was nothing if not resourceful when properly motivated.

I grabbed the comm Torran had given me and shoved it in my other pocket. I hadn't had time to set it up yet, but I'd figure it out if I needed it.

Torran held a finger to his lips and then we slipped from the room. The dim hallway lights provided just enough visibility so that I didn't run into anything. We slid from the house into a chilly night. Unfamiliar insects filled the night with soft sounds.

We took a path toward the back of the property and the building I'd seen when we'd walked the perimeter earlier. The door opened at our approach and we eased inside. Torran pulled a slim light stick from his pocket and the interior of the building became a little clearer.

Torran had called it a workshop, but it was more a workshop-garage combo. A line of small vehicles glinted in the light. Torran headed for the smallest, a two-seat lev cycle that was vaguely ovoid—as if someone had squished an upright egg mostly flat without cracking it.

The outer shell protected passengers from the elements, but that was about it. It was molded around the lower half of the vehicle, which included the engine and skid plates. Torran opened the hatch and pulled out a set of Valovian armor.

I raised an eyebrow at him.

"This was the shortest set I could find," he said. "It may still be a little tall for you, but we should be able to make it work."

"Are we going somewhere where I'm going to need armor?"

"Hopefully not. But it'll disguise your identity in addition to offering protection."

I stripped off my outer layers and worked my way into the armor. It was a snug fit, because I had more curves than it was designed for, but overall, it was far more lightweight and flexible than I'd expected.

I tucked both comms into a hidden compartment against my ribs, but I couldn't figure out how to attach my blade and pistol.

"Leave them," Torran said.

"Easy for you to say," I grumbled. "You can just smush people without lifting a finger. Some of us need a little help."

Torran hadn't donned his helmet yet, so I caught the tiniest hint of a smile before his expression turned serious. "I will protect you. You have my word."

"Thank you, but that won't help me if someone smushes *you*."

His grimace had a wry twist. "If I go down, then you should already be running," he said quietly, "because neither of your weapons will help."

I sighed and left the pistol and blade with the stack of my clothes. I felt naked without a weapon, but Torran was right. If he couldn't protect me, then escape would be my best chance of survival.

Torran handed me a helmet designed for long hair and showed me how to put it on and remove it. Once it was on, the face shield slid closed and the night vision kicked in. I looked around the workshop now that I could see far better. The kidnappers' transport was in an area by itself. I could see where Kee and Anja had crawled around under it, removing the shielding to get to the data stores.

Torran put on his own helmet, then held the lev cycle's hatch and gestured for me to climb in. Inside, a padded seat was meant to be ridden astride. At the front, manual controls were more prominent than the embedded control panel. If I had to guess, this vehicle was very quick and very fun to fly.

And we were going to be tightly pressed together.

"This is the best option?" I asked, my voice muffled by the helmet. When the comm didn't automatically pick it up, I frowned. I tapped on the side of the transport. I could hear that fine, so the helmet was piping in outside sounds, but it wasn't transmitting.

"How do I turn on the comm?" I pointed at my mouth in case he couldn't hear me.

Torran leaned in. "These are untraceable helmets and don't have comms built in," he said, his voice barely audible. "Communicating will be easier if I can speak to you telepathically. Will you allow it?"

I froze. The memory of our last interaction was still fresh in my mind. I had not handled myself well. I swallowed down my fear. "Will you be able to read my thoughts?"

"No, I will keep the touch very light. If you want to say something, tap me or make a noise, and I will listen more carefully. If we are separated, you will need to mentally shout to get my attention."

Alarm slithered through me. "*Are* we going to be separated?"

"No. But it's something you should know, just in case."

"This is such a bad idea," I muttered. Louder, I said, "Fine. I agree. Don't break my trust."

I felt the lightest brush of coolness against my mind, then Torran's voice whispered directly into my head. "You have my word: your thoughts are your own."

Goose bumps rose on my arms, and I shook off the strange feeling.

I tapped Torran, so he would listen, and the coolness came back a little stronger. "Are you sure this is the best vehicle?" I asked again. I asked the question aloud because I wasn't quite comfortable with mental-only communication.

It seemingly worked, because Torran said, "This is the one that won't be tracked."

I shivered again and ducked inside. I swung a leg over the seat and sat in the passenger position, such as it was. As much as I wanted to fly the thing—and it was a very great deal indeed—I decided that whatever Torran had to show me took priority over a joyride.

For now.

Torran climbed in, and the narrow cabin immediately felt far more cramped. I moved back as much as I could while he swung his leg over the seat.

I tried to leave space between us, but he reached back and pulled me snug against his back. "The safety system is going to engage. Don't be alarmed."

Flexible clamps closed around my ankles, calves, and thighs. I could still move, but not much. Torran was similarly locked in.

"You can hold on to me, or there's a handle under the seat," he said. "We're going to be traveling at speed, so pick whichever is more comfortable and secure."

I tried the handle under my seat, but it did not feel secure at all, so I tentatively wrapped my arms around Torran's waist. He pulled them tighter, until I could feel the firm press of his armor under my gloved fingertips.

All of the feelings I'd been trying to ignore came rushing back. We were pressed together about as tightly as two people could be, but I wished the armor wasn't separating us. I liked Torran, despite everything that stood between us. That alone was enough for my body to get ideas about what we could do when pressed together like this—preferably sans clothes.

Before I could worry about whether Torran had picked up that delicious—and mortifying—thought, the lev cycle rose from the ground. The control panel remained off and a single light indicated that the vehicle was on at all.

"Ready?" Torran asked.

I must have been getting used to his mental voice, because I barely flinched. "Yes."

He eased the vehicle out of the garage without turning on any external lights. Outside, the starlight was bright enough that the night vision in the helmet made it seem like daytime. I could see, in color, with incredible detail. I wondered if Torran would notice if this armor went suddenly missing when we returned.

Rather than letting the autopilot, if there was one, take over, Torran manually piloted the small craft. As soon as we cleared the residential area, Torran opened the throttle. The lev cycle darted forward, fast and nimble. We floated a meter above the ground, stabilized by an internal gyro and Torran's skill.

We stayed off the main expressway, which still had some traffic despite the hour, and kept to the smaller, slower roads. Not that Torran paid any mind to a speed limit, assuming there was one.

We wove around the few other transports we encountered, but more often than not, Torran would alter the route rather than passing too close. Clearly, we were trying not to be seen, but it became more difficult the deeper into the city we delved.

The buildings climbed around us, first a dozen stories, then fifty, then more than a hundred. At one of the tallest buildings with an elegant sign in Valovan that I couldn't read, we turned into a parking garage. Only then did I realize why this street had seemed familiar—I'd watched the kidnapper's transport emerge from this exact spot.

I looked around with new interest but there wasn't much to see. Even an alien civilization hadn't figured out how to make parking garages interesting. A long row of open spots lined one wall. Each spot was marked for storage and retrieval. Park a transport in one, agree to the terms, and the machinery would whisk the vehicle away to an underground storage area. When it was time to leave, the client would request their transport before they left the building above, and the vehicle would be ready and waiting for them.

Based on the number of spots, this building must cater to high-end clients, because most normal city dwellers just used the shared transports available on nearly every corner. At least, that's how it worked in human cities. Maybe Valoffs were different.

The garage was well lit, and suddenly the armor made sense because surveillance cameras likely covered everything. If Torran was supposed to keep his investigation quiet, then showing up with an unknown human woman in tow wasn't the best way to go about it.

Torran parked the lev cycle in the first spot. I expected the restraints to release, but they remained securely strapped around my legs. I tapped Torran and waited until I felt the telltale mental coolness. "What are we doing?"

"The kidnappers were in the vehicle when it exited the storage area. We're going to look around inside."

"We should've brought Lexi. This is her thing."

"I did not expect this opportunity tonight or I would've given you more warning. I apologize for startling you and disrupting your sleep."

"So this isn't a sanctioned visit?"

Torran's mental voice was quietly amused. "Not exactly."

The garage machinery clamped around the lev bike's landing pads and swept us deeper underground. The night-vision helmet became useful once again as the lower garage was barely lit. A few emergency lights indicated exits, but the rest of the large area was dark.

Spaces for vehicles lined the garage from floor to ceiling. There were no stairs or walkways because a vehicle wouldn't be moved into storage with passengers inside. Torran must've overridden the safety controls.

Our vehicle settled into a narrow slot with a jolt. We were on the lowest level, just a couple of meters from the floor. At least I wouldn't have to figure out how to climb down from the top.

The safety restraints released my legs, and I scooted back so that Torran would have room to stand up. It took a little more maneuvering, but he eased out of the vehicle and held the door for me. If the cycle had been any wider, we wouldn't have had room to exit. As it was, Torran had to crouch so he wouldn't hit his head on the platform above us.

Torran jumped to the ground, a trick I wasn't about to copy. My knee had been a lot better since Havil had healed it a second time, but I wasn't going to take stupid risks.

"I've got you," Torran said a moment before his power clamped around me. It felt different in armor, not as personal, and I could still breathe. Well, that was handy.

I landed softly next to him. "Thank you." I looked around, then tapped him. "Where are the access points?"

Torran pointed at the three emergency exits indicated by the lights. "All entry points are monitored, yet none of the cameras caught the kidnappers."

"They overrode the system?"

"If so, they did it surgically. No data breaches were recorded, and the video has no obvious loops."

"Do you still have access? Lexi and Kee might find something."

"No. We barely got access the first time. The main part of the building is a financial institution with a great deal of influence. The upper floors are apartments for the rich and powerful. Without an official investigation, they will give us nothing. My original access was a favor from a friend."

"Why doesn't the empress make up something to investigate? Surely she has the power."

Torran paused, and when he spoke again, his mental voice was filled with frustration. "Her reasons are her own."

"Her reasons suck," I muttered.

"I agree," Torran responded, very quietly.

CHAPTER TWENTY-ONE

Torran climbed to the top of the room with nothing but strength and determination. I watched him until my nerves couldn't take it anymore, then I went to investigate the entrances. The kidnappers hadn't materialized in here, so how did they get in?

"Don't open the doors," Torran warned. Despite the physical distance between us, his mental voice sounded exactly the same, like a comm. "The cameras are down in here, but not outside."

"Noted."

Two of the doors had matching labels with a pictogram of what looked like stairs. The third door was an elevator. If I were sneaking in a team, I would use the stairs. Service stairways often had access hidden from public view, especially in fancy buildings where the clients didn't want to see maintenance personnel. A pair of loose, slightly dirty maintenance coveralls was the easiest way to make yourself invisible to the types of people who inhabited these buildings.

But in the video from Torran's house, the kidnappers had been wearing armor. Building security would not have allowed a team of armored soldiers past the front door, even if the video surveillance was down or altered. And while it was *possible* that security was in on it, the more likely answer was the soldiers had been disguised. None of the reports mentioned clothes in the transport, so I started looking for a place where they could have stashed their extra gear. It might give us the clue we needed to trace them before they arrived at the building.

My frown grew as I searched. Why pick a building in the middle of the city in the first place? It made sense only if they didn't want to burn their home base, either because they still needed it or because of what—or who—it would reveal. Stealing and hiding a transport early added a lot of additional risk if they were planning to abandon the city anyway.

My gut said they were still in Zenzi. If not in the city proper, then at least nearby.

Whoever had picked this building had done their research well. They knew that it wasn't likely to be investigated, and even if it was, the occupants would not be overly helpful. And because of the residences, a transport staying for a while wouldn't be unusual.

I slowly walked the perimeter of the room, looking for hidden entrances or areas big enough to hide a change of clothes, but despite my careful perusal, I almost missed the square vent cover. It was about a meter wide and as black as the wall around it. Tucked in a corner behind one of the massive legs of the transport storage tower, it was nearly invisible.

My pulse leapt, even as I tried not to get my hopes up.

I wedged myself into the narrow space and examined the vent cover. I couldn't find any attachment points, so I pulled on one corner, but my gloves made it hard to get a grip. I adjusted my hands, but my fingers slipped again, and I cursed under my breath.

"Tavi?" Torran's voice whispered across my mind.

"I'm in the corner opposite the stairs," I said while focusing my thoughts toward him. "I need your help, if you're back on the ground."

I heard faint footsteps approaching, then Torran peered into the narrow gap where I'd wedged myself. "What are you doing?"

"I'm trying to get this vent cover off, but I can't get a good grip. Do you have anything flat to pry it with?"

"Move back."

I eased away from the cover. As soon as I was clear, it popped away from the wall, held aloft by Torran's power. Right. *Telekinetic.*

"Damn. That's handy," I murmured.

While he moved the cover aside, I knelt to peer into the exposed vent. The duct ran straight back for a handful of meters before disappearing upward, and on the floor, a pile of suitcases gleamed faintly in my helmet's night vision.

Jackpot.

I pulled the nearest suitcase to me and opened it. A jumble of clothes slipped onto the floor.

"What is that?" Torran asked.

I looked up at him, wishing that I could see his face. "This is the disguise the kidnappers wore to enter the building."

"How do you know?"

Suspicion filled his tone and I rolled my eyes. "Because

I was here and I helped them plant it, of course." When he didn't respond, I sighed and said, "It's what I would do."

"How did they get past the cameras?"

"I don't know." I considered the vent. "Maybe they came in through here. Maybe they had someone as good as Kee who could override the surveillance system without leaving a trace. Kee could probably figure it out if we gave her access."

"That's not possible."

Virtually nothing was impossible for Kee, but I let it go. "I'm going to pull the rest out. Let's see if they left anything else behind."

Torran crouched next to me and the suitcases slid toward us. As I pulled each one out, another moved to take its place so I didn't have to crawl into the vent. "You're useful to have around, has anyone ever told you that?"

"Once or twice," he murmured, amusement threading his mental voice.

We moved to the clear area in the middle of the garage and opened the suitcases. They each contained a cheap suit sized for a tall, fit adult—like, for example, a soldier. Some of the cutouts in the suitcase lining made me think that they had originally contained weapons and armor. So the soldiers had snuck in, swapped into their armor, and left the disguises behind.

"Do you have someone who could examine these?" I asked, after tapping Torran's shoulder to get his attention again. "They might have fingerprints."

I'd been careful while opening them with my gloved hands, but the odds of pulling a usable print were still pretty low. We were clearly dealing with professionals. They knew the game as well as I did, so they would've wiped everything down if they'd had time.

"I do, but we will have to come back for them. We don't have room to take them with us tonight, and technically, we're not here."

"At least this gives us somewhere to start looking. If Kee can pull the surveillance video from the surrounding area, we might be able to track them back to their base."

Torran remained silent. I touched his arm. "Why aren't you happy about this? This is exactly the sort of thing we came to find."

Torran shook his head. "I'm sorry. Of course, this is amazing. I had people scour this whole area, and they missed something you found in ten minutes. That's incredible. *You're* incredible."

"But?" I prompted when his mental voice faded out.

"Nothing." He shook his head again. "We'll see what else your team can find. For now, let's put this stuff back so we can return for it later."

Most of the suitcases were already back in the vent when Torran cocked his head. "Someone is coming."

I shoved the remaining suitcases in the duct and waved for him to replace the cover. Once it was in place, I tapped him and pointed up. "We need to hide. Boost me up a level."

"Why?"

"Because we're not supposed to be here?" It came out a question, because I wasn't sure which part of my statement *he* was questioning.

"It's too late," he said calmly. "They'll be able to sense you in a moment or two."

"So shield me!"

"Last time—"

"Just do it," I demanded.

The cool feel of Torran's power swept over me, and I

pulled my own shields closer. Rather than lifting me up a level, Torran pressed me farther into the narrow space between the wall and the transport storage tower.

My back hit the wall and Torran pressed closer, trapping me in the corner. My heart rate rose from a combination of fear and desire.

"I will protect you," Torran murmured in my mind. "You are safe. Nothing will get past me."

As strange as it was, I believed him. With his power wrapped around my mind, I should've been terrified, and part of me *was,* but I also felt *protected.*

Desire wove delicate tendrils through my veins. Torran was prepared to put himself between me and danger, and we were squeezed close together in a dark corner. Yes, we were hiding, but my libido apparently hadn't gotten the memo that this was business and not pleasure.

I wished the armor wasn't in the way so that I could feel the press of his body against mine.

A tiny groan came from in front of me, one I hadn't heard across our telepathic link. "Try not to think too loud," Torran whispered into my mind. "I'm trying to stay away from your thoughts, but it's harder when I'm shielding for you."

A flush rose in my cheeks at exactly what thoughts he might've caught. True telepathy must be even more sensitive than subvocal comms because I *had* been thinking quietly—or so I'd thought.

Before I could ask him about it, the distant sound of a door opening caused me to freeze. A beam of light bounced around the space, but the main lights, if there were any, remained off.

"Security guard," Torran said over the telepathic link.

The guard muttered something in Valovan. I didn't understand the words, but the mocking tone came across just fine. Someone wasn't happy that they'd been sent to peer around in the dark.

With nothing better to do until the guard left, I focused on my shields. I could feel Torran's power around me, like a cool bubble, but like last time, I couldn't sense anything else.

The flashlight beam moved closer, and I froze again. I *really* did not want to be caught breaking and entering on Valovia.

Torran shifted in front of me and the sound seemed incredibly loud. I raised my face to hiss at him, only to find that he'd opened the visor on his helmet. He lifted his hand and pressed the release on mine, so that we were face-to-face.

"Stop fighting me," he whispered, his voice barely audible. It was too dark to see the colors shifting in his eyes, but I caught a glint of dark and light.

I shook my head. "I'm not," I murmured.

"You didn't hear my last question and you nearly broke through my shield."

"I'm not doing it on purpose," I clarified.

The flashlight beam bounced off the ceiling of the pod next to us. We were about to be caught. I began contingency planning. Could we make it to the lev cycle before the guard called for backup? I could take a single Valoff, assuming they weren't telekinetic. But what if they were?

I was so focused on planning that the shock of Torran's lips against my cheek took a second to register. The moment stilled into crystal clarity. Torran's lips were firm and his breath gently warmed my cheek. He pressed softly against my skin, barely touching.

"Torran?"

Torran pulled back until he could meet my eyes. "Tavi, may I kiss you? Properly?"

My chin dipped in agreement before I could overthink it.

Torran leaned in slowly, giving me time to change my mind, but instead, I met him halfway. His lips covered mine, warm and delicious. I licked his bottom lip and the resulting jolt of desire slammed through me. Torran groaned softly, deep in his chest, and then he moved, sliding his tongue against mine. I arched into him, pressing as close as I could get with the armor in the way.

It wasn't enough.

I wrapped my hand around the back of his helmet and pulled him closer, fusing our mouths. When my tongue slipped past his lips, Torran made another low sound of pleasure, and my stomach clenched.

I wanted to hear that sound *again*.

One kiss became two, then three, then more, blending together until time and place lost all meaning. A light, fluttering touch ran down my back under my armor, and I gasped into Torran's mouth. "Was that you?" I whispered.

He nodded, breathing hard, his mouth flat, and I wished I could see his expression. "I'm sorry. I should've asked. You drive me—"

"Do it again," I demanded.

This time, the phantom touch was firmer, and I bit back a moan as it ghosted over my breasts and between my legs. I trembled and my knees turned to jelly. If not for Torran's weight pinning me to the wall, I would've melted to the floor.

"How?" I whispered in awe.

A tiny smile pulled at the edges of his lips. "Very precise control. It's far more difficult with you in armor."

"Are you going to suggest that I take it off?" I asked with a smile of my own.

"Only if you want to." His lips touched mine as his power stroked down my body again, and pleasure surged through me. Was there anything I wouldn't do if he asked like this?

The sound of a door slamming closed sent me crashing back to reality. We were in a parking garage, about to be discovered by a security guard. Now was not the time for making out. I pulled back and sucked in a deep breath, then held it, trying to calm my racing pulse—and quell the heat flooding my body.

A moment later, the cool feel of Torran's power slipped away, leaving me feeling shaky and exposed, even though my own shields were still in place. "What are you doing?" I whispered.

"The guard is gone."

How much time had I lost in the pleasurable haze of desire? Most of the guard's visit, that much was certain. And had Torran kissed me just to distract me? Lingering pleasure turned to outrage, with a heaping side of embarrassment.

"I didn't kiss you to distract you," Torran said calmly, then corrected himself. "I didn't kiss you *only* to distract you. And if you think I did, then you haven't been paying attention."

My eyes narrowed. "You said you wouldn't read my thoughts."

"I also told you to mentally shout to get my attention and that thought was incredibly loud. I kissed you because I wanted to. I've wanted to for days, but I wasn't sure my attention would be welcome. If we hadn't had an audience on the ship, I would've asked to kiss you after we sparred."

"Oh." All the times I'd thought I'd seen heat in his eyes hadn't been my imagination, even before our unmistakable almost kiss on the wall. The desire that I'd been fighting rose higher, stoked by the knowledge that it was mutual, that he really did want me as much as I wanted him.

A thought occurred. "You could've used your power to carry me to the medbay without touching me."

His grin was quick and wicked. "I could've," he agreed. He stepped back but held my arms until he was sure my legs would support me. He gestured at the vent. "I think we've found everything we can here, so let's head out before the guard returns. I'll send someone to retrieve the suitcases later. For now, I have a few more places to show you, if you're not too tired."

My mind immediately jumped to exactly *which* places I'd like him to show me, but I figured he had less exciting things in mind. I sighed. Work needed to come before play, sadly.

With thwarted desire still simmering through my veins, I wasn't sure I'd ever be tired again. Plus, I was in that weird, wired state that came from too little sleep. I would crash eventually, but I would be okay for another few hours. I followed Torran out of our hidden little corner and back into reality.

I nodded. "Let's go."

WE MADE IT OUT OF THE GARAGE WITHOUT BEING STOPPED, which I considered a minor miracle. Torran took us on the same route the kidnappers had used. With our visors down for night vision, we had resumed telepathic conversation.

Well, telepathic on Torran's end, and half mental, half verbal on my side.

The route wasn't the most direct way to get from the garage to Torran's property, but it did seem to avoid most of the late-night traffic. Torran stopped at the corner of his property where the kidnappers had exited the transport.

There wasn't anything particularly exciting about this corner, except that it was near the point they'd chosen to scale the wall. We were close to the house, so I sent Kee a message confirming I was still alive, and letting her know what we'd found.

"Some of us are *trying to sleep*," she replied. Then she added, "But I'm glad you're not dead. I'll start looking for the outside surveillance tomorrow. Let me know when you get in."

I promised her that I would.

Torran turned to me, though all I could see was the gleaming visor of his helmet. "Ready to continue?"

I nodded. "Show me the rest."

We took the same circular route the transport had taken, passed by Torran's front gate, and then headed away from the city. The edge of the forest wasn't that far from the Imperial Palace, so the houses we passed were hidden behind high walls and ornate gates.

The road ended in a wide circle without much fanfare. It was like a switch had been flipped: city on one side, nature on the other. Trees and plants stretched as far as I could see.

Torran ignored the barriers at the end of the road and continued into the trees. After a dozen meters, a narrow path became visible. It was cleverly hidden from the road with plants and a natural rise, but the trees had been cleared enough to allow a transport to pass through.

I tapped Torran. "Is this route well known?"

Torran shook his head. "And the owners around here fight to keep it that way."

"Where does it go?"

"There's a monitoring station a few kilometers out."

I sucked in a surprised breath. That hadn't been in the brief. I figured the answer was obvious, but I had to ask anyway. "Did you check it?"

"Extensively."

"Show me where they dumped the transport."

Torran nodded and we continued deeper into the forest. The trees were tall, with glossy, deep green leaves and pale bark. Straight trunks branched into wide canopies at the top, and the dense foliage prevented any view of the sky. All in all, it was an excellent place to disappear, given the right equipment.

We continued deeper into the forest, until I could see nothing but trees. Unease slithered down my spine. This would also be the perfect place for an ambush.

I tapped Torran's shoulder. "Is this area under surveillance now? Did you tell anyone we were coming here tonight?"

"We're monitoring the entire area. No one has returned. My team knows that we're out."

Torran's team seemed loyal, but most traitors seemed loyal right up until the hidden knife slid between your ribs. My unease crept higher.

We stopped at a seemingly random point. The only thing that differentiated it from the rest of the path was the trampled undergrowth. The lev cycle settled to the ground, and we climbed out.

The soft sounds of nature filtered through my helmet. I opened the visor and gave my eyes a minute to adjust, then waved my hand in front of my face. I couldn't see it. I could hear Torran moving around, but I couldn't see him, either. It made me worry about what *else* might be creeping through the dark.

I hurriedly closed the visor, and the night vision returned, brightening the night to daylight once again.

I waved my hand at Torran and asked, "Can you see without your helmet?" I knew Valoffs had better natural night vision, but I wasn't sure how good it actually was.

Torran's helmet clicked open, then a moment later he said, "Not much."

"I couldn't see my hand in front of my face. How much better is 'not much' than that?"

There was a long pause, then he said, "I will show you, if you are willing."

When I murmured my assent, an image formed in my mind, much like when Luna sent me a picture of her empty bowl. The night wasn't nearly as dark for Torran, but while he could see somewhat, the details were hazy. It took me a second to figure out that the person-shaped blob in the middle of the image was me standing next to the lev cycle.

No wonder Valoffs had such excellent night-vision tech. They could definitely see better than humans, but with so much of their time in the dark, boosted night vision helped fill in the details.

"Thank you," I said. I tilted my head as I considered the trampled plants. "So even if the soldiers had Valoffs with them, the team had to have night-vision gear because neither of us can see well enough to change vehicles quickly."

"The moon was up that night. In moonlight, a Valoff could see well enough to navigate the trees."

I looked at the thick canopy and shook my head. "Then the humans, at least, had night-vision tech. That doesn't tell us too much, because it's pretty common, but they had to get it somewhere." While we sometimes caught a lucky break, most of our cases were solved by dogged pursuit of the details.

I circled the lev cycle, looking for tracks, but the trees were far enough apart that a transport could've left in any direction. Rather than waving at Torran again to get his attention, I tried to think loud thoughts. "Which way did they escape?"

It took a couple of tries, which hopefully meant he really wasn't listening to *every* thought, but eventually he turned to me and waved an arm off to the left side of the route we'd been following.

"Their getaway vehicle was hidden off the main path. After that, we were unable to track them."

"You don't have any thermal satellites that might've caught their engine exhaust?"

"We checked, but the tree canopy reflects so much heat that it would hide a small transport engine."

"Seems like a security issue with the palace so close." It was also data the FHP would probably find very, very valuable.

"The palace is well protected," Torran said, his mental voice cold and stiff.

"Show me where the other vehicle was."

Torran waved me closer, then headed deeper into the

trees. I was glad for the Valovian armor because the sharp undergrowth slid past the synthetic material without catching—or cutting.

After a few minutes, we came to another area where the plants had been trampled. The tree trunks were far enough apart that a good pilot could navigate through them without too much trouble, but they wouldn't have been moving at a great deal of speed.

"How long did it take you to find this after Cien was taken?"

"Four hours, but three of them were wasted because no one knew he'd been kidnapped until I returned and reviewed the backup footage. The primary surveillance system had been disabled, likely the bodyguard's doing."

"He didn't know about the backup system?"

Torran shook his head. "No one did, until now. It was the last line of defense."

I briefly wondered if Kee had us under some sort of secret backup surveillance before chuckling to myself. Of course she did. There was no question.

"So the trail was already cold by the time you arrived," I said, returning to the conversation.

Torran dipped his head in agreement.

Four hours was certainly long enough to put the kidnappers out of sensor range, even at the slow speed navigating the forest required.

But they wouldn't *know* that Cien's absence would be undiscovered for so long.

So if they'd made their plans on the assumption that they'd be tracked within an hour, that limited their options. Still, with no idea what kind of vehicle they'd taken—or how many—tracking their return to the city was impossible.

"Was the forest searched?" I asked at last.

"Yes, from the air. Ships with sensors designed to penetrate the canopy were deployed to scan the entire area, even farther out than the kidnappers could've possibly made it. They found nothing."

So that left the city or the monitoring station. "Are there other monitoring stations like the one nearby? And were they checked?"

"They were all searched," Torran snapped, frustration evident. "We did *everything* right. We still failed."

I approached him slowly, like I would a wounded animal. When I was close enough, I opened my arms and waited.

"What are you doing?"

"I'm offering you a hug, no strings attached."

His helmet turned away. "I don't need a hug. I'm not a child to be coddled."

"First of all, hugs are for anyone who wants one. Second, I'm offering you comfort, not coddling. And finally, 'no strings' means exactly that. You don't have to explain why you want a hug or what's bothering you or anything else. I'm just offering one hug, freely given. Here." I opened my visor and blinked at the resulting darkness. "Now I can't even see who I'm hugging. Could be anyone. Maybe a bear wandered by. No one knows."

Torran eased into my arms, body stiff and not just because of the armor. I let him settle for a second, then pulled him closer and gave him a gentle squeeze. Slowly, so slowly, his arms crept around me.

We stayed like that for a long minute. When Torran straightened, I let him go. "Thank you, *cho udwist diu*," he whispered.

I recognized the middle word was stubborn, but I didn't know the rest. From the tone, it was likely an endearment rather than an insult, so I let him get away without explaining it.

But I would definitely look it up later.

THE MONITORING STATION GATE SLID OPEN AT OUR APproach. The building was a squat, square, unsightly little thing that wasn't helped by the large antenna mounted on top. Around the perimeter, a tall fence and more of the spiky *vomosulabr* shrubs warned trespassers to keep their distance.

I tapped Torran's shoulder. "Why is this building so . . ." I trailed off and gestured, trying to find a tactful word for "ugly."

I could feel Torran's laughter against my chest from where we were pressed together on the lev cycle.

"It was built in the early years of the war, when they were more concerned with speed than beauty," he said. "Except for occasional maintenance checks, no one ever sees it, so it never got an update."

We exited the vehicle. The building's aesthetics did not improve upon closer inspection. I walked around the outside, but there wasn't much to see. A single door was set in the wall that faced the gate. There were no other doors or windows of any kind.

A narrow ladder on the back wall led to the roof. One short climb later and I could say that the roof *also* didn't improve the building's looks. The antenna anchors took up most of the flat space, and what was left was crowded with buzzing, unfamiliar equipment.

I climbed down to find Torran waiting for me at the base. "Find anything?" he asked.

I shook my head. "Just a bunch of old equipment."

The inside didn't reveal anything, either. The lights worked and the air was warm, but that was about the end of the positives. Because, while the lights worked—*technically*—they cast everything in a sickly yellow tint. The floor was cracked and chipped, and the paint had started to peel from the walls.

Around the edges of the room, a few older workstations that hadn't been upgraded in twenty years still hummed along, doing whatever it was that this station did. A raggedy rolling chair with a chunk missing from the cushion and a wheel that wouldn't turn was the only other furniture.

I felt bad for anyone who had been stationed here. Maybe I would find their vengeful ghost, and it would crack the case wide open. I looked around. No ghost appeared.

I sighed. I'd been so sure that this place was important. After all, why choose *this* route for escape? But I'd seen enough coincidences to know that not every clue led to an answer. The easiest answer was often the right one, and this path just happened to be the closest forest access to Torran's property.

Still, I would have Lexi look into it, just in case. There was no reason not to run down every possible option. And with less than two weeks remaining, we had to work fast *and* smart.

CHAPTER TWENTY-TWO

Torran and I returned to the workshop where we'd started. He didn't say anything, but I could *feel* his disappointment. Like me, he'd hoped that I would just waltz into the right answer and find Cien, but real life rarely worked like the entertainment vids.

If it did, my job would be so much easier.

I quietly stripped off my borrowed armor, until I was left in my tank top and leggings. I shivered as I pulled on my outer clothes. By the time I'd strapped on my weapons, Torran had changed back into the tunic and pants he'd been wearing earlier.

"Thank you for coming with me," he said quietly. "I apologize again for disrupting your sleep."

"You're welcome. I'm sorry I wasn't more useful, but the visual of the path does help cement the timeline in my mind. And now Kee has some idea what to search for on the surveillance videos in the time leading up to the transport leaving." It was something, but it wasn't enough. I ran a frustrated hand through my hair.

Torran held out his arms, an unreadable expression on his face in the dim light from the light stick he'd activated when we removed our helmets.

My eyes shot to his face. "What are you doing?"

"I am offering you one hug, freely given, no strings attached." A tiny smile hovered at the corner of his mouth. "I was led to believe that this is how it is done."

I stepped into his arms. Hugging him without armor was a completely different experience. His chest was warm and firm, and I could feel the muscles in his back when I wrapped my arms around him. He was solid and alive, and I didn't realize how much I'd actually needed a hug until his arms were around me.

My frustration melted under the gentle pressure of the embrace. We would find his nephew. We just had to keep looking. I had the best team in the system, so I just had to have a little faith.

I squeezed Torran and pulled back just far enough that I could meet his eyes. The colors were muted in the low light, but I could still see the silver streaks branching across his dark gray irises. This close, I could see that the colors shifted as his pupils dilated.

The rest of his face was just as interesting. He had the fine bone structure common to Valoffs, with sharp cheekbones and a strong jaw. His short black hair just touched his forehead where the helmet had plastered it down. When my gaze dropped to his mouth, one corner quirked up in a half smile. I remembered the feel of his lips on mine, and I wanted to feel it again, without the armor between us.

"I'm going to kiss you," I murmured.

The smile bloomed, and he nodded his agreement.

I put my hands on his shoulders, then lifted onto my toes and brushed my mouth against his. Little sparks of pleasure danced across my nerves. When he opened his mouth, those sparks roared into an inferno.

Torran buried a hand in the hair at the back of my head and I shivered in appreciation. His other arm clamped me tight against his body and the heat of him seared through my clothes—clothes that felt more and more unnecessary as the kiss continued.

I slid one of my hands up his neck, pulling him closer as I settled back on my heels, and he groaned against my mouth as he followed. My other hand moved down, tracing the firm muscles of his chest and abs. When I didn't find the hem of his shirt, I growled in frustration and pulled at the fabric.

Torran let me go long enough to yank his tunic up, then my hand splayed across the warm skin of his side. We both hissed in pleasure. His mouth caught mine and I lost myself in the feel of his lips until the heat of his palm glided up my side and stopped just under my breast.

I didn't know when he'd gotten under my clothes and I didn't care. Instead, I held my breath, but he didn't move. I glanced up at him, struck by the stark longing on his face. "Don't tease," I whispered.

His hand eased upward, and when his palm met my nipple, I'd never been so glad that I hadn't taken the time to put on a bra. Then he dipped his head and licked me, and I buried my fingers in his soft hair and clutched his head as delight raced along my nerves.

He pushed up my shirt and paid the same attention to my other breast, and my legs, already wobbly, decided that now might be an excellent time for us to get horizontal. But before I could sink to the floor, Torran caught me, brushing featherlight kisses over my jaw. His late-night stubble added a delicious friction that I wanted to feel *everywhere*.

Instead, using the tiny sliver of self-control I still possessed, I pressed my fingers against his chest. He pulled back, his gaze hot and hooded. My resolve wavered. I was caught in a tornado of conflicting emotions. My body demanded satisfaction, but my head warned of danger and my heart wanted more.

Torran must've sensed my hesitation, because he lifted my fingers to his mouth and pressed a gentle kiss against them, then he let me go.

The workshop had never felt colder, and not just because my chest was exposed to the air.

I fixed my shirt, then stared at his gorgeous face and distinctly Valovian eyes and made a decision—I wanted him. He was a Valoff, and a client, and that complicated everything, but I wouldn't be here long enough for it to get awkward if things didn't work out. I would guard my heart and have a little harmless fun.

I lifted my face and brushed a kiss against his lips. "Come back to my room with me," I murmured.

He groaned and something like pain flashed across his face. "I can't."

I frowned at him. "Are you saying that because you want me to persuade you or are you saying it because it's true?"

A muscle in his jaw flexed. "It's true."

"Then why—" I bit off the question. It was his right to refuse for any reason, even if he'd just had my nipple in his mouth. The rejection stung, but I cleared my throat and pretended that it didn't. "Okay. Please let me know if any new information comes in."

Torran's expression had gone unreadable once again, but even that couldn't completely snuff out the little flickers of heat between us. "I will share what I can," he said at last.

All of my frustration came roaring back, but I kept the bitter words locked behind my teeth. Apparently, I was good enough for furtive kisses and groping in the dark, but not good enough to trust or to fuck.

That thought hurt far more than it should've.

TORRAN LEFT ME OUTSIDE MY BEDROOM WITH A LINGERING look and no kiss. I firmly told myself that I wasn't disappointed.

It was a lie.

Luna opened one eye and chirped a sleepy greeting before closing the eye again and settling her nose more firmly under her tail. She had the right idea. Torran and I had been gone for so long that the sun was already peeking over the horizon, but if I didn't get a few hours of sleep, I'd be worthless.

I sent Kee a message letting her know that I was back safe and planning to crash for a few hours, then I messaged everyone on my team, asking them to keep digging, specifically on the parking garage building and the monitoring station. I let them know that they were on their own for food until I felt human again.

That done, I flopped into bed, clothes and all. Luna moved from the other side of the bed to curl up on my chest.

It was her favorite spot, and I'd learned to breathe with her weight compressing my lungs.

I fell asleep to the low rumble of her purr.

I AWOKE TO SHARP CLAWS PRICKING AT THE SKIN UNDER MY collarbones. Luna stretched again and the claws dug deeper. As soon as I grumbled at her, she sent me a mental picture of her empty food bowl.

I was contemplating her murder when she blinked her big, violet eyes at me and rubbed her head against my chin. The little devil knew exactly how far she could push me *and* how to win her way back into my good graces. It would be impressive if it wasn't so annoying.

I petted her for a few minutes while the fog of sleep slowly lifted. A check of my comm proved that I'd been asleep for a little over three hours. It wasn't nearly enough, but it would have to do.

A hot shower knocked most of the cobwebs from my brain, and by the time I opened the door, I was ready to face the day.

Which is the only reason I didn't trip over the tray on the floor.

The tray had two covered dishes with accompanying labels. Someone had written my name in a neat block script on the larger container's label, and the smaller one had Luna's name on it.

I squinted at the text. Was this Torran's handwriting or had one of his staff taken care of it?

I carried the tray to the kitchen. If I was up anyway, I might as well be sociable. Both the kitchen and dining area were empty when I arrived. Unsurprising, since it was well into midmorning.

The bowl labeled with Luna's name contained a mix of meat, vegetables, and a grain that looked like rice, all cooked. It wasn't too different from what I cooked for her when we ran out of her normal food. A sniff didn't detect anything out of the ordinary, so I dumped it into her food bowl, and she dug in with a happy little sound.

I took my plate to the long dining table. It could seat twelve easily, but I hadn't found a smaller breakfast table, so I sat at the end and pretended I wasn't uncomfortable. The padded chairs were white, which was just asking for trouble, but they went with the pale wood of the table.

I couldn't believe Torran had a young nephew stay with him often and the cushions were still pristine. Maybe Valoffs had figured out some miraculous anti-staining technology.

My plate was a mix of unfamiliar fruits, nuts, and what I assumed was cheese. Another note had been tucked half under the plate. When I drew it out, I realized that it was a guide to everything included, written in Common in the same neat hand. There were even tasting notes that included things like sweet, bitter, and spicy, along with a recommended eating order.

Someone had gone to a lot of trouble to ensure I was comfortable with Valovian food.

I finished everything on my plate. It wasn't all exactly to my taste, but none of it was terrible and I appreciated the work someone had done on my behalf.

I left Luna to continue enjoying her food and carried our plates to the sink in the butler's pantry. Anja and Eli had been unable to find a sanitizer after dinner last night, so they'd washed the dishes by hand. I did the same this morning, then carefully balanced the plate and bowl next to the sink to dry. Once I found Torran, I'd ask him to give me a proper tour.

More food had been left out on the kitchen island, with the same Common labels that explained what it was. Torran needed to give his staff a raise.

"Where is everyone?" I asked over the comm.

Eli was the first to respond. "Good morning, lazybones. *Some* of us are earning our keep while you get your beauty rest."

The comm caught Lexi's snort. "I saw you 'earning your keep' in the gym earlier. It looked a lot like flirting."

"You sure you want to go there, Lex?" Eli taunted. "Because I saw—"

"Children, focus," I said.

"Kee is out at the transport with Varro," Eli said. "Anja and I are in the war room with Chira and Havil, going over surveillance footage. Lexi had to take a walk to clear her head after a certain someone who shall not be named got under her skin while they were discussing ways into the building you apparently visited last night."

"He didn't get under my skin," Lexi ground out.

I grinned to myself but didn't comment. "Did you all eat?" After I got back a chorus of agreements, I asked, "Lexi, if I let Luna out, will you keep an eye on her?"

"Of course. I'm close to the front door if you want to let her out now."

I called Luna to my shoulder, then stepped outside. The air was crisp, but the sunlight made it slightly warmer. I soaked up the rays for a few minutes, aware that the sun was already dipping toward the first sunset of the day.

As soon as Lexi appeared, Luna went to greet her with a happy chirrup. Lexi looked cool and untouchable in a slim pair of black slacks and a long-sleeved blouse. I wondered if she realized that the shirt was the same green as a certain Valoff's eyes. With Lexi, it could go either way.

I waved to her and headed back inside. I stopped by the war room, but Torran wasn't there, so I kept looking. His office door automatically opened as I approached, but the room itself was empty. Two stops later, I found him in the gym, sweaty and shirtless, as he fought an invisible foe masquerading as a punching bag.

The muscles in his arms and back rippled with every strike. Clearly the universe was trying to tempt me, not that I needed much help in that arena.

If Torran was feeling the short night, I couldn't tell from his movements, which remained light and fast. He'd been holding back when we'd sparred. So had I, but not to the same degree. Even Eli would be hard pressed to keep up with him.

Torran bent to retrieve the towel on the ground before turning to face me. Something dark flickered through his expression as he met my eyes, but before I could guess what it meant, he asked, "Did you eat?"

"Yes," I said, watching him closely. "Someone left a tray at my door. Who should I thank?"

He rubbed the towel over his head before answering. "I wanted to apologize for keeping you up so late. You didn't appreciate my last gift, so I tried something new."

"You didn't need to apologize, but I enjoyed the food. Thank you. When you have time, I'd like a tour of the kitchen, so I don't have to guess how things work."

"Of course. I'm sorry I didn't do it yesterday."

I shrugged. "There was a lot going on. I made it work." I kept my eyes firmly above his neck, even though they kept trying to drift down. "Did any new information come in?"

"No."

It was the answer I'd expected, but it didn't make it any easier to hear. I sighed. "Come find me once your workout is done. I want to talk about the kidnappers themselves—what you know, what you don't, that kind of thing."

"I'm finished. I'll meet you in my office after I get cleaned up."

I would not think about him in the shower, I would not think about him in the . . . *dammit*. I jerked my eyes away from his chest and nodded. "Sounds good. I'm going to go check on Kee, then I'll meet you there."

I left the gym before I got myself in trouble.

The workshop was closer to the house than I'd thought—the trip had seemed longer in the dark. I stepped inside the warm interior. Two pairs of legs stuck out from under the stolen transport, and Nilo crouched beside them, looking under the vehicle. One pair of legs was obviously Kee's, and the others likely belonged to Varro.

"Yes, right there," Kee murmured, her voice coaxing. "Just like that."

I chuckled to myself. I'd heard Kee talk to her electronics before. That, plus the fact that the two sets of legs were fairly far apart, made me pretty sure that I wasn't interrupting anything private.

"Have you found something?" I asked.

Nilo turned to me without a hint of surprise. He'd likely known I was here since I'd stepped in the door. He was dressed from head to toe in unrelenting black, but he made it look chic. He glanced over my shoulder, but his mask didn't reveal any of his feelings when it became clear that I was the only one here.

"This damn machine tried to lock me out," Kee said, outrage in her voice. "Me! As if I'm going to let that happen."

I crouched down next to Nilo and peered under the transport. Kee and Varro were on their backs, their arms in the transport's guts. They both had on the long-sleeved shirts and sturdy pants that had become the unofficial uniform on *Starlight*. Varro held a light with one hand while the other braced a part that was half out of the undercarriage. Kee fiddled with something on the part, a slate on her chest.

She concentrated for a second, a scowl on her face, then with a final wiggle, she made a sound of victory. "If you won't come to me, I'll come to you," she said, easing a small flat box out of the part that Varro still held.

"Tavi, grab this, would you?" She lifted her head so she could see me. "Don't drop it."

She handed the little box over as if it were a baby bird, and I cradled it just as gently.

Kee squirmed out from under the vehicle, then helped Varro out. "Thanks, Varro. If your boss gets mad about the transport cost, remind him that we're on the clock."

I scowled at her. "Kee, did you break this transport?"

She looked at me, her eyes wide and guileless. I didn't believe it for a second. "*Break* is a strong word," she started.

I waved her off. "I don't want to know. Plausible deniability. At least tell me it was worth it."

She shrugged. "I hope so." She took the box back from me and popped it into the hacked-together contraption next to her. "I should be able to get the data this way. I extracted a little bit overnight before the security features booted my script, but it didn't tell us anything new. The points I care about are the beginning and the end, and I haven't gotten either, yet."

She tapped on her slate for a moment, then turned it to Nilo and pointed to something on-screen. "See, this is how you know the data is there."

"How did you know that this would work?" he asked, leaning closer.

Kee grinned at him. "I didn't."

Nilo laughed. "So what are you going to do now?"

The two of them broke off into a technical discussion, their heads close together, while Varro watched with cool reserve.

"Kee, do you need anything from me?" I asked.

She shook her head, already absorbed in whatever was happening on-screen.

"Keep me posted," I said, then turned to Varro. "Make sure she eats and stays hydrated."

He nodded, his expression grave. "I will," he promised. He slanted an unreadable glance at Nilo, then added, "She is safe with me."

I believed him. I said farewell and received a distracted nod from Kee as she explained something to Nilo. I didn't take it personally. She would be lost to the world until she bent the data to her will—and I had no doubt that she would.

By the time I returned to the house via a long walk around the property, Torran was in his office, having showered and changed into another tunic and slacks. The deep blue color of the tunic complimented his fair skin and dark hair.

I plopped into one of the guest chairs in front of his desk before I did something foolish like climb in his lap and kiss him senseless. Last night had been an aberration brought on by close quarters and not enough sleep. I didn't need to continue making a fool of myself, especially after he'd set his boundaries. He didn't want more, and if I kissed him again, I *would*.

"Tell me about the kidnappers," I said when it became clear that Torran wasn't planning to start the conversation. "We know that they're human and want power. What else? Why did they target Cien? How did they know he was here?"

"As you thought, they are hoping that Cien is the lever they need to move the empress." He sighed. "I suspect they turned Cien's bodyguard long before the attack, and that's how they knew when he would be here alone. My house is easier to breach than the Imperial Palace."

"Does your nephew stay with you often?"

Torran shrugged. "Often enough."

So the team had been on-planet for a while, but maybe weeks rather than months. Humans weren't exactly forbidden on Valovia, but they weren't encouraged to visit, either. The number of full-time human residents was probably in the low thousands. Without special flight authorization, visitors had to take approved ships from Bastion in order to reach Valovia. A team of nine would've likely come in on several different ships.

Even with an inside informant, planning an operation of this size and complexity took time and skill. Disappearing wasn't easy. Disappearing with a Valovian child on a planet full of telepaths was even more difficult.

"Tavi, are you armed?" Eli asked over the comm. His voice was tense and urgent.

"Just a blade," I responded subvocally. I'd left my guns behind this morning because I hadn't planned on leaving the house.

"I need you to come to the war room. Ditch Fletcher if you can."

A glance at Torran revealed his eyes were distant. Whatever Eli had found, Torran already knew about it.

I stood. "Eli needs my help for a moment. I'll be right back."

Torran stood as well. He looked like he wanted to say something, but he just inclined his head in acknowledgment.

Then he followed me out.

Kee, Lexi, and Anja were crowded around Eli's station. All bristled with weapons but none of them was drawn. Whatever Eli had found, he'd relayed it to the others first, which meant he expected trouble with Torran.

Chira, Havil, Varro, and Nilo stood nearby, expressions guarded. The lines had been clearly drawn, and it was humans versus Valoffs.

That was proved true when Eli leveled his flat, cold, killing gaze on Torran the moment he walked through the door.

"Tavi, you need to see this," Eli said without taking his eyes off the threat.

I eased closer. The screen showed the outside of a low building. The video was likely from a traffic or security camera. "What am I looking at?"

"I've been tracing the origins of all the transports that entered the garage in the hours leading up to the attack. This is one of them." He pressed a button and the video began to play.

For a long moment, nothing happened. Then a transport pulled up outside the building. The entrance door opened and nine people walked out. They were dressed in suits, but the clothes couldn't disguise the fact that they moved like soldiers.

Or the fact that they were carrying the exact suitcases I'd found hidden in the parking garage last night.

The nine soldiers loaded into the transport. Their disguises were clever. If the transport was stopped, they just looked like tourists or businesspeople going about their day.

Eli held up a finger, telling me to wait, as he sped up the footage. People and transports sped by at an accelerated rate, but the door to the building remained closed.

Until it didn't.

Eli paused the frame and expanded it, but he needn't have bothered—I would recognize the son of a bitch on-screen at a thousand meters: Commodore Frank Morten, the asshole in FHP Command who had ordered me to blow up civilians.

None of the Valoffs in the room showed a trace of surprise. Either they didn't know who Frank Morten was or they'd *already* known.

I rounded on Torran, unwilling to believe that he'd betray me like this, but unable to deny what was right in front of my face. "Tell me you didn't know."

Torran's jaw clenched, but he remained silent.

"Why, out of all the bounty hunters in the galaxy, did you pick me?" I asked, my voice deadly quiet. I wanted to be wrong. I wanted to be wrong *so much.*

Torran met my eyes, his expression stark, and shattered all my dreams. "Because you're the hero of Rodeni."

The knife slid into my back without so much as a whisper of warning.

CHAPTER TWENTY-THREE

At Torran's words, my team closed ranks around me, weapons drawn. The Valoffs didn't move. I mentally snorted. Of course they didn't. They didn't have to. Torran could incapacitate us all before a single shot was fired.

I straightened my spine. "Is your nephew even missing?"

Torran nodded, his expression turning haggard before the mask smoothed it over once again.

The pieces came together, and I didn't like the picture they painted. "I suppose that whatever happens in—what is it, ten days, now?—has more to do with me than your nephew, doesn't it? If Commodore Morten doesn't bow to the empress's wishes, then you have me as a backup plan. I'm a valuable hostage."

Torran's gaze dropped away from mine.

I shook my head. "Not a hostage, then." I took a stab in the dark. "The execution of an FHP hero would send quite the message, I bet."

Torran flinched but denied nothing.

Tears pricked at the backs of my eyes, but I refused to acknowledge them. "Let my team go, right now, and I'll be your little scapegoat," I said. "I'll even keep looking for Cien."

"Tavi, no," Eli growled. "If you think we'll just leave you—"

"You'll do as I order," I interrupted, sinking command into my tone.

"I won't," Kee said from my right. "Consider this a mutiny if you must, but I'm not abandoning you, no matter *what* you order." She looked around at the Valoffs in the room, all of whom towered over her. "And if you all think you're safe just because you have a telekinetic, then you don't know us very well."

Torran held up his hands in a placating gesture. "No one is going to die."

"So we're free to go?" I challenged.

He held my gaze even as he continued to stab me. "Not exactly."

"Then that sounds *exactly* like we're prisoners." I shook my head as a bitter smile twisted my lips. "Very clever, getting us to lower our guard. Effective, too. I thought we were friends." I'd thought Torran and I could be more, too, but I was bleeding enough without acknowledging another wound. My laugh was small and harsh, and it rang with the hurt buried deep in my soul. "Shows what I know."

"Tavi," Torran started.

I slashed a hand through the air. "No. You may address me as Captain Zarola or not at all."

Something raw and bleak crossed his face before he

bowed his head in acknowledgment. "Captain Zarola, it was not my intent to mislead you. I didn't know about the empress's plan until we returned."

And still he'd kissed me. The knife of betrayal dug deeper, and I wanted to hurt him as much as I hurt. "You knew that you were to return with the hero of Rodeni." I scoffed. "Surely you had *some* idea of my fate. And yet you promised me safe passage, knowing that it was a lie. You've lied to me from the beginning."

Torran stiffened as if struck, but he didn't deny my words. So much for the famed Valovian personal honor.

"If we rescue Cien," Chira said, her voice fierce, "then the empress will let you go. Torran made her vow—"

"That's enough," Torran said.

Chira glared at him, but he stared her down. She dropped her eyes to the floor, though her expression remained furious.

Torran ran a hand down his face, then straightened. His expression turned cold and harsh, and it transformed him into the general who'd thwarted FHP forces again and again. The stark difference highlighted just how much he had relaxed around us in the past few days. Or at least how much he'd *pretended* to.

And I'd fallen for it. I bit my lip against the fresh wave of pain.

"FHP is denying all involvement," Torran said at last. "They say that Commodore Morten was discharged over a year ago and that he doesn't represent FHP interests."

"Of course they are," I muttered. They could be in it up to their eyeballs—and likely were—and they'd still deny everything. "What are the kidnappers demanding?"

When Torran hesitated, I laughed without humor.

"Your empress is going to kill me. I deserve to know why I'm dying."

"They want guaranteed shipping rights in Valovian space," Nilo said, "and access through all of our wormholes."

I rocked back on my heels. So not much then, just what we'd fought a decades-long war for, until both sides had determined that it was too costly for too little gain. The resulting peace treaty had returned us to the status quo, with neither side happy about it.

Were the Feds reevaluating that decision, or was the Valovian Empire using a convenient kidnapping to justify breaking the treaty?

Either way, war loomed on the horizon.

And an innocent seven-year-old kid was smack in the middle of it. None of us had asked for this shitty hand that life had dealt, but it wasn't Cien's fault that his uncle was an enormous asshole.

I met Torran's eyes. "We're going to find Cien. And when we do, you're going to board *Starlight* with us and escort us all the way back to Bastion, where we'll happily boot your ass out. If your empress has other ideas, then you'll voluntarily become *our* hostage until we get to Bastion. Refuse and you won't make any progress on the kidnapping at all because you'll be too busy trying to keep us pinned down."

"You're not really going to help him, are you?" Lexi asked.

"No, I'm not. I'm helping the kid, and I'm helping myself, and I'm helping you all. General Fletcher can fall in a volcano as far as I'm concerned."

"I agree to your terms, Captain Zarola," Torran said.

"At least until some better deal comes along," I taunted. "I've seen exactly how much your promises are worth."

He flinched again.

I spun away from him and landed in the first chair I found. My ragged, bleeding wounds were dangerously close to becoming visible. "Let's get to work," I snapped.

"Tavi," Kee said over the comm. The compassion in her tone was nearly enough to smash the fragile hold I had on my emotions.

"Later," I commanded, my voice harsher than it should've been. I winced and stared at the display in front of me without seeing anything.

It took a few blinks, but eventually the image resolved itself into the zoomed-in picture of Commodore Morten. I stared at the face of the person I hated most in the galaxy—at least until Torran had done a bang-up job trying to steal the title.

I turned to Chira, determined to completely ignore Torran for the next ten days, and pointed at the screen. "Was this building searched?"

She glanced at Torran, but when I didn't move my attention from her, she nodded. "Nothing was found."

"Were their locations before this traced?"

"No. As far as we can tell, they'd been inside for a week without leaving, and the surveillance video doesn't go back far enough to catch their entrance."

"So they knew about the surveillance capabilities of the city. Who has that information?"

She shrugged. "Too many people to run down."

"I want a list." I turned to Kee. "How long until you'll get the data from the transport?"

"I should have it by tomorrow morning," she said. "I will let you know when it's ready."

I nodded my thanks. "Until then, I want you tracking Morten. The asshole isn't as smart as he thinks he is, so he made a mistake. We just have to find it."

"I'll find him," she promised.

Finally, I turned to Nilo. "I want a new brief, one that includes *all* of the information you have, not just the pieces you feel like sharing. You have one hour."

He raised an eyebrow. "Or?"

"Or I start making your lives very, very difficult." My lips curved but it was less smile and more warning.

Nilo grinned at me, unfazed. "I'll have it ready."

THE REST OF THE DAY PASSED IN COLD SILENCE. MY HEART was bleeding, and I couldn't get it to stop, so I ignored the wound. I didn't know how Torran had burrowed quite so deep, but it just made the betrayal sting all the more.

He tried to talk to me three times, and three times I ignored him.

Dinner was grim and quiet, and no one lingered. The door to my suite had barely closed behind me when it opened again, and Lexi stepped inside.

I summoned a wan smile. "You drew the short stick, huh?"

Her answering smile was kind. "Someone had to beard the lion." She switched to sign language. "Do you want to leave tonight? Kee and I can get us out, even with the telekinetic."

I shook my head. They would be expecting us to make a break for it tonight. I had no doubt that Kee and Lexi *could* do it, but we didn't need to take extra risks. Torran wasn't the only one who knew how to lull someone into lowering their guard.

And there were still too many unknowns. If Morten *wasn't* sanctioned by the FHP, then I needed to stop him before he started another interstellar war.

"The kid isn't at fault," I signed. "And until we know what's going on, we need to keep digging."

Lexi sighed and flopped into my guest chair. "I told them you'd say that," she said. She opened her arms and Luna hopped into her lap. She gave the little burbu a good petting before she looked up and met my eyes. "Want to talk about it?"

I sat on the edge of the bed. "I thought Morten was done fucking us over." It wasn't what she meant, but it was the only thing I could talk about without wanting to cry.

Lexi's face darkened. "I should've stabbed that little weasel when I had the chance."

"Then we would've never gotten out. We did the best we could with what we had." Just like we were doing now.

"For what it's worth, Chira said Torran really *didn't* know about the empress's plan," Lexi said, "and that he was furious when he found out." I glared at her and she raised the hand that wasn't petting Luna. "Don't shoot the messenger."

"What if I just *stab* the messenger, instead?"

"I'm not making excuses for him, because what he did was shitty, but I can tell you care for him, at least as a friend." She raised her eyebrows but didn't comment on whether she thought it was more than that. "You don't have to forgive him, but you should at least hear him out before you chuck him into a volcano."

Based on my current level of anger, a volcano might be too good for him.

A bitter smile touched Lexi's mouth. "Kee said you told him about Rodeni, or at least enough that he could draw the right conclusions about what really went down. But before you explained, how did it look from his side? Like you ruthlessly murdered a bunch of innocents. Every story has two sides." She eased Luna off her lap and stood. "Just think about it."

"It *hurts*," I whispered.

Lexi sat next to me and wrapped her arms around me. "I know," she murmured.

My control snapped and the pain and grief poured out of me in a silent deluge of tears. Lexi procured a handkerchief from one of her hidden pockets and pressed it into my hands, then went back to hugging me, offering quiet strength and support.

After I'd finally cried myself out, I squeezed her tight. "Thanks, Lexi."

"Of course." She leaned back and pinned me with a hard stare. "Don't forget, while you're so busy taking care of everyone else, that it's okay to let someone take care of *you,* occasionally, too."

"I don't—" Her stare got fiercer, so I raised my hands in surrender. "I'll try."

She squeezed me again. "Get some sleep. Tomorrow is a new day."

I bid her good night and she left with a final wave. My room felt emptier without her presence, but overall, I felt better. The emotional maelstrom had settled a bit, bringing clarity. I would find Cien, I would stop whatever war was brewing, and then I would get the hell out of Valovian space.

If the thought made my heart ache, I ignored it.

CHAPTER TWENTY-FOUR

I slept poorly and arose far too early again. It was becoming a bad habit, but it likely wouldn't get better until my team and I were safely back in Fed space. Then I would sleep for a week and forget I'd ever met General Torran Fletcher.

A breakfast tray was waiting outside my door, topped by a beautiful envelope with my name written on it in the same strong hand that had written yesterday's note.

I stepped over it without stopping.

In the kitchen, I fed Luna the food I'd brought for her. Once she started eating, I made my way to the gym. I felt an urgent need to punch something.

Unfortunately, the gym wasn't empty. Torran and Varro were sparring. I averted my eyes and steeled my spine. I wasn't a coward, so I wouldn't run like one. The two of them weren't using the punching bag, and they were far enough away that I wouldn't interrupt them.

Since I didn't know how to use any of the other equipment, it was either boxing or dynamic stretching. I probably *should* do some fluid, meditative stretches to recenter myself, but I felt like some old-fashioned violence.

I wrapped my knuckles with the wraps I'd brought with me, then did a few minutes of warm-up. The first punch connected hard and sent a satisfying jolt up my arm. I fell into the rhythm, dodging and weaving to avoid imaginary blows.

By the time Eli appeared behind the bag to stabilize it, I'd worked up a sweat and my lungs were heaving like bellows.

"You done?"

I could barely hear him over the sound of my own breathing. But if I quit, then I had to face the rest of the day. "Five more minutes."

"You want to beat on a live target instead?"

I stopped long enough to look him up and down. Eli wasn't the least bit sweaty, which meant he hadn't even started his workout, and my arms felt like lead weights. He outclassed me on my best day and today was far from that. "No, thanks. I'm not volunteering to be your punching bag."

"Spoilsport." He grinned at me, but under the grin, I could see the concern lurking in his eyes.

"I'm fine," I told him. "Go beat up someone else."

His gaze cut to the two Valoffs sparring nearby. "I would, gladly, but I don't think you'd let me."

"You'd be surprised," I muttered.

Eli barked out a laugh. "Just say the word, Captain."

I pressed my lips together and spent five minutes trying to drive the bag through Eli's grip. It didn't work, and my arms felt like wobbly pudding by the time I was done.

Eli shook his head. "You're going to feel that tomorrow."

I bent over and shook out my arms. "I feel it today."

"You should soak in the heated pool," Torran said. "It is good for sore muscles."

I flinched in surprise, mostly because he was closer than I'd expected. As much as I wanted to ignore him until the end of time, I was a damned adult. I could act like it, even if it killed me, so I straightened, turned to him, and stared at his chin. A smile was beyond me, so I didn't even try to summon one.

"Thank you for the suggestion, General Fletcher." The words were exquisitely polite, but my tone screamed, *Now kindly hurl yourself into the nearest star.* "If you'll excuse me."

I left without waiting for acknowledgment.

AFTER A SCALDING HOT SHOWER AND AN HOUR OUTSIDE with Luna, I felt marginally better. And every time I stepped over the tray at my door, I got a little stab of vicious satisfaction. The meal bar I ate tasted extra delicious with a side of spite.

I was going through Nilo's new brief for the third time when Kee bounced into the war room, slate held high. "I got it," she crowed. "It's just raw numbers right now, so I still need to sort through it, but I got it."

"Excellent work, Kee." I raised my hand for a high five, and she slapped her palm against mine. "Do you need help?"

She waved away the offer. "I think I can write a script to translate the coordinates into map locations." Her eyes lit up. "Maybe I can plot it in VR with street-level imagery."

"Time, Kee. Start with the basics—where it went and for how long. You can play with virtual reality once Cien is safe."

Kee wrinkled her nose at me and heaved out a dramatic sigh. "No one appreciates my art." When I just stared at her, she cracked and smiled. "Fine, fine. The basics first."

I suppressed my own grin, but it was difficult when she was so jubilant. "Thank you."

She sank down at the workstation beside me, humming under her breath. Her hands flew across her slate as she lost herself in the world of numbers and code. In her element, Kee was irresistible, and all of the Valoffs watched her with a kind of awed fascination.

Nearly everyone carried scars from the war, but Kee's were deeper than most. By the time she'd landed in my squad, she'd been so close to breaking that I'd stayed up nights watching her. But Kee was nothing if not resilient, and she'd refused to give up.

I would do *anything* to keep her and the rest of my team safe.

And, right now, that thing was finding a scared child who didn't deserve to be treated like a pawn. The new brief didn't shed much light on the kidnapping. If this really was everything that the Valoffs knew—and that was questionable—then we were all working with the same data now. Commodore Morten meant to use Cien as a lever, and the empress meant to use me. One wrong move and we'd face a return to war.

No pressure.

A shadow fell across my screen. "Have you eaten?" Torran asked quietly.

Out of the corner of my eye, I saw that he held the tray

that had spent the morning outside my door. "I ate a meal bar," I said without looking up. "You may dispose of that."

"Tavi, please—"

I sucked in a sharp breath. He'd so rarely called me by my first name and now it cut like a knife.

"I am sorry," he murmured. He left with a whisper of sound.

Kee slanted a glance at me, proving that she wasn't as oblivious as she seemed. "You okay?"

I shook my head slowly. "No, but I will be."

I SPENT THREE HOURS TRYING TO TRACE COMMODORE Morten's movements on the surveillance videos before giving up. The transport that he'd entered had made more than a dozen stops, half of them inside buildings with large amounts of traffic and no significant importance. Morten might be an asshole, but he knew how to run an operation. He had likely switched vehicles multiple times.

With no other leads, I watched the video of the kidnappers' transport again. It stopped at Torran's gate for pickup, then continued on to the edge of the forest, where it disappeared. I checked that final camera's video, watching two days flash past at high speed, but nothing else appeared.

Still, something about the dingy little monitoring station in the middle of the forest wouldn't leave me alone. I tried researching it, but the public data on it was surprisingly scarce. Torran wasn't kidding about the landowners' desire to keep people away. Trespassing in that part of the forest carried a hefty fine due to its proximity to the Imperial Palace, and the surrounding owners were all too happy to turn people in.

"Lexi," I asked over the comm, "did you look into the monitoring station?"

"Yes, but I didn't find much. It was built during the war as part of the global network of stations scanning for ships approaching from the wormhole closest to the human sectors. Several of the other stations have fallen into disrepair, but this one was deemed strategically important, so they've kept it running."

Her information matched mine. When I didn't respond, she asked, "Do you want me to look again?"

"If you have time, but your current project is higher priority." She, Eli, and Anja were quietly looking for signs the FHP had operatives on-planet. If we could find them, then they would likely lead us to Cien. And at this point, we needed to follow every possible lead.

My stomach rumbled and a glance outside confirmed it was fully dark. Midday had arrived, if it could be called that. I stood and stretched. My arms were already tightening up. "Has anyone seen Luna?"

My team shook their heads. It wasn't too odd for her to disappear, but it was strange that she hadn't let me know about her lack of lunch. That probably meant that she'd conned one of the Valoffs into feeding her, so I started my search in the kitchen.

I heard Luna before I saw her. When I rounded the final corner, I found her sitting on Torran's shoulder, watching him cook. She turned and chirped at me in greeting, then sent me a wave of affection that nearly buckled my knees. At least one of the monsters in the room was happy to see me.

The bubbling pot on the stove smelled delicious and my stomach rumbled louder. Torran glanced at me without ever meeting my eyes. "This is ready if you are hungry."

Pettiness warred with hunger.

When Torran didn't say anything else and didn't press, hunger won. "I could eat," I said stiffly. "Thank you."

Rather than lessening the tension in Torran's spine, my words seemed to make it worse. He pulled two bowls from the cabinet and filled each with rice and what looked suspiciously like my favorite tomato and chickpea curry.

Someone on my team had sold me out.

Rather than handing me one of the bowls, he carried them both to the table. He murmured something to Luna, and she jumped down and returned to her food bowl, which was filled with the same meat and veggie mixture that had been on the tray for her yesterday.

"Captain Zarola, please join me."

I narrowed my eyes and remained where I was. "Who told you about the curry?"

One corner of Torran's mouth tipped up. "Your recovery specialist might've mentioned something about it after Eli attempted to break my face this morning."

Lexi was giving Torran a chance to explain himself, and a reason for me to stay long enough to listen to it. I wondered if he knew that she'd provided him with an opening, and if he'd use it or throw it away.

Eli, on the other hand, had just wanted to smash in Torran's face, and right now, I was firmly on Team Eli. I stopped avoiding Torran's gaze and traced my eyes over his features. Sure enough, a bruise had started to darken his jaw. "You let him hit you."

"'Let' is a stretch. I agreed not to use my ability and Eli was highly motivated. The hit was fair." Torran gestured at the food on the table. "We should eat before it gets cold."

I stared at the table as if it were a dangerous animal and didn't move.

"I will eat elsewhere if you prefer," Torran said, his voice quiet.

I reminded myself that I was an adult, and Lexi wouldn't have given him my favorite recipe if she didn't think he deserved a chance to be heard. And like it or not, I had to work with him for the next nine days, and likely longer, since I doubted the empress was just going to let us go even if we found her nephew. Why would she voluntarily lose a valuable bargaining chip?

I gingerly slid into the closer chair. When Torran remained standing, I waved at the seat opposite me. "It's fine."

He sat, and we dug in. The delicious flavor of the curry warmed my mouth and soothed the ragged edges of my soul. I could tell that he hadn't had quite the right spice blend, but he'd gotten surprisingly close. I focused on my food and let the silence stretch. It felt tense and awkward, but breaking it meant that I'd have to reveal exactly how much he'd hurt me.

I had nearly finished my bowl when Torran said, "I can get you and your team out tonight. You'll have to leave your ship, for now, but I'll return it as soon as I am able."

I blinked at him. "Is this some kind of test? I take the offer, and the empress shoots me out of the sky and kicks off another war?"

Torran's mouth flattened into a grim line. "No. You would be snuck out. Empress Nepru would not know you were gone until you were already in Bastion."

"And what of your nephew?"

His gaze slid down and away. "My team and I will continue to search."

"What aren't you telling me?" I demanded.

"It doesn't concern you."

"If the empress is willing to sacrifice Cien, then what will she do to you once she realizes you've let her backup plan slip through your fingers?"

"It doesn't concern you," he repeated. "I vowed safe passage. I will keep the promise. If your ship cannot be recovered, I will replace it."

The thought of losing *Starlight* was enough to steal my breath for a moment, but I returned to the question at hand. "What will happen to you?" I demanded, enunciating each word.

Torran sighed and rubbed his face. "I don't know. Perhaps nothing."

"And if it's not nothing?"

"Then I'll be tried for treason."

I blew out a slow breath. I might be furious and hurt, but despite all my talk of volcanoes, I didn't want Torran *dead,* if for no other reason than his nephew was going to need all the support he could get once he returned home. "Why the change of heart?"

He shook his head. "It's not a change. I told you yesterday that no one was going to die. The preparations were underway, but tonight was the soonest I could get you out. I had hoped . . ."

When he didn't finish the thought, I prompted, "Had hoped what?"

"I had hoped that Cien would be found before you needed to leave," he said.

I stared at him for a long moment, weighing his sincerity. It could've easily been emotional manipulation, but it didn't feel like it. I tapped the table while I thought. "Tell me how you plan to get us out," I said at last.

"I have an acquaintance who makes regular supply runs to Bastion. She is strong enough to shield you from detection, and her ship is outfitted with appropriate hiding places if the authorities start searching."

"She's a smuggler."

Torran nodded. "One of the best."

I watched him carefully. "If we don't go tonight, could she get us out later?"

"Her normal supply run is next week, and that was my original alternative plan. But the longer you wait, the more danger you'll face." He met my eyes, his expression calm and clear. "You should go tonight."

"Did you really make the empress vow to let us go if we find your nephew?"

Torran sighed. "She made the vow, but Chira and I are the only witnesses."

I filled in the blanks for what he refused to say. "So if you were to sadly perish during the rescue, no one would know about the promise." I scoffed. "That's one way to treat personal honor."

Torran's eyes darkened, but he didn't comment one way or the other.

"Did your sister really want to marry into that family?"

"My sister and I are . . . not close. I cannot speak to her decision process."

I took a deep breath and blew it out slowly, then dropped my eyes to the table as I thought. Torran had been keeping secrets from the beginning, but I believed that his offer to get us out was genuine. So should we stay or go?

The pragmatic half of my brain wanted to leave immediately, as soon as I could gather my team and get us to safety. But a child's life was at stake, and none of this was Cien's fault. If we left, would Torran be able to find his nephew before something terrible happened to him?

I couldn't be responsible for a child's death, even indirectly. Torran loved his nephew, but he had still urged me to leave tonight. That, more than anything, made me believe that he sincerely desired to fulfill his vow of safe passage.

But belief wasn't enough. We had to come to a real understanding, and the only way to do that was to have a conversation guaranteed to be painful. I raised my eyes so I could watch his expression.

"Twice you've lied to me by omitting important information that I needed to know," I said, my tone unyielding. "That's two times too many. If you'd just told me the truth, then we could've worked together on a solution, but instead, you let me think that you'd stabbed me in the back. Why?"

Torran's spine straightened. "Some of us *do* care about keeping our promises, and I warned you that I was bound by many oaths. I had hoped that you would be safely off-planet before it became an issue, but I underestimated your team's skill and determination once again."

"How many more times is this going to be a problem? How many more secrets are you keeping?" I stabbed a finger at him, temper rising. "I may be only human, but I care about promises, too. And yours are putting my team in danger."

Torran stared at me for a long time, his expression intent. He seemingly came to a decision, because he stood and circled the table. When he knelt next to me, I frowned down at him. "What are you do—"

The rest of the question was lost as he silently raised his left arm, flipped open a knife with his other hand, and sliced the blade across his exposed wrist. He met my eyes. "*Cho wubr chil tavoz,*" he said, voice calm, as if deep red blood wasn't pouring down his arm.

"What the fuck?" I demanded. Torran didn't move. I grabbed the cloth napkin from beside my bowl and wrapped it tightly around his wrist, pressing on the wound to stanch the bleeding. "Havil!" I shouted before I remembered that I had a comm. I activated it and didn't bother to speak subvocally. "Someone get Havil to the dining area now. It's an emergency."

"On it," Eli responded.

A few moments later, both teams ran into the room. The Valoffs slid to a stop with shocked looks while my team shared my confusion. "What happened?" Lexi asked.

"Torran cut himself. Havil, don't just stand there. He needs medical attention."

Havil shook his head. "I cannot intervene."

I pinned him with a furious stare. "What do you mean? You're a medic and Torran needs help. Help him!" Under my fingers, the white napkin was slowly turning red.

Havil's expression went through a flurry of changes before he carefully asked, "Are you specifically directing me to stop the bleeding on your behalf?"

I blinked at the strange wording, but the ever increasing bloodstain held most of my attention. "Of course I'm asking you to stop the bleeding. What did you think I was doing?"

Havil sagged in relief and rushed forward. At his direction, I peeled back the impromptu bandage, and Havil gripped Torran's hand. As I watched, the deep gash in

Torran's wrist knit itself back together until only unblemished skin remained.

And through it all, Torran knelt silent and still.

Once Havil was done, he ushered everyone else out of the room, leaving Torran and me alone once again.

My heart thundered in my chest, and I took a moment to just breathe before I spoke. "Explain."

"You were right that my previous promises conflicted with my promise to keep you safe," Torran said, his voice quiet but firm. "Now we are a single unit by Valovian law and custom. Anything I know, I may share freely with you, prior oaths notwithstanding."

"What do you mean 'a single unit'?" I waved at his now-healed wrist. "What did you do?"

"I offered you a life debt and you accepted."

CHAPTER TWENTY-FIVE

I held up a hand as if I could physically push Torran's words away. "I did not accept. I don't know what a life debt is, but I don't want it. I release you."

Torran clasped my hand and pressed a gentle kiss to the pads of my fingers. "Thank you," he murmured.

My eyes narrowed. "That didn't do anything, did it?"

He shook his head, expression unreadable. "No, but I appreciate the sentiment." He rose and returned to his seat. Only the bloody napkin and the stained arm of his tunic indicated that anything unusual had happened.

Torran's hands rested on the table and his fingers slowly curled into fists. "The day after Cien was taken, Empress Nepru summoned me to the palace. The kidnappers had already been in contact, and the empress suspected that the FHP was involved. I was tasked with retrieving one of several prominent FHP heroes. I refused, but I was not given a choice. You happened to be in the right place at the right time—and you seemed like you might be able to find my nephew. You were my top pick."

"So you knew I was going to be in danger but promised me safe passage anyway."

"It was a promise I made with every intention of keeping. The empress has her agenda and I have mine. I want Cien found. I don't want another war."

I leaned back in my chair. So I wasn't the only one who thought war was on the horizon. "How do we stop it?"

"We can't, not if they're determined, but we can find Cien and get you off Valovia. They'll have to find something else to fight about."

I pivoted the conversation without warning. "What is a life debt and why was your team so shocked?"

Torran steadily met my gaze. "It is a very old custom. When *vosdodite* isn't enough or when honor demands more, a life debt is offered. If accepted, the two individuals are bound."

"How did I accept without knowing?"

"You stopped the bleeding."

I spread my hands in a gesture of helplessness. "So I was supposed to just let you bleed to death without doing anything about it?" I frowned. "This system seems rigged."

Torran smiled gently. "The bleeding would've stopped on its own, eventually. Deaths are rare, unless the cut is careless."

Realization dawned. "You tricked me. How do I release you?"

"You don't. Life debts are freely offered and withdrawn only once the debt is paid. It is up to the debtor to determine when that is."

I relaxed. "Okay, so you can just tell me everything I need to know and then withdraw the offer."

"I could," Torran agreed, something odd in his tone.

"Don't tell me you intended to do more than that? What *else* does a life debt entail?"

"The reason that a life debt binds two people so tightly that they are seen as one in Valovian law is because I became your shield the moment you accepted." He put his left wrist over his heart and met my eyes, his expression searing in its intensity. "I will put your life above my own until the debt is paid. I will protect you from dangers seen and unseen, from every quarter, until I prevail or my body fails. Your happiness and safety are my singular goals."

I swallowed the wave of emotion that rose at his words. My heart, being the soft thing that it was, attempted to leap out of my chest and straight into his arms. It didn't care about betrayal or lies or impossibility. It knew what it wanted—and it wanted Torran.

"How long do you think it'll take you to feel like you've paid the debt?" I asked.

"Once I've regained your trust and returned you safely to human-occupied space, I will reevaluate," Torran said with every indication that he was serious.

"That's a lot to do this afternoon if you still think I should leave tonight."

"I will travel with you."

My mouth popped open. "But what about your nephew?"

"My team will search in my absence. Putting your life above mine wasn't just words, Tavi. A life debt supersedes all other ties."

I sighed and pressed my fingers together. I wanted to trust him, but he'd burned me before. "If you're doing this just to manipulate me, then I'm going to make your life debt literal and kill you. You know that, right?"

He flinched and bowed his head. "I am sorry that I've given you reason to doubt my honor so thoroughly. It is an error I intend to fix, starting now. Ask me anything and I will answer."

I didn't even hesitate. "Did you know the empress planned to kill me when you asked me to take the job?"

"No. But after we arrived, Nilo informed me that he'd been hearing whispers about *something* happening in less than two weeks, which is why I urged you to work quickly. I did not know the full extent of those plans until yesterday morning when I spoke to Empress Nepru. Chira and I both tried to talk her out of it."

I did the mental math. Yesterday morning was *after* we'd investigated the garage and the route the kidnappers had taken. The tight knot of hurt unclenched in my chest. He hadn't known that the empress was going to kill me when he'd kissed me.

"How did you get her to promise to let me go if I found your nephew?"

Torran gave me a grim smile. "I have a few levers of my own, things she would not like to be made public. I will not say more than that."

I drummed my fingers on the table. "If I ask you to do something, do you have to because of the debt?"

He shook his head. "It doesn't work like that."

"What if it'll make me happy?"

His expression softened. "Your happiness is my goal, but the debt doesn't require me to do anything against my will. I might *choose* to do something that will make you happy, but it's still my choice."

I let out a slow breath, relieved. I could deal with the debt as long as I knew that he was free to make his own choices. "What did you say after you recklessly cut yourself?"

"*Cho wubr chil tavoz.* My life is yours."

"That doesn't sound like you have much of a choice," I said with a frown. "What am I supposed to do with you? Do I need to look after you or something? Is there a manual for this stuff?"

Torran's eyes crinkled at the corners as he fought to keep a straight face. "I'm not a pet. I can look after myself. There's no manual because you don't need to do anything. I am here to look after *you*." He leaned back in his chair. I thought it was meant to make him look nonthreatening, but it emphasized the breadth of his shoulders and the hard planes of his chest.

"Were we ever really friends, or was all of this"—I waved at his relaxed pose—"designed to get me to lower my guard?"

He sat forward, searing honesty on his face. "It was not a trick. I had intended to keep my distance, to stay cold and aloof, but you weren't the person I expected. You were kind and caring even when it was more work. You snuck past my guard and were impossible to resist. Your friendship means a great deal to me, and I am sorry that I made you feel otherwise."

I believed him, if only because he'd snuck under my guard, too—in more ways than one. "Why did you kiss me, really?" The question popped out without thought.

Torran's mouth tipped into a slow, melting smile that matched the heat in his eyes. "I wanted to." His eyes dropped to my mouth. "Shall I demonstrate again?"

I shifted in my seat as the ever-present chemistry between us burned brighter. "No," I said, my voice unsteady. "Not while you're bound to me with a life debt."

He rose and stalked around the table. Sheer instinct forced me to my feet, but I was torn between standing my ground and fleeing like a scared rabbit. Staying won, but only because my feet felt glued to the floor.

Torran stepped so close that our chests brushed, and I had to tip my head back to hold his gaze. Desire thundered through my veins, driven by my pounding heart and the stark hunger carved into his face. He leaned down, and my eyes dropped half closed. But rather than kissing me, he brushed his cheek against mine in a barely there caress.

"My choices remain my own," he whispered into my ear, his voice dark with promise.

He could read a dictionary to me, and as long as he used that tone, I'd never ask him to stop.

My hands flexed at my sides as I forced myself to resist the temptation of his body. The last two days had been a whirlwind of wild emotions. We'd barely started back on the path to trust. No matter how much I wanted him—and desire pulsed with every beat of my heart—a physical relationship was the worst possible idea.

Even if my body *vehemently* disagreed.

"Why did you say you *can't* go to bed with me?" After I'd gotten over the hurt of the rejection, I'd wondered at the slightly odd wording.

"There were too many things unresolved between us. Too many secrets. It would've been a betrayal, even if you didn't know about it." The searing heat of his expression weakened my knees and made my body throb. "But that is no longer an issue," he growled. "Ask me again."

Backing away from him felt like losing a limb, but the second step was easier. "Not while you're bound," I repeated. I glanced up at him from under my lashes. "But if you'd like to renounce your debt . . ."

"Clever," he murmured, "but you'll have to try harder than that to get rid of me."

I couldn't hide my grin. "It was worth a shot."

I shook my arms as if I could shake off the desire simmering in my blood. I gathered up our dishes and headed for the sanitizer. I hadn't found it the first day because it looked nothing like I'd expected, but it cleaned the dishes and that's what mattered.

Torran followed me.

"What are you doing?" I asked once I was done with the dishes. When he didn't answer, I asked, "Is this part of the debt?"

"I'm ensuring your safety," he said. The tone was light, but his expression was deadly serious.

"Is there some reason you think I'm *not* safe in your house?" He shook his head, so I waved my hands at him. "Shoo. Go bother someone else."

He didn't move, but one side of his mouth curled up into a delicious grin.

"I *order* you to go away," I tried.

Instead of leaving, he stalked closer. "I'll remind you once again," he murmured, "that I don't have to follow your orders."

"You may not *have* to," I said, secretly relieved that orders didn't actually work, "but you'd better consider doing it anyway or you are not going to appreciate where I put my boot in relation to your posterior."

He chuckled as the threat bounced off him without making the slightest impact.

I sighed. "If you're going to tail me anyway, we might as well go see what my team thinks about leaving tonight."

I had a pretty good idea how they would vote, but I wanted to discuss the decision. And the comm had been unusually silent since Torran's little stunt, so I needed to head off any rumors before they got started.

"After you," Torran said, sweeping his hand toward the war room.

I rolled my eyes, but I led him out of the kitchen.

AFTER AN HOUR OF DISCUSSING IT, MY TEAM DECIDED TO STAY. Lexi and Eli voted to leave today while Anja, Kee, and I voted to stay for another week to try to find Cien.

Lexi and Eli were the most pragmatic members of the group. It wasn't that they hated kids, it was more that they had weighed the risks and decided to protect the ones they loved. But once they were outvoted, they threw themselves back into the search without a single grumble of complaint.

Much to my relief, Torran did eventually leave me on my own. But as soon as he'd cleared the door, Kee spun her chair around to face me. "Spill."

"About what?" I tried.

Kee just tilted her head and gave me an unamused look.

"Torran vowed a life debt to me."

Kee waved at the other Valoffs still in the room, all of whom were eavesdropping and not even being subtle about it. "They explained that part. Why did he do it?"

"I told him that his promises were putting my team in danger and that I was tired of it. Apparently, a life debt was his solution."

Kee sighed, and I knew that sigh. I shook a finger at her.

"It wasn't romantic. It was scary and traumatizing, and he won't take it back, so now we're bound together until he decides the debt is repaid."

"It's a little romantic," Anja said from my other side.

I spun to face her and caught Eli nodding behind her. I pointed at him. "Not you, too. You punched him in the jaw."

Eli lifted one shoulder. "He deserved it, but now he seems like he's making up for it."

I tossed up my hands. "Traitors, every one of you."

"A life debt is an extraordinary step," Chira said quietly. "It was not something he did at the spur of the moment, no matter what you said to him. I'm sure he had been considering it since our meeting with the empress."

I glanced at her and found Varro and Nilo nodding along with her words. "Is it true that he doesn't have to do what I tell him?"

Chira chuckled. "Does he seem like the type to do what you tell him?" She laughed again and then shook her head when she saw that I was serious. "A life debt is complicated, but it won't force him to act against his will. Order him around all you want—it won't do anything."

"Except amuse the rest of us," Kee added. "Though him having to obey your orders would've been fun, too."

"No, it wouldn't," I murmured.

She cocked her head at me, and I saw the exact moment the lightbulb went off. "You and him—oh." She scowled. "Oh. Yeah, that would be bad if he couldn't say no."

"You want to enlighten the rest of us?" Eli asked.

"No, she does not," I interrupted before Kee could speak. "Where are we on the investigation?"

"My script is almost done," Kee said. "I haven't found any sign of Morten, but I'm still looking."

Lexi said, "I'm tracking down a possible lead on the monitoring station, but I haven't found anything else."

"Something good?" I asked.

She shook her head. "I don't know yet."

"We haven't found anything, either," Eli said. Over the comm, he continued, "If FHP is here, they're staying well under the radar."

I fought the urge to move, to act, to do *something*. Zenzi had a population of more than two million. I wasn't going to just bump into one of the kidnappers by wandering around aimlessly. Sorting through the data was the best option, but it felt like doing nothing.

TWENTY MINUTES LATER, KEE BOUNCED IN HER SEAT WITH A TRI-umphant sound. "The script is done. Who wants to see what this transport was up to, hmm?"

Torran returned to the room, and we all crowded around Kee's workstation—everyone except Lexi. "Lex?" I asked.

She waved her fingers without removing her focus from her workstation. "I'm busy. Don't wait. I'll get the highlights later."

Kee nodded and pulled up a map that had a few points marked. "This is the transport owner's house," she said, pointing at the first. She moved to the rest of the marks, naming them as she went. "Parking garage, Torran's house, and where the transport was abandoned."

The first few minutes were all trips to and from the owner's house, but the date in the corner jumped wildly between each trip. "This is the data from before the vehicle was stolen," she explained.

As we watched the little animated transport on the map,

it left the owner's house and drove straight to the parking garage. "Is this the theft?"

"No, this is a month ago," Torran said.

Sure enough, the transport returned to the owner's house. It made a few more trips to unlabeled locations, then sat for a week. Finally, it moved to the garage and stayed there.

"I want a list of all of these locations," Torran said.

Kee smiled at him. "I'm way ahead of you. I have a raw data list I can share, and my new script is working on auto-tagging all of the locations."

"For someone who doesn't use their transport often, that seemed like a lot of trips," I said. "Did you check the owner's connections?"

"We didn't find anything," Torran said, "but you're right, the data is suspicious."

The next time the transport moved, it followed the route the kidnappers had taken. After the final pickup, it moved toward the forest, but rather than stopping at the marked abandonment point, it kept going. Kee zoomed in, and the map location perfectly overlaid the monitoring station. The transport paused for a moment, then turned around and returned to the expected point.

"Why would it go to the monitoring station?" Eli asked. "What's there?"

"There's nothing there," Torran said. "We checked it after the kidnapping, and Tavi and I checked it again yesterday."

Lexi cleared her throat and pointed at her workstation. "Yes, but did you look *under* it?"

CHAPTER TWENTY-SIX

Lexi's smug expression meant she was very pleased with herself. She looked at me. "I started digging again when you asked me about it the second time," she said. "I know you said it wasn't a priority, but I figured whatever was bothering you was worth looking into, and I was right." She winced apologetically. "But it wasn't cheap."

I suppressed my own wince. Lexi's "not cheap" generally meant thousands and thousands of credits—if not tens of thousands. But if it led to Cien, then it would be worth it, especially because I totally intended to hold Torran to his promise of bonus pay.

Lexi's screen displayed a scan of a very old set of blueprints. It took me a moment to figure out exactly what I was looking at because all of the labels were in Valovan. The blueprints showed a cross-section of the monitoring station. The little building sat on top of a much larger underground structure.

I sucked in a sharp breath. "All the equipment on top of the building isn't for the monitoring station itself, but ventilation for the underground rooms. *That's* what was bothering me about the building."

"There's also this," Lexi said, pointing at a tunnel that led off the page. It was labeled with an arrow and Valovan text. "I'm not a fluent reader, but as far as I can tell, that says 'to palace.'"

"It does," Nilo confirmed quietly. The charming Valoff had used the excuse of looking at the screen to ease closer to Lexi. She didn't seem uncomfortable, so I left it alone.

I turned to Torran and pointed at the screen. "Did you know about this?"

He held my gaze, his expression shuttered. "No."

"Does the empress?"

This time he hesitated. "I don't know, but it is likely because it seems as if it was designed as an emergency shelter."

Dread pooled in my stomach. If it had taken Lexi this long to find the information on the monitoring station, then a group of FHP soldiers wouldn't have just stumbled across it. But if someone had tipped them off . . . Surely the empress wouldn't use her own nephew as a pawn to start a war.

Right?

The grim set of Torran's mouth told me that his thoughts tracked with mine. "Perhaps we should keep this information to ourselves for now," I said. "Just in case someone in the palace isn't trustworthy."

Eli looked at the map still up on Kee's screen. "Is the monitoring station far enough away that Cien couldn't contact someone in one of those fancy houses at the edge of the forest?"

"No," Torran said. "Cien is strong enough that he would be able to reach me here from that distance."

"So he's either drugged or being shielded," Havil said. He took a deep breath. "I will need to accompany the assault group in case it's the former."

The Valoffs offered him sympathetic looks. As an empath, being in the main assault group would be miserable, but he still planned to do his duty.

"Cien might not be there," Lexi pointed out. "Just because this exists doesn't mean that it's the answer."

It was the bucket of cold reality we all needed, but that didn't make it any more pleasant to hear.

"We still have to check it out," Kee argued. "It's too much of a coincidence to ignore."

"I don't disagree," Lexi said. "But I don't want you to be heartbroken if all we find is dust and rats. Temper your expectations."

Kee grinned at her. "You know I won't."

Lexi's sigh covered a grin of her own. "I know."

"Assuming we don't want to get permission from the empress to enter from the palace side, how do we get in?" I asked.

Nilo and Lexi both pointed at the same corner of the building. Nilo gestured for Lexi to explain. "There is an access ladder here," she said, "but it wasn't meant to be the main entry. The landing is twelve meters down. Our best bet will be to skip the ladder entirely and fast rope in."

I squinted at the blueprint, trying to see what they saw. "Where's the door? I would've noticed an unexplained door, but there wasn't one. It's just a room full of old equipment."

Lexi pointed at a tiny squiggle on the blueprint. "The hatch is in the floor. If you didn't notice it, then it must be controlled remotely. This blueprint doesn't include a wiring diagram, but Kee and I can find the control."

I rubbed my eyes and tried to think of all the things that could go wrong. "If the bunker is supposed to be an emergency shelter for the palace, then the monitoring station will likely be under surveillance. We need to figure out how and where so whoever is downstairs—if anyone—doesn't know we're coming."

"I'm on it," Kee said. "Though if it's truly an emergency shelter, then it may be a closed system. In that case, I'll need to be nearby to figure it out."

"I can take you," Varro said, speaking for the first time. The weapons specialist seemed content to remain in the background, observing everyone around him, and I got the impression that he saw more than he let on.

And it did not escape my notice that he volunteered every time it involved spending time with Kee. I wasn't sure if he was still trying to make up for his terrible first impression or if he had an entirely different motivation, but Kee smiled at him. "Thank you."

Eli grimaced. "I just love attacking an unknown number of soldiers in a fortified underground bunker," he said. "It really livens up my day."

"At least we have a telekinetic on our side this time," Anja said with a grin. "*They'll* run away from *us*."

I didn't exactly share her optimism, but I hoped she was right. "Do we have everything we need, or do we need to make a trip to *Starlight*?"

"Going to your ship is not a good idea," Torran murmured.

"Chira will get you whatever you need, and it would be best if you wore Valovian armor."

"We'll need the armor soon, then, so we have time to get used to it," Eli said. He glanced out the window at the dark sky. "It's already after midday, so tonight will be cutting it close, even if Kee and Lexi can get us in."

"Not tonight," I said. I held up a hand to ward off the protests. "You know I don't want a child to suffer for any longer than necessary, but if we go in half-cocked, then we're more likely to run into problems. We'll plan for tomorrow night when most of the guards will be asleep. That gives us a day and a half to come up with a solid plan, do some training together, and get used to the armor. If Lexi and Kee can't find a way in, then we'll reevaluate tomorrow afternoon. Objections?"

No one objected.

"Okay, Kee and Lexi, you're on access. Figure out a way to get us in without being seen. Take Varro with you if you need to be on-site."

"I'll go with them," Nilo said. The charming grin was back, filled with mischief. "I know a thing or two about getting into a building unseen."

Lexi rolled her eyes but didn't object.

I turned to Eli and Anja. "Work with Chira to get us the weapons and armor we're going to need." When they nodded, I moved to Havil. "Gather medical supplies. I know you can heal, but if you are hurt or overtaxed, then we'll have to triage injuries ourselves, so we'll need bandages, medicine, and trauma kits."

He dipped his head. "I will have everything ready in an hour."

"Torran and I will do some initial planning, then we'll

talk everything through once you all are done with your individual pieces. Sound good?" Everyone nodded. "Then let's get to it. Good luck. Be careful."

TORRAN AND I RETREATED TO HIS OFFICE SO WE COULD TALK without interrupting Lexi and Kee, who were trying to find a remote way into the underground bunker. We pulled the blueprint up on the wall display, and I stared at the little squiggle that was going to be our entrance point.

I was kind of with Eli on this one—attacking an unknown number of fortified enemies wasn't my favorite thing. I wanted to save the kid, but not at the expense of my team.

"I don't suppose you have a whole squad of telekinetics who would like to take this mission?" I asked.

Torran grimaced. "No. There are a few in the imperial guard, but alerting them isn't the best idea for obvious reasons."

I paced, too antsy to sit still. There were too many unknowns, and I wasn't sure any of them would be resolved by tomorrow night. "This is such a bad idea," I mumbled to myself.

Torran stopped me with a hand on my arm. He waited until I met his eyes. "You don't have to go," he said. "You and your team can remain here."

I sighed. "We have to go. Now it's about more than a missing child. I don't have much of a voice with the FHP, but I will do everything I can to prevent another war."

"And if it *is* the FHP?"

"Then I'll go public. Normal citizens don't want another war. We still haven't recovered from the last one. If I can sway public opinion, then it might be enough."

"And what will the FHP do?"

My smile was grim. "They'll try to silence me, of course."

"They'll hunt you," Torran said. "You won't be safe."

I nodded once, sharply. If it came to that, I'd have to send my parents into hiding—my parents, who'd lived in the same house for forty years. It would break their hearts, but they would understand. They knew the cost of war.

We all did.

I smiled at him, trying to lighten the mood. "So make sure you fulfill your debt before it comes to that, okay?" I turned to the displayed blueprint before he could respond. "Now, let's see if you live up to your reputation, General. How do we get in safely?"

Torran's gaze lingered on my face for a long moment before he reluctantly turned to the display. "The entrance is designed to be easy to defend, so we need to get past it before they know we're there. That means speed and stealth. Your team will need to allow my team to mentally shield them at least until we're inside."

I remembered the cool press of Torran's mind against my own in the parking garage. Then I remembered what had happened next. My cheeks heated. A peek at Torran revealed that his gaze was fixed on me, a hungry expression on his face.

He stalked closer, the silver in his eyes expanding. "Perhaps we should practice," he coaxed, his voice deep.

A throb of yearning tugged on me, but I straightened and put a hand on his chest. "Not while you're bound," I reminded him quietly.

His eyes dropped half closed and his mouth curled into a tiny, satisfied smile. "I was referring to the shielding, Captain."

"Sure you were," I whispered. I bit my bottom lip and his gaze zeroed in on the motion. His muscles locked tight before he growled something under his breath. He pivoted away before he spun back and opened his arms, a challenging light in his eyes.

"Torran," I protested.

"Are hugs forbidden now, too?"

With the way I felt right now, they probably should be, but I just shook a warning finger at him. "A hug *only*."

"On my honor," he agreed quietly.

I eased into his arms and knew immediately that this had been a mistake. Because under all of the hungry looks and burning desire, there was a deep well of care. And my heart was far more susceptible to caring than it was to lust.

He held me lightly, gently, and when I remained tense, he ran a soothing hand down my back and played with the ends of my hair. "Relax, Tavi," he murmured, his voice a low rumble.

I wanted to hear it again. I gingerly laid my head against his shoulder and demanded, "Tell me something about yourself. Why did you join the military?"

"It was expected," he said. "My father was a general, a decorated war hero, as was my grandfather. I learned strategy from the best." He sighed. "I rose through the ranks quickly and everyone assumed it was nepotism. And it was, of a sort. I'd been taught by two of our greatest military strategists. They didn't have to help me get promoted because they'd already taught me everything they knew."

"You were one of our primary targets," I admitted. "But you never got close to the front lines."

His chuckle had a bitter bite. "I spent plenty of time at

the front," he said. "Telekinetics, even generals, are not to be wasted. But we didn't announce my presence. I'm not *that* bad at strategy." He paused, as if weighing his words, then admitted, "I was on Rodeni the day you attacked."

I leaned back and met his eyes. "Really?"

He nodded. "I was a few kilometers away from the blast, organizing the assault that would've wiped out the remaining FHP forces." His eyes darkened. "The attack on civilians changed my plan."

I thought of Lexi's words about how every story had two sides. I wanted to explain more of my side, but it wasn't only my life on the line if word got back to the FHP. I clenched my teeth and stared at his chin.

Torran's fingers ghosted along my jaw. "Someday, when I've earned your trust, I would like to hear the truth of what happened. It will go no further than me, I swear it, but my decisions that day haunt me."

I closed my eyes against the agony of memory. "That day haunts me, too." A piece of the truth slipped out. "I lost half my squad trying to disable the bombs, and the rest of us barely made it out because Command left us to die. I resigned the same day."

Torran frowned. "But they flaunted you for months after that."

A bitter, self-mocking smile twisted my lips. "I'm aware. It was the only way to save Eli, Kee, and Lexi." I slid out of his arms and away from the horrors of memory. "So you will need to shield us. Can you shield everyone?"

The change of subject wasn't subtle, but Torran didn't call me on it. His fingertips hovered in the air for a second before he dropped his arm. "I can't shield all of you *and* communicate *and* fight. We'll have everyone pair up. My team members are strong enough to shield multiple people, but it's easiest one-on-one."

I turned back to the blueprint. "How many Valoffs are we going to find in the bunker?"

Torran's expression hardened. "I hope none."

I raised an eyebrow. "Does that seem likely?"

"No." He stared at the display. "Two or three mid-level civilian telepaths is most likely. In the worst case, it'll be at least two telepaths and a telekinetic, all military trained."

I rocked back and forth between my toes and heels. The thought of a telekinetic waiting for us in an underground bunker was the stuff of nightmares. "Can you subdue another telekinetic?"

His smile was quick and fierce. "Yes. But it is highly unlikely that it will be necessary."

I pointed at the cross-section of the underground bunker. Lexi hadn't been able to uncover a floor plan, so this was all we had. It didn't tell us how wide the bunker was, just how deep. "If you were using this as your base, where would you be?"

Torran pointed at a large room in the middle. "Somewhere on this level. It's easily defendable from either direction and most likely where bunks are."

I nodded my agreement. That's where I would set up, too. Now we just had to figure out how to get in without getting killed.

OUR FIRST TRAINING SESSION PROVED THAT THE VALOFFS WERE so used to telepathic communication that it was going to be a problem for the humans in the group. Sure, my team could communicate with our comms, but more often than not, we ended up going a completely different direction than Torran's team because our base strategies were so different.

Lexi flatly refused to accept telepathic communication from any of the Valoffs. It was her decision, so after a few experiments, I became the link between the two teams. Kee fitted Torran with an earpiece so he could hear our comms. It had a built-in mic, but he forgot to reply aloud often enough that we eventually nixed it. Instead, Torran looped me in to his telepathic orders, and I relayed them over the comm to my team. It wasn't perfect, but it worked well enough.

Luckily, the Valovian armor was much easier to get used to. It was lighter and more flexible than the armor we normally wore, and the protection was even better. We didn't look very much like Valoffs, not with our curvier builds and variable heights, but at least we were unrecognizable.

And it might be enough to cause another Valoff to hesitate.

It took several tries, but we finally moved enough as a team that we successfully cleared the shared hallway and all of its various rooms without anyone stepping into the line of fire or moving in the wrong direction.

Torran led, and I was positioned directly behind him. Half of his commands I could relay via hand signals and skip the comms altogether. Everyone had paired up with the most vulnerable team members—Kee and Havil—roughly in the middle. Lexi and Nilo were behind me, followed by Havil and Anja, then Kee and Varro. Eli and Chira brought up the rear.

If we had to split up, Eli and Chira would take Havil, Anja, Kee, and Varro while Nilo and Lexi joined Torran and me.

Torran didn't have anywhere to practice with ranged

weapons, so we decided that we would use our own plas pistols and rifles. Valovian weapons weren't that different, and we'd had some limited experience with them thanks to the war, but a delicate rescue mission wasn't the place to test our knowledge. We'd spent countless hours with our weapons. Familiar was better.

By the time we stripped off our armor and did a debrief, it was nearly dinnertime. Torran cooked us a local meal that was as delicious as it was unfamiliar. We'd all taken to sitting in the same seats we'd had on *Starlight* and yesterday's grim silence had been replaced by laughter and teasing.

But as the sun sank behind the horizon, my tension started climbing. Kee, Lexi, Nilo, and Varro planned to visit the monitoring station as soon as it was fully dark. Kee and Lexi hadn't been able to find a remote way to override the surveillance system, so they were going to have to get close to breach it.

I knew they could take care of themselves, but I never liked it when my team was in danger—especially when I wasn't there to watch their backs.

Havil and I cleaned the kitchen while the others went to get ready. "Are you okay?" Havil asked once we were alone.

"Yeah, I just overdid it this morning in the gym, and I'm worried about Lexi and Kee. Once they get back, I'm going to spend fifteen minutes in the heated pool."

Havil dipped his chin in acknowledgment. "I know that Nilo can seem rather frivolous at times, but he is an excellent soldier. He and Varro will keep your team safe."

I smiled gently at him. "Lexi and Kee can keep themselves safe. But that doesn't mean I don't worry about them."

CHAPTER TWENTY-SEVEN

It took Lexi and Kee four excruciating hours to break into the surveillance system without getting caught. But when they returned, just before dawn, it was with proof that *someone* was in the bunker. It was just a short clip, and it didn't show Cien or Morten, but it did show a person in dark armor walking across one of the underground rooms. It was all Kee could pull in the time she'd had.

We decided that it would be better to discuss it after sleep, so everyone headed to bed. I'd been up for nearly twenty hours, but the adrenaline of the last few wouldn't let sleep come easily.

I needed to relax, and short of sex—which I firmly put out of my mind before I could think about taut muscles, black hair, and dark eyes streaked with silver—the heated pool was the next best thing.

Since I didn't have a swimsuit, I changed into a pair of boyshorts and a sports bra, then covered them with the short robe I'd found in the bathroom. I piled my long, curly hair into a messy bun on top of my head. I looked ridiculous, but everyone else was either asleep or heading that way, so no one would know.

A fifteen-minute soak and then I would sleep.

The hallway was quiet and dim. I slipped through the house on silent feet and smiled when the pool room door slid open at my touch. The air was warm and humid, and I could already feel the heat working the knots from my sore arms.

I was so focused on getting into the heated water that I failed to notice the pool wasn't empty until I'd already dropped my robe and dipped a foot in. Movement in the corner of my eye startled me so badly that I screamed and flailed.

I lost my balance, but before I could flop into the water like a drunk fish, Torran's power clamped around my body and set me back on my feet.

"Are you all right?"

I glared at him. "You're supposed to be asleep!"

He tilted his head. "So are you."

Torran wasn't wearing a shirt and I could see the tops of his broad shoulders. The water obscured the rest of him. Was he wearing anything at all? I paused, torn. Getting into the pool with him was such a bad idea, but my arms ached. The heated water would do them good, and a shower just wasn't the same.

"Join me," he invited, his voice neutral.

Still, I hesitated. "You don't mind?"

He gestured around. "The pool is big enough for both of us."

I wasn't sure that statement was true, not with how

flushed I felt from looking at his shoulders, but I eased into the water with a hiss. It was delightfully hot, just shy of scalding. I wouldn't be able to stay long, but already I felt better. I tipped my head back against the edge and closed my eyes.

I dug my fingers into my left triceps, working on the knots. What I wouldn't give for a massage right now . . .

"Would you like some assistance?" Torran asked.

I opened my eyes, but he hadn't moved from his spot on the other side of the pool. "Are you reading my mind?"

"No." The corner of his mouth tipped up. "Were you thinking about my hands on you?"

Heat that had nothing to do with the water temperature burned through me. I hadn't been, but now I was. "I was wishing for a massage, if you must know. I overdid it a bit this morning."

This morning that felt like a hundred years ago.

"Come here and I will massage your arms for you."

Temptation, thy name was Torran Fletcher. I cleared my throat. "It's probably safer if I stay over here."

Torran frowned. "You think I'm a danger to you?"

"No," I said, drawing the word out. "Not like you're thinking."

His frown melted into a heated smile. "Then let me help you. I would do it from here," he said as his power gently clamped around my biceps, "but I need to reserve my strength for the attack." His tone turned gentle and coaxing. "And you need to be in top form, too. Let me help you. Please."

Despite the tumult of the past two days, I trusted him. He'd been looking out for me, in his own way, even when I thought he'd betrayed me. I crossed the distance separating us, until I was within arm's reach.

I held out my right arm. "Okay."

His long fingers circled my wrist and drew me closer. "Shh," he murmured when I stiffened. "I'm just making you more comfortable. I remember and respect the boundaries you've set."

Not while we're bound by a life debt.

Torran drew me into his lap, with my back against his chest. I found it impossible to relax when I was so close to him. Then his strong fingers started kneading the muscles of my shoulders, pressing into an incredibly tight spot just below my neck. I groaned and let my head drop forward.

Torran paused. "Tell me if it's too much."

"Keep going," I demanded.

His chuckle vibrated through me, but he returned to the massage. By the time he turned me so that he could work on my right arm, I'd forgotten everything except how good his hands felt. He had remained coolly professional, but I burned everywhere he'd touched.

And some places he hadn't.

Perched on his thigh with my right side facing him, I could feel the muscles of his leg shifting to keep us balanced on the edge of the pool. I wanted to straddle that thigh and rock against it until pleasure blotted out everything else.

I searched desperately for a distraction. Sitting like this, I could see his face and the careful concentration furrowing his brow. Tiny water droplets clung to his eyelashes, sparkling in the low light. The man was incredibly handsome. My eyes traced the line of his nose, the arch of his cheekbones, the lush slash of his lips.

And I knew exactly how good those lips felt against mine.

He glanced up, and I sucked in a breath at the sight of his eyes. Molten color—silver and teal and copper—blazed across his dark gray irises.

He froze, his hands hovering, not quite touching. "Are you okay? What's wrong?"

"Your eyes . . . are *you* okay?"

A grin pulled at the corner of his mouth. "You're in my arms, practically naked, and I get to put my hands on you. Did you expect me to be unaffected?" His expression turned serious. "But it doesn't matter. You are safe with me."

I swallowed. "I believe you. Do you want to stop?"

"*Nidru chich,*" he murmured. "But I will if you are uncomfortable."

I didn't know much Valovan, but every good soldier knew *nidru* was the word for "fuck" because we were all twelve at heart and learning foreign curse words had passed the time. If I had to guess, I'd roughly translate it as *fuck no*.

I smiled at his vehemence. I didn't want him to stop, but I *was* uncomfortable, just not for the reason he thought. I shifted, trying to ease the ache that burned low in my belly. I buried my head against his shoulder and told him the truth. "I wish we weren't bound by a life debt."

"Why?"

"Because I would really like to take you to bed."

He turned to stone under me before groaning, low and deep. "Shall I renounce the debt and redeclare it in the morning?"

I chuckled against his shoulder and shook my head. "How do you know that I wouldn't just let you bleed to death if you tried?"

"You wouldn't," he whispered. "Even if you hate the debt, you would still stop the bleeding."

He was right, of course. I wouldn't let him hurt for longer than necessary, no matter how much I disliked the life debt. Just the thought of the blood pouring from his wrist was enough to turn my stomach.

"I don't want you to be hurt again," I said. "If you insist on remaining in my debt, then you must *remain* in my debt."

He brushed his lips against my temple. "My debt is not yet paid, so I will remain. Will you wait?"

I lifted my head. "You want me to wait for you to fulfill your debt? Then what?"

His eyes gleamed with wicked heat. "Then I will take you to bed and pleasure you so thoroughly that you will forget the rest of the world exists—until you writhe and beg, and only then will I give you the relief you crave."

It should've sounded like the worst kind of braggadocio, but instead, it sounded like a promise, and I couldn't help the tiny moan that slipped past my lips as desire overwhelmed me.

He swallowed and his hands tightened against my skin, then with extreme self-control, he smoothed the burning hunger from his expression. "But for now, I will continue to work the knots out of your arms." He paused and met my eyes. "With your permission."

I shifted again at the thought of him touching me after all of that, knowing that he wanted me as much as I wanted him. "Won't that be torture?"

"I'll still be touching you. That's not torture."

"Maybe not for you," I grumbled. "I'm dying over here."

The silver swallowed his irises, and he went absolutely

still. The groan sounded like it was torn from the bottom of his soul. "*Now* it's torture," he murmured. "If you won't let me help you, then you should help yourself."

Was he saying what I thought he was saying? My face flamed red. "Help myself how, exactly?"

His eyebrows rose and his expression was pure sin.

Did I think my face was red before? It had nothing on the inferno in my cheeks now. "Here?" I squeaked. "Now?"

"Yes. I won't touch you," he vowed, his voice a deep, dark rumble.

I wrinkled my nose and waved an arm through the heated water around us. "In the pool?"

His grin was quick and fierce. "Is that your only objection?"

"What? I don't know. Maybe." Clearly, the thought of touching myself with him nearby had scrambled my brains.

I faintly heard a shower turn on, then Torran lifted me out of the water. The cool air caused goose bumps to rise across my skin and my nipples tightened into hard peaks. At least my sports bra was padded, so it wasn't completely obvious.

I wrapped my arms around his neck, surprised anew at the ease with which he carried me. "Where are we going?"

"Not the pool," he said, heat in his eyes.

Oh. *Oh.*

Before I could become too chilled, we reached the locker room, where one of the showers was already sending steam into the air. The lights were low, soft, preserving the intimacy of the moment.

Torran eased into the steamy water, then let go of my legs. I slid down his body until my toes touched the ground. I could feel him, hot and hard as steel against my belly. A peek revealed he had on tight black swim shorts that left very little to the imagination—and I had a fantastic imagination.

I reached for him, then aborted the motion halfway. Not while he was bound. I curled my fingers into a fist. "I should return to my room," I whispered.

"Will you think of me?" he demanded. I wordlessly nodded. "Then think of me *here*. And I will finish your massage afterward."

I shivered from head to toe, then ran my eyes down his body. "What about you? That seems unfair."

A wild smile, hotter than a burning star, bloomed on his mouth. "I didn't promise not to touch *myself*. And I get to watch you come apart. Seems fair to me."

My breath caught, but while the large, tiled shower had a frosted glass door for privacy, the walls didn't go all the way to the ceiling. Anyone who entered the locker room would hear us. I glanced around uneasily. "What if someone comes in?"

"The outer door has been locked since you arrived. You're safe." He gently herded me toward the side wall, so the water sprayed our bodies and not our faces. He turned me around and put my hands on the wall, then carefully caged me in with his body, not touching, but so close that I could feel the heat of his skin.

"Okay?" he asked.

His voice danced down my spine, and I nodded. I couldn't see him, except for his arms, and I felt protected and sheltered. It didn't hurt that the rumble in his voice arrowed directly from my ears to lower.

Much lower.

"You're so gorgeous," he murmured, his voice husky.

"So strong and fierce and caring. I wanted you from the moment I saw you, when your eyes spit fire and you refused to back down. I want to kiss you again. I want to kiss you *everywhere,* until you're all I taste, and then I want to watch you come apart on my tongue."

My embarrassment slowly melted away under the rough burn of his words. One of my hands left the wall and crept down my body. The first touch sent bolts of delight skating along my nerves, and I sighed out my pleasure.

Torran's breath caught and his arms flexed as he fought to keep his hands on the wall. "That's it," he groaned. His power flowed down my body, caressing everything that his hands could not.

My skin lit with pleasure, but worry gnawed on me. "Torran—" I started to protest.

"That wasn't touching," he growled, his voice as deep as I'd ever heard it. I shivered, caught in a web of heat and longing. "But it requires precise control, and mine is slipping away," he continued, his words soft and caressing. "I will not touch you, but let me show you what I would do if I could. Let me feel what you're feeling."

I curled the fingers that were still pressed against the cool tile wall. I could not touch him. I *would not* touch him. With the addition of his power, we were already skating dangerously close to the boundary I'd set. He might say his decisions were his own, and he might think it was true, but until I knew for sure, I wouldn't cross the line.

Still, I dipped my head the tiniest amount, and that was all it took. Torran's mind touched mine with a cool rush of power, and I could *feel* the desire he'd leashed under tight control, but deeper, I could feel his care and respect. Then he sent me a mental image of me splayed on dark sheets, his head between my thighs.

I sucked in a breath as sharp, pulsing desire pushed me to the brink of release.

"Touch yourself, *cho orchobr diu*," he demanded roughly, his fists clenched on the wall.

With Torran surrounding me with strength and care, I felt safe and secure and *treasured*. My fingers stroked through slick heat until pleasure drowned out everything except his whispered encouragement in my ear.

His desire burned brightly in the back of my mind, driving mine higher and higher, and I wanted nothing more than to turn around and lose myself in his lips, in his body.

Only hard-fought control kept me in place.

But even without physical touching, this was the hottest thing I'd experienced in a very long time, and it did not take me long to find release. Waves of pleasure detonated, and I slumped forward until my forehead pressed against the cool wall, trembling from head to toe.

The cool touch of Torran's mind withdrew, and his hands swept down my back, massaging the muscles that ran along my spine. I groaned as he hit a particularly tight knot. He continued for a few minutes as I caught my breath and remembered how to stand.

When I straightened, I felt him, hot and heavy against me before he stepped back. I glanced at him. "You didn't . . . ?"

"I'm good. Give me your arm."

I lifted my right arm and he pulled me deeper into the spray of the shower, then began working on the knots in my upper arm muscles. "But," I protested, with a wordless wave downward.

He tipped my chin up until I met his eyes. "I'm good," he repeated. "I am not some untried youth with no patience. I can wait for what I want."

"And what do you want?"

"You," he said, expression fierce. "When you are ready and comfortable. Until then, I will wait."

CHAPTER TWENTY-EIGHT

I awoke around midday, feeling rested and relaxed. I'd fed Luna before falling into bed this morning and had left her roaming the house, so I hoped all of Torran's furniture had survived her curiosity.

At the thought of Torran, a warm flush washed through me. True to his word, last night he had massaged my arms, wrapped me in a long, fluffy robe, and sent me off to my bedroom—alone. Lines had been bent but not crossed, much to my mingled relief and regret.

I dressed in the base layers required by the Valovian armor and then put my normal pants and shirt on over them. Tonight we would infiltrate the bunker under the monitoring station. I tried to temper my expectations, but, like Kee, I wasn't very good at it. If we didn't find Cien tonight, I would be devastated.

A tray was waiting outside my door with my name neatly written on a luxurious envelope. I turned it over and found a wax seal set with the same looping insignia that lived on Torran's transport and gates.

I slid a finger under the seal and popped it open. Inside, a single card with Torran's bold script waited. The note was short and sweet: *Dearest Tavi, I hope you had pleasant dreams. If you need anything, I am at your service.* Torran had signed it with a spare, neat signature.

I tucked the card back in the envelope and then slipped it into my bag of personal belongings. Maybe it was sentimental, but I wanted a little token of my time here, even if things didn't work out.

I picked up the tray and made my way to the kitchen. It was late enough that Eli, Chira, and Havil were eating lunch. They all poked good-natured fun at me, but admitted that Kee and Lexi were still asleep, and Nilo and Varro had awoken only a little while ago.

"Have you seen Luna?" I asked. "I'm surprised she's not demanding lunch."

"She's outside with Torran," Chira said.

My gaze leapt to the door, and I wondered if he would mind if I joined him.

The two Valoffs watched me from the corners of their eyes, but Eli wasn't so subtle. "Kee was right," he mused. "You do have a thing for him. I'm glad I punched him. I'll do worse if he breaks your heart."

"I don't need you sticking your pretty little nose in my business, Bruck. That's a good way for it to get broken. And don't forget that I can order you to scrub toilets for the rest of your natural life."

Eli's grin was cheerful and teasing. "Aww, you think my nose is pretty. What about the rest of my face, Captain? Does it pass muster?" He fluttered his lashes at me.

I bit down on my smile. "You have a face only a mother could love," I lied. "And the Valoffs will back me up, right?"

Chira and Havil froze. Chira's eyes traced over Eli's face. When he smiled at her, her cheeks slowly bled pink, warming the cool tone of her pale skin. Oh ho, I'd wondered, and now I knew.

"Is Eli not considered handsome by human standards?" she asked.

I shook my head, my voice grave. "He's hideous, I'm afraid."

Eli flashed the grin that had single-handedly dropped underwear at stations across the galaxy. I clutched my chest. "Turn that away. My poor heart can't take the horror."

"She's lying," he told the Valoffs across the table. "She has to delude herself lest my incredible good looks scramble her brain."

I snorted. "So modest," I said, deadpan. I shook my head sadly. "I've lived in close quarters with you for years. I'm immune to your looks *and* your charm—or lack thereof."

Now it was his turn to clutch at his chest. "You wound me, Tavi."

"Luckily we have a medic here who can fix you up," I said, rolling my eyes.

Eli gave Havil a soft look. "That *is* lucky," he murmured.

Havil ducked his head and focused on his plate, but he couldn't hide the smile that pulled at his lips.

And now I knew—Eli was flirting with them both, at the very least, and neither of them seemed to mind. I hoped that he wasn't stepping on Anja's toes, but I hadn't sensed any tension, so I figured the four of them could sort it out.

I finished my breakfast and headed outside to find Luna and Torran. Chira gave me a soft light that cast a golden glow around me and barely illuminated the path. It was very pretty but not very useful.

I found the gorgeous Valoff before I found my wayward pet. Torran smiled as I approached. "Did you eat?"

"Yes, thank you." I tilted my head as I considered him. "What's the deal with you trying to feed me all the time?"

"It is honorable to provide for those under one's care."

My eyes narrowed. "Did you leave trays for the rest of my crew?"

"No, although I did provide them with food." His eyes sparkled. "I do it for you because I enjoy taking care of you."

My cheeks heated, and I cleared my throat, thrown by the simple honesty in the words. "Well, thank you. I appreciate it." I glanced around at the greenery that was barely visible. The light made it feel like Torran and I were enclosed in our own little bubble, and I began to see the appeal. "Where's Luna?"

Torran turned and pointed just off to our left.

I held the light up, and it caused the burbu's normally violet eyes to reflect a bright, glowing blue from deep in the leaves of a short tree. "Did Torran feed you, hmm, or are you out here hunting for a tasty snack?"

Luna chirruped at me and leapt for my shoulder. I turned to absorb her momentum and scratched her under the chin. She sent me a wave of affection. "I missed you, too, darling," I murmured.

Torran watched us with an unreadable expression.

"Is everything ready for tonight?" I asked. "No new updates?"

"Nothing has changed since this morning. Nilo has

been monitoring the bug they planted, but he hasn't heard anything."

"And he's sure that we can get in?"

"Yes." Torran stepped closer. "What is bothering you? Do you regret this morning?"

"What? No. This morning was fantastic, but I always worry about operations, especially one with this many unknowns. And our bounties don't usually have a chance of leading to an interstellar war." I laughed without humor. "Or a public execution."

"You will not die," Torran said, his voice firm. "I will not allow it."

I nodded and turned for the house. "In that case, let's go over the plan again."

WE SPENT THE REST OF THE DAY PLANNING, PREPARING, and practicing. After dinner, my team and I packed all our stuff onto a levcart and left it in the hallway. If we found Cien, we wouldn't have a lot of time to make our escape, so we needed to be ready to leave as soon as we returned.

Once the packing was finished, we all took a couple of hours for ourselves because we wouldn't leave until the darkest part of the night.

I returned to my suite with Luna. If Torran wasn't set on keeping the damn life debt, I would've invited him to join me so we could both blow off some steam. Instead, I watched a vid in Valovan that I didn't understand and thought about all the ways the job could go wrong.

Luna snuggled herself into my lap, and I absently petted her while plotting how to keep my people safe in the event everything went massively sideways. It was something I did before every big job, but it seemed especially important this time.

The hours crept past both faster and slower than I wanted. I filled Luna's water bowl and set out a heaping bowl of dry food. When she cocked her head at me, I said, "You have to stay here, my fluffy little friend. If I don't come back, make a hellacious noise until someone comes and finds you, okay?"

She chirped at me, then leapt up onto the bed and curled into a ball, her nose tucked under her tail. If the worst happened, she would be fine for a few days until someone found her.

I gathered my gear and slipped from the room. Eli and Kee were in the hall. They had their mission faces on and I knew my expression matched theirs. When Lexi and Anja joined us, we headed for the workshop-garage, where we'd change into our armor and take a transport to the monitoring station.

"Everyone has their comm?" Kee asked.

One by one, we nodded. Our comm implants could be used in an emergency without requiring a separate device, but the range was extremely limited. By linking to a standalone comm, we could communicate over longer distances, even if we couldn't tap into the Valovian networks.

We slipped into the workshop and found the Valoffs already inside. Torran had donned his armor, leaving the helmet open, but the others were in various states of dress. We joined them, shimmying into the black, close-fitting armor.

Once we were armored, we attached our weapons. Our guns wouldn't connect to the attachment points built in to the Valovian armor, but my plas blade snapped right into place along my right thigh.

Our rifles were designed to be carried via a cross-body sling, but our pistols required holsters, so my team wrapped the same utility belts we'd used during training around our waists and called it good. We didn't look very Valovian, but our movements would also give us away, so it wasn't a big loss of surprise.

"Ready?" Torran asked once I had checked on each of my team members.

I wasn't, but delaying wouldn't make me any readier. "Yes."

"Will you allow me to speak to you telepathically?"

I shivered at the memory of what he'd used his telepathy for earlier, then put it out of my mind. I didn't have time for distractions, no matter how pleasant. Torran had asked every time we'd practiced, too, so I gave him the same answer. "Yes. Don't read my thoughts."

He smiled softly. "Your thoughts are your own." I felt the lightest brush of his mind against mine. "Stay close to me tonight," he said telepathically. "The life debt demands that I keep you safe. If you fight me, you'll end up distracting us both."

"I will try," I murmured.

He stared at me for a long moment, then dipped his head in acknowledgment.

After a final check, we all loaded into an unmarked transport. We had discussed leaving from a different location just in case the empress was more involved than she seemed, but speed had been deemed more important than stealth.

This transport was smaller than the one we'd used coming from the spaceport, with overhead handles rather than seats. I still wasn't used to seeing all of the Valoffs in their armor, and I shivered as painful memories tried to rise.

I focused on my team instead. They were easier to tell apart. Kee was the shortest and she was fussing with a slate, cursing and coaxing at turns under her breath. Anja and Lexi were about the same build, but Anja was just a little taller. And Eli towered over us all.

"Teams, begin shielding," Torran said. I relayed the command so the cool feeling of the Valoffs shielding our minds wouldn't startle my team.

"I'm never going to fucking get used to that," Lexi muttered loud enough for the comm to pick up. "If that asshole reads my thoughts, I'm going to gut him."

"Just don't think loud thoughts," Kee said with a snicker. "Shouldn't be a problem for you, right?"

We'd practiced the shielding, and while Lexi didn't love it, she tolerated it because it was necessary. But she always warned Nilo that his life was over the moment he dipped into her thoughts. I had a feeling I knew exactly what she was so desperate to keep secret.

The transport lifted from the ground, and we were on our way. I said the same prayer that had gotten me through the war: I prayed for strength and guidance and safety.

The ride was quiet. We were all focused on the upcoming operation. I could still feel Torran's presence in my mind, but it was distant.

When the transport settled to the ground in the forest just outside view of the monitoring station, I touched each person in my squad. My team, used to the tradition, raised their hands for high fives as I came by. It was a ritual that I'd done countless times. After a moment's hesitation,

I turned to the Valoffs. We were all teammates now, so I clapped them on the shoulders or gave them high fives, too.

I saved Torran for last. He took my hand in his, then his voice whispered into my head. "We have a plan. We've trained. We're ready."

"Let's get your nephew," I responded mentally. I was getting better about projecting my thoughts at him without having to verbalize them.

We piled out of the transport and took up our positions within the group. Kee would loop the surveillance footage while Lexi got the floor hatch open. Then we needed speed to carry us into the main part of the bunker before the kidnappers could mount a defense and trap us in the entryway.

Eli and Chira carried the heavy rope and floor anchor that would allow us to bypass the ladder. This afternoon we'd practiced fast roping off Torran's roof just to refresh our muscle memory.

We crept through the trees, sticking to the darkest shadows. The heavy red moon was barely a sliver in the sky, so we didn't have to worry about moonlight giving us away, but we were careful anyway.

Torran called us to a halt at the edge of the forest, and I relayed the signal to my team. "Kee, you're up," I said over the comm. "Lexi, you're on deck."

"On it," Kee confirmed.

She pulled a slate from its attachment point on her thigh. A few minutes later, she said, "Surveillance is looped. I didn't see anyone on the cameras below."

A moment of doubt struck. Was the person we'd seen before just a palace guard on a random sweep? If not, where was everyone? I shoved the doubt aside and tapped Torran's shoulder. "We're good to go," I said aloud so the comm would pick it up for my team.

Torran led us to the gate and it took Lexi less than ten seconds to slide it open. Torran could've gotten us in with his access, but we'd decided to be as stealthy as possible in case someone was watching for him.

The door to the building opened just as easily, then Lexi moved to one of the machines along the wall that looked exactly like every other machine. Rather than tapping on the screen, she flipped a manual switch, one of ten seemingly identical switches. How long had it taken her to find the right one? No wonder they'd been gone for hours last night.

The floor split along what I had thought were natural cracks, revealing a square about a meter wide. Thanks to the night vision in my helmet, I could see the ladder leading down, but the slightly off color made me think it was pitch-black.

Chira and Eli set up the rope while the rest of us kept an eye on our surroundings. After Chira placed the anchor, Eli gave the rope a hard yank, then dropped the rest of the coil into the hole. I heard a soft sound as the end hit the ground.

Torran moved to the rope and disappeared. As our strongest fighter, he would go first to secure the room. And as a telekinetic, if anyone fell too fast, he could catch them. Eli and Chira swung their rifles up and watched the door. They would come down last.

"It's clear," Torran's voice whispered in my head.

"Room is clear," I relayed. "I'm going down. Follow like we practiced."

I wrapped my legs in the rope, got a good grip, and then swung into space. Once my head cleared the floor, the night vision adjusted and I could see the floor, twelve meters down. I loosened my legs and slid down the rope, thankful for the gloves that covered my hands.

Once I was on the ground, I moved away and pulled my rifle up into a low ready position. The room was small and roughly square, with a single door I could see. So far, this was exactly what we'd expected.

Eli was the last one down. As soon as his boots hit the ground, Torran led us to the door. It was weird, following someone else's lead after leading my own squad for so long, but it absolutely made sense for Torran to go first. Not only could he incapacitate the enemy with just his mind, he could protect the rest of us as well.

The door was hinged rather than sliding and had a manual doorknob. On Torran's signal, I swung it open and he swept into the corridor. I followed on his heels, my rifle covering the left half of the hallway. Nothing moved and it was still and dark.

We cleared the short hall and came to a second doorway that opened into the main part of the bunker. I tapped Torran's shoulder. "Can you sense anyone?"

"No."

I moved to the door control panel. This one slid open and as soon as it did, we wouldn't have any cover. "Ready when you are," I said.

Torran glanced behind us, then returned his attention to the door. A flat, black disk about a half meter across lifted from its attachment point on his back and moved around to hover in front of him. I hadn't noticed it against the black of his armor, and he hadn't had it in training. I flinched at the sight.

The solid, armored disk was part shield and part

weapon, and in the hands of a telekinetic, it was lethal as either. The spiked edges had been sharpened into deadly points, and the thick metal body could block plas pulses.

I'd wondered at his lack of weapons—he carried only a plas pistol and blade—but now I knew why. The disk was plenty. I'd only ever seen it wielded in a training video, but the horror had stuck with me.

"Are you okay?" Torran asked, concern in his mental voice. My emotions must have bled through our connection.

I swallowed. "I didn't expect the . . ." I trailed off and waved at the disk.

"The *nimtowiadwu*? It is the traditional weapon of telekinetics."

I nodded. "I'm aware." I swallowed again as bile tried to climb up my throat. If Torran used it anything like in the training video, I wasn't sure I could stop myself from vomiting in my helmet. The telekinetic in the video had taken unholy pleasure in ripping his opponents to shreds.

Literally.

Toran stepped closer and put his hand on my shoulder. "What is wrong?"

I tried to shake off the memories and failed. "They showed us a training video of a telekinetic using one. It left an impression."

His mental voice was very, very gentle. "I believe I've seen that video. That is not how a *nimtowiadwu* should be used, but I will leave it behind if you are uncomfortable."

He would hobble himself for my comfort. The thought steadied my nerves. "No," I said. "Keep it. It might be the thing that saves your nephew."

He hesitated a moment longer, as if judging my sincerity, then he nodded. "Ready?"

I lifted my hand and let it hover over the door control. "Yes."

"Go."

I pressed the control and relayed the command. Torran swept through the door as soon as it slid open, the *nimtowi-adwu* leading the way. I followed him, my rifle sweeping the left half of the room.

We were in the main area that connected all of the rooms and hallways. The lights were off and it was quiet. Were the kidnappers so confident that they didn't even post a guard overnight?

Torran led us to the right, down the first hallway. We cleared rooms as we passed. From the peeks inside, it seemed like they were offices and meeting rooms. An undisturbed film of dust coated everything.

My sense of dread grew stronger as we moved deeper into the bunker. Each new doorway revealed a whole lot of nothing. We swept through bedrooms and barracks, rec rooms and a medbay, and none of them looked like they had been used in months or more. Someone must clean occasionally because the dust was a fine layer rather than a blanket, but otherwise, the rooms were untouched.

We turned down the final hall and I mentally crossed my fingers. Maybe they were all holed up in a single room. It would make saving Cien trickier, but I would take it at this point. However, as we delved into the rooms, my hope died. Torran stopped in the final room, his shoulders stiff, and bowed his head.

The bunker was thoroughly, completely empty.

CHAPTER TWENTY-NINE

I shoved down the frustration and focused on the problem. "What did we miss?" I demanded, both over the comm and by directing my thoughts at Torran.

"This should've been it," Kee murmured. "We saw someone in here on the video. Where are they now?"

"We need to check the tunnel that leads to the palace," I said.

Torran's head jerked toward me. "No, absolutely not. If the empress catches you trespassing, I won't be able to protect you."

"Then we need to ensure she won't catch us."

"It's risky," Eli warned. "We don't know what's down there."

"We don't, but it could be a scared child," I argued. "We owe it to him to at least check."

"Or this could be Morten's plan all along," Lexi said.

"Feed us enough clues so that it looks like Cien is here, and then wait for us to blunder into the palace fully armed and start a new war."

I winced. She made a fair point.

"I think we should check," Anja said quietly. "We need to be careful, obviously, but if we run into trouble, we can haul ass out. This is the only lead we've found. If we don't check, we'll always wonder, and coming back is more dangerous than checking while we're here."

Eli and Lexi both sighed, but neither of them protested.

Torran should've heard our conversation thanks to his earpiece, but he, too, remained silent. "My team is going to check it out," I told him. "You are welcome to keep your team here while we do."

"It's too dangerous," Torran's voice growled in my head.

"It's over a kilometer to the palace. Let's at least check the first part of the tunnel. If it looks like it's full of imperial guards, then we'll head back."

"Tavi . . ."

"Please, Torran. Your nephew could be down there."

"If we get caught, stay still and let me do the talking. And if I tell you to run, you run."

That was easy enough to agree to because he hadn't specified which direction I should run. So I could run *to* him and drag him out with me.

After a final pause, Torran led us to the only door we hadn't opened. Like the doors before it, it wasn't locked, and I wondered about the palace's security. *Someone* knew this tunnel was down here. Perhaps the empress should be more concerned about that.

I opened the door and Torran stepped through. Like

where we'd entered, this side also had a short hallway with another door at the end that swung inward on hinges. I checked on my team before swinging the door open.

Torran disappeared through the doorway without a word. I followed him and found myself in a wide, semicircular tunnel. The walls and ceiling were curved, but the floor was flat. At a little over three meters across, it gave our teams some room to spread out.

Far in the distance, a wide double door in a solid wall blocked our line of sight. We approached it cautiously. Unlike the doors before it, this one was locked.

"Kee, Lexi, you're up," I said over the comm.

The two of them got to work on the electronic lock. A minute later, I heard the bolt slide back. It seemed incredibly loud in the quiet tunnel.

Torran pulled the door open and then froze in the doorway. "Lights," he said telepathically.

I relayed the news to my team, then peeked around the doorframe. Sure enough, far in the distance, a doorway set into the wall spilled light into the tunnel.

And there was exactly zero cover between us and it.

Beyond the light, another doorway across the tunnel blocked the view. I glanced back the way we'd come. The bunker was perhaps three hundred meters behind us, which meant we weren't even halfway to the palace.

Without access to the blueprint, there was no way to know what was behind the door—or why it needed a light. But if I were designing a bunker to protect myself from an invading force, I'd put strongholds along it where soldiers could set up defensive positions.

Torran must've decided the same thing, because he sped up until I had to jog to keep up. We were still ten meters from the door when it opened, sending more light into the tunnel.

Torran came to a silent halt, and I narrowly avoided crashing into his back.

"I'll check it," a man grumbled loudly in Common. "You lazy bastards keep sitting on your asses," he continued quietly to himself.

The man stepped out into the tunnel wearing the type of body armor preferred by FHP soldiers, but without a helmet. Plas rifles were relatively quiet, but this close to the door, a single shot would bring everyone else. Still, if we didn't shoot him, he'd raise the alarm.

I brought my rifle up but before I could draw a bead on him, his head twisted a different direction than his body. When the body gently lowered to the ground, I realized what had happened.

I swallowed, glad that Torran was on our side.

"Kee, can you get me visuals on that room?" I asked.

She pulled out her slate and tapped on it for a few moments. "No, not unless I can find a hardline connection. There's no wireless network here."

So going in blind was it. "Plan?" I asked Torran.

"Same as before. Clear each room and find Cien. I can't sense any of the humans even from here, so there's at least a Valoff or two inside."

"Are we going to cause a war if we kill them?"

Torran shook his head. "They've sided with the enemy."

I updated my team and we moved closer to the door. I could feel Torran heavier in my mind, and I wondered if he'd increased my shielding, but there was no time to ask.

The door slid open and we entered a bright space. My

helmet adjusted for the light and I could see we were in an entry with rooms to our right and left. In front of us, a hallway led to a larger room.

"Back already?" a gruff man asked from the left.

"Probably forgot his gun," a woman taunted with a laugh.

We flowed into the room as if we'd been working together for weeks rather than hours. It was a rec room, with a sofa and chairs facing a vid screen. The man and woman, both human, sat with their backs to the door, a tactical mistake considering they were on guard duty.

Torran and I went right. I shot the woman before she could raise her weapon. Behind me, someone's gun pulsed and the man fell dead.

"Whoever is shielding them is going to know we're here," Torran said. "Keep moving."

The room on the other side of the entryway was empty, so we moved down the hall toward the main room. This area also had sofas and chairs surrounding a vid screen, but it was empty. Doors and hallways branched off on every wall. To the left, I could see a slice of what looked like a kitchen area.

I heard a faint whistling sound just before Torran's *nimtowiadwu* jumped in front of my face. A heartbeat later, something heavy and metallic crashed into it, and Torran grunted.

"Telekinetic," he warned, his mental voice strained. "Strong."

I relayed the warning. I'd never seen two telekinetics fight, and I'd hoped to keep that streak going. I searched the part of the room that I could see, looking for a target, but no one was visible. "Where?" I asked.

"Right back," he gritted out.

I *focused* on the area and ignored the immediate stab of a headache. Even though I couldn't see the telekinetic, I could see the edge of a bright orange Valovian aura peeking out from the hallway in the back of the room.

I raised my rifle, trying to get a bead on the telekinetic while staying behind the cover Torran provided. Instead, my rifle jerked forward, dragging me with it by the sling.

Torran grabbed for me, but he was too late. Someone telelocked my armor and lifted me into the air. I felt like I was being held in a giant's hand as their fingers tightened around me. I cursed and tried to move but nothing happened. At least I could still breathe—for now.

My team shouted over the comm, and a light, unfamiliar voice called something in Valovan.

I strained against the hold, remembering the lessons from *Starlight*. It might not save me, but it might keep the telekinetic busy enough that someone else could take them out.

The armor tightened around my body, and I groaned. Breathing wasn't getting any easier. I panted, sucking in shallow breaths. I couldn't believe I'd survived a decade of war just to die in an underground bunker on Valovia itself.

Clearly, the universe had a dark sense of humor.

Below me, I heard plas pulses ricocheting around the room. One hit the ceiling above me and fine dust rained down. Not being able to breathe properly wasn't fun, but not being able to see what was happening was almost worse.

I kept straining against the hold, until my muscles trembled. If I was going to die like this, then I was going to fight until the end.

I felt a pop, and then I fell. Torran snagged an arm

around me before I hit the ground and his support allowed me to get my feet under me. I felt bruised from head to toe, but I lifted my rifle and looked for a target. A soldier wearing full FHP armor was down at the far edge of the room. A dead man in Valovian armor—without a helmet—lay next to them.

My focus had snapped during the telelock, so I couldn't see any auras. "Is the telekinetic dead?"

Torran shook his head. "I broke her hold on you, so she retreated, but she's just licking her wounds until the next fight."

He sounded weary in a way I'd never heard before. "Are you okay?"

His chin dipped. "I will protect you."

That wasn't what I'd asked, but now wasn't the time to argue. "Can you sense Cien?"

"No."

Delving deeper into an unknown structure where a telekinetic waited for us was a nightmare scenario, but I firmed my resolve and sucked in a deep breath, beyond glad that I *could* breathe. With the telekinetic pressure gone, my armor had returned to its previous shape. And without the armor, I would be dead.

It was a sobering thought. I'd skated close to death before, but it never got any easier. I let the adrenaline drown out the terror and signaled for my team to move to the left. We'd need to keep an eye on this main room, or the kidnappers could slip out while we cleared the rest of the building.

Unless they already had a secondary way out.

Unlike the rest of us, Kee carried a rifle and no other weapons. Instead of a pistol or blade, her slate was strapped to one leg and the other had a small case of gadgets that she thought might be helpful. On the inside of her left arm, a mini comm screen displayed real-time data from her linked slate. Varro, Nilo, and Lexi watched over her as she pulled a pair of tiny drones from the case she carried.

She unfolded the drones and activated them, and they hovered in the air, waiting for her command.

"Where do you want these?" she asked over the comm as she closed the case and returned it to its position on her thigh.

Presumably the telekinetic had retreated to the right, so I waved to the left. Kee tapped on the display strapped to her arm and the drones zoomed off in a searching pattern.

The drones had tiny cameras, but they flew so fast that watching the video was nauseating. Instead, Kee relied on their software to flag any potential enemies using a combination of heat signatures, sounds, and visual recognition.

Drones weren't quite as good as an in-person search, but they were way, way faster. Of course, they also gave away the fact that someone was here searching, but in this case, that ship had already sailed.

While we waited on the drones to finish their sweep, we split up the team and took defensive positions in the rooms the drones had already cleared. Torran and I were in the kitchen, a spare room that was meant to feed soldiers, not win interior design contests.

The telekinetic did not return, and every second that ticked past brought more worry. Was she escaping? Was Torran's nephew in danger? Were they setting up an ambush?

At least one of those was certainly true. I wanted to press ahead, but doing so when we didn't know if more soldiers would come in behind us was a good way to end up dead, so I stared at the slice of the main room I could see and forced myself to stay put.

"This side is clear," Kee said a few minutes later. "Checking the other side."

The drones split and each one took a hallway on the other side of the room. The first one returned quickly and headed down the hallway that the telekinetic had taken.

"Front is empty," Kee said. "Only one hallway left."

Torran and I eased out of cover. Our team fell in behind us as we headed for the hallway in the back of the room.

When we reached the doorway, Kee groaned. "First drone is down. It registered three people before it died, but there might be more."

"Do you have a map?"

She moved closer and held up the arm with the display attached. Reading drone maps was something of an art, but luckily, I'd had plenty of practice. The drones built a rough floor plan as they went, thanks to the scanners, but they were often incomplete.

For Torran's benefit, Kee pointed at a large room that was the intersection of several of the lines. "We're here, and the drone died here." She pointed at the room where one of the lines ended. Only the first part of the room had been mapped, so I didn't know how big it was, but it was at the end of the main hallway. We'd have one corner for cover, pretty far back, and that was it.

The other drone filled in a few of the missed spots, but it hadn't reached the room with the people in it yet. "Any way you can get the second drone past the room? I'd like to know if they have another exit."

Kee grunted and tapped on the screen. "I'll try, but I

doubt it, considering how fast they took down the first one. The telekinetic is likely in the room."

I forced down the fear. Attacking a fortified telekinetic would be suicide without Torran's assistance. But since he was going to be the first through the door, I assumed he knew what he was doing.

We entered the hallway with Torran's *nimtowiadwu* leading the way. It seemed like scant protection, but it was better than nothing. I took a deep breath and let it out slowly.

We'd made it only a few meters when Kee cursed again. "Second drone is down. It registered four before failing."

Four soldiers could probably hold the room, especially if they had cover. But were they merely buying time for the rest of their squad to escape, or were they fighting for their lives? The first meant they'd break and run if they met too much resistance, but if it was the second, they would be relentless.

At the final corner, Torran paused and peeked around the edge of the wall. I'd gotten used to the cool feel of his mind against mine, but the temperature dropped until it felt like I had an icicle in my brain. Torran jerked back and a plas pulse sailed by. It hit the far side of the hallway with a sizzle.

"Come out, General, and bring your humans with you," the telekinetic woman called in heavily accented Common. A child cried out in pain. "Unless you want this one to die."

"How many did you see?" I asked, directing my thoughts at him.

"The telekinetic, two humans, and Cien."

Cien's voice broke on a scream, and Torran's fists clenched. "Stay here," he ordered, then he surged around the corner, the *nimtowiadwu* floating in front of him.

Shit.

I couldn't let him face the enemy alone. I muttered a string of curses and followed. The rest of the team fell in behind me. I didn't want to give the telekinetic another chance to grab me, so I stayed behind Torran, my rifle covering his left. His broad shoulders blocked most of my view, but I quickly snuck a glance past him and wished I hadn't.

The telekinetic wore a full set of Valovian armor, hiding her face. Two soldiers in human armor stood next to her with their plas rifles trained on Cien. Based on their height and thick builds, they were likely both men.

The child floated in front of them, his arms and legs splayed wide like the telekinetic was trying to tear him limb from limb. His clothes were filthy, and his dark hair was matted and unkempt. His head lolled on his neck like he was barely conscious, but even so, I could see the tears glistening on his face.

And if that wasn't bad enough, a vest filled with explosives hugged his small torso.

My heart broke as his back bowed and he cried out again, but I couldn't save him quite yet, so I turned my attention to the room. It was smaller than the one where we'd fought the telekinetic before, but it had just as many exits. Hallways led off both sides, and on the far wall, a heavy, reinforced door blocked our view.

The room itself looked like it had been set up for planning with long tables and displays on the walls, but everything had been pushed to the edges. A table on its side blocked the end of our hallway. It was meant to slow us down, but it also provided a tiny bit of cover. It wouldn't stop any plas pulses, but it was better than nothing.

Marginally.

As soon as Torran reached the table, the telekinetic spoke, her voice amplified by the armor. "That's close enough, General. Try anything and these men will kill the child—if the explosives don't get to him first. I am keeping the trigger depressed. Kill me and you'll kill him."

The two men next to her didn't remove their attention from the kid. If they weren't trained soldiers, then they were at least trained mercenaries. Cien's body didn't cover them completely, so I could hit them somewhere fatal without hitting the kid, but we needed to keep the telekinetic alive long enough to get Cien out of the vest. I couldn't do both at once, so I bided my time, discarding plans as quickly as I thought of them.

"Release the child immediately, and I will spare your life," Torran said, his tone dangerous. His armor also amplified his voice. That was a neat trick that would've been useful to know about.

The telekinetic laughed. "You will spare my life anyway, unless you want the child to die."

I tapped Torran's back and directed my thoughts at him. "Can you break her hold?"

"Not without risking Cien."

"Kee, can you jam the signal for the explosives?"

"I'm looking into it," she said, "but it'll be a temporary fix at best."

Torran minutely shook his head. "The trigger will be on his vest somewhere. There may also be a remote detonator, but as soon as she lets go of the telekinetic pressure, it will trigger."

"Find it," I told him, then relayed the information to Kee.

"What do you want?" Torran demanded aloud. "Why are you working with the humans?"

"Why are *you*?" she countered, ignoring the first question.

"They are helping me retrieve something that was stolen from me."

"It's not like you to be so sentimental, General," she taunted. "Or perhaps you just don't care about anyone but yourself." The bitter words hinted at deeper resentment, but she shook herself, and her tone returned to the light taunting she'd been using all along. "If you cooperate, you can have the child back in a little while. We no longer need him."

Well, *that* sounded extremely ominous.

"Where are the others?" Torran demanded.

The telekinetic tilted her head. "What others?" she asked innocently.

"They left her behind with two flunkies and the kid," Lexi said. "Why? And why is she stalling?"

"She's waiting for the others to escape," I murmured.

"Or she's waiting for someone else to show up," Eli said.

"Or both," Lexi growled. She was ever the optimist, our Lexi.

The telekinetic spoke. "You have something that I want. I have something that you want. Let's trade."

"No," Torran said flatly.

"Don't be so hasty, General. I'm not asking for anything you aren't willing to part with. Give me the humans, and I'll return Cien to you safe and sound."

Torran remained silent for a beat, then he shrugged. "Deal." Telekinetic power wrapped around me, and my feet lifted from the ground.

CHAPTER THIRTY

The comm exploded with outraged voices as my team turned on their Valovian counterparts, weapons drawn. The telekinetic holding Cien laughed in delight. "I want the hero of Rodeni alive, but you can kill the rest," she told Torran.

My team lifted into the air, their weapons useless.

Just how strong *was* Torran?

"Quiet," I demanded over the comm. "He's not going to betray us." I sounded confident to my own ears, but it was difficult not to harbor doubts. His power held me gently, not at all like the crushing grip of the other telekinetic. I *wanted* to believe that it was because he wouldn't hurt us, but were my feelings getting in the way of reality?

No. Torran had vowed a life debt, and the care I'd felt from him wasn't faked. He had a plan; I just wished I knew what it was. And how to help.

"Remove Cien's vest and I will hand over the humans," Torran said.

The other telekinetic laughed. "Give me the humans, and I will show you where the trigger is, but know that I also have a remote override. You will let me leave, and I will not use it."

It was Torran's turn to scoff. "And you expect me to trust you?"

"I suggest you work fast, General."

"Kee, did you find the remote signal?" I asked.

"Yeah, but it's hard to do anything about it while I'm dangling like a hooked fish," she griped. "I can jam it, assuming I can reach my arm, but not for long."

"How long is not long?"

"Thirty seconds, give or take," she said. "Longer than that and we risk a backup timer setting it off."

Once Torran had control of the physical trigger, we would have to get the vest off Cien, and then retreat far enough that the explosion wouldn't kill us, while also fighting a telekinetic and two trained soldiers. We outnumbered them, but it was still a lot for thirty seconds.

Torran had continued trading barbs with the other telekinetic, but I hadn't been paying attention to what exactly they were saying. "I'll be the distraction," I said over the comm. "I'm the one she wants. Trade me for Cien and figure out where the trigger is. Kee can block the signal from the remote detonator while you remove the vest."

"Tavi, no!" my team shouted.

I ignored them. "Once Cien is safe, you can worry about me. My armor will protect me until then." I hoped.

"I grow bored of this," the telekinetic said. "Give me the humans now or watch the child die."

Torran waved aside the table blocking the hallway and

stepped into the room. I hovered by his side, the *nimtowi-adwu* in front of me.

The telekinetic held up a hand. "Careful, General."

"Show me the trigger," Torran demanded. When it seemed like she might balk he continued, "Or do you not have an override after all?"

Cien groaned as his body was spun around.

"Tell Kee to jam the signal, then be ready," Torran whispered in my mind. I relayed the order. I wasn't sure exactly what I was getting ready for, but if it was anything like before, it was going to be a shitload of pain.

"Signal is jammed," Kee said over the comm.

A control box in the middle of Cien's back had a depressed red button. "It's all yours," the telekinetic said, "but you don't know where the override is. Try anything and I'll kill him."

"Go," Torran said telepathically.

A Valoff appeared in front of Cien. Based on the height and build, I guessed it was Nilo, but I had no idea how he'd gotten there without me noticing. I hit the ground as the two soldiers' plas rifles jerked toward the ceiling.

Nilo reached up and Cien fell into his arms. They dropped backward and by the time they hit the ground, Cien's vest was gone.

Not taken off, not removed—*gone*.

Nilo rolled over and covered Cien's body with his own. I snapped out of my shock and brought my gun up. I hit the soldier on the left, but his armor protected him from the worst of the damage.

Our team swept into the room on a wave of plas pulses. The telekinetic shouted something that I couldn't make out over the sound of shots, and her power crashed around me. She jerked me toward her until I hovered in front of her, where Cien had been before.

I felt Torran's rage a second before his presence in my mind dimmed, replaced by a squeezing pressure filled with knives as the other telekinetic tried to smash through my resistance. I poured more energy into my mental shields, but it was like stopping a tidal wave with a toothpick.

The telekinetic spun my body around so I faced Torran and my team. With a flick, she opened my visor then wrenched my helmet off. "Move and she dies," she said, wrapping a cool, gloved hand around my throat.

I fought to move, to do anything, but she had telelocked my armor, freezing me in place. With her power clamped around me, my body was beyond my control, and even blinking was difficult. I couldn't see much, but Nilo and Cien had made it to safety behind Torran and the others. Both remained on the ground, so Torran must've dragged them closer, but I would take it.

If this was my last stand, then at least my life had saved a kid.

I focused all of my energy on moving a single finger. The telekinetic shook me like a rag doll. "Stop resisting, human, or I'll rip you piece from piece."

Pain stabbed into my brain as she again tried to pierce my mental shields, but I could feel the tiniest hint of Torran's power still protecting me. No matter what happened next, I hoped he wouldn't let me turn my weapon on my friends.

I kept trying to move my fingers. The enemy telekinetic's power spiraled higher, and I clenched my teeth against the urge to scream. I lost precious seconds as I fought to stay awake and aware. Once I could think again, I redoubled my efforts. Torran was helping me, and if she could feel the resistance, then it meant my focus was doing *something*. If only I could reach my plas blade, I'd have a chance.

A very tiny, nearly impossible chance, but a chance nonetheless.

"You have already lost," Torran growled. "Let her go and die with honor." His eyes bored into mine. He was trying to tell me something, but I was in too much pain to figure out what it was. But if he could get me free, then I'd do my best to stab the bitch holding me.

The telekinetic dragged me backward, toward the reinforced door. Locked in her power, I floated along like a balloon—not a comforting thought. One of her soldiers was down but still alive. She left him where he lay. When the other tried to help him up, she snarled, "Leave him!"

Clearly her love for humans extended to her allies, too.

I heard the door behind us open. If I let her drag me through it, I was finished. Pain, terror, and furious, burning anger bloomed. Rather than pushing it aside, I focused on it, letting it bolster my mental shields.

I had thrown Torran out of my mind during our shielding practice. *Once.* But if I'd done it once, I could do it again.

Then I'd show this smug Valovian traitor exactly how I'd survived a decade of war.

My finger moved. Not much, but it was a start. The hot rush of victory was nearly drowned by a wave of pain, but I pushed onward. Slowly, so slowly, I wrapped one finger, then two, around the hilt of my plas blade.

The loud squeal of metal tearing came from behind us and the telekinetic's mental vice grip loosened for a fraction of a second. It was enough. I shoved her from my mind with a roar, and in her surprise, the telelock faltered. My feet hit the ground, and I spun, operating on muscle memory and adrenaline.

I drew and activated my blade in one move, then closed the distance between us and drove it upward, under her chin, into the weakest part of her armor.

The red blade sank a centimeter, right on target, and I pushed harder, so focused on her death that I didn't notice she'd lifted her hands until she *shoved* me away. The blast of power flung me across the room. Torran shouted, and I jerked to a stop so close to the wall that I could see individual dust particles clinging to the flat surface.

For a moment, the cool comfort of Torran's power wrapped around me before the mental ice pick returned. Something yanked viciously on my head, and I arched my back, trying to save my neck. Bones cracked and the pain became a suffocating blanket that stole my breath. It felt like I was being torn in two.

I groaned in agony. My mental shields were shot. I'd failed, and now I didn't have the energy to throw her out again. Distantly, I heard a heavy, metallic crash and the sound of plas weapons, but it was all I could do to cling to consciousness.

Then strong arms wrapped around me and the pain receded slightly. "Hang on, I've got you," Torran murmured.

It was the last thing I heard before my overtaxed brain shut down and everything went dark.

I AWOKE TO THE GENTLE ROCKING OF SOMEONE CARRYING me. For a brief, fuzzy moment, I enjoyed the sensation. Then my memories caught up, and I cracked open my eyes to see where I was.

Pure darkness met my gaze.

My head felt better, but had something happened to my vision? Terror dug in with sharp claws.

"You're safe," Torran whispered in my mind.

"Why can't I see?" I asked. My voice echoed oddly, and now that I focused, I could hear people moving around us.

My team shouted in relief over the comm, but Torran's mental voice cut through the noise. "You lost your helmet and we're still in the tunnels. Havil healed some fractures in your ribs and neck before we moved you. You've been unconscious for about ten minutes."

"And the telekinetic?"

Torran's arms tightened. "She brought the tunnel down behind her. The two humans didn't make it, but she escaped."

"Oh, shit," Kee breathed.

Her voice came over the comm, so I had no idea where she was relative to me. That didn't prevent me from craning my neck, trying to see. "What?"

"I left a couple of cameras behind in the tunnel, just in case the kidnappers came back. They didn't, but a dozen Valoffs in imperial guard uniforms *did*."

It took my brain far longer than it should've to connect the dots. The kidnappers were trying to frame *us* for the kidnapping.

Or the empress was.

That's why the telekinetic wanted me. If the hero of Rodeni had stolen the empress's grandson, then it would be easy to sway public opinion toward another war. After all, if Cien wasn't safe, then who was?

"Move," Torran shouted. The easy swaying turned into a harsh jostling as he broke into a run. I wanted down, but

I wasn't sure my legs would work, and even if they did, I couldn't see a damn thing.

We slowed, near what I hoped was the door into the underground bunker. The door opened and the sound changed.

"Wait," Kee hissed. "There are more guards outside the monitoring station, at least three. They haven't overridden my surveillance mods yet, so they likely think the building is empty, but it's only a matter of time until one gets curious and sees our rope."

"Torran, can you bluff my team past them?" I asked over the comm. He was a high-ranking general and Cien's uncle. In the dark, and with minimal contact, my team might pass for Valoffs if Torran kept the soldiers off balance. Without a helmet, though, I was fucked.

Torran didn't answer. Instead, he asked, "Nilo, can you get Tavi's team out?"

I didn't catch Nilo's response, but Torran's arms tightened around me. I assumed that was a no, then.

I steeled my courage. "Take my team with you and leave me hidden in one of the rooms in the bunker. Once it's safe, you can come back and get me, or I'll crawl out on my own." Being left alone in the dark would be a nightmare, but I'd faced worse.

"We're not leaving you here," Lexi said, no give in her voice.

Torran's voice whispered into my head. "Nilo can get you out, but once he does, he'll be down for a few hours. I need you to watch over him until we catch up."

"What about the rest of my team?"

"They'll come with me. I will get them out, Tavi, I

swear it. Their lives are your happiness. I will not let them be hurt."

I swallowed, then nodded and relayed the message to my team.

There were a few grumbles, but Kee opened a private comm channel with me. "Do you trust him?"

"Yes." I trusted Torran, not just with myself, but with the people who were most important to me. I knew what that meant, but now wasn't the time for grand declarations.

"That's good enough for me," Kee said. "I'll tell the others. Stay safe."

"Thank you. You, too." When she closed the connection, I pulled Torran's helmeted face down to mine and pressed a kiss against the smooth armor that protected his jaw. "Be careful. Take good care of my team."

Torran hugged me close. "I will be, and I will." He carefully set me on my feet, aware that I couldn't see a thing. "Nilo needs to touch you. Don't be startled."

A gentle hand wrapped around my upper arm, and Torran let me go. "I'll see you soon," he promised.

I nodded, my throat clogged.

Next to me, I heard the sound of a visor opening. "I'm going to port us out," Nilo whispered, his voice stripped of its usual charming inflection. "The first time is disorienting, so I need you to kneel down with me."

I instinctively turned my head to him, though I couldn't see him. "You mean *teleport*? Is that even possible?" I'd thought Cien's missing explosives vest had been a trick of the light or something explainable, but *teleportation*?

"Yes, port is short for teleport. It's perfectly safe."

"For humans?"

There was a long pause before he said, "Probably? I've ported animals with no trouble."

"You suck at comforting," I growled.

His chuckle was nice, but it didn't curl into my chest like a gift. So far, only one person had that effect, and I was about to leave him behind.

"Torran wouldn't ask me to take you if he didn't think it was safe," Nilo murmured. "If you don't trust me, then trust him."

My nerves steadied. "Okay."

We probably looked hilarious to the rest of the team, since with his visor open Nilo couldn't see, either, but eventually we fumbled our way to the ground.

"Eli, take care of everyone," I said over the comm.

"Will do, Captain."

"Are you ready?" Nilo asked.

No, I wasn't, but I nodded anyway, until I remembered that he couldn't see me. "I'm ready."

"Close your eyes, take a deep breath, and hold it."

I did as he asked and the cool feel of Torran's power was replaced by something colder and sharper. Not painful, but not exactly pleasant either. My stomach dropped, and it felt like my head went one way while my body went another—while upside down and spinning.

I clenched my jaw to keep my stomach contents where they belonged, and just when I thought I would lose the battle, light shined through my eyelids.

"Safe," Nilo gasped as he slumped against me. "Open . . ."

I opened my eyes in time to catch him as he lost consciousness. I wasn't *too* worried, since Torran had warned me that it would happen, but I didn't want him to get a concussion from bashing his head into the floor.

I looked around, then blinked as if that would change the view.

We had landed on the padded sparring floor of the gym in *Starlight's Shadow*. The automatic lights had turned on with our movement, but the ship remained quietly sleeping around us.

I eased Nilo to the ground, then gently removed his helmet. I wasn't sure what he was wearing under the armor, so I didn't go any further, but I made sure that he wouldn't wake up with a crick in his neck.

His pulse beat strongly under my fingers and a check of his breathing confirmed that he was unconscious rather than dead. I could probably drag him to the medbay, but I risked hurting him in transit, so I left him where he was.

Torran wouldn't have sent me to the ship if he didn't think we'd need to leave in a hurry. I tried to raise my team on the comm but got nothing but silence in return. I knew the distance was too far, but worry pressed on me.

I'd lost my weapons at some point during the evening, so I stopped in the cargo bay to restock. I kept the Valovian armor. If I had to leave the ship, it would let me blend in better than my own armor.

I undid Kee's lockdown protections on the ship, but I left the cargo bay door closed and locked. It would take her only a few seconds to open it, and there was no reason to let anyone watching know that someone was getting the ship ready to launch.

On the bridge, I started the process of bringing the ship out of standby. The routine was so familiar that it did nothing to distract me from my worries. Would Torran bring my team straight here? If so, I'd be forced to leave Luna behind. Pain stole my breath. The ship would be far too lonely without the little burbu, but my team's safety came first. Maybe Torran would meet me in Bastion, once it was safe, and return her to me.

A different kind of pain rose at the thought of parting from Torran. I'd gotten used to his quiet presence. Maybe it was better that I hadn't taken him to bed. I already felt too much. Letting him go was going to leave a scar.

With the ship as ready to go as I could make it without alerting anyone outside, there was nothing left for me to do but wait. I checked on Nilo—still out—and stalked through the ship, letting my booted footsteps echo in the empty halls.

When my comm implant finally crackled to life, I held my breath.

"We're on our way," Eli said. "We need to buy some time, though, so turn off the cargo bay lights. We'll sneak aboard."

I swallowed my relieved tears and focused on what needed to be done. "Will do. What's your ETA?"

"Ten minutes." He paused, then continued. "I'm glad you're okay."

"You, too."

I didn't ask him all of the questions burning on my tongue. We'd worked together a long time. If he hadn't mentioned the team, that meant they were okay—or at least okay-ish. My questions could wait.

I snagged a pair of night-vision glasses from our supply, then went about shutting down all the lights in the cargo bay, including the emergency backups. At nine minutes, I opened the cargo bay door just enough that someone could duck under it, then I crouched on the floor with my plas rifle and waited for my team.

I'd expected them to arrive in a transport, but they slipped across the spaceport grounds on foot. Eli, Kee, and Lexi were the easiest to spot, thanks to their distinctive heights. The rest were more difficult, but it looked like Varro had an arm around Havil, half carrying him. Chira carried Cien. The boy was awake, but he huddled against Chira's chest like he wanted to crawl inside her to hide. Anja was next to Eli, bringing up the rear and watching over the others.

My eyes flickered over them again, searching for the person who was missing, but the results remained the same. Torran wasn't in the group.

They ducked into the cargo bay, but I kept my eyes on the spaceport. Nothing moved. Kee stopped beside me. "He got held up with the imperial guards," she said, her voice soft over the comm. "He sent us ahead. We're to leave without him if he's not here in twenty minutes—or earlier if someone tries to stop us. Without him, *Lotkez* will protect us on our way to Bastion. They are already in orbit."

Even without being here, he protected me still.

I swept my eyes over the spaceport one last time before reluctantly turning away. "Is anyone injured?"

"No," Kee said. "Havil overdid it with the healing, but otherwise he's okay. The rest of us have a few bumps and bruises, but this armor is fucking unbelievable. I mean, I *knew* it was, logically, but having it on is a whole other experience. I took a close-range plas pulse to the chest and barely felt it. No wonder Valoffs are so damn hard to kill." She shook her head. "I'll never understand why the FHP didn't steal the tech. We fought in tissue paper by comparison."

I nodded. It was an exaggeration, but not by much. I likely would not have survived tonight in my standard armor, and I wondered if Torran had known that.

"Get to the bridge," I told Kee. "I've brought the ship out of standby, but we'll need to be ready to launch as soon as Torran gets here. Just don't let ground control know what we're up to until the last minute."

Kee nodded and left the cargo bay just as Varro returned, without Havil. The remaining members of both teams kept their weapons close and their attention trained on the cargo bay door. I didn't know if Torran had warned them to expect trouble or if they were just as on edge as I was, but I appreciated the backup.

Chira tried to carry Cien deeper into the ship, but he shook his head and babbled something in Valovan. When he squinted at the door, I realized he couldn't see.

I pulled a second pair of night-vision glasses from our supplies and quietly approached the pair. I activated the lenses, then held them out, keeping a bit of distance between us. I didn't want to make the kid any more nervous than he already was. "If he wants to see, he can use these," I murmured softly. "They'll be a little big for him, but they should work okay."

"Thank you," Chira said. She spoke to Cien in Valovan, then handed him the glasses.

The child put them on, blinking around in wonder until his gaze settled on me. Then he jerked back, fear stark on his face. He spoke quickly to Chira, his tone urgent. I couldn't understand what he said, but I did catch *droch*, the word for "human."

Valoffs might've kept his abilities suppressed, but humans had frightened him.

While Chira reassured him, I carefully turned and moved back to the door, keeping my motions as soft and nonthreatening as possible. I returned to my former position, crouching so I could see outside.

The spaceport remained empty.

As the minutes ticked past, my anxiety climbed higher and higher. I'd always had a fabulous imagination, and now it worked against me, reminding me of all of the terrible things that could've befallen Torran.

The allotted twenty minutes were nearly up—not that I was planning to leave until I was forced to—when Torran's voice whispered across my mind. "I'm on my way. Wait for me if you can."

The connection disappeared before I could respond. "Torran is on his way," I said over the comm. "He seemed to think we might not be able to wait for him, so I want everyone on alert."

"The spaceport is quiet," Kee said, "and I'm ready to launch on your command."

Eli crouched on the other side of the door and together we waited, staring into the starlit night. The sun would creep over the horizon soon, and I hoped to be off-planet before it did. Not that darkness would hide us from Valovia's sensors, but maybe the empress would be less likely to blow us up if we left before we were seen.

Or maybe not.

The seconds trickled past, each an eternity. Finally, Kee said, "We have incoming. Small vehicle, no registration, no insignia."

I waved Chira and Cien to the side of the cargo bay so

someone outside couldn't see them. And they would be out of the line of fire, if it came to that. Varro moved with them, shielding them further.

Anja joined Eli and me at the door. "Is it Torran?"

"I hope so," I said.

"Uhhh, three more transports just came into range," Kee said. "They're all broadcasting imperial registrations. They are approximately ninety seconds behind the first."

"Spin up the engines."

"That will—"

"I know, do it anyway. As soon as he's aboard, get us off the ground. Override ground control if you have to."

"On it," she confirmed.

I opened the cargo door a little wider. The faster we could get Torran inside, the faster we could launch. I hadn't expected him to bring his nephew and the rest of his team along for the ride, but with Cien's parents still away and the empress under suspicion, Torran didn't have many other options.

Hopefully he had a plan that would prevent the empress from pinning the entire kidnapping on me.

A sleek black vehicle slid into view, moving faster than was safe or prudent. It raced across the spaceport and jerked to a stop at the base of *Starlight*'s cargo ramp. I lifted my rifle as the side door opened.

"It's me," Torran whispered, his mental voice weary.

I lowered my rifle and waved the others to do the same.

Torran pushed a levcart out of the vehicle, and I rushed to help him guide it up the ramp. He still wore his armor, but he moved like he was in pain. Once we were inside, I snapped commands over the comm, and my team rushed to get us in the air.

Torran handed me a large black bag. "Sorry I had to contain her, but she couldn't be seen," he said, his voice amplified by his armor.

When the bag gave an indignant chirrup, I knew exactly what he'd given me. I lifted the top flap and peeked inside. Round, fuzzy ears and big, angry eyes stared back at me. Luna did not like to be contained, a lesson I'd learned early. I cooed at her and gently lifted her out of the bag, sending her as much affection as I could.

I turned back to Torran. I couldn't speak around the lump in my throat, and my expression had to be openly adoring, but I didn't care. This was the greatest gift he ever could've given me.

"Thank you," I whispered. "Thank you so much."

He nodded. "I'm glad you're okay."

I dipped my chin. "Thanks to you. And Nilo."

The cargo bay door sealed closed and the lights came on. I blinked as my eyes adjusted.

Cien said something, his voice soft, but Torran jerked in his direction. He pulled off his helmet and crouched down with a barely audible groan. It took a beat for Cien to recognize him, then the boy dashed into his uncle's arms with a choked sob.

I knew exactly how he felt.

CHAPTER THIRTY-ONE

I didn't know how Torran managed to pull it off, but the Valovian authorities let us launch without trying to stop us. Perhaps the empress was just waiting for us to reach deep space so she could kill us without witnesses, but I would deal with that issue when it became a problem.

Valovia receded on our rear cameras and nothing but stars stretched out ahead of us. Thanks to my late morning, I hadn't been up long, but the day had taken a toll. I rolled my head, stretching the muscles in my neck.

I still felt the telekinetic's harsh grip. Havil had healed me, so it had to be phantom pain, but he couldn't erase the sound of my neck bones cracking. The rest of the fight was somewhat foggy and distant, but that sound lived in my memory now.

Luna, sensing my mood, purred louder. She'd been stuck to me like glue since we'd returned to the ship. I petted her for a minute, then scooped her up and stood. I handed her off to Kee, who cooed at her like they'd been parted for weeks.

Luna soaked up the attention.

I stretched. Restlessness pulsed under my skin. I needed to move, not sit here and watch Valovia shrink on the displays. It was only evening standard time, so it was too early to sleep, even if I could get the adrenaline to subside long enough to attempt it. I didn't trust Empress Nepru, and I kept waiting for the other shoe to drop.

I wasn't the only one who was nervous. The bridge was full, even though we were almost a day and a half away from the first wormhole. My crew had changed out of the Valovian armor, but Torran's team still wore theirs. I wasn't sure if that was a bad sign, or if they were just more comfortable in armor than clothes.

"Eli, you have the bridge. I'm going to check on the others and then make a snack for anyone who wants one."

"I have the bridge," Eli acknowledged. "And if you're making a snack, I vote cookies."

"Oooh, yes, please," Kee said, looking up from Luna. "I'm dying for some sugary goodness."

I grinned at them. "I'll see what I can do."

I left the bridge with a wave and made my way to the crew quarters. Nilo had been put in Havil's room while he recovered, so the doctor could keep an eye on him. The door slid open at my knock, and Havil smiled at me from where he was propped up in bed. Nilo remained out cold.

"Everything okay?" I asked.

"Yes, I'm feeling better," Havil said. "And Nilo will be fine with a bit more rest."

"Good. Let me know if you need anything."

Havil nodded, and I waved before sliding the door

closed. I moved down the hall and knocked on Torran's door. I waited for a long moment, but no one answered. Worry nipped at me, but Torran could take care of himself. Maybe he'd decided to take Cien down to the medbay with him.

My stomach rumbled as I headed to the galley. Between the time changes and the weird double sunrises, my body had no idea what time it was supposed to be, but stress burned a lot of calories. Cookies sounded amazing.

The galley wasn't empty. Torran and Cien sat at the table eating what looked like pasta and cheese. Torran still wore his armor, but Cien had obviously had a bath.

When Cien caught sight of me, he froze, his eyes huge and scared. I stopped near the door. Rather than focusing on him, I turned my attention to Torran. "Kee has requested cookies. Would you like to help me make them, or should I come back later?"

Torran turned to Cien. "Would you like a cookie?"

The child hadn't taken his eyes off me, his food forgotten. He mumbled something in Valovan, but Torran just waited. Cien sighed. "What is a 'cookie'?" he asked in Common, his tongue tripping over the unfamiliar word.

Torran said something in Valovan and Cien's eyes widened, but he didn't immediately agree. Instead, he watched me like a hawk. It broke my heart to see the kid so scared.

Then I felt the cool touch of a mind against mine, but rather than the light, delicate touch I associated with Torran, this was heavier, clumsier. "Reading a human's mind without their permission is extremely rude," I said, my voice gentle but firm. "It can be viewed as an attack."

Cien's chin tilted up. "Your shields are terrible."

He looked so much like Torran right then that I had to

bite my lip to suppress my smile. "Even if I didn't have any shields at all, it's still rude."

He frowned. "Humans are strange."

"Maybe it's Valoffs who are strange," I said. "But I bet you wouldn't read another Valoff's mind without permission, shields or no."

Cien ducked his head and his pale cheeks flushed red.

"If you want to know something about me, just ask."

"You could lie."

"I could, but I won't." I waved at Torran, who'd been quietly watching our conversation. "Ask your uncle if you don't believe me."

Cien's attention turned to his uncle, but he still watched me out of the corner of his eye. They spoke telepathically for a moment before Cien turned back to me, his eyes wide. I would've given just about anything to know what Torran had told him.

After a long pause, Cien asked, "Will you hurt me?"

"No. Nor will I allow anyone else to hurt you if I can prevent it."

The suspicion didn't drain from his expression. "If you make cookie," he started, then paused with a questioning glance at Torran. After a bit of silent communication, Cien corrected himself. "If you make *cookies,* can I have two?"

I smiled at him. "Well, you'll have to ask your uncle for permission, but as far as I'm concerned, you can have as many as you want."

That earned me a shy smile, just the barest twitch of his lips. He inclined his head, as regal as the emperor he would one day become. "Okay. Make cookies." At Torran's pointed cough, he added, "Please."

"I will have to enter the galley to cook," I said. "Is that okay with you?"

Tension tightened his small frame, but he nodded.

I took the long way around so that I would pass behind Torran rather than Cien. As I did, I felt the lightest brush of a mind against mine. "Thank you," Torran whispered into my head. The touch vanished before I could respond, but I gently tapped my fingers against his shoulder in acknowledgment.

"Cien is in the galley," I said subvocally over the comm. "Avoid it for now because the kid is shaken. I'll bring the cookies out when they're done."

I got back a wave of agreement.

I checked our supplies and decided to make two batches, chocolate chip and snickerdoodle. I worked on the chocolate chip cookies first, mixing the batter and dolloping it out on a tray. I felt Cien's eyes on me the whole time.

Once the first batch of cookies was in the oven, I held out the spoon. "Want to lick the spoon?"

A brief flash of longing crossed Cien's face before he shook his head. I shrugged and moved to pop it into my own mouth.

"I do," Torran said.

I smiled and moved to hand it to him. "Good thing you weren't any slower or you would've been too late."

Rather than waiting for me, he stood and approached. I frowned at the way he favored his side. "Has Havil checked you over?" I hissed once he was close enough that Cien wouldn't overhear.

"I'm fine," Torran murmured.

So, that was a no, then. Before I could press him to go to the medbay, he wrapped his fingers around my hand that held the spoon. He lifted the spoon to his lips and licked the batter from the back of it, his eyes hot on mine. Desire blindsided me, and I shifted as I noticed just how close he was. I could just lean over and . . .

I shook myself. He hadn't renounced the life debt yet.

He brought the spoon to my lips. "Try it," he urged, his voice deep and tempting.

"There is a child in the room," I whispered.

"And I'm showing him that you are trustworthy," Torran replied just as softly, but his tone held a wicked edge of heat. "Touching you is just a bonus. As is tempting you." He brushed the spoon against my lips.

"If I lick it, will you go to the medbay?" I asked, then immediately groaned at myself. Had I really just said that out loud?

Torran's expression told me that yes, I had. "If you lick it," he said, his voice a rumble of desire, "then I'll go wherever you like."

I leaned forward and took the spoon in my mouth, making sure that Torran caught sight of my tongue curling around the end of it. I hollowed my cheeks, far more than was necessary to lick a spoon, but if I was going to play with fire, I was going to do it right.

I moaned low, just loud enough for Torran to catch it.

Then I released the cleaned spoon and grinned at him. "I'll expect you in the medbay as soon as I put this next batch of cookies in the oven."

He blinked, his eyes silver and teal, and then he chuckled. "Well played," he murmured.

IT TOOK ME THE BETTER PART OF TWENTY MINUTES TO PEEL Torran out of his armor and cut away the base layer he wore. Underneath, his skin was livid with bruises. I gently traced my fingers over a particularly bad one on his ribs.

"What happened?" I breathed. "Why didn't your armor protect you?"

He chuckled without humor. "It did."

I looked up and met his eyes. "Explain."

"The telekinetic figured out pretty quickly that I was more interested in protecting you than myself." He gestured at the bruises. "She tried to break my concentration. She failed."

"Was she caught?"

Torran's expression hardened. "No. The guards caught a pair of humans, but Morten and the telekinetic were not with them."

I sighed and dropped my gaze to the floor. "If only I'd been faster. I *had* her. Another second and my blade would've done more than piss her off."

Torran tipped my face up with gentle fingers. "You overrode a powerful telekinetic, injured her, and made her lose concentration long enough that she stopped using you as a shield, giving us a chance to attack. If not for you, we would not have escaped so easily."

I huffed a laugh at him. "I don't know about easy. I can still hear my bones cracking."

His expression darkened until something dangerous lurked in his eyes. "I failed to protect you."

"We're both still alive, so let's call it a win, okay?"

Torran looked like he wanted to argue, but when I just stared at him, he reluctantly nodded.

I pulled out the salve we used to treat bruises and unscrewed the cap. "This will ease the pain until Havil can heal you. Do you need help applying it?"

Cunning lightened some of the darkness in his eyes. "If I say yes, are you going to apply it for me?" Without waiting for an answer, he lay back, and pointed at the vibrant bruise over his ribs that dipped all the way down until it disappeared beneath his underwear. "I'm not sure I can reach it all. Would you mind?"

From his expression, I knew exactly what he was doing, but I would take the flimsiest of excuses if it meant I got to put my hands on him. I warmed the salve between my palms, then smoothed my hands over his bruised body.

He sucked in a breath between his teeth.

I jerked my hands away. "Too much?"

"You didn't hurt me," he said, which didn't answer the question. His fists clenched. "Please continue."

"If you are uncomfortable—"

"If I'm uncomfortable, it's because I want to pull you on top of me and drive us both to the edge of sanity. I thought the pain would blunt the need, but it seems my body has other ideas. If proof of my desire makes *you* uncomfortable, then I will do it myself."

I swallowed and my eyes dropped to the growing bulge barely hidden by the low-slung briefs that wrapped around his hips. The desire that always simmered in my blood around Torran flamed higher. "You could renounce the life debt," I suggested. "If you're not too hurt."

He shook his head immediately. "Not until we're out of Valovian space."

I licked my lips. "You could, ah, help yourself."

His eyes brightened as the silver grew. "If I wasn't hurt, I would, *cho akinti*. But for now, I'll just enjoy your hands tending to me, if you don't mind."

The endearment washed over me. I didn't know what it

HUNT THE STARS

393

meant, and I was too shy to ask, but his voice caressed the words like they were precious.

Like *I* was precious.

I returned my hands to his ribs. His chest expanded, but he didn't say anything, so I smoothed the salve over the worst of his bruises.

And there were *a lot*. His body was littered with so many deep purple marks that I worried about internal bleeding. I didn't know what I'd looked like before Havil healed me. Maybe I'd been just as bad, since I'd felt the telekinetic crushing me with my armor, but I winced at every bruise on Torran. If he hadn't been protecting me, he could've protected himself.

"Why did you let her hurt you like this?" I murmured.

"Because the moment I took my concentration away from you, she would've killed you. It was all I could do to keep her from crushing you or your mind, and you were still severely injured. I didn't expect a telekinetic of my level. We are very rare." He said it without a hint of boasting. "My pride nearly cost your life."

I perked up. "If telekinetics at your level are rare, does that mean you know who she was?"

Torran sighed and closed his eyes. "I believe she is one of Empress Nepru's *Fiazefferia*."

I sucked in a breath. That was a word I knew. It roughly translated as Sun Guardians, and while I didn't know much about Valovian culture, even I'd heard of the famed Sun Guardians. Part assassin, part protector, and part advisor, they were the empress's right hand, and their identities were guarded at the highest level.

They were also known to be fiercely loyal.

"Did she betray the empress?" I whispered, already suspecting the truth.

"I don't know, but it would surprise me if she did. More likely the empress sent her to infiltrate Morten's team and keep an eye on his plans."

"But she had Cien. She put him in an explosive vest and *hurt* him."

Torran shook his head. "She could've killed him at any point, but he barely had a bruise on him. I didn't have time to examine the vest, but my guess is that it was a convincing fake."

"She wanted me and my team dead so the empress could blame us for the kidnapping and restart the war. Will the captured human kidnappers be enough?"

Torran's mouth compressed into a flat line. "I don't know. Depends on how strong their tie to the FHP is."

I closed my eyes. "Why? Why does the Valovian Empire want another war?"

"Empress Nepru fears what the FHP is planning on Bastion. It would take us years, maybe decades, to build a similar station on our side of the wormhole, while Bastion continues to grow unchecked. If FHP operatives truly have infiltrated Valovia, she'll take it as a sign that the FHP is actively working against her and Bastion is an immediate threat."

It was a valid concern, but starting a war over it seemed drastic. However, maybe she had tried diplomatic routes and had gotten nowhere. I wouldn't put much of anything past the Feds.

"Will you be pulled back into the military if there's another war?" I asked.

His expression grew pensive. "I don't know. I've served my time, and I've seen enough death, but I can't stand by and watch our people be overrun, either. I would much rather stop the war before it starts."

I sucked in a breath, connecting the dots. "You intend to go after Morten and the telekinetic, with or without the empress's blessing."

He nodded, watching me closely. "They are instigating war. I want to know why. It'll be harder if Empress Nepru decides to try me for treason, but I'll still do what I can."

"Does the empress know that you have Cien? And that you're on my ship?"

"Yes."

"Was she happy about it?"

One corner of his mouth lifted. "No."

That wasn't the answer I'd hoped for, but it wasn't unexpected. "Will she really try you for treason?"

"That remains to be seen," he said, his voice grim. "After we found Cien, she ordered me to bring him to the palace and remain with him while you returned to FHP space. I refused on the grounds that my life debt overrode the order, but she let us go only because we launched with him on board. She has a few reasons to keep me alive, but that won't stop her forever."

"Well, if she declares you a traitor, you're welcome to bounce around the galaxy with us." I grinned, trying to lighten the mood. "We could charge a *lot* more with a telekinetic on board."

Torran stilled, his eyes on my face. "Do you mean it?"

The comment had been spur of the moment, but I wouldn't have offered, even teasingly, if I didn't mean it. I nodded. "You risked your life and position to get us out.

And while it was your fault that we were on Valovia in the first place, I believe that you didn't know we'd be in mortal danger from the empress. So, yeah, if you need a place to crash, you'll always have one with us."

He put his left arm over his bruised chest and bowed from the waist.

Once he straightened, I said, "I would like to help you chase Morten, too, but I can't make the decision on my own. The FHP has already fucked us over, and I won't put my crew back in their sights without permission."

Torran cupped my cheek, his thumb brushing a burning path across my skin. "I understand. I'm glad that you would consider it at all."

I stared at him for a long moment, then made my decision. "I need you to swear that you will never repeat what I'm about to tell you, to anyone, for any reason."

He once again crossed his chest with his left arm. "I swear it, on my honor."

"The FHP invaded Rodeni with too few troops and too much ambition," I started, voice rough. "Rather than fortifying a forward base, Command spread us too thin. We kept fighting a losing battle while we waited for backup that never arrived. Then we received intel about an inbound Valovian strike group."

Torran's jaw clenched before he nodded. "Those were my troops."

"There was no time to retreat. All of the FHP forces were going to be slaughtered. I volunteered for a last-ditch attack on what I thought was the Valovian command center, and despite my protests, my squad came with me."

Dread and anger and grief churned in my stomach as the memories rose, but I forced the words out. "A transport got us to the edge of the small city, then we worked our way closer on foot. We didn't see a single person, so we thought that everyone had been evacuated."

"They were all hiding in the strongest central building, waiting for rescue."

I nodded, throat tight. "We planted the charges, amazed that we'd made it, that it had been so easy. Then I saw the little boy." My night-vision helmet had washed the color from his Valovian eyes, but his face was burned into my memory.

"I contacted Command and called off the attack. I told them about the civilians. They didn't care. They ordered us to leave." I swallowed down a fresh wave of rage and pain. "I gave my squad a choice, and they chose to stay with me. We tried to disable the explosives before they could be detonated, but we failed. Three of my squad died in the blast. Another died from her injuries as we fled."

Torran's expression didn't change, and I couldn't tell what he was thinking. Perhaps this would be the thing that caused him to renounce the life debt and leave *Starlight*— and me. But now that I'd started, the story spilled out, an unstoppable torrent of words.

"We dragged ourselves back to where the transport was supposed to be waiting, but it wasn't there. After I disobeyed orders, Command removed our escape route without telling me. It took us ten brutal hours to find another way off-planet."

"How did you do it?"

"We stole a Valovian ship. The Feds nearly shot us down before they realized I had the correct FHP protocols. I went to Command—to Commodore Frank Morten, as a matter of fact—and turned in my resignation on the spot. Eli, Kee, and Lexi did the same.

"But Morten isn't stupid, and he used the expedited discharge to secure our silence, with the understanding that if any of us spoke about what really happened, we'd quietly disappear, along with everyone else on the team. Then the Feds paraded me around as a hero to really rub salt in the wound, knowing that I had to grin and bear it."

Torran's power hummed against my skin and his eyes glowed silver and teal. I stood my ground, but remembered fear whispered at the edges of my mind. Had I made a mistake in trusting him?

"Frank Morten is dead," Torran growled, dark promise in his tone. "I will see it done, you have my word."

Before I could protest, Torran wrapped his arms around me in a gentle hug, tucking my face against his shoulder. "Thank you for telling me," he whispered into my hair.

I tried for a casual shrug even as my tears dripped onto his skin. "You deserved to know, but I've put the safety of my team in your hands. Please don't break my trust."

His arms tightened around me. "Never," he vowed quietly.

THE NEXT TWO DAYS PASSED IN INCREASINGLY STRESSFUL increments. We'd passed through the first wormhole without being challenged, but I decided to wait until we were safely in Fed space before talking to my team about continuing the hunt for Morten and the telekinetic. We were already under enough stress, and there would be time to talk later.

Assuming we made it.

Lotkez once again escorted us, allowing *Starlight* to skip the checkpoints, but I wasn't sure if they were more protection or threat. With Cien on board, perhaps they were some of both. I hadn't seen any other ships stalking us, but a battleship waited at the final wormhole that would send us back to human space.

A battleship we were nearly within range of.

Cien, Kee, and Havil were in the galley, ostensibly making lunch, but really Kee and Havil were keeping the kid off the bridge in case things went sideways.

With her colorful hair, delicate build, and bright personality, Kee was the least threatening person on board, and the only human Cien trusted enough to let close. He had tolerated the shared dinners, and had even cracked a smile once or twice, but the rest of the time, we gave him his space. The kid deserved it.

Everyone else was on the bridge. I scratched Luna under the chin as the minutes crept past. Finally, *Starlight* pinged a warning—we were within range of the battleship's guns. I brought up our weapons and defensive systems.

Not that it would be much help against a battleship.

But even though Empress Nepru had very likely used her grandson as a pawn, she'd also kept him safe, so I didn't think she would kill him now—and a hit from a battleship would absolutely destroy *Starlight*.

Torran's expression went distant. I pretended everything was normal and confirmed our course through the wormhole. After a heart-stopping moment, the anchor put us in the holding pattern.

Was the empress going to let us leave?

Lotkez entered the pattern behind us, and Torran blew out a low breath.

"Everything okay?"

He smiled at me. "Yes. They're letting you leave. Your bounty has been permanently rescinded."

My eyes narrowed. It couldn't be that easy. "But?"

"You are strongly discouraged from ever visiting again. And while I won't be tried for treason, I'm being stripped of my diplomatic status and all standing within the empire. She's made me a pariah, and my team with me." Bitterness coated his tone.

"Why is *Lotkez* following us through if you don't have any diplomatic standing?"

"They will ensure Cien's safety in FHP space, and then return me to Valovia."

My heart skipped a beat. Of course he would want to return. Even stripped of standing, he still had a life on his home planet. And as soon as we made it to Fed space, his life debt would be over. He could do whatever he wanted.

Lexi asked, "Did the empress freeze your accounts?"

Torran grinned at her. "She tried, but thanks to the kidnappers, I'd already moved a great deal of my money elsewhere." He turned his attention to me. "Your payment should already be in your account. I doubled the completion bonus, as we discussed."

"You didn't have to—"

"I did," he said, his expression fierce.

"Yeah, he did," Lexi and Eli agreed over the comm.

I ignored the peanut gallery. "So you can return to Valovia?" I asked. I was happy he had the option—truly, I was—but I'd hoped that maybe he'd hang around for a while longer. However, if he didn't *have* to avoid Valovia, then there was no reason for him to bounce around the galaxy with us, especially not if he wanted to hunt Morten and the telekinetic.

"Yes," he said slowly, his eyes on me.

I nodded and buried my hand in Luna's soft fur. She

purred at me, trying to soothe my frayed nerves, but it was a losing battle. I'd already told him he could stay. But staying meant giving up his life on Valovia, at least for a while, so it had to be his decision. I wouldn't try to influence him, no matter how much I wanted to.

I returned my attention to my terminal. The empress might've said she would let us go, but I wouldn't completely relax until we were through the wormhole. And maybe not until we reached Bastion, where Cien's parents were supposed to meet us. *Lotkez* wouldn't dare attack us at the busy FHP station.

As the wormhole got larger on-screen, Cien slipped into the bridge and climbed into his uncle's lap. It seemed he, too, could feel the energy in the air and didn't care for it.

Luna stretched, then leapt to the communications terminal and flopped over with her fluffy belly on display. Cien glanced up at Torran. When his uncle nodded, Cien reached out a tentative hand and stroked his fingers through Luna's fur.

She purred and rolled over, her feet in the air, shamelessly angling for more petting.

Once again, I wondered just how smart she was because she kept the kid occupied all the way through the wormhole.

The bridge let out a collective breath as we popped back into human space. I checked the sensors and kept us on course out of the danger zone. There were a few ships waiting to traverse, but no armada waiting to turn us into tiny little pieces of debris.

Carrying the heir to the Valovian Empire into human space was a huge risk. The empress had let us go because of it, but if we lost Cien, she wouldn't need any flimsy, manufactured excuse for war because we would have delivered the perfect one right to her door.

Lotkez came through behind us, and I felt the lightest brush of a mind against mine. I glanced at Torran and he raised an eyebrow. When I dipped my head, he whispered into my mind, "We need to change course."

"Why?" I asked mentally. With practice, I was getting better at directing my thoughts his way.

"We're going to meet with my sister and her husband nearby rather than on Bastion."

It was almost scary how often his thoughts mirrored mine. "You expect trouble?"

"Not expect, exactly, but I would prefer if trouble didn't find us."

He sent me the coordinates and I punched them in. Eli and Kee cut me looks across the room, but they didn't question our new heading.

Starlight estimated we would arrive in twenty minutes. Torran hadn't been kidding about it being nearby. In less than half an hour, his debt would be fulfilled, and he could leave with his nephew.

And I would just have to learn how to live with the empty ache in my chest.

CHAPTER THIRTY-TWO

Twenty-five minutes later, we docked with a large, sleek ship broadcasting a Valovian diplomatic registration, and *Lotkez* hovered nearby. Both teams had gathered in the cargo bay while we waited for the docking tunnel and airlocks to confirm a solid connection.

Torran had gone around to each person on my team, presumably saying his good-byes, but I didn't know because he hadn't talked to *me*.

The ache in my chest deepened.

"Anyone who wants to return to Valovia early may board *Nirpaf*," Torran said. "My sister returns to the capital directly and has vowed safe passage."

Nilo's gaze slid toward Lexi without ever quite reaching her. His expression went distant, and Torran nodded at him. No one else spoke.

Torran's team wore their armor, and my team was armed with whatever weapons we could successfully conceal from Cien. We didn't want to make the kid nervous, but we didn't want to face potentially hostile Valoffs without weapons, either.

I had a small plas pistol tucked in a shoulder holster hidden by an open jacket, and Eli had hidden a rifle in a pile of cargo, which he now leaned against.

We were as ready as we were going to be.

The airlock connection turned green, and I opened both hatches. A short, five-meter tunnel connected to the airlocks on *Nirpaf*'s side. A brief inspection confirmed that the connection was solid. These docking tunnels were built to be nigh indestructible. Even if the Valovian ship tried to pull away, they'd just drag *Starlight* along with them.

As soon as I returned to my cargo bay, *Nirpaf*'s hatches swung open. Past the crew securing the doors, I caught sight of a beautiful woman in a dark dress. Her careful makeup couldn't hide the circles under her eyes and the wan pallor of her skin. Cien caught sight of her and dashed through the tunnel with a cry.

She bent, catching him, and clutched him to her chest. She buried her face in his hair with a choked sob. This woman loved her child. If the empress had used him, it had not been with his mother's permission.

I relaxed a fraction. Now that she knew the danger, she would keep him safe.

Torran stepped into the tunnel, and my heart cracked. He was going to leave without a word. I stood frozen, unable to tear my eyes away as he stopped just before the airlock on the other side.

Torran's sister asked him a question and he shook his head. She raised her left arm, still wrapped around Cien, and covered where her heart would be. She bowed her head.

When she lifted her eyes, her gaze sought mine and she repeated the gesture. I thawed just enough to dip my head in acknowledgment.

Without a word, her crew closed the hatches, preparing to disconnect, and Torran returned to *Starlight*'s cargo bay. I blinked at him. "You're not leaving?"

He tilted his head. "Did you expect me to?"

I waved at the tunnel. "I thought—"

"We are still bound, *cho akinti*. You will not be rid of me so easily."

"That would've been good to know ten minutes ago," I grumbled under my breath. Relief washed through me, but I knew it was only a temporary reprieve. Torran had asked if his crew could remain until we reached Bastion, and I'd agreed.

I would still have to say good-bye far before I was ready.

I swallowed as Torran started closing the hatches on our side. "No one else is transferring, either?"

"We go where the general goes," Chira said.

"Not a general anymore," he said quietly, looking over his shoulder. "My military record has been expunged."

She rolled her eyes and repeated, "We go where the general goes."

Once the hatches were closed, I initiated the decoupling process. *Nirpaf* had already initiated it on their side, so as soon as I approved, the airlocks began pumping air out of the tunnel in preparation for separation.

"Eli, to the bridge. Watch them as they leave. Keep an eye on *Lotkez,* too."

He ducked into the main part of the ship with a grim nod.

I stood by the cargo bay terminal as the tunnel disconnected and returned to its place, then the outer shield slid over it. I watched on-screen as the other ship pulled away. This was the most dangerous part. *Nirpaf* might mean "peace," but they were armed with a lot of very nice, very dangerous weapons. With Cien safely on their ship, they might decide we were no longer useful.

"I'm on the bridge," Eli said. "So far they are moving away smoothly. Wait, *fuck. Nirpaf* is bringing up their weapons." He paused. "But they're targeting *Lotkez*?"

I turned to Torran. "Why is your sister targeting our escort?"

"Just a precaution," he said, "in case the empress has decided that we are at the end of our usefulness. *Nirpaf* will escort *Lotkez* through the wormhole."

I relayed the information to Eli, who remained tense, but said, "I'm plotting a course to Bastion. I'll keep an eye on the other two."

"Thanks," I murmured back, then turned to Torran. "Won't that get your sister in trouble? And how will you return to Valovia now?"

"She owes you." He frowned at me. "What makes you think that I want to return to Valovia?"

I waved my hand around the empty cargo bay. "You said good-bye to everyone. You made no mention of staying. You were halfway into your sister's ship without so much as a word to *me*—" My composure broke and I blinked back tears.

Torran drew me softly into his arms. "Oh, *cho akinti*, I am sorry that I did not explain, but I thought you understood. I talked to your crew to ensure that they were okay with us staying for a while longer. I spoke to my sister because I had to ensure that Cien would be looked after, and that Feia would prevent *Lotkez* from trying anything. I did not mean to cause you pain."

"So you're not leaving at Bastion?"

"No, not unless you ask me to."

I wrapped my arms around him and held him tightly. "I'm so glad," I whispered.

He ran a soothing hand down my back, and I slowly relaxed against him with my head on his shoulder. My mind drifted back over the brief meeting with the imperial princess. She wasn't what I expected. "Your sister loves Cien."

"Yes. We don't see eye to eye on many things, but we would both die to protect the boy." Torran held me for a few more minutes before pulling back and meeting my eyes. "We are in human space. You are safe."

My heart kicked. "Your debt is paid." The thought was more bittersweet than I'd expected. I *liked* the thought of us as one entity. If I could keep that without the rest, I would, in a heartbeat.

Torran knelt, held his left wrist over his heart, and looked up into my eyes. *"Cho wubr chil choz de cho arbu chil tavoz."* His voice was deep and sure, and I didn't know why my eyes were misting over, but I blinked the tears away before they could fully form.

"What does it mean?" I whispered.

"My life is mine, but my heart is yours."

I cleared my throat, trying to speak around the lump in it. "Is that the traditional saying?"

He smiled and pressed my fingers to his lips. "'My life is mine' is how a life debt is traditionally ended."

"And, ah, the other part?"

"The truth. It is also a traditional phrase used during courtship."

I smiled down at him and cupped his gorgeous face in my hands. "Used how?"

He coughed. "It is usually used to move the courtship to its final stage before a life bond—a marriage."

So it was something like an engagement. That didn't bring the terror I thought it would. Instead, warmth nestled in my heart. "Teach me the words?"

He did, repeating them until I had the pronunciation correct.

I knelt in front of him and took his hands in mine. "*Cho arbu chil tavoz.*"

As soon as the words left my lips, Torran crushed me to his chest. His mouth slanted over mine, hot and needy. I moaned and parted my lips, desperate to have him closer. Just when I thought he would comply, he pulled back with a groan. "Can your crew get us to Bastion?" he asked, his eyes on fire.

I nodded and licked my lips.

"Good." He stood and scooped me up in his arms. "Your room or mine?"

"Mine."

He pressed another kiss to my lips, like he couldn't wait any longer, then headed into the main part of the ship, where we promptly ran into Lexi and Kee. Lexi smirked and Kee gave me a thumbs-up.

"Tell Eli he's in charge for a while," I called over Torran's shoulder when he didn't break stride. "And I don't want to be disturbed unless the world is ending."

"Don't worry. We've got it!" Kee shouted back.

I disabled my comm implant. If they needed to get ahold of me, they could use the ship's intercom. The door to my quarters slid open at our approach. Torran glanced around at the office, then unerringly strode for the bedroom.

Despite my desire, the nerves that I hadn't experienced earlier decided to make their presence known. I wanted Torran and he wanted me, but getting completely naked with someone for the first time was always a little awkward.

Rather than placing me on the bed, Torran let my legs down and carefully set me on my feet. He ran his hands from my shoulders to my fingertips, then held my hands. "I would very much like to take you to bed," he growled, his pupils blown. Silver spread through his irises, brightening his eyes.

"I would like that, too," I assured him. I glanced up at him from under my lashes. "I seem to recall a certain former general making some very bold promises a few days ago."

Torran gave me a look of such intense, searing yearning that I nearly combusted on the spot. "And I plan to keep every one," he ground out, his voice gravel and sin.

I reached up and wrapped my hand around the back of his head. I played with his short hair for a moment, loving the soft feel of it against my palm, then I drew his head down and met him halfway. Firm and warm, his lips glided over mine with gentle pressure.

Until I licked him.

Then the kiss changed, deepening and heating. His tongue slid into my mouth with greedy little licks, sending shivers down my spine. I arched into him and his arms supported me and clutched me close. I felt desired and protected.

And so very, very hot.

Torran's hand crept up my ribs and glided over my breast. My nipples tightened, and I sucked in a breath.

He pulled back and met my eyes. "Okay?"

"So good," I assured. I tapped his armor. "Let's peel you out of that, yeah?"

I helped Torran remove his armor and base layer, and he helped me remove my shirt and pants, leaving us both in our undergarments. I wished I had worn something sexier, and I wished my skin wasn't marred with scars, but based on the heat in Torran's eyes, he didn't mind at all.

I ran my hands up his chest, something I'd wanted to do ever since I'd seen him in the pool. His skin was flawless once again, thanks to Havil's healing ability, and his muscles tensed and flexed under my exploring fingers. I pressed a kiss to his pec and let my tongue flicker out for a taste. He groaned deep in his chest.

He guided my mouth back to his, kissing me deeply before sliding his lips across my jaw and down my neck. He fingered the edge of my bra. "May I remove this?"

Rather than answering, I unclasped it and let the fabric slide down my arms. He tossed it away and then his hot mouth closed around my nipple at the same time his power swept down my body, phantom fingers against my skin. Pleasure exploded and I arched into him, holding him in place.

My legs turned wobbly. "Bed," I gasped.

Torran lifted me and I wrapped my legs around his waist. Two thin pieces of fabric were all that separated us, and his length nudged exactly where I wanted him. Maybe beds were overrated.

Torran turned his attention to my neglected breast and I briefly wondered if anyone had died of pleasure—right before I lost the ability to think at all.

I rocked against him, mindless and wanting, while he whispered Valovan endearments against my skin.

"What are you saying?" I asked with a moan as he hit a particularly fantastic spot. I slid against him again, chasing bliss.

"My darling, my love, my precious heart," he murmured, his voice dark with an edge of a growl. "So beautiful and desirable. I want you so much."

"Then have me," I demanded. "Now."

"Patience," he growled.

"Patience later. Satisfaction now." I let my legs drop from around his waist and shimmied my underwear off, beyond awkwardness. The proof of his desire was unmistakable, and his words had driven me to the edge.

His power swept down my body again, and it felt like he touched me *everywhere*. I sucked in a breath as invisible hands caressed my breasts. I glanced up and found Torran watching me closely.

"Are you okay with me using my ability like this?" he asked.

I nodded, beyond words.

He tipped my head back, his thumb tracing a burning path across my skin. "Will you allow me to share your pleasure?"

"Like in the shower?" At his nod, I shivered, remembering the feel of his desire. How much better would it be now that I could touch him? My stomach clenched, and I demanded, "Yes."

His mind brushed against mine with a cool rush that couldn't disguise the burning desire he felt. "You are so lovely," he murmured.

I could feel the truth in the words, and in this moment,

with his power swirling around us and his fiery gaze tracing over my body, I felt like it. And I wanted him to feel as good as I did right now.

I touched his waistband and waited for permission. He nodded, his jaw clenched, and I slowly slipped the last piece of clothing down his legs. He was perfect, long and thick, and I found some patience after all.

I slid to my knees before he could stop me and licked him once, twice. His groan sounded like it was torn from the bottom of his soul, and fiery pleasure burned through our connection. I gasped against the onslaught as every muscle tightened.

"Bed," he growled. "Now."

The demand brought me back to myself, and I grinned up at him, pleased by how the tables had turned. But before I could lick him again, he picked me up and tossed me onto the bed as if I weighed nothing. I bounced once and then he was there, caging me with the lean, hard strength of his body.

His hand slipped down my chest and over my belly until he found the proof of my desire, slick and hot. He stroked me with light teasing touches, feeding my desire back to me tinged with the scorching heat of his. His power skimmed over my skin, until I writhed under him and threatened him with death if he didn't give me what I wanted.

Only then did he slide a finger deep, hitting a place that made the world explode with pleasure. Torran groaned against my shoulder as he shared the shattering bliss through our connection.

I was still riding the ripples when he was there, hard and broad against me. I could feel the iron band of his control, and I wanted nothing more than to drive him past it. I lifted my hips and he sank home, one delicious centimeter at a time.

My desire ignited anew, stoked by his, and I shifted under him, chasing the friction that would push us both over the edge. He groaned into my neck, then his lips covered mine in a fierce, frantic kiss. "Open your eyes," he whispered.

My eyes flew open, and I realized that we'd left all the lights on. I could see the silver, teal, and copper spreading across his eyes. I could see the sweat beading on his skin. And when he levered himself up on his forearms and drew back, I could see where we were connected.

I clenched around him and he froze and cursed in Valovan, but I was done with his control. "Can you feel how much I want you right now?" I asked, staring into his eyes. "Can you feel how my body clings to yours?" I tweaked my nipple and hissed as sensation arced through my nerves.

Torran's eyes went solid silver, and I was rewarded for my boldness with a deep thrust that sent pleasure ricocheting through my veins. "Yes," I growled. "Just like that."

"Say you are mine, *cho akinti,*" he groaned, driving me toward another explosive release. With him in my head, the endearment translated. *My love.*

"I'm yours, *cho akinti,*" I gasped, tripping over the words but not the meaning. Torran's eyes widened and his rhythm faltered as his control snapped.

Then he surged into me, and his power crashed over me, igniting all of my nerve endings with unending pleasure. Desire, his and mine, blended together and blazed higher and higher. My eyes tried to drift closed, but I fought the urge. Torran drove into me again and again, each time better than the last. When I tipped over the edge into oblivion, I took him with me, staring into his gorgeous eyes.

My love.

SEVERAL HOURS LATER, EXHAUSTED AND CONTENT, I lounged on Torran's chest and listened to his heart beat steady and strong. He ran a hand down my back, then pulled a sheet over my cooling skin.

"What are you thinking?" he murmured.

"I'm just basking in how happy I am right now," I told him honestly. "And wishing you'd dropped the life debt earlier, because this was so much better than our time in the shower."

He chuckled. "You were an incredible temptation," he admitted. "Keeping my hands to myself nearly killed me."

"But now you don't have to."

He smoothed a hand down my back again, proving my point. "Have you talked to your team about hunting for Morten and the telekinetic yet?"

I sighed, but even the uncertainty of the future couldn't pierce my little bubble of happiness. "Not yet. I thought we might do it together."

"Of course," he murmured, then he paused. "Would you be upset if some of my team decided to stay on *Starlight,* too? If your team agrees to help, I mean."

I lifted my head so I could meet his eyes. "Your team is always welcome on my ship, whether or not we end up helping with Morten."

Some of the tension that had crept into his frame melted away. "Thank you. I don't know who will want to stay, if anyone, but I want to give them the option."

"Of course," I agreed gently. "Family is important, and even if they're not your family by blood, they're still family."

He nodded, his expression solemn. "They are," he admitted. "They saved me as often as I saved them."

I smiled. "That's what families do. Now, I suppose we should get up and get the conversation over with so I can stop worrying about it."

He grinned and rolled me under him. "We could. Or we could *not* do that."

"What did you have in mind instead?"

He slid down my body with a wicked smile and pressed a kiss against my stomach. "I believe I still have some promises to keep. Let me show you."

His mind touched mine as his head settled between my legs and our shared desire blotted out everything else.

IT WAS AFTER DINNER BY THE TIME TORRAN AND I EMERGED from my quarters. We grabbed a quick meal of leftovers, then I gathered everyone in the rec room for a meeting.

Torran and I fielded a lot of knowing smiles and sly glances, but no one looked unhappy at the latest developments. I hoped that would remain true at the end of the meeting.

"What's up?" Kee asked once everyone was settled. Varro sat next to her, but I still couldn't get a read on him. He wasn't sitting any closer to her than he had been that very first night when we'd watched vids, while Anja, Eli, Havil, and Chira were happily wedged onto a sofa together. And even Lexi and Nilo sat in individual chairs that just happened to be next to each other.

I looked at each member of my team. "I've offered Tor-ran a place on *Starlight,* as well as a place for any of his crew that want to remain with him," I said, ripping the first bandage off without warning.

I didn't get the shocked expressions that I'd expected. Instead, I got nods and knowing looks from my team. "Sounds great," Kee agreed easily.

I looked around with narrowed eyes. "I expected more pushback. I made the decision without your input."

Kee's smile was gentle. "You're the captain. And, be-sides that, we know you're gone for him, Tavi." She winked at Torran, then continued, "Of course we're not going to push back on keeping him around." She waved at the rest of the human crew. "We're just happy that it sounds like *you're* planning to stay with *us.*"

Her words soothed a secret worry that I'd carried for a while. I grinned at her. "As if I could ever get rid of you lot. Without me, you'd fall apart in ten minutes."

"Probably less," Eli agreed.

I paused before moving to the next topic, and Torran clasped my hand, offering me strength. I flashed him a smile, then turned back to my crew. "That's not all. Torran plans to hunt Morten and the telekinetic. He thinks they're instigating a war and he wants to know why. I would like to help, but this is not a decision I will make without your input, especially because he believes the telekinetic might be a Sun Guardian."

My team shifted uneasily, and Lexi hissed out a curse. "Sun Guardians don't fuck around. Hunting one is danger-ous."

"It is," I agreed. "And if it was just the FHP at risk, I'd

happily let them go down in flames. But you know that if we return to war, people will suffer. We might be able to stop that."

She scoffed. "If they want to go to war, nothing we can do will stop them."

"True enough. But it's also possible that the kidnappers *weren't* working on FHP orders, and if we expose them, tensions will decrease."

Lexi shook her head but didn't contradict me.

Eli stared at me, his expression unreadable. "Do you really think we could help stop a war?"

"I don't know. Maybe Morten is neck-deep in some FHP plot. Maybe the empress contracted the whole kidnapping just so she'd have a reason to break the treaty. There's no way to know unless we dig into it."

Eli sighed. "This is a very stupid idea, but I'm in."

"Me, too," Kee said.

"I'm in," Anja said quietly. "If my vote matters."

"Unless you want off at Bastion, you're part of my crew now. Your vote matters."

She smiled at me. "I'd like to stay."

Kee clapped her hands. "Yay! I never have to work with Eli on delicate electronics ever again!"

Eli snorted and made a show of rolling his eyes, but a grin hovered around his mouth.

"We're in," Chira said quietly. "If you'll have us."

"All of you are welcome," I said. "I meant it."

She bowed her head, her left wrist over her heart. The rest of the Valoffs did the same.

I nodded at them, then turned to Lexi. "I know you're going to be off relieving someone of their hard-earned credits, but what do you think?"

"I think it's a terrible idea," she said bluntly. "But I think you're going to do it anyway, and I would be disappointed if you didn't. One of us has to fight for the greater good, and it's not me."

My smile softened. Lexi liked to think she wasn't a good person, but her actions proved her wrong. Sure, she took some questionable jobs, but when I'd needed help, she'd dropped everything to go to Valovia with me. "Thanks, Lex."

She nodded, her expression fond.

"So, we're decided then?" I asked. Everyone nodded, and Torran squeezed my hand with a smile. I grinned. "Then let's go stop a war."

Octavia "Tavi" Zarola and her motley crew are back with another thrilling adventure in the Starlight's Shadow series. This time it's up to sunshiny information-guru Kee and grumpy weapons-expert Varro to save the day.

Coming out July 2023

ABOUT THE AUTHOR

Jessie Mihalik has a degree in computer science and a love of all things geeky. A software engineer by trade, Jessie now writes full-time from her home in Texas. When she's not writing, she can be found playing co-op video games with her husband, trying out new board games, or reading books pulled from her overflowing bookshelves.